RISE OF THE DEAD

An Earth-Shattering Anthology of Zombie Terror

I0561327

Edited by
Andy Rausch
R.D. Riley
Rich Bottles Jr.
Gary Lee Vincent

Burning Bulb
PUBLISHING

Rise of the Dead: An Earth-Shattering Anthology of Zombie Terror
Edited by **Andy Rausch, R.D. Riley, Rich Bottles Jr.** & **Gary Lee Vincent**

Burning Bulb Publishing
P.O. Box 4721
Bridgeport, WV 26330-4721
www.BurningBulbPublishing.com

Cover designed by Duy Phan.

First Burning Bulb Publishing printing.

Edition ISBN Paperback 978-0692341476

Printed in the United States of America

Library of Congress Control Number: 2014957996

Contents

FOREWORD
ZOMBIE ROOTZ IN THE SIXTIEZ
by John Russo

By now almost everyone knows that the concept of the modern flesh-eating zombie originated in the sixties with *Night of the Living Dead.* That's why I think that this anthology of short stories paying homage to that fact is a wonderful idea. When I was asked to write such a story, I was told that each and every story in the book would have to take place in or around the time, in 1968, when the horror classic that I co-authored took place.

I came up with two key ideas that made *Night of the Living Dead* possible. Namely, that the threat in the movie would be the recently dead; and that they would be driven to go after live human flesh. George Romero had written a story that essentially became the first part of our screenplay; a girl and her brother were in a cemetery, where they both got attacked by a being whose exact nature was at first unclear; the brother loses an all-out fight with this creature, and the girl is chased into a farmhouse in the middle of nowhere that is gradually surrounded by more and more of these demented beings. When I read what George had written, I said, "This is good. It has all the right suspense, all the right twists and turns – but you never say who it is that is attacking the girl. So who are they?"

He said, "I don't know."

I said, "Well, when I was reading it, it seemed to me that they could be dead people."

He said, "That's good."

And I said, "But you never say what the attackers are after."

He again said, "I don't know."

3

And I said, "Well, why don't we use my flesh-eating idea?" because at the time I was working on a script dealing with aliens from another planet who came to earth in search of human flesh.

George said, "That's good." And that's how the terrifying beings in our movie became flesh-eating dead people.

When we told those ideas to others in our group, someone said, "How are we going to do that? We can't afford to film people coming out of their graves."

So I thought it over for a few moments and said, "Well, then, only the recently dead can come back. People from morgues, hospitals or funeral homes, or people killed as the result of the catastrophe that has occurred."

After we beat around some more ideas and developed the overall plan for our story, I re-wrote the part that George Romero had written, putting it into screenplay form, and wrote the second half of the screenplay myself, because George got tied up on a commercial job. In those days, we worked that way as a matter of course. If someone couldn't complete a project, then someone else would pick up the ball and carry it forward. I was afraid our feature film would die before it got off the ground if I didn't at least finish the screenplay, and I did so in about three to four weeks.

The rest is horror-film history. *Night of the Living Dead* took off and became a monster hit, and has been in almost constant distribution ever since. The movie had its world premiere in Pittsburgh on October 1, 1968, and the flesh-eating-zombie phenomenon took off fast and has never really slowed down. By creating flesh-eating dead people we tapped into an atavistic fear that has been at the core of mankind throughout our evolutionary process; human beings were prey for vicious carnivores such as cave bears and saber-toothed tigers, and now, in books and movies, we are prey for our own dead-but-still-hungry friends and relatives.

4

Night of the Living Dead has a raw, elemental aspect to it that is a source of its strength. I retained that raw power when I came up with the original concept for *Return of the Living Dead.* I'm not talking about the version written and directed by Dan O'Bannon, I'm talking about the stark-horror version developed by me, Russ Streiner and Rudy Ricci when we were partners in a company called New American Films, Inc., in Pittsburgh. We had split away from George Romero to form our own filmmaking company. By 1972 he had written a script called *Dawn of the Dead*, which bore little relationship to the movie of that same title that he later directed, because it was a very claustrophobic script about a man and a woman hiding in the crawlspace of a shopping mall. He and I read each other's scripts, and he later totally changed his script to incorporate the kind of action he had seen in ours. He raised money to do his first, and that kind of knocked the pins out from under us in our own effort to get financed.

Rudy Ricci was delegated to write the first draft of *Return of the Living Dead*, and as I received comments and critiques from different potential distributors, I went on to do a couple of extensive re-writes. The script opens with the funeral of a child, and at the peak of the ceremony a preacher hands her distraught father a spike and he drives it into the forehead of his dead little girl. Thus, we learn immediately that a religious cult has sprung up after the first "zombie crisis" that maintains the belief that the dead must be spiked or burned. I think that if the dead really did come back to life and went after human flesh, such cults really would spring up. The concept of *Return of the Living Dead* was to deal with, not just another zombie uprising, but also with how humans might behave toward one another in the midst of such a crisis. There was a raiding party in our script, a gang of rapists, murderers and thieves, who were in some ways a worse threat to the main characters than the living dead were.

Well, to date this original stark-horror version of *Return of the Living Dead* has yet to be made. Instead Dan O'Bannon was hired to turn it into a horror comedy, which he did very well and very successfully. It was a big hit and has spawned numerous sequels. And so there are two novels of that title, one based on my screenplay and one based on Dan O'Bannon's, and both written by me.

My purpose in relating all this is to illustrate how the terrific impact of *Night of the Living Dead* immediately created a sub-genre that was developed and exploited, at first, by its original creators, including me and George Romero, each going in different directions with our own individual perspectives on the zombie phenomenon. George Romero has made *Dawn of the Dead, Day of the Dead, Land of the Dead, Diary of the Dead* and more, and I was involved in *Return of the Living Dead, Night of the Living Dead 1990,* and the totally awful *Children of the Living Dead* which I neither wrote nor directed but was roped into producing. Meantime, other filmmakers, such as Dan O'Bannon with his horror-comedy version of *Return of the Living Dead Parts I and II,* and Sam Raimi with *The Evil Dead,* picked up the baton and kept running with it. More and more filmmakers saw a way to jump-start their own careers, and so more and more zombie films got made over the years, and are still getting made, right up to things like *28 Days Later, Shawn of the Dead, The Walking Dead,* and many, many more.

Currently I have two published zombie-type novels in distribution: *Escape of the living Dead* and *Living Things.* I also have written several screenplays, *Tau Kappa Zombie* and *My Uncle John is a Zombie*, both of which are zombie comedies, and *Children of the Dead* and *Spawn of the Dead,* which are straight horror. When *Escape of the Living Dead* was developed into a series of comic books and two graphic novels, published by Avatar, the stories were set in the early seventies, not in a contemporary time period. None of these movies have gotten made as yet, but there are deals in the works on some of them. So stay tuned to my website and Facebook pages.

There has been an argument raging about "slow zombies versus fast zombies." I am not a purist in this regard; if you can make it work either way, more power to you. Furthermore, when Russ Streiner, George Romero and I, as executive producers of the authorized stage play, *George A. Romero's Night of the Living Dead Live,* were appearing before a packed house in Toronto, George said that he thought it made no sense to have zombies cracking open human skulls to eat brains, like they did in *Return of the Living Dead* -- but I disagreed with him. I said that in a way certain kinds of zombies have become supernatural, not a purely "natural" and "realistic" phenomenon, the way we first portrayed them. I also told him it was useless to argue with the success of Dan O'Bannon's movie, which did millions of dollars' worth of business and spawned a slew of sequels, and to this day is one of the films that fans constantly tell me is their favorite of all time.

Perhaps, for you, dear reader, some of the stories you will read in these pages will take their place as some of your very own favorites. Please step back with me into the 1960's – a time of peaceniks, rednecks and unspeakable zombie horror!!

THE FIRST ONE
by John A. Russo

With twenty books published internationally and nineteen feature movies in worldwide distribution, John Russo has been called a "living legend." He began by co-authoring the screenplay for NIGHT OF THE LIVING DEAD, which has become recognized as a "horror classic." His three books on the art and craft of movie making have become bibles of independent production, and one of them, SCARE TACTICS, won a national award for Superior Nonfiction. Quentin Tarantino and many other noted filmmakers have stated that Russo's books helped them launch their careers.

John Russo wants people to know he's "just a nice guy who likes to scare people" — and he's done it with novels and films such as RETURN OF THE LIVING DEAD, MIDNIGHT, THE MAJORETTES, THE AWAKENING and HEARTSTOPPER. He has had a long, rewarding career, and he shows no signs of slowing down. Recently his screenplay for ESCAPE OF THE LIVING DEAD was made into a five-part comic book released by Avatar to great acclaim; it made the Top Ten of Horror Comics nationally and spawned two graphic novels and ten sequels.

Russo's latest novels THE ACADEMY, THE AWAKENING, BOOBY HATCH, DEALEY PLAZA, LIMB TO LIMB and LIVING THINGS are published by Burning Bulb Publishing. His short story "Channel 666" appears in THE BIG BOOK OF BIZARRO, also by Burning Bulb Publishing.

There were many causes for the outbreak in 1968 and no one understood any of them. The manifestation of it, when it finally burst forth, was too sudden, too incomprehensible. The people were terrified. The scientists were puzzled, perplexed and overwhelmed. They tried their best, but no vaccine existed, and none could be developed very quickly, if at all. For reasons of self-preservation and for the good of society, crude but temporarily effective methods were employed in an attempt to defeat or at least slow down the epidemic. The creatures had to be shot in the head, spiked in the head or incinerated.

Armed posses stopped the first outbreak. *Bang! Bang! Bang!* One ghoul after another was gunned down. Then they were dragged onto a huge bonfire. This was the recommended method of disposal.

But down through the decades more outbreaks have occurred, and they remain just as incomprehensible as the first one, back in 1968. I hate to admit this, because I am a scientist, but I have gotten accustomed to futility while passionately devoting the last four decades of my life toward solving problems that have remained largely unsolvable – a desperate situation that has prevented me and many other dedicated scientists from totally eradicating the most insidious, frightening disease known to man. As I have said, there are apparently many causes, many ways to become infected, and so the disease persists in being unfathomable and largely unstoppable by any known medical treatment or injection.

However, there is one particular case which I have been able to fully study and analyze, and from my investigations to make certain deductions. It is the case of Roger Dowman, a vicious serial killer, who did not start out that way, but eventually succumbed to the darkest side of his forsaken humanity. As far as we know, he was the first man to become undead and to exhibit a lustful craving for live human flesh.

In June of 1966 Roger came back from Vietnam after fighting for thirteen months in jungles polluted with Agent Orange. It was a chemical defoliant relentlessly sprayed from planes and helicopters to kill the thick, impenetrable jungle vegetation, which became brown and withered, giving the Viet Cong nowhere to hide, so that they could more easily be flushed out and killed. During his combat tour, Roger Dowman killed a dozen or more of these short, skinny enemies in black pajamas, and kept their ears for trophies on a cord tied around his neck, first soaking them in formaldehyde to keep them from rotting and stinking, which did not entirely work.

Before he was sent home from his tour of duty, Roger passed an extensive physical exam given by army doctors. He appeared to be totally normal, and was given a clean bill of health. But troubling symptoms began to appear over the succeeding months as he tried to adjust to civilian life. And presently his affliction got worse and worse. In those early days, no one attributed it to Agent Orange. Instead, Roger was diagnosed with Combat Fatigue, as it used to be called before a more accurate term came into use, Post Traumatic Stress Disorder, or PTSD.

His wife, Molly Dowman, was deeply in love with him, and so she valiantly tried to cope. In spite of what the doctors said about Roger's condition, she knew that *something mysterious* had to be wrong with him – something that could not be denied any longer, when he developed asthma, emphysema and heart failure at age 26 and the mottled flesh of his chest and underarms started to peel and rot off.

Scrambling for an answer or a cure, Molly delved obsessively into medical texts both ancient and modern, and the nearest description she could find of what was happening to Roger was *leprosy*. But the doctors almost laughed at her for mentioning it. They insisted that her husband was mentally ill in some strange way and that his symptoms were psychosomatic. They gave her the example of Padre Pio, an Italian priest whose hands, head and feet would spontaneously bleed on Good Friday, in imitation of the crucified Christ. The padre was beatified as a saint of the Roman

Catholic Church, even though un-superstitious scientists knew that his stigmata were created by the inner workings of his fervently religious mind, and that is how he had subconsciously willed tiny capillaries of his body to rupture and bleed. Each time he did this, the capillaries became thinner and weaker, making the psychosomatic effect easier and easier to pull off.

Molly and Roger tried everything they could think of, or were told about, out of desperation to find a remedy. Acupuncture. Hypnosis. Homeopathic medicine. Herbs and potions and vitamins galore. Alas, nothing worked! Deteriorating mentally as well as physically, in his addled brain Roger developed the notion that his wife was a demon who had cursed him and was making him ill. By this time, he was not holding down any sort of job, his unemployment compensation and army medical benefits had run out, and his wife and mother-in-law were the breadwinners. All three were living in the same shabby apartment together because it was the only way they could take turns caring for Roger while at the same time barely making ends meet.

Roger eventually came to believe that his mother-in-law and his wife were *both* demons and they were inhabiting his brain and making parts of his body rot off till there would be nothing left – if he didn't take an immediate step to abort the process.

The proper step was to strangle them to death.

Surprisingly, he enjoyed doing it. He raped his own wife and sodomized his own mother-in-law, then killed them. Their bodies were found a day or two after they were dead, but Roger somehow evaded capture for weeks, by living in the woods like an animal. Maybe he actually *was* a wild animal now. Maybe the Agent Orange had eroded his brain down to its primitive, animalistic elements. He was far better adapted to living in the wild than living among civilized humanity, now that his own inner humanity was gone.

He went on a rampage of rape and murder that absolutely terrified the small farming community where he and his wife and mother-in-law had been living. The police had smears of his seminal fluid but they didn't know where he was or how to track him down. This was decades before DNA testing, which was to come into play much later, at my behest.

He began to believe that he could not ever be captured or killed. He became imbued with the idea that he was immortal and omnipotent. He was an evil spirit who could never, ever die. He was no longer a mortal, but a sort of god, a specter, a sex-obsessed ghost.

One night in June of 1967 after he had already raped and murdered seven women during his time on the loose, he sneaked into the home of a beautiful young bride-to-be named Judy Scranton. He crept out of the surrounding woods and onto her patio, and pried open a sliding glass door while no one was home. He had what to him was a supernatural intuition that since Judy's wedding rehearsal was that afternoon, she would return to the isolated house where she lived with her policeman father, as soon as the rehearsal was over. He hated anyone who led a normal life, because he was incapable of doing that. He told himself that he no longer needed or wanted a life of that mundane sort. He was beyond that now. He was above it all. He was immortal. He was omnipotent.

***

Judy's father, Norman Scranton, was actually at a crime scene right then. He was there because Roger had provided him with a decoy -- something to keep him away from home long enough for his daughter to meet her fate. Roger had purposely left the lieutenant the dead body of another young girl that he had raped and killed previously. He had dumped the girl's body at the side of a well-traveled road just so it would be promptly discovered and reported and thus drawing the lead investigator there while his daughter was being horribly ravaged.

Norman and the coroner, Stan Jenkins, were standing over the nude body, staring at it, shaking their heads. They knew her personally. She was 17-year-old Nancy Jansen, the daughter of a local handyman. She was nude, and her throat bore strangulation bruises. Stan Jenkins said, "She's been dead only a few hours. I'd guess it's the work of Roger Dowman, and if so this makes number eight for him. Frustrating as hell, Norman – to know who the killer is but not where to find him."

Norman said, "Sooner or later he'll make a mistake. My men will finish combing the area after you get her out of here. Do you believe it? This was my day off. I was supposed to be at my daughter's wedding rehearsal."

***

In a fury, Roger Dowman started trashing the game room, tearing framed photos and mementoes off the walls and stomping the glass into the carpet. The whole place completely turned into a wreck, but Roger continued his frenzy for quite a while longer, screaming in rage, tears running down his face as he vented his hatred and self-pity. He stopped briefly and leaned against a wall, panting. Then he snatched a police bowling league trophy from the mantel and hurled it against the fireplace bricks, loudly shattering it to pieces.

In the moments of silence that followed, he heard a car pull onto the gravel driveway. He crept to the living room. Peeling an edge of window curtain aside just slightly, he snooped and eavesdropped. Judy and her betrothed, Steve Adams, came up onto the porch. They embraced and kissed. Roger heard them talking about the bachelor party Steve had to go to tonight. Good.

He was soon to depart. He would leave Judy alone. The way Roger wanted her. Roger needed "quality time" with her before her policeman father should arrive home.

Smiling after kissing Steve good-bye, Judy unlocked the front door and entered the house. Roger heard Steve slam his car door, start his engine and pull away. Roger was listening from a hiding place, a place where Judy wouldn't immediately discover him. She went into her bedroom, kicking off her shoes. She put her purse on her dresser, then looked at her reflection in a full-length mirror, turning this way and that, assessing her attractive figure. Then she began to undress, removing her blouse and skirt first, getting down to bra and panties. She stepped out of the panties and put them on the dresser. Then she unsnapped her bra.

Roger leapt out of her closet and pounced on her!

She screamed as the bra fell, exposing her breasts. He cut her scream short by seizing her by her throat and forcing her down onto her bed. She whimpered, trying to resign herself to being raped. Her eyes bulged wide with terror, and with the choking. For a long time he continued his assault on her. When he finished, crying out in extreme pleasure, he slowly realized she was already dead. He hadn't meant to finish her so soon. He had meant to drag out the experience so as to enjoy it to its fullest.

He was zipping his pants up when he suddenly heard a key in a lock. The front door! Someone was entering!

Roger ran into the kitchen to grab a knife. He knew that Lt. Norman Scranton, Judy's father, must be arriving home too soon – and of course he would have a gun. Roger seized a huge butcher knife from the knife block, but he didn't feel he could go up against the gun, and he had no place to run to, except down the basement stairs. He made a dash for them as Norman fired a shot that splintered the door jamb. But Roger wasn't hit. He jumped rather than ran down the basement stairs, taking two or three steps at a time. Norman fired at him again, but the basement was almost totally dark, and the shot went wild. Soon, Roger feared, he would lose the shelter of darkness – Norman would surely flip a switch and turn the lights on. Before that could happen, Roger reversed himself, hoping to gain an element of surprise. He ducked low and charged back up the stairs at Norman, instead of going farther down, as any normal pursuer would expect, especially one with a gun.

Roger tackled Norman on the stairs – and the gun went flying as Norman fell hard and Roger stabbed him in his shoulder. They grappled with one another. Norman, twenty years older than Roger, was still stronger than Roger expected, and he managed to twist the knife out of Roger's hand. Amazingly, Roger was losing the battle – maybe because of the depredations of Agent Orange. He had heard the knife clattering on the concrete below, out of reach. He was desperate to get it back. So he let himself fall over the edge of the staircase. And miraculously he fell on the knife, but not onto the sharp point of it – it was lying flat and so it didn't harm him.

He knew once more that he was immortal and omnipotent. And he grabbed the knife by its handle as Norman was about to pounce on him again. He got up smiling an evil smile, and Norman backed off, looking scared, ready to beg for mercy. But Roger jabbed the knife hard at him – and Norman barely managed to spin and duck. The blade of the knife entirely missed Norman's body – and slammed instead into the basement fuse box. It was the old-fashioned kind, not one replaced by modern circuit breakers.

And Roger's knife thrust went deeply into the electrical wiring!

There was a loud ZAP!! And then a SIZZLE!!

Roger was electrocuted. He jerked and writhed in his death throes as the current coursed wildly through him. And as he died he cried, "I am immortal! I can never die! I am the undead! And I will be back to devour you!"

Where these prophetic words came from, nobody exactly knows. They sounded like the farfetched delusions of Roger Dowman's chemically altered brain – the same ugly and fearsome alterations enabled by Agent Orange, eventually making him into a demented rapist and serial killer. Viewed that way, it is relatively easy to concede that he was not responsible for what was done to him, nor for what he became.

As a scientist who knows more about such things than other scientists in other disciplines do, I have come to the belief that Roger Dowman was destined to become the first of the undead. I cannot absolutely prove this, but I firmly believe it. Call it intelligence enhance by intuition. The same kind of intuition that manifested itself in a more perverse fashion inside Roger Dowman's ravaged mind. I think that what he became was due to a combination of the chemical effects of his exposure to Agent Orange combined with the ravaging effects of his unintended and untimely electrocution during the fight with Lt. Norman Scranton.

In any event, the pure unadulterated fact is that, when Roger Dowman's body was about to be lowered into a pauper's grave, the grave diggers took a break and left him lying there while they lit up cigarettes. They stared at his body and made jokes about it. They agreed that he met a fate that he richly deserved. They even told stories about some of his victims and the ways in which he killed them, for the gravediggers knew some of the victims personally.

But the next morning Dowman's intended grave was not filled in, and his body was nowhere to be seen. Instead both of the gravediggers were found dead, and parts of their flesh had been devoured.

Four decades after all the sad, terrifying events of Roger Dowman's life and his, perhaps, lack of staying dead, it was possible to test for his DNA in the semen smears taken from his wife and mother-in-law, and to compare them with DNA taken from bites into the flesh of the two gravediggers. It was a match, to the exclusion of all other persons inhabiting the earth.

And that is why I think that Roger Dowman, undead, was the entity who attacked the brother and sister in the cemetery in 1968.

HOME COOKIN'
by Tyson Blue

Tyson Blue, a true eminence grise in the world of horror criticism, has been reviewing books, stories, films, and audiobooks in the genre since the late 1970's. He is considered an expert on the work of Stephen King and the various media projects related thereto, and has lectured extensively on the subject around the country. His THE UNSEEN KING, the first definitive study of King's lesser-known and unpublished work, was for years the standard work on the subject. A Contributing Editor to Castle Rock: the Stephen King Newsletter, and Cemetery Dance for many years, Blue has also written and published a number of short stories for various anthologies. The story in the present volume was originally written in 1989 for consideration for Skipp and Spector's classic zombie anthology BOOK OF THE DEAD. This marks its first publication. Blue lives with his wife, Janice, near Rochester, New York, and practices law in his spare time.

The last thing Wilmer Warner ever saw was his own heart being eaten by a dead black man as Warner lay at his feet in a puddle of gasoline and blood. (The blood was his, the gasoline wasn't.) Warner was not the first person in Shannon to die that night, and he wasn't the last, but if the survivors could agree on nothing else in the days that followed, they agreed that he was the most deserving.

Warner was a lawyer, and a damned good one, which meant that even his own clients thought he was a mercenary, heartless son of a bitch—which turned out to be true in the final analysis. He had resented being called away from the annual Larey County

Leadership Ball which had been in full swing at the country club earlier that evening to bail out a client charged with DUI—as things turned out, it probably allowed him to live for a few more hours.

When Luther Mullis had made his one phone call to Warner's answering service, who then dutifully passed it along to him, Wilmer had been hobnobbing with the judge who had appointed him as juvenile court judge three years before. Warner was grateful to the judge for that step, at least in public, and always swore that out of gratitude, he would never run against him for Superior Court judge, when in point of actual fact he was gearing up to do just that.

In order to understand precisely how Wilmer Warner came to end up as a hot lunch for a walking dead man, it is necessary to shift the scene a bit, from the country club to the woods nearby. In those woods was located a secret graveyard where the Larey County Sheriff's Office had seen fit to carry out a few clandestine burials of individuals who had died at the county work camp, a penal facility which, albeit somewhat Byzantine by most people's standards, precisely suited the sensibilities of the average citizens of Larey County, Georgia.

Deaths happened at the County Farm from time to time, but most there were a result of attempts to escape, or from accidents which were a natural concomitant of the type of heavy labor which one would expect in places like this. The persons buried in the woods near the second tee at the country club, however, had died from beatings administered by the guards at the facility, and these inmates simply disappeared, buried at night and listed on the official records as escapees.

Now while Wilmer Warner was brown-nosing potential voters among the hoi-polloi attending the country club dance, and while Luther Mullis, who had in fact had a few while fishing down on the river that evening, was driving toward the club, the former inmates of the County Farm began bursting out of the ground and tottering through the scrub pines toward the road. There were an even dozen of them, in varying degrees of decomposition from a nearly-mummified fat man to one particularly grotesque young man who had been added to the "cemetery" only a week before.

This last man had been carried out of the County Farm in a wooden crate which had originally been used to ship a new engine which drove a saw at the Farm's mill; and because the man was too tall to fit into the box intact, that very saw had been used to saw off his legs at the knee. Although no one knew it at the time, when the corpse had awakened in the box, he had devoured both of his legs before digging his way to the surface, and he had tottered out onto the roadway by walking on his hands just as Luther Mullis was driving by.

Luther saw the legless man waddle into the road almost under his bumper and slammed on his brakes so hard that his last two "Pony" bottles of beer flew off the seat beside him and shattered on the dashboard, soaking him with beer and thus furthering the suspicions of the deputy who would soon charge him with driving under the influence.

Luther unwrapped himself from around his truck's steering wheel, eased his grime-crusted gimme-cap back into its customary place atop his head, and nervously stepped out of the cab. His truck had stalled out, and there was dead quiet around. He came quickly around to the front of the truck, his face flushed.

"What in the sam hill you mean, boy, walkin' out in front 'a me like 'at —" His incensed tirade broke off abruptly as he saw the unmistakably dead man perched before him on its hands, the truncated legs swinging back and forth with pendulum-like regularity. The lifeless eyes stared up at him from a slack face. As Luther watched, the mouth writhed in a grin, and clots of dirt and pine straw oozed out.

"Oh, my Gawd," Luther choked, and felt his stomach roll over. Just before he puked, he felt both of his sphincters let go. As the dead man in the road began waddling toward him, looking almost like one of those Weeble toys his sister's boy had, Luther broke and ran for his life. He tore the door of the pickup open and leaped inside, slamming it and locking the door. As he frantically tried to restart the flooded engine, he first became aware of the other figures which were shambling toward him out of the woods. Their stick-like, dead arms flailed out, finger scrabbling over the windows, trying to get in.

Just as he felt his sanity was about to go, the engine caught and the truck roared into life. He threw it into gear and stood on the gas, the wheels crunching over the skull of the legless man as two more of the walking corpses were spun off into the ditches by the fenders. The legless man flopped on the blacktop like a beached fish for a few seconds, then lay still.

Luther had just about enough time for his heart to begin slowing down once more when the backlight window of his truck cab smashed inward and a vile-smelling black arm began flopping about, hand clutching the air in search of something living. Luther screamed. There was one of them in the payload.

Howling with fear, Luther began weaving back and forth in the road, trying to shake loose his undead rider. He could see patches of mold growing on the arm which groped for him, and the smell of something long in the earth was filling the cab. It was while he was trying this maneuver that Luther was spotted by a sheriff's car, which gave chase, blue lights flashing and siren wailing.

So intent was Luther on getting rid of this man in his truck that he didn't notice two things. The first one was the deputy chasing him. The second one was the curve where Country Club Road ran into the highway which led into Shannon. He ran a red light and plunged straight across the highway, went over the embankment and then was thrown from the truck as it rolled over three times and exploded, taking with it Luther's ghastly rider.

The luck which attends drunks and other fools was with Luther, who came out of the accident with only cuts and bruises and a few new additions to his traffic record, the latter courtesy of the deputy who helped him up the bank to the highway before handcuffing him and thrusting him into the back of the patrol car. Having arrested Luther a time or two before, Deputy Lucius Cole didn't bother to listen to his frenzied tale of walking dead men.

He would listen soon enough.

While Lucius was booking Luther, and Luther was interfering with Wilmer Warner's political aspirations, and while the remaining revenants from the secret graveyard near the country club were shuffling slowly toward Shannon, things were happening all over the city. The secret cemetery was not the only graveyard in Larey County whose natives were restless this foggy night. Among many other incidents which were later discovered were these:

Pretty young Carrie Smith was lying on the front seat of the Mustang which belonged to her boyfriend, also named Carey Smith (a subject of endless jokes from the couple's friends at Shannon High), her legs resting on the ground. She wore only her blouse, which was wide open.

The car was parked in what, in retrospect, was a pretty stupid place—Shannon Rest Cemetery. But they didn't know that then; they only wanted a little privacy.

Carey was kissing her with total absorption, moving down her neck, over her breasts, then down her belly. Carrie had her eyes closed, letting her other senses carry the load. Carey jerked away from her for a moment, making a funny choked sound.

Carrie hardly had time to register the icy cold of the mouth on her crotch before it bit her.

A five-year-old boy who had gone out his back window after his bedtime for a last-minute check on the backyard grave of his beloved cat, buried the day before, was so frightened he couldn't even scream before the animal, which was halfway up out of the ground as he arrived, sprang at him and buried its filthy, needle-sharp teeth in his carotid artery. Boy and cat fell back, a thin fountain of blood spraying up over them. Undisturbed, for no one knew the boy was gone, the cat began to feed.

Mildred Coffey, unable to sleep, to relax, to do anything, sat and sipped a glass of sherry. She had buried her husband Edward that very afternoon, and she wanted only to have him back with her again. It is uncertain whether Mildred ever heard the old Chinese proverb about being careful what she wished for, but at any rate, the doorbell rang, and she got it.

Daisy McHenry was an old black woman whose modest brick home bordered on the African Baptist Church graveyard. She had read her Bible until it got too dark to see any longer without turning on the lights, then gone to bed. She was awakened by a crashing of brush in her backyard, and when she went to her back door and turned on her porch light, she found the yard teeming with a crowd of people, some wearing dirty, torn dress clothes, others in nightclothes or winding sheets.

They spotted her, and began shuffling purposefully toward the door. It wasn't a sturdy door; it didn't hold them long.

Daisy was a small meal.

Mark Henderson was the orderly working the night shift in the morgue at Shannon's Broadview Park Hospital. He had nearly dozed off over a thick paperback novel when a sudden pounding began on the doors of the lockers where the bodies were stored, bringing him bolt upright.

Dr. Singh was the pathologist on duty that night. He'd done an autopsy earlier on a man who'd died during surgery that day, and gone off to grab a bite to eat before coming back to sew up the body. Mark thought at first that the doc might have sneaked back in and gotten in the locker to scare him (he wouldn't put it past him), but he wasn't about to check it out alone.

Not taking his eyes off the metal doors, which were beginning to dent with the force of the internal blows raining on them, Mark backed up and headed toward the table behind him, where the body of the autopsy subject, its chest still cut wide open, sat up. The unrestrained organs flopped out of the body cavity and onto the floor. Mark stepped in them and slipped. His feet left the floor and his head landed in the dead man's lap. Before Mark could scream, the dead mouth closed on his face.

In Stumps Park, Shannon's central greensward, Buzzy Jones prowled among the trees in search of a little late night action. Shannon didn't exactly have what one could call a gay scene, and it was tough to score these days. That might be the reason Buzzy so readily approached the young boy who tottered dazedly through the park. Buzzy thought he'd lucked out, though—the boy didn't bat an eye when Buzzy squeezed his ass; in fact, he put his close-cropped head on Buzzy's shoulder and nuzzled his neck.

Buzzy's dreams of a perfect evening began dissolving when the boy's rotted stench seared his nostrils, and collapsed entirely when the boy tore his throat out.

Red Sheftoe was Shannon's designated town bum, and was asleep in an alley between Pa Dawkins' Restaurant, a downtown greasy spoon, and the local gold and silver exchange. It was a good place to sleep, as the heat from the restaurant kitchen would keep him warm most of the night. This was the sort of survival tip you picked up living on the streets for five years. When the two dead men sloughed down the alley, they stepped over him and kept right on going. Why they did this is uncertain—perhaps he smelled so bad they thought he was already dead, maybe they even thought he was one of them. It doesn't really matter.

R.L. Thompson was an old man who lived in a fenced-in mini-fortress on the edge of town. Although no one suspected it, he had kidnapped and murdered fourteen children over the last ten years and buried them under trees set out in his vast wooded backlot. He was awakened this evening by a scraping on his back door, and was surprised to find his previous victims gathered around him like a group of gruesome Trick-or-Treaters, come to repay him for his hospitality.

The party at the country club was in full swing, managing somehow in spite of the unexpected absence of Wilmer Warner. The glass windows of the club's terrace dining area offered no obstacle whatsoever to the efforts of the nine remaining men who had arisen from the secret graveyard in the woods and made their way to the club after their run-in with Luther Mullis. None of the former inmates of the County Farm had been members of the country club, nor was their present appearance likely to make them candidates for admission, but none of the attendees of the party seemed to consider that.

Wilmer Warner need not have concerned himself with running for judge, since he would not have been opposed after this night. The incumbent was dragged down and disemboweled by two of the creatures before they moved on to some of the others. In all, twenty of the cream of Shannon high society were either killed outright by the shambling revenants, or died from heart attacks or strokes and were gobbled up along with the rest. The fortunate few who did manage to escape headed for home and called the

Sheriff's Department, adding to what soon became the general hysteria.

And finally, Sid Gregory, an officer of the Georgia Department of Transportation, arrested the driver of a tanker truck loaded with ten thousand gallons of gasoline for a violation of the state's interstate transport laws. This required the driver to be taken to the County Jail, where he would be allowed to call his employers, who would then wire him money to pay a fine and he would be allowed to go on his merry way. Since he refused to leave his rig out on the highway, he drove it into Shannon and parked it across the street from the courthouse.

The DOT officer had dumped the fuming driver on Deputy Sgt. Phillip Taylor and then left. This had been a busy twenty minutes or so for Taylor. He had just finished booking Luther Mullis on a DUI charge—he was cooling his heels in an interview room while that hot-tempered racist sumbitch Wilmer Warner came in from the country club to bail him out—and now Taylor had to stand there and nod quietly and listen to this loud-mouthed asshole spout off about the inherent unfairness of the state's highway laws, the outrageous fines and all the drunks that seemed to be wandering around along on the highways tonight.

Taylor was just finishing up the paperwork on the DOT case when Wilmer Warner entered the waiting area. He stood there a moment, his feet planted apart, his thin slit of a mouth tight and his beady eyes glaring out through the huge lenses of his glasses. He reached out to shake the handle of the locked door of the Sheriff's Office, looking to Taylor like the world's biggest little kid, peering through the screen and wanting to be let in to go to the bathroom.

"Are you going to let me in," he hissed, "or am I going to stand out here all night?"

"Just let me finish with this gentleman here and I'll be right with you, Mr. Warner," Taylor answered. He didn't like Warner – the man was a juvenile court judge, but he acted like a high-school hall monitor or a highway flagman, getting a little power and acting like he was King Shit on Turd Mountain.

"While you do that, can I see my client?" Warner snarled.

"Certainly, sir," Taylor said, getting up and opening the door to let the fuming Warner in. He told him where Luther was waiting, and the lawyer stepped into the interview room and slammed the door.

"Sometimes," he told Luther with a meaningful twitch of his head in Taylor's direction, "I remember why it is that I've always had a distaste for dark pigmentation."

"Hey, Mr. Warner, listen, am I glad to see you!" Luther rose and pumped Warner's hand. Warner, getting a whiff of Luther's unique perfume blend—beer, piss, shit, and the miasma of dead flesh—grimaced and tore his hand free, then wiped it on his pants leg. "God-DAMN, boy, where have you *been*?"

Before Luther could answer him, the driver of the tank-truck screamed.

Taylor had let him out the door, and as it shut behind him the outer door opened to admit a shambling dead man. The man was wearing an old blue suit, which hung loosely over his stick-like limbs. Patches of bone showed through his forehead, and a fine fuzz of brown mold covered his face. The eyes were gone, but he was drawn to the trucker by feel, the champing jaws closing on his shoulder as he turned to head back into the office where it was safe.

The trucker screamed as the dead man tore a quivering chunk of meat out of his shoulder. Blood sprayed everywhere, drenching Taylor. The shambling monster sought to tear the trucker away from the counter, but his fingers were clenched through the heavy steel mesh. The keys to his truck lay on the edge of the counter where he had dropped them. As Taylor watched in horror, the thing tore the poor bastard loose, leaving one finger hanging in the screen, and fell with him to the floor, where frenzied chewing sounds rose up as the screams fell off and finally died.

Warner and Luther had flown out of the interview room to watch the awful scene, and Taylor shoved them aside to get to the radio. Warner absently rubbed at the place where the black deputy's hand had touched him. Taylor keyed the radio and spoke into the microphone.

"Central SO to Unit 1263," he said. "What's your 20?"

"We're right downtown en route back to your location," came back the reply from Roger James, one of the three deputies on the road. "This is unreal, Sarge. I know you're not going to believe this, but the whole damn street is full of dead people!"

"That's what I tried to tell y'all," Luther whined, "but you wouldn't listen!"

"I believe you," Taylor answered. "One of 'em's here in the outer office eating up a trucker the DOT brought in."

"Holy God," screamed James. "We're comin' in ASAP."

"Just don't let those things get you."

All of the major highways and small roads in Larey County naturally funneled traffic into the center of Shannon's main drag, which ran from the county courthouse at one end to City Hall at the other. Since the army of walking dead had tended to follow the roads, they had almost all ended up there.

A few had followed the bypass and were wandering through residential streets and pouncing on anything and anyone that moved. Others had been drawn to the lights at the hospital and were having a field day with those patients and personnel who had not already fallen victim to those in the morgue who had gotten a head start.

Oddly enough, none of them went to the Shannon Mall. Evidently, it had not been an important part of their lives.

"Is there another way out of here?" Warner asked Taylor.

Taylor glanced at him, then went on loading the M-16 he'd broken out of the riot locker in the back.

"There's a side door in Sheriff Webster's office," he said, jerking his head in their direction. He then set the gun down beside him and went back to work on the radio, taking calls from the city police and the Georgia State Patrol. The reports confirmed, that evidently, most of the creatures were presently massed downtown between the courthouse and City Hall.

Taylor spotted the trucker's keys on the counter, and remembered the man bitching at him about how he hoped the cops didn't mind ten thousand gallons of gasoline sitting out there in the middle of the street while he wasted his time farting around in here, and an idea began to germinate in the back of Taylor's mind. He chambered a round in his rifle and reached for the key ring.

As his fingers closed around the ring, the dead thing reared up on the other side of the mesh, gobbets of meat and shredded cloth clinging to its gaping, champing maw. Taylor screamed, flung the key ring to the floor behind him and squeezed off a full clip from the M-16 on auto burn. The dead man's skull disintegrated in a foul mist as the slugs tore through it.

While this was going on, Warner grabbed Luther by the arm and headed for the side door.

"Come on," he told his client. "We're getting out of here."

"Wait a minute," Luther protested. "Don't you think we'd be safer in here?"

Warner jerked him along.

"I'm your lawyer, you listen to me!" He shook Luther like a rag-doll. "We have to get out to my car, where we have some mobility! These things'll break in past that nigger and get us if we sit there and wait for them."

He opened the outer door, which let into a corridor running along the outer wall of the Sheriff's Department. Looking through the window of a door at the end of the corridor, Warner could see his Cadillac. Pulling Luther with him, he headed for the car. Suddenly, three shambling corpses blocked his way.

Without even a moment's hesitation, Warner flung Luther at the three. Luther screamed like a woman as they fell on him. Warner wrenched open the door of his Caddy and flung himself inside, locking the door. He started the car and roared out of one end of the Sheriff's Department parking area as Roger James' car pulled in from the other side. James screeched to a halt and flung his door open, drawing his Colt Python .357 Magnum, which boomed as he snapped off shots at the creatures around Luther Mullis' partially-devoured body.

Taylor came out the door, the trucker's keys in one hand and the reloaded M-16 in the other. He spotted the truck across the street and headed for it. There were a few of the things shambling along, but he downed them with controlled bursts of fire. He reached the truck and started it, driving it around the courthouse to stop it so that the tanker hoses faced down the street where most of the zombies were milling about aimlessly.

Jumping down, Taylor raced to the tanker and unlimbered the two hoses. He dropped them into the street pointing downhill toward the undead horde and turned the valves as quickly as he could. Slowly, ten thousand gallons of gasoline began to flow down the street, toward the milling horde of creatures, which filled the main drag of Shannon. Taylor was only dimly aware of Warner's Cadillac racing down the street past him, ignoring the ominous tide through which he drove and the mob toward which he was headed.

At the last minute, Warner suddenly saw the shuffling things in front of him. He hissed and wrenched his wheel to the right. The Cadillac rolled and became airborne, smashing through the window of a dress shop. Warner shoved the door open and rolled from the upside-down vehicle. As he landed on the sidewalk, his broken left leg folded up under him, the bones bursting through the skin. He screamed and dragged himself into the street.

Although he was too frenzied with fear and pain to notice it, gasoline was soaking his clothing. And even if the living dead into whose midst he was crawling were aware of their danger, the presence of food in their path overwhelmed them. They surrounded him, grasped him, tore at him, ignored his babbled appeals. A black man knelt on his stomach and tore open his chest and rooted around with gnarled fingers.

And as we have said earlier, the last thing Wilmer Warner ever saw was his own heart being eaten by a dead black man. He never saw the gnawing at his broken leg, and he never saw Phil Taylor fire a quick burst from his M-16 at the street, never saw the bullets strike sparks from a manhole cover, never saw the eye-searing fireball which consumed Warner and all the creatures around him, before it rolled up into the night sky over the busily-burning ruin that had been, mere moments before, the main street of Shannon, Georgia.

The mop-up came the next morning. The fire which had destroyed most of the creatures (along with Wilmer Warner and the majority of downtown Shannon) was not cool enough for anyone to approach the wreckage. The initial blast had killed Phil Taylor, and the secondary explosion caused by the ignition of fumes inside the tanker had flattened the courthouse behind it, killing Roger James and his partner, along with a few more of the creatures. As the courthouse fell, it took with it the radio antenna which broadcast signals for all three major law enforcement agencies, forcing the survivors to rely on hand-units while they roamed the streets in pairs, destroying those few of the walking dead who had not been incinerated in the fire the night before.

One enterprising State Patrol officer lured a handful of the things into the woods behind him, perched in a deer stand high in a tree—the creatures could not climb trees—and picked them off with a high-powered rifle while they milled around below him.

All of the survivors were quite self-satisfied with their day's work, and were heartily congratulating themselves on how well they had come through this horrifying ordeal when someone in their midst pointed out just how many cemeteries there were in Larey County, and that no one had yet thought to find out if the problem was, as they had assumed, a strictly local one...

THE LAST MINISTRY
by E.L. Stice

E. L. Stice is an author who lives in Kansas City, Missouri, with her husband and three cats, mostly acquired by accident. In a past life, she was a technical writer and snooty grammarian but now has embraced the more ambiguous existence of fiction writer, sometime blogger, and intermittent poet. You can visit her at cheekyginger.com.

And this shall be the plague with which the LORD will smite all the people that have fought against Jerusalem: Their flesh will decay while they stand on their feet, their eyes will rot away in their sockets, and their tongues will dissolve in their mouths. — Zechariah 14:12

Reverend Thomas Daniels opened his eyes to darkness. The room was chilly, wood being difficult to come by lately. Little wood meant little hot water for washing, so the sheets—and the man—had taken on the stale, greasy odor of unclean humanity—dirty clothing, rank sweat, oily hair. That was all right. There were worse smells.

From out of the night came the familiar, relentless tick of the clock he'd wound before sundown; silence reigned otherwise. Nonetheless, something had awoken him. He was reassured by the feel of the shotgun, cleaned and loaded, under his hand. A box of shells was within reach. The hunting knife strapped to his thigh was gleaming and sharp. These were the important things now. What used to be the important things? He almost couldn't remember anymore. It wasn't just that he was too focused on survival to think about it; a fence had been erected in his mind. There was THEN, and there was NOW. THEN, he had known everyone in this small town and had, in the way of small towns, been well-known and revered in turn. THEN had been a time of Bible reading, preparing and delivering sermons, Sunday dinner with parishioners, officiating the occasional wedding, visiting the sick, sending off the dead. The dead. That job, at least, had persisted. As had, on occasion, the Bible reading. That was the NOW.

Slowly, carefully, Daniels slipped out of bed. He kept the springs of the narrow bed frame oiled, but still, occasionally, they creaked when he got in or out. Tonight they did not creak. Good. Holding the shotgun, he crept toward the window that overlooked the front yard, then moved the curtain back a fraction of an inch, just enough to allow him to see outside. Nothing. He saw nothing. But he was not reassured. He remained still for a full minute longer, peering into the darkness, willing his ears to detect the slightest sound. Finally, he let the curtain close and turned toward the bedroom door but did not move. No rush. The undead were in no hurry, so neither was he. Time passed. Still he waited as silently as possible. As far as he had been able to discern, in general the undead couldn't see well, but they had keen hearing.

Snick.

That had sounded like the deadbolt. Not likely. He'd been alone in this house for weeks, with the exception of brief forays outside for supplies and what he had begun thinking of as hunting missions, and in all that time he had not seen another live human being. It wasn't past reasonable that one of *them* could get in with brute force, despite his fortifications—but working a lock? No. His ears were misleading him. Or the undead were smarter than he'd realized. Or. Or. Or.

Death was a reality, his and everyone else's, but he wasn't in any rush to get there … especially now. Best to deal with whatever was waiting, then. He was out the bedroom door and on the landing almost before the thought had come to him. In one smooth action, he cocked the shotgun, raised it to his shoulder, and aimed it down the stairs. Let them come, the unholy bastards. Maybe they could learn, *would* learn, to recognize that sound, at least.

"Don't shoot!"

He was so startled that he almost did. Later, he would wonder how pulling the trigger might have changed things.

Reverend Daniels peered down into the darkness. The moonlight from the window did not reach the bottom of the stairway. "Who's there?"

"It's Paul, Paul Aikins," came the clear voice.

Paul Aikins, the town atheist and resident long-hair, at the preacher's house. That was almost funny. When Daniels spoke, he kept his voice low, but still loud enough to be heard. "Step out where I can see you, Mr. Aikins. Come up the stairs. Slowly." He kept the gun pointed down the stairs as the tall, shadowy figure came into sight, hands raised. "Now stop." Daniels hadn't heard the undead talk before, and Aikins didn't look or move like one of them. Still, it was better to be cautious. "How did you get in?"

"I used the key under the mat."

In other circumstances, that *would* have been funny. But now it was just unnerving. All his precautions—boarding up the first floor windows, making sure there were no hiding places near the house, staying quiet—and he'd left the spare key under the mat. Not that the undead could ever figure out how to use it, probably, but still, leaving it there was careless. Though he was sure now that Aikins was not one of them, it would be even more careless to assume that meant that his survival up to this point was because of anything but dumb luck. "Did you lock the door behind you?" Daniels asked.

Aikins actually chuckled at that. "Yeah. It'd be a shame to find probably the only other person alive in this town and end up getting us both killed because a walker managed to open the door I was too stupid to lock."

At that, Daniels lowered the shotgun. "A walker, eh? I call them undead, or sometimes just 'them,'" he said. "Come on up, and we'll talk."

Talk they did, in low, measured tones, wasting few words as they traded information and observations until sunrise, starting with how they'd realized what was going on. Paul—they took to using first names after the reverend observed that if the only other live person in town was an atheist, his title no longer had much meaning—described how he'd been driving to his house just outside of town one early evening a few weeks ago and had seen someone walking, stumbling, slowly up the road toward him. As he drew closer, he could see that the black suit the big man was wearing was filthy and torn. He started to brake and rolled down his window, intending to ask the man if he needed help. The man began shuffling toward the car, and a shock of unreasoning fear spurred Paul into action. "I floored it. Got home as quick as I could, ran in the house, locked the door. For a while I just sat in the living room, shaking. I asked myself why I would do that, what I was afraid of, why didn't I give the man a ride to the hospital, what was wrong with me. Finally it hit me. I knew him. *It was Dave Carpenter.*"

Thomas looked at the other man carefully before speaking, trying to determine if Paul believed what he was saying. In his experience—the reverend had always had a peculiarly practical bent and believed there was no point in pretending humans were less flawed than they were—people lied to their religious leaders only slightly less thoroughly than they lied to their doctors. But then, he wasn't Paul's minister, and Paul clearly believed what he'd just said, however unlikely it seemed. When he spoke, he spoke slowly, articulating every word. "That doesn't make any sense, Paul. Dave Carpenter passed away over a month ago. He would have been dead and buried three weeks by then."

"Buried, yes." Paul looked away. "But not dead. At least, not normal dead. It was him, all right. Taller than me, big as a house, that ugly mole on his chin like a fat black raisin …"

"Still, it might have been someone visiting or traveling through," Thomas said. "Someone who looked like Mr. Carpenter and got in an accident, maybe."

Now it was Paul's turn to try to reason with the unreasonable. "THOMAS. The thing was wearing a black suit, a funeral suit. Covered in mud from head to toe; where do you think that came from? *Jesus H. Christ, the goddamn eyes were still sewn shut.*" He shuddered.

Thomas still wasn't convinced. "I've seen dozens, maybe hundreds of them in the past few weeks, none that looked like they came out of a grave. In fact, I knew most of them before they turned."

"No surprise there," Paul said. "I think Carpenter was the only one who came back that way, the only corpse fresh enough to. I think he started the whole mess. You've seen how it works, how it spreads, right?"

Thomas had, of course. People got attacked, died, then came back, but not as themselves. Not as human. Paul's theory made sense, in a way. John Carpenter was the first person who'd died around their little town in the past few years before this had started. Maybe the rest of the local graves contained bodies too far gone to have been infected by the contagion. Or at least too far gone to be able to claw their way to the surface.

"You may be right. I've seen plenty of corpses in my line of work, but until a few weeks ago, they all stayed dead. None of this makes much sense to me," Thomas said. "Let's get some rest. We'll think more clearly when we're not so tired."

That afternoon, after they'd both slept—or tried to—the men took stock of their situation. The advantages of staying together were clear and could be summarized best by a phrase every schoolboy who'd ever walked through the woods after dark knew: safety in numbers, even when it's just holding hands and whistling in the dark. Everything else beyond that, however, was a difficult choice.

"Stay or go, that's the question," Paul said. "I'd been thinking about getting out of town. It's a Morton's Fork, though: if we stay in the middle of their hunting ground, we might end up joining them because of their numbers. But if we leave, abandon what safety we have, and can't get out of their territory ..." He let that hang.

"I hadn't planned to leave. Leaving feels wrong. But maybe that's just habit talking, because these people were my charge." The look Thomas shot at the other man was straightforward but contained a hint of defiance. "That probably doesn't make any sense to you."

"Why, because I don't believe in God? I don't think it matters why you were a leader, just that you were. And good leaders don't abandon their followers. I get that. But you said it yourself: they're gone. These are just walking corpses."

Thomas looked thoughtful. "You're probably right. I haven't seen a living soul for days, besides you. And I've been looking. Going on hunting expeditions, visiting their houses, hoping—"

"To find someone alive. But you never found anyone," Paul finished for him, not without sympathy.

"No. Not yet. But I'm not quite done, and if I do leave, I won't go before I've checked every one of their houses. They trusted me. We're alive. Someone else might be too."

Well, that was that. Sometimes a man's mind was made up, that's all, and there was no talking him out of it. That could be a good thing, or it could be a bad thing, but either way it had to be accepted.

Paul looked thoughtful for a minute. "Okay. I'll help. It'll be faster and safer. We can start tomorrow morning."

As day broke, they were already nearly finished packing: food, flashlights, rope, first aid kit, and perhaps most importantly, weapons. Both men had hunting knives, Thomas carried his shotgun, and Paul had the axe he'd brought with him. "Dual-purpose," he said as he saw Thomas looking at it. "Firewood—and walkers."

"Use it much?" asked Thomas. He didn't have to specify on what.

"A few times. Mostly I've tried to avoid 'em, especially in groups, but twice I've killed stragglers. The first time, I hit one in the middle of the back. Swung at it as hard as I've ever swung at any tree."

"It didn't go down?"

"Oh, it went down. I chopped it nearly in half because it was already half-rotted. But it didn't even seem to notice, just kept coming for me, dragging itself along with its arms. My second swing did the trick, though. Split the head open." He looked at Thomas. "You gotta get 'em in the head." Thomas nodded. This he knew already.

They walked through the streets mostly in silence, Thomas leading the way. Both men were hyper-vigilant, watching for any sign of danger. After they'd been walking 15 minutes, Paul lightly touched Thomas's arm to get his attention, then pointed down a side street. A quarter mile away, a walker was slowly shuffling around, without any clear intent. Thomas looked at Paul and shook his head. No point in engaging that one. They kept on. The thing did not seem to register their presence.

The men had walked perhaps three miles when Thomas stopped in front of their destination, a simple, small, white house, well-kept. Under different circumstances, it would have been a real estate agent's dream. He walked up the front steps, and Paul followed him. When the door proved to be locked, Paul motioned Thomas back, bent down, and lifted the welcome mat. Nothing. He shrugged, half-smiling; it had been worth a try. They stepped off the tiny porch and slowly walked to the back of the house, weapons raised. The back door was also locked, but this time they got lucky; the spare key was under a rock in the tidy flower bed.

Because the house would be such close quarters, Thomas unlocked the door as silently as possible, motioning to Paul to head in first. Paul raised his axe and gently pushed the door open. Both men gagged and backed away as the unmistakable odor of advanced decomposition washed over them. Putrid, yet sickly sweet, it was nothing either had smelled before a few weeks ago, and yet, however many times they had smelled it since—the undead rotted like any other human, once taken down, and sometimes they left the remains of victims too badly mutilated to turn, so those rotted too—it was impossible to get used to and something neither would ever forget. Paul closed his eyes and swallowed, trying not to vomit. Thomas understood, but standing outside any longer was a luxury they could not afford. He squeezed the other man's shoulder, and when Paul opened his eyes, Thomas again motioned him in. Paul nodded. They stepped over the threshold, locking the door behind them.

The stench was even worse inside, but both men knew what was at stake and kept on. They walked through the small but tidy kitchen, its homey neatness a grotesque pretense; it was as if hell had been whitewashed and turned into a diner serving poisoned apple pie. The living room was in the same state; the normal had become the obscene. Obviously they were looking for the source of the putrefaction, but the smell was so thick that they could not detect the source using their noses. Every door, then, was potentially THE door.

Thomas led the way now. He knew this house, had eaten dinner here any number of times with its owners, a kind middle-aged couple who, having no children of their own, had become honorary grandparents to the neighborhood's youngsters. Though they'd clearly made peace with the situation, he had always been aware of a slight undercurrent of sadness, the type that only the accidentally childless seem to put off. But then, perhaps that was for the best, considering the current circumstances.

Focus, he told himself. And so he did, walking to the short hallway that led to the couple's bedroom. Paul saw that two other doors led off the hallway, so he turned his back to Thomas, so as not to be ambushed in that tight space, trusting the other man to be his eyes as he backed into the room behind him. Thus he heard, rather than saw, Thomas walk around the bed, crouching down and looking beneath it, before opening the closet. "Nothing," whispered Thomas.

They followed the same pattern as they walked into the spare bedroom facing the couple's own. Again, there was nothing out of the ordinary. Except, of course, for the odor. At this side of the house, that left the bathroom. Paul stood at the ready, keeping one eye on the living room, as Thomas quickly opened the door. "Jesus!" said Thomas, at the same time Paul uttered his own, "Oh, fuck."

Mr. Henry Carnahan, liked by his neighbors and loved by his wife, an honest merchant, intelligent, mannerly, considerate, owner of a well-behaved dog, weekly trimmer of front yard shrubbery, yearly hanger of Christmas lights, and possessed in life of a calm and cheerful demeanor, lay in the bathtub alongside a shotgun that he had probably fired only once. Part of his face stared back at them in a frozen rictus. The other part of it, along with plenty of dried blood, teeth, hair, bits of skull, and gray clumps of brain, was imbedded into and plastered onto the tile surrounding the tub. "Jesus," said Thomas again.

"I'm sorry," Paul said. "I know—"

"No," Thomas said sharply, looking at him. "You don't. You don't know." Paul remained silent but nodded, and Thomas turned back to the corpse.

"Thomas," Paul said gently, after a few minutes. Thomas turned to face him, but for a moment it seemed as if he was elsewhere. In hell, maybe. He closed his eyes for several seconds, and when he opened them again, he was back. Paul relaxed and let go of the breath he hadn't realized he'd been holding. Then he gestured at the mirror, where there was a piece of paper taped up that read, simply, "Attic." Thomas nodded and led the way without a word. It wasn't as though they had a choice.

Thomas had been in the attic once, but only once, when Mr. Carnahan's natural reticence had given way to a moment of exuberant pride in his favorite hobby: ham radio. Mrs. Carnahan had mentioned it as an aside over dessert and coffee one fine spring evening, the reverend had expressed genuine interest, and so while she had cleaned up after dinner, the two men had pulled the rope that lowered the attic stairs and headed up, just as Thomas and Paul were doing now. That day, the reverend and Mr. Carnahan casually discussed how ham radio could be a very useful hobby in certain circumstances, such as emergencies. This certainly qualified.

Neither Thomas nor Paul expected the attic to conceal danger, thinking the walkers incapable of entering a locked house or, barring that, working the attic stairs once in, and their assumptions were correct. At first glance, the space seemed harmless. On one side were neatly labeled boxes full of seasonal decorations, summer clothing, and the sort of paraphernalia—old photographs, letters, white elephant gifts, the detritus of young adulthood—one finds tucked into attics. On the other side was a desk with a ham radio setup and, perhaps more interestingly, a journal.

Though the journal had been started months before, it was opened to a page dated three weeks ago, about when the scourge had begun. It was written in a precise, easy-to-read hand that belied the nature of the increasingly disturbing content.

Monday, April 29, 1968

Mary called me at the store today and asked if I would close up shop and come home early. Very unlike her. When I got home, she told me that on her way back from buying groceries she had seen a few people stumbling around like they were sick. She said something about it had spooked her, so she tried phoning a few neighbors when she got in the house, but none of them answered. I've never known her to imagine things before; I'll stay home tomorrow to keep an eye on her. Maybe I'll call the doctor. George can open up the store.

Tuesday, April 30, 1968

I called George last night and again this morning. He didn't answer. Neither did Robert. Very strange. Mary is still insisting that she saw ... what she saw, but she seems fine otherwise. The doctor is also not answering his phone. I'm not sure what is happening in this town.

Wednesday, May 1, 1968

After I took Duke out today, someone came to the back door, banging on the door and moaning. I looked out the window. It was Mrs. MacDermott from across the street, but she was ... something was wrong with her. It was her, but it wasn't. Duke growled like I've never heard him do before. We turned off all the lights and made sure all the doors and windows were locked. Finally she went away.

Something is wrong.

Thursday, May 2, 1968

These things (I don't think they are people anymore) walk the street constantly. They are dangerous, I think. Mary and I have not seen any normal people in two days. I go outside only to take the dog out and won't let her go out at all.

The power has gone out. We are on generator. I'm not sure how long it will last.

Friday, May 3, 1968

Today I got on the radio. I thought I might be able to find help. It took me a while to find anyone on, but I finally did. The news is not good. This is happening everywhere. Apparently, these things are humans that have died and revived, somehow. They eat human flesh, and when they do, they turn living people into more of themselves. But the worst part is that even when people die natural deaths, they are coming back as ... as what is being called "undead." You can only kill them by damaging the brains.

If I hadn't seen it with my own eyes, I wouldn't believe what I'm hearing, but I have no good reason to doubt any of it. I'm trying to keep up appearances for Mary's sake, but I don't know what we're going to do or where we're going to go. There is nowhere safe, at least nowhere I know of. Dear God, is this how the world ends?

Saturday, May 4, 1968

Mary is gone. She opened the door—I don't know why—and Duke ran past her. An undead was in the yard, and Duke went right for it. And then Mary ran to try to get the dog. It ... the thing got her. I shot it in the head. But Mary was bleeding so badly. I got her into the house, into the kitchen. There was so much blood. The blood was everywhere. It got her neck.

She went so fast. One minute she was there, and I told her to hold on, that I would get help. But she just ... there was so much blood. Then she was gone. When she started moving again, I knew. I knew I had to make it final. She wouldn't want to come back like that. I stabbed her through the head. No. It. Not her. My beautiful Mary was already dead. I buried her in the shed. My beautiful Mary.

I don't know what happened to Duke.

Sunday, May 5, 1968

If this isn't the end of the world, I can't imagine what it is. I won't become one of them, though. I won't! Maybe it's a sin to do what I'm going to do, but surely, letting myself become one of them would be a worse sin, and it would only be a matter of time. My only hope is that I will open my eyes to see my Mary once again.

The men took turns in the shed, one digging while the other stood watch. Paul let the other man do most of the digging, only taking over when he thought Thomas might otherwise collapse; the former reverend seemed to be working something out in his head while he fought the soil. They did the rest together, using a few tarps they'd found in the shed. The grave was shallow, by necessity, but Mr. Carnahan got as proper a burial as time allowed.

When it was finished and the two men had rested a while, they walked back home as silently as they'd come. Foolish, perhaps, but neither could stomach staying where they were. By chance, or perhaps not, they made it. The axe remained clean, and the shotgun remained loaded. After they'd climbed the steps, let themselves in, and made sure all was secure, Thomas turned to Paul. "I was called to minister to people. The people are gone. Or going. What now?"

"Now we do what humans have always done," Paul said. "We do what we have to. We try to stay alive. We try to find others like us. Kill those who want to kill us. Kill those who used to be us. Survive. Help others survive, if there are others. Isn't that what a ministry is anyway?"

Thomas was silent for a minute, then he spoke. "I suppose it is. Even if it is mostly a ministry to the undead."

"The last ministry."

"Yes. The last ministry."

THE TURBULENT FLIGHT HOME
by Nelson W. Pyles

Nelson W. Pyles is an author of horror fiction currently living in Pittsburgh PA. He is novelist and author of several short stories. His first novel, DEMONS, DOLLS, & MILKSHAKES is available from Post Mortem Press. He is a member of the HWA.

Nelson is also the host of the popular "The Wicked Library" on the Society 13 Podcast Network, available to hear for free on iTunes and Stitcher.com

He was discovered by Burning Bulb Publishing for his short story contribution, "Decorations," which appears in THE BIG BOOK OF BIZARRO. A year later, his story "Just Enough Rope" made it in WESTWARD HOES.

Somewhere over Eastern Europe, approaching Germany, October 1ˢᵗ 1968 1348 hours

Paul's head rested against the green metal wall. He'd been in the air for about three hours and the plane stank. This was made worse with the sun still beating on the plane and the 30 other grunts sitting around him. They were all laughing, talking about going home. Paul was just grateful that no one had tried to shoot him for three hours.

The thrumming of the plane's engines normally soothed his over active mind, but not today for some reason. He was going home and he should have been excited, but all he wanted was to pass out.

That, he decided, wasn't going to happen any time soon.

He picked up little bits of conversation. Some folks were talking about sleeping late for a month. Others talked about girls, jobs, friends and TV shows. The one show that kept coming up was some space bullshit called *Star Trek*, or something like that; Paul had seen a few episodes of it before he deployed out of Pittsburgh.

His brother James liked it just fine, but Paul had no interest in it at all. Paul was the younger of the two and although both brothers got along well, James had always been the intellectual one. He was creative and serious. Paul was far from serious; headstrong, funny and always with an eye for the ladies. He flatly told James he'd watch the show with the sound off and a joint, maybe some Hendrix while he watched that Uhura chick shake it in space.

Man, he couldn't remember the last time he got high.

James never liked pot, but Paul had been ready to make it a life avocation; he wanted to be a guitar player in a band like his hero Jimi Hendrix. That or a pot farmer in Jamaica.

And of course, James disapproved.

James wanted him to go to college like he did.

"You can be anything you want," James said. "But not if you rot your brains with that shit. That'll get you nowhere."

"Look at Hendrix," Paul would reply. "The man is a genius."

"You watch. He's gonna drop dead one of these days from all of that junk he does. And, news flash little brother, Hendrix was already making something of himself. He was in the Air Force. He was working as a musician when he got out, making money. You can't even play."

Paul would be damned if he was going to join the Air Force, and he said so too.

Three weeks later, the Army didn't give him a choice of where he went.

And now, two years later, he was finally going home.

He felt like a different man now. He still wanted to play guitar, but now he had a plan of how to go about things. James had said the Army would straighten him out and much to Paul's surprise, it did. Probably not in the way either of them had thought, but it did snap him into focus.

For one thing, Paul had never liked white people.

It was a huge bone of contention between the brothers and frankly, their father who had raised both boys on his own. The phrase "don't trust whitey" was used frequently. James never bought into it, much to the dissatisfaction of their father.

"They always gonna keep us down," he said. "Ain't never done nothing for us. We on our own."

James didn't buy it. Paul did.

Now, Paul understood things even his brother couldn't possibly understand. When you're in a jungle surrounded by people trying to kill you, you'd better trust the guy next to you – black or white, or you're dead.

He'd become a soldier. He learned to trust his platoon, not because there was a choice. You're stripped of your identities in basic. You're all shit, regardless of your skin color. You're all torn down. Then, you're remade. By the time he was ready to hit the jungle, he got it. He was surprised at the transformation in him and his fellow soldiers. Of course, not all of them got it. He still heard "nigger" under people's breath, but now, he didn't care. He knew who he was. What he was.

He was a soldier.

He was a man.

That didn't mean he necessarily liked being in the middle of a conflict that most of his friends were back home protesting. He spent the war being mostly terrified. But, he was a goddamn soldier with a mission.

Kill the enemy.

And he did for two years with his brothers. His new brothers.

Now, he was going home with a plan and he couldn't wait to see his brother to tell him.

If he could only sleep.

Most of the passengers were from his unit, but there were a few guys he didn't know. Everyone was now quietly talking, a few guys sleeping, with only the engines of the C-97 to remind them they were all alive and going home. Paul rested his head against the metal hull again and tried in vain to at least pass out.

Thump.

Paul sat up and looked around. No one reacted to it.

Turbulence, thought Paul. *Must be it.*

He put his head against the hull again.

Thump. Thump.

He sat up again and looked around him. He looked to Smitty, a soldier from his unit.

"Smitt, you hear that?" he asked.

Smitty turned slowly to him, a half grin on his face.

"Yeah, a whole lotta nothing for like three hours. It's kinda nice, ain't it?"

Paul smirked.

"I guess, but it sounded like something knocking into the plane."

"You're hearin' shit, Paulie." Smitty said, chuckling.

Thump. Thumpthump.

Smitty's smug expression changed.

"Okay, that's what you heard?"

Paul nodded.

Smitty stood up.

"Anybody else hear that?"

The soldiers were looking at each other and then, the thumping increased.

"What the hell is that?" asked Smitty.

Smitty moved himself into the long aisle and motioned for Paul to come to him, which he did.

"We should go talk to the pilot," Paul said.

"That's what I'm thinking. Ain't no turbulence I ever heard, man."

The two men walked to the cockpit carefully, and about ten feet before reaching it, one of the cockpit crew opened the door.

"Hey, you boys hear that?" asked Jessup, the navigator. "The hell are you guys doing back here?"

"That's why we were coming to see you," Smitty said. "Sounds like you're hitting potholes and shit."

"That's odd," Jessup said. "Sounds like it's back here by you. No turbulence at all so far."

Thumpthumpthump.

The three men all looked toward the back of the plane. The passengers also looked toward the back when more thumps came in a flurry.

Paul looked down.

"What's in the cargo hold?"

"Hang on," Jessup said and disappeared back into the cockpit.

Smitty and Paul looked at each other.

"Why'd you ask what was in the hold?"

Paul turned and started to walk back to the rear of the plane.

"Cause that's where the sound is coming from," Paul said as he walked. Smitty followed, frowning.

Paul walked past the seats to the thick metal plate covering in the floor. The noise was louder now, and seemingly concentrated.

"Smitty, it's here. Help me with this," Paul said, reaching down.

"Hold on, man," Smitty said, grabbing Paul by the shoulder. "We ought to find out what's down there first."

Turk, a big soldier who hadn't said a word to anyone since the flight took off said, "That's where the bodies are."

They all took turns looking at the large man, who didn't even bother looking up from his book.

"Who are you, big guy?" Smitty asked.

"I'm the guy mindin' his own bees wax," Turk said quietly. "Whatever the hell is down there can't be good. Y'all should just let it ride."

Jessup burst through the cockpit door and nearly ran down the aisle.

"We're carrying back the dead," he said, nearly panting. "Somebody down there might still be alive."

Paul and Smitty looked at each other.

"Well, you wanna go or shall I?" Smitty said, smiling an unhappy smile.

"Damn," Paul said. "I guess I could go."

Turk chuckled.

"Sure as fuck ain't gonna be me," he said to no one. "Might as well let the boy go in."

Paul flinched, but that was all. He wasn't going to wait around to debate if Turk meant boy because of his age or otherwise. He let it go. Smitty however, had other plans.

"No one was asking you anyway, ya fuck." Smitty said and then did smile. Paul chuckled as he tried to figure out how to open the floor hatch. Turk didn't say anything.

Paul grabbed the latch, turned it and yanked it open. The smell hit him first and he nearly threw up. The other soldiers gagged and backed away from it. Grimacing, he looked down and saw nothing but darkness.

"I'm gonna need a light," he said in a shaky voice.

Jessup made his way through.

"It has lights, but they don't operate while we're in flight."

"Well that's kind of useless," Paul said quietly. "I guess I can use a zippo,"

"No," Jessup replied. "And you're not going down there. I am." He pulled a flashlight out from his camo.

"Hey, fine by me," Paul said getting up. "I wasn't really looking forward to going down there anyway."

"I'll bet, boy," Turk said, chuckling.

Paul forgot his nausea and snapped his head in Turk's direction.

"You best knock that 'boy' shit off, Private." Paul said.

"I'm a specialist," Turk replied. "I reckon I can call you boy if I feel like it."

"Nice, asshole," Smitty said smiling. "Guess they didn't tell you Corporal is kind of a higher rank, right?"

Turk actually moved in his seat to look at them.

"They making niggers corporals now?" he asked no one in particular. "Hmmm. Glad I'm getting out I guess."

Smitty went for him, but Paul held him back.

"We ain't doing this, Smitty. Fuck that asshole. We got shit to do."

Smitty was actually growling and the Turk laughed.

"We get off this plane," the Turk said. "You can try and teach me something. Listen to your boy over there."

Paul held onto him for a moment longer and Smitty began to relax.

"Sounds like a plan, asshole," Smitty said finally through gritted teeth. He looked at Paul.

"Why didn't you let me at him?"

Paul smiled.

"Ain't worth it. Trust me."

"If you guys are done," Jessup said, sounding a little relieved the situation was diffused. "I'm gonna head down there. Might be a VC in there, so you boys be ready up here."

Jessup pointed the light into the hold which revealed a thin looking staircase leading down.

"Hello?" he called out. "Anybody down here?"

Thump.

It came louder now that the latch was open and everyone flinched.

"Okay, going down," Jessup said, and he slowly descended.

"Guy's got some balls," Smitty said.

There was a general agreement among the soldiers and they waited for anything other than the thumps, which were now increasing.

"I'm gonna go to the cockpit—see if there's any more flashlights up there," Paul said and quickly walked up the aisle. He knocked on the door and heard the pilot grunt.

He opened the door and saw the pilot and co-pilot doing what they do.

"What's up soldier?" the pilot said without looking.

"You got anymore flashlights available? In case something happens to your guy in the hold?"

The co-pilot turned to Paul.

"There's a couple in the storage box right behind us. About three of 'em in there. Don't all you boys start going in the hold, though? Just wait till Walt gets back up."

Paul nodded and closed the door.

The utility crate was where the co-pilot said it was. He opened it and grabbed two more flashlights. He headed back and that's when he heard the scream.

"Hey, what's going on?" Smitty yelled in the hold.

Another scream followed by another volley of thumps, but now there were multiple thumps.

"Paul? You find 'em?"

"Yeah," said Paul, handing one to Smitty. "Let's get down there."

The other soldiers parted like the sea and made room for the two men to go down below when they all heard another scream, this one calling out to God.

Smitty pointed his flashlight into the hatch.

"Hey, somebody's coming up! It's one of us."

They looked and a soldier, covered in dirt and gore, was stumbling up the stairs slowly, as Jessup screamed in the background.

"Soldier, you okay? What the hell is going on down there?"

The soldier ignored this and continued to shamble up the stairs.

"He was probably marked as dead by accident," a soldier named Peters said. "Looks like they was wrong."

"Let's help him up here," said Smitty as Peters and Paul reached into the hatch to pull the man up. Each grabbed the man under his arms and pulled him straight up.

"Give us room!" Paul said as they went to lay the guy on the floor. The other soldiers moved back as the injured soldier struggled with Paul and Peters.

"Easy fella," Peters said. "Looks like you're gonna be alright now."

"Who else is down there?" Paul asked, but before there could be an answer, Smitty jumped into the hatch, yelling, "Holy fuck!"

Paul looked at Peters.

"Try and calm this guy down. Put your hand on his chest and keep him still." He stood up. "Someone get a blanket to cover this guy. I'm going down."

He made his way to the latch, but then saw Smitty running back up.

"Stay the fuck up there!" he yelled, staggering up the stairs. "Holy living fuck!"

Behind him, Jessup still screamed and something else…something like…moaning.

Smitty nearly fell onto the floor. He was bleeding from several wounds on his arms and his hands.

Paul bent down and helped him up.

"What the hell is going on down there?" Paul nearly yelled.

"Close the fucking hatch!" Smitty spat out. "Now!"

"What about—" a soldier started to say.

"Now!"

Someone kicked the hatch closed.

"Stand on it!" Smitty said, trying to get to his feet and failing. "A couple of you guys, fucking stand on it."

Two men did, as Paul helped Smitty into a seat. Peters was still on the floor with his hand on the injured soldier's chest. The soldier was still struggling and beginning to moan.

From below, the thumps were coming from seemingly everywhere, and the screams of Jessup were getting quieter.

The thumps were moving to the hatch.

"Smitty, what the hell—" Paul started.

"All of 'em," Smitty gasped. "Every fucking soldier down there. They attacked Jessup."

"But why would they do that?" Paul asked.

"They fucking attacked *me*, Paulie. They're crazy or something. Moaning and shit. Like they're…I don't know, dazed? High? But man…" He started to sob.

"Calm down, Smitt," Paul said. "What the hell are these wounds?"

"Bites," he replied. "They were biting me. They were…*eating* that guy."

"Eating him?" Paul said, and then everyone looked at the injured soldier that Peters was attending.

No one looked harder than Peters himself.

He looked down at the soldier, who was still struggling, but now was snarling.

It all happened quickly for Peters. The soldier grabbed Peters' arm and pulled him off balance. Peters fell across the soldier's midsection, which is where the soldier hooked his arm over Peters' head and his other arm across his back. He pulled Peters toward his face and the soldier bit into the side of his chest.

Peters screamed as the soldier pulled back with a mouth full of uniform and flesh; it pulled off surprisingly easy as the soldier began to chew. Peters struggled to get away, but was held firm by the soldier, who went and took another bite. Peters screamed again.

The surrounding soldiers were stunned. With all of the violence they had seen during the war, nothing compared to the scene before them. As Peters screamed, Martinez, a small soldier, snapped out of his daze and pushed forward to help. He grabbed Peters and tried to pull him off of the other soldier, whose face was now covered in blood.

"Come on, man help me out!" Martinez yelled, struggling with the now screaming and squirming Peters. Paul jumped over and tried to pry the death grip the soldier had on Peters' neck. The soldier snarled and tried to bite Paul. Paul put his boot on the soldier's neck and pulled.

The soldier's arm came off, tearing a chuck of Peters' neck with it.

Someone yelled "Aw, fuck!" as a stunned Paul threw the arm toward the cockpit.

The soldier was unfazed, but Martinez managed to get Peters up and off of the soldier. The other soldiers moved in and began to kick the soldier on the ground, who still seemed unfazed by all of this. He just gnashed his teeth and snarled.

"What the hell happened to that guy?" asked Martinez, trying to stop the bleeding coming from Peters' neck, and failing.

Paul was trying to get Smitty to lie down on the seats when he heard three very loud thumps. The two soldiers on the hatch made startled noises. Paul stood up and looked at the hatch. With two men on it, it was still opening. The two men wavered on it and the hatch opened just enough that a hand shot through. The hatch came down on it and the hand struggled. One of the men jumped on the hatch and it cut into the hand. No screams came from below, just more moans and grunts. He jumped again and the hand came completely off.

Turk stood up and moved into the aisle. He pulled his service revolver.

"Maybe we should let 'em up." He said.

A few of the soldiers nodded in agreement, One of the soldiers kicking the injured soldier on the ground pulled his Colt and aimed it at him.

"Watch the windows!" someone yelled.

"Back away," the soldier said, and when it was clear, he shot three times into the downed soldier's chest.

Two things happened at once.

Three black holes appeared in the man's chest and absolutely nothing else. The shots didn't seem to do anything to the man except renew his resolve to stand up. The other soldiers backed away as he stood up clumsily. He hauled himself up and turned to face the shooter, who was now stunned. He held the gun up.

"Back off!" he yelled and fired another shot into the snarling soldier now advancing toward him. The shot had no effect as the shambling soldier grabbed the shooter and toppled onto him, knocking them both down.

"What the hell!" Paul nearly screamed as the skin of the shooter's face was grabbed by the cheek and torn off in a solid piece. A thick, gurgling scream erupted from the unfortunate soldier's mouth as Paul chose to help the downed soldier and nearly ran toward them. He grabbed the snarling soldier by his hair and pulled. He had hoped the pain and the snapping back of his head would be both distracting and successful. It was neither. He came back with two fistfuls of hair and scalp. He gagged and threw the chunks onto the floor.

"Somebody help Paul!" Smitty said, sitting up and watching in horror.

Turk, revolver still in hand walked into the aisle behind Paul, who had no idea what to do next. He pushed Paul roughly aside and put the butt of the gun directly against the temple of the ghoulish soldier, who was eating the chunk of flesh ripped from the screaming, struggling man underneath him.

The gun exploded and the bullet tore through the man's head, travelling violently through the other side of his skull, spraying three soldiers with bone, blood and brain matter. The three soldiers, now covered, didn't have time to react as the plane violently pitched forward.

The bullet had gone through the cockpit door.

For twenty seconds, the plane was in a freefall and the bulk of the soldiers, both alive and not, slid and crashed against the cockpit. Smitty managed to hold onto the seat in front of him that he was thrown into. The two soldiers standing on the hatch collided and slid violently down the aisle, desperately trying to grab onto something to prevent their descent.

Twenty seconds later, the plane slowly began to correct and level out. The battered men slowly and unsurely got to their feet. After a minute Paul asked, "Everybody okay?"

Peters mercifully had passed out and the poor bastard who Turk had saved was unconscious as well.

That left the biter.

He lay still and unmoving at last; his blood all over the floor, but he wasn't biting or trying to do anything anymore.

He was decidedly dead.

Paul made a break for the cockpit to check on the pilots. He hoped they had just been startled by the gunshot. When he opened the door, the co-pilot, Hennessey was barking into the radio. The plane's captain had a valley in the back of his head as he sat slumped to one side, dripping blood. Blood was all over the left side of the interior windshield.

Paul gagged a little and asked the co-pilot, "Are you okay?"

Hennessey jerked his head around.

"Do I goddamn look okay?" he said. "Hell no, I ain't okay. Which one of you assholes shot the Captain?"

"It was an accident. One of the soldiers below…" Paul's voice trailed off.

"Below?" Hennessey said. "There's nothing down there but dead soldiers."

"They ain't all dead, but they are pretty fucked up."

"Ain't dead? Explain that."

"I can't," Paul said. "Let me see what's going on back there. I just wanted to make sure someone was flying this thing."

"Yeah, yeah…we're okay. He's not though…" Hennessey said, nodding to the dead Captain. "Keep me posted about what's going on back there, you got me?"

"Yeah," Paul said and left the cockpit.

Paul closed the door behind him and looked around in the cabin into a sea of expectant eyes.

"What's up, Paul?" Smitty asked through gritted teeth. He looked bad, but so did everyone else.

"Turk shot the captain, but the co-pilot has it under control."

Turk, who had gone back to sitting down as if nothing had happened, jerked his head up.

"Shot the captain?"

"Yeah," Paul said trying not to glare at Turk. "Right in the head."

"Humph," Turk said, dismissing it all as he went about reading his book.

"Unbelievable," Paul said, walking to Smitty,

"Hey, you alright?" Paul asked. Smitty looked up at Paul with bloodshot eyes.

"Man, I feel like I have the goddamn flu now and these bites hurt like a bitch. So yeah, it's like, Tuesday in Da Nang."

Paul smiled and looked away for a moment. Something wasn't right and he noticed it too late.

Not only was the hatch open, but three bodies were half out of it.

The bodies were moving out slowly and onto the floor. It was happening slowly and Paul took a quick look around to see if anyone else had noticed.

They hadn't.

"Smitt, can you get up?"

"Man, I ain't movin'."

Paul grabbed the big man and hauled him up onto his feet.

"Get the fuck off of me, Paul. Jesus—" and then he saw them too.

"Guys, we got problems!" Paul yelled as he moved Smitty toward the front of the plane.

Heads whirled around and the soldiers got up, or turned, and drew their side arms.

"What the fucking—"

Shots rang out as three of the soldiers fired into the three shambling soldiers who had somehow managed to not only stand, but advance.

"Stop firing!" Paul yelled. "That shit don't work!"

Turk moved his big self into the aisle, gun drawn and walked toward the advancing soldiers.

"It does if you head shoot 'em, *boy*," he said and raised his gun, taking his time to aim. A smile broke out across his face as he fired into the forehead of the nearest one. The soldier's head snapped back and he collapsed to the knees before falling forward, down and unmoving.

Turk turned around and faced his audience.

"See? That simple. This will be easy."

The other soldiers motioned for Turk to turn back around, but it was too late. A fourth biter on the floor that no one had managed to notice, and was missing his lower torso, grabbed Turk by his legs. He pulled himself up slightly and bit into Turk's calf. Turk screamed and fell over backward.

"Holy shit," Smitty said. "It's Jessup."

Paul looked, and indeed, it was the flight navigator, biting and chewing on Turk's leg like a ravenous dog.

"What happened to his legs?" someone else asked.

"Fuck you, what about my legs?" Turk screamed. He was punching Jessup in the head, having dropped his gun.

Paul looked at Smitty.

"I don't wanna shoot Jessup in the head," he said quietly.

"Paulie," Smitty said. "That ain't Jessup anymore, I don't think."

That fixed it, and Paul walked to Jessup and shot him, point blank in the head.

Jessup stopped moving, but Turk didn't. He began to crawl backward away from the thing that had tried to eat him.

He backed into the two remaining ghouls that he had targeted originally. They fell on him and began to tear him to pieces.

Paul slowly backed away. He looked behind the grisly feast in front of him and saw more soldiers with the same glazed look coming through the hatch.

"Alright men," Paul said, raising his Colt. "Take your time, fire at the head. They ain't in no rush and neither are we, but be careful. No way we know how many is down there."

Paul carefully aimed at one still eating Turk's face and decided to shoot the one chewing into his mid section. He found it difficult and missed the first two shots. It was hard to break the training to shoot for center mass and switch to head shots, but improvising was Paul's best trait. He took a deep breath and shot the next one.

"Don't need everybody right now," Paul said lowering his gun. "Let's not empty it all into them. Take your time."

Paul holstered his gun as two soldiers took his place. He went to talk to Smitty, who was sitting at an odd angle and looking dazed.

"You alright?" Paul asked.

"No," Smitty croaked. "But I would like to tell you that I'm not as bad as those two motherfuckers over there." With a shaky arm, Smitty pointed at Peters and the soldier with the half torn face. "You may consider a pre-emptive bullet or two in their skulls." He laughed. "And, mine."

Paul looked and shuddered.

"Yeah, I ain't popping you," Paul said.

"Right, I can do it."

Paul looked at him.

"The fuck you can, you can't shoot nothing," Paul said flatly. "Hell, only reason I shot VC was because they were laughing at your bad shooting ass."

Smitty coughed a laugh and then it turned into just a thick, choking cough.

"No one shoots you, not even you," Paul said and stood up.

"Anybody on here got any fucking idea what the hell this shit is?"

No one said a word. They just looked at Paul, or just shot into the heads of the folks coming through the hatch.

"And how about some of you guys moving ahead and closing the fucking hatch?" Paul walked and looked at the two unconscious men. He grabbed the nearest soldier and said, "If either of these two move and start doing that shit. . ." He pointed down the aisle. "Give a bullet in the head."

The soldier shrugged and looked at him.

"You ain't my fucking CO," the kid said, but Paul's return look told him otherwise.

"Before you shit your pants, kid," Paul said. "Right now, I am your CO. Me and that guy." He pointed to Smitty. "Don't shoot him."

Paul went into the cockpit once again.

He closed the door behind him.

"How we doing back there?" Hennessey asked.

"Not fucking good," Paul said.

"Well, we ain't doing much better up here either. I was getting static on the radio and just started getting really weird radio updates."

"How weird?"

"Fucking weird. Tell me what's going on back there."

Paul described what was going on in the back. Hennessey shook his head, and every now and then, would swear under his breath.

When Paul was done, Hennessey simply turned on the radio.

"You turned off the radio?" Paul said.

"Listen," Hennessey replied.

The broadcast was from the US Military. It was a looped repeating message. It was brief and to the point.

"This is Oberschleissheim Army Airfield. The base is currently quarantined. Please coordinate your flight with one of the other airfields."

"Quarantined?" Paul said.

"Right. And I checked the other airfields. Same message."

"Well, we can't land there. Where then?"

Hennessey shook his head.

"I'm going to start hitting up the UK, but we'll be making it on fumes. Can't get any response from anyone just yet."

"You think…" Paul began but stopped.

"Think what?" Hennessey asked. "And what's all the shooting back there?"

Paul shook his head.

"I think we're quarantined too. Maybe what's going on here isn't just here."

Hennessey visibly shuddered. He turned and looked at Paul, almost pleading.

"Can you get the captain out of that seat?" he asked. "It's making this hard to do."

Paul nodded.

Ten minutes later, the soldiers in the cabin had managed to close the hatch and pile the bodies on top of it. It was a grim scene Paul walked back into from the cockpit. He had taken the captain's body and moved it from the pilot's seat to the navigator's chair and threw a spare utility blanket over him.

Paul looked at Smitty, now lying down across two seats and twitching slightly. He looked at Peters and the young faceless soldier who didn't move at all.

The soldier he had told to watch them came over to him.

"I think they're dead," he told Paul.

Paul nodded.

"Well, I guess we know what we gotta do," he said.

The soldier nodded back and drew his gun, but Paul put a hand on his shoulder.

"Use a knife or something. I think we're all goddamn sick of gunshots."

The soldier nodded and holstered his gun.

Thump.

Paul sighed and looked down the aisle. There were at least ten bodies on the hatch, so no one was coming back up unless the plane started to pitch like that again. He took the chair in front of Smitty and leaned over to take a look.

66

He looked bad. *Really* bad. He was breathing short, shallow breaths and his skin color was going from pale to gray. He wasn't gonna make it. If the plane couldn't land, none of them were gonna make it.

He was going to have to take care of Smitty sooner or later.

He turned around and sat hard in the seat. He looked down at his boots, caked with blood and gore. He looked at his hands. He wished he had a guitar.

He wished his brother was there for the first time. Not to tell him he was sorry for how they left things, but to see his brother. Give him a hug. Tell him he was right. See that big ass grin on his face.

Thump Thump.

Paul started to laugh.

What would Hendrix be doing right now?

Thump.

Thump.

Moan.

That came from directly behind him and he knew what it was.

Paul swallowed hard and drew his knife to say goodbye.

THE SOUTH WILL RISE AGAIN
by Andy Rausch

Andy Rausch is a freelance journalist, celebrity interviewer, and film critic. He is the author or co-author of nearly twenty books on the subject of popular culture. These include MAKING MOVIES WITH ORSON WELLES, THE FILMS OF MARTIN SCORSESE AND ROBERT DE NIRO and THE WIT AND WISDOM OF STEPHEN KING. He is also the author of the novels MAD WORLD and BLOODLETING: A TALE OF REVENGE and ELVIS PRESLEY, CIA ASSASSIN is published by Burning Bulb Publishing. His short story collection DEATH RATTLES is also published by Burning Bulb Publishing.

Andy has also worked as an actor, film producer, composer, casting director, and as the screenwriter of the cult film DAHMER VS. GACY. He is a regular contributor to SCREEM magazine, and his work has appeared in such publications and online journals as FILM THREAT, SHOCK CIMENA, and BRIGH LIGHTS FILM JOURNAL. He resides in Parsons, Kansas.

It was a warm mid-March evening, and the guys were flying down a Tennessee back road in Wilson's new 1968 Cadillac Eldorado. They were having the time of their lives. The three of them—Cleavon, Marshall, and Wilson—were driving from American Baptist College in Nashville down to Atlanta for spring break. The radio station they were listening to was breaking up, George Jones starting to bleed through, and Marshall turned the knob. "I'm not listening to any of that hillbilly cracker music," he said, twisting the knob until he found James Brown howling "I Feel Good."

"Now *that's* music," said Marshall.

"How many girls you think are gonna be there?" Cleavon asked.

"In Atlanta?" Wilson asked. "Lots of girls, man. More than you can even imagine. It's gonna be black girl heaven, with fine-looking sisters everywhere, as far as the eye can see."

Cleavon grinned. "Sounds good to me."

"Don't it?" said Marshall.

"Why are there so many black girls in Atlanta?" Cleavon asked.

Marshall said, "Morehouse is there, and there are a whole bunch of black colleges within a day's drive. Where else are they gonna go for spring break?"

"I might just catch me a woman to settle down with," Marshall joked.

Wilson chuckled. "You'll be lucky to catch crabs."

Marshall thought about that. "You had crabs before?"

"No, but my friend Jerry had 'em once."

"Were they bad?"

"Well, they weren't good. But he said they weren't really as bad as you might think. More of a pain than anything. He had to shave off all his pubic hair and put on some kind of ointment down there."

"And that killed 'em?"

"Deader than a Kennedy."

"Hmmm," Marshall said. "I think I'll just use a rubber."

This made Cleavon and Wilson laugh.

Cleavon said, "Good policy."

"Besides, there are all kinds of things you can catch having sex these days," Wilson said. "I hear brothers are comin' back from Vietnam with all kinds of crazy shit from having sex with those Vietnamese girls. And now all that nasty shit's here, too. So yeah, wearin' a rubber's the way to go. Besides, you don't wanna have a baby at nineteen."

Marshall chuckled. "You're right there. I'm not ready to be a father. Maybe one day, but not now. There's still a lot of stuff I want to do before I settle down."

"Like what?" asked Cleavon.

"I wanna go to Paris. I wanna see the champs-elysees. I wanna write a novel."

"You wanna write a novel?" asked Cleavon.

"I wanna write a *bunch* of novels."

"What kind of novels?"

Marshall said, "Whatever kinds I feel like. Look at Gordon Parks."

"*The Learning Tree*," said Wilson. "That's a good one."

"I wanna go to Paris and write about being a black man abroad," Marshall said.

Cleavon nodded. "Yeah, I could see that. Kind of a fish-out-of-water thing."

"And think of all the Parisian women you could have sex with over there," Wilson said.

Cleavon chuckled. "Leave it to you to bring the conversation back around to sex."

"I hear those white women over there like black men," said Wilson. "Have you *seen* those French women? Man, they look fine as hell. They look better than American models, and that's just their normal, every day girls."

Cleavon put his hand up for Wilson, who smacked it with a five.

"You tell me when you're goin' to Paris, I just might go with you," said Wilson. "We'll be a couple of uppity brothers, writin' novels and screwin' Parisian women."

Cleavon looked at Wilson. "You're gonna write a novel, too?"

Wilson said, "I'm gonna be the black Mickey Spillane!"

Marshall laughed. "Sounds like a plan."

The James Brown record ended, and a Nancy Sinatra song came on.

"Turn off that noise," said Marshall.

"Nah," Cleavon said. "Leave it on. That's my girl, Nancy Sinatra."

"What're you talkin' about, Nancy Sinatra?" asked Wilson.

"Have you *seen* Nancy Sinatra?" Cleavon asked.

Wilson nodded. "She's got a nice, round ass on her."

"So because she's got a nice ass," Marshall said, "we've gotta sit here and listen to her crap music? You know, she's not here. She's not giving out head to anyone who can make it all the way through her awful goddamn song."

"You don't like it?" asked Cleavon.

"Hell no!" said Wilson. "I'd rather hear your dumb ass sing."

So Cleavon started singing the Nancy Sinatra song.

"Oh, man," Wilson said. "I shoulda known."

The three of them roared with laughter.

Marshall asked, "What would you do if *you* got a girl pregnant?"

"I'd take her back home to see Doc Sonny and get fixed," said Wilson.

"Doc Sonny?"

"Yeah. He's a veterinarian by day, and he gives women 'the operation' at night."

"You sound like you know all about it," Marshall said.

"Maybe I do," Wilson said. "When I was seventeen, I got this girl named Dorothy Carter pregnant. I knew if I told my father, he'd skin my hide. And if her mean old grandmother found out— boy, there would have been hell to pay!"

"So she got it taken care of?" asked Marshall.

Wilson nodded.

Cleavon asked, "Do you ever feel bad about it?"

"I try not to think about it," Wilson said. "I'm not exactly happy about it, but when I think about it, I ask myself where my life would be today if I'd had a baby with that girl."

"And where's that?"

"I'd be working in that factory right there alongside my father, and that's no life at all. I've watched him work his fingers to the bone all these years, and it's killing him. He's gonna be dead before he's fifty. And do you think anybody at that factory cares? Hell no. They'll just get someone else to take his place before he's even cold and in the ground."

Cleavon lit a cigarette, and the pungent odor of smoke filled the car.

"Dammit, man," said Wilson. "The least you could do is roll down the goddamn window when you're gonna smoke."

Cleavon rolled down the window, but said nothing.

Marshall turned to Wilson. "So you're meeting your girl in Atlanta, huh?"

Wilson grinned. "Yes, sir. Me and Mary Lou are gonna have a good old time."

"How long's it been since you saw her last?" asked Cleavon.

"Almost a year." Wilson now had a photograph of her out and was kissing it.

"Man," Cleavon said, "you don't bring your girl to spring break. Don't you know anything?"

Wilson laughed.

"It's like taking a bologna sandwich to an all-you-can-eat buffet," said Marshall. "That shit doesn't make any sense."

Wilson's eyes narrowed. "You callin' my Mary Lou a bologna sandwich?"

"Yes, I am," said Marshall. "She's a damned good-lookin' bologna sandwich, but you can have her any time. Spring break is for meeting new girls. Man, I thought I taught you better. You're disappointing me, son."

"You guys can have all the crabs and Vietnamese diseases," Wilson said. "I'll be just fine with my Mary Lou."

The Nancy Sinatra song ended, and Sam and Dave came bursting onto the radio singing "Soul Man."

"Now that's my song right there," Cleavon said. "Why don't you turn that shit up a little bit?"

"Don't mind if I do," said Wilson, turning up the volume. The sounds of "Soul Man" now filled the automobile, and each of the three men snapped their fingers and danced in their seats.

Cleavon said, "They should make more music like this."

Marshall nodded. "They should definitely do that."

Then, out of the blue, the song went off and an announcer interrupted. "We are getting reports that..."

"What the fuck?" asked Cleavon. "I really wanted to hear that."

"Quiet," said Wilson. "I wanna hear this."

The reporter said, "large groups of what appear to be walking corpses attacking and killing residents in Pittsburgh, Pennsylvania. We have received reports of these incidents from all across the country now, from Los Angeles to New York City. At this time, government officials are unable to speculate on the cause of this outbreak, but promise to keep us posted as new details emerge. I repeat, large groups of people appearing to be walking corpses are attacking people and killing them. Most of Atlanta is shut down, and the city has issued an alert. Local authorities are asking travelers not to try and enter the city. Residents of Atlanta are asked to stay inside their homes until the threat can be contained."

"Do you think it's real?" asked Wilson.

"It's on the radio," said Marshall.

"Yeah," Wilson said, "but so was that *War of the Worlds* thing."

"Go ahead and turn it," Cleavon said. "See what they're saying on other stations."

Wilson turned the knob and changed the channel. Soon an old, white, southern minister came over the radio. "This is it," he said. "The rapture is upon us. Our Lord Jesus Christ is coming back to take his followers to the Promised Land..."

"Different station," said Cleavon.

Wilson turned the knob again, and a country-western station came on. He continued turning the knob, and the next station was saying basically the same thing as the first had.

"Shit," Marshall said. "What do you think it's all about?"

"Well, I know what I *don't* believe it is," Wilson said. "I don't believe it's corpses walking around killing people. That sounds like a load of horse shit to me."

Cleavon said, "Agreed."

"Maybe it's Communists," said Marshall.

"Or maybe aliens," said Cleavon, getting in on the joke.

Marshall added, "It's those damn Vietcong."

"So really, what do we do now?" Cleavon asked.

"I think we've got to go to Atlanta," said Wilson. "We've got nowhere else to go. Besides, everything looks completely normal out here. It can't really be all that bad. I mean, if I saw hordes of crazy people walking around out here, I might be inclined to believe that something's going on. But I haven't seen shit."

"I don't know," said Marshall. "The radio said—"

"The radio said there were dead people walking around killing people," Cleavon said. "And dead people don't do anything. They're just dead. So who cares what that damned thing says?"

"I've got a bad feeling about this," Marshall said.

"Well, where would you wanna go?" Wilson asked. "I mean, we're out here in the middle of nowhere. We at least have to drive until we reach a town with a motel."

Cleavon said, "I hope they've got a pool."

Marshall rolled his eyes. "I hope they don't have any walking dead people. That's what I hope."

Wilson nodded. "Yeah. That would be good, too."

"But a pool," Cleavon said. "I could definitely go for a swim right about now."

"Yeah," Marshall said. "I say we stop at the next motel and stay there until we find out what the hell is going on."

They drove until they reached the next town, Dead Possum, which was a rundown little bit of nothingness that fully lived up to the expectations set by its moniker. The town seemed to have nothing more than a few houses and a filling station. But there was no motel and no walking corpses to be seen. There were also no people anywhere in sight.

"Well," Marshall said. "We might as well stop and stretch our legs. We need gas anyway."

The others agreed, and Marshall turned the Eldorado into the lot of the filling station, pulling up in front of the pumps. They waited several minutes, but no attendant came out. Finally, they approached the station itself, but found that the building was locked up and there was no one around.

"Shit," Marshall said. "We really need gas."

"Any idea how far it is to the next town?" asked Wilson.

"No idea."

"I guess there's no reason to stay here."

"Guess not," said Marshall.

They climbed back into the Eldorado and pulled the doors shut. Marshall started it up, and they pulled out of the lot and got back on the road.

"We're really low on gas," Marshall said. "I hope we find another town soon."

They listened to various reports on the radio, but no one seemed to have anything new to say. It was all just a rehash of what they already knew.

"What if it really is the apocalypse?" asked Wilson.

Cleavon said, "Nothing feels any different. I doubt it's the apocalypse. It seems like that would be a big enough thing that you'd know something was happening."

"I guess," said Wilson.

"Can you believe they're actually saying those groups of people may be corpses?" Cleavon asked. "That's just crazy-talk. I don't even know what to make of that. How could that many people be seeing the same crazy thing at the same time?"

"Mass hysteria?" asked Wilson.

"Maybe."

Marshall looked at him. "I wonder how they're killing people."

"What do you mean?" Cleavon asked.

"Those groups of crazy people or corpses or whatever they are," Marshall said. "They didn't say exactly how they were killing people. I mean, are they using guns? Knives? Are they beating people to death?"

"That's a good question," said Wilson. "I hadn't even thought about that."

"The question is, if you were a corpse, how would you kill people?" asked Marshall.

"This is ludicrous," Cleavon said. "Do you guys hear what you're saying?"

"It may be nonsense, but it's what they're saying on every single radio station," said Marshall. "How do *you* explain it?"

"I don't know," said Cleavon. "I'd have to see those mobs of crazy people first to assess what in the hell it is we're actually talking about. But I don't at this moment have it in me to believe without seeing them that they are actually dead people come back to life."

Marshall nodded. "I guess so."

"Besides, dead people *couldn't* come back to life," Cleavon said.

"Why is that?"

"They take out their blood and fill them with embalming fluid when they die," Cleavon said. "I don't think it would be possible for anything to live with a body filled with embalming fluid."

"Hmmm," said Marshall. "That's interesting."

"Is there any music on at all on that radio?" Cleavon asked.

Marshall turned through the channels, but found nothing.

"Sorry," said Marshall. "No music. Just more dead-people talk."

"I miss Sam and Dave already," said Wilson. "We were having a good time there for a minute."

"Yeah, those were better times," Cleavon said. "And that was only, what, an hour ago? And now we're talking about... I don't even know what we're talking about."

Wilson said, "Madness."

"No shit," said Cleavon. "This is just crazy."

"Indeed," said Marshall.

"If there are dead people out there," Wilson said, "what do you think brought them back to life?"

Cleavon said, "Damned if I know."

They drove for an hour, but did not come to another town.

Soon the car started sputtering and shook for a moment, running out of gas. Marshall maneuvered the dying Eldorado off the road.

"Fuck," said Marshall.

"Now what?" asked Wilson.

"We've gotta walk to find gas," Marshall said.

Wilson frowned. "Walk where?"

"How the fuck do I know?" Marshall said. "I've never been here before."

"You don't have a map?" asked Cleavon.

"Sadly, no," said Marshall.

"Good planning," said Wilson.

"I don't see you with a map either," Marshall said.

The three friends climbed out of the Eldorado.

"You got a gas can?" asked Cleavon.

Marshall shook his head. "No."

"What will we use for the gas?" asked Wilson.

"We'll have to improvise," Marshall said. "We'll figure it out when the time comes."

Marshall locked the car doors, and the three friends started to walk down the road. They walked for what felt like an hour or so, but did not see any houses or towns.

"Taking back roads kind of seems like a bad idea now, in retrospect," said Cleavon.

"Hindsight is 20/20," said Marshall.

They continued to walk until they came to a cemetery on the right side of the road. It was a large, lavish cemetery, unlike anything they had ever seen. As they approached it, Cleavon said, "I don't like being near a cemetery while they're talking about corpses attacking people."

"I thought you didn't believe that," said Wilson.

"I don't," Cleavon said. "But I don't wanna take any chances either."

"There aren't any dead people walking around over there," observed Marshall.

"Maybe they were just cadavers from universities that got loose," Wilson said. "I mean, how could dead people get out of the ground if they were alive?"

Cleavon nodded. "True."

The three friends walked towards the cemetery to see what exactly it was, why it was so lavish.

"This is a strange place," said Wilson.

"It is," said Marshall. "I've never seen anything like it."

There were huge statues of men riding on horses with swords, and hundreds of tiny Confederate flags adorned the graves.

"Is it a Civil War cemetery?" asked Cleavon.

"No," said Wilson, now understanding what this place was. "It's a Klu Klux Klan cemetery."

"It's a *what*?" asked Marshall.

"You heard me."

They saw a huge marble sign in front of the cemetery that read: THE NATHANIEL BEDFORD FORREST MEMORIAL CEMETERY FOR FALLEN SONS OF THE SOUTH.

"I didn't even know there was such a thing," said Marshall.

"Neither did I," Wilson said.

"Weird that it's out here in the middle of nowhere, on some back road," said Cleavon. "Really strange place for such a fancy cemetery."

"Well," said Wilson, "this may not have been a back road back when this cemetery was established. This may have been a fairly-busy road back then, before the highways came in."

Cleavon nodded. "Makes sense."

"Should we check it out?" asked Wilson.

"I vote no," said Marshall. "We need to find gas, and it'll be dark soon. Besides, I don't want to run into the crackers who maintain this place. Do you? Something tells me they aren't partial to Negroes lurking around here."

"A few minutes won't hurt anything," said Cleavon. "Besides, I've gotta take a leak."

Marshall and Wilson looked at each other as Cleavon approached the cemetery gates. Wilson shrugged.

"Maybe you ought to just piss out here by the road," Marshall said. "That way we don't have to worry about any racist rednecks showing up and getting mad because you're desecrating Uncle Wilbur's resting place."

Wilson chuckled.

Cleavon kept walking. The gate was unlocked. He unlatched it, and walked into the cemetery. He looked around, eyeballing the huge statues of Klansmen riding with their sabers raised. He also looked around at the lavish mausoleums.

"They really keep this place well-maintained," said Cleavon.

"Yeah," Wilson said, entering the cemetery gates. "This place is nicer than our school. This is nuts."

Cleavon found a grave with an engraving on its headstone of a Klansman being carried to heaven by an angel.

"Looks like as good a place as any," he said, unzipping his pants.

He let his penis hang out and started urinating on the headstone, turning to spray the little Confederate flag next to it, as well.

"Uncle Wilbur's gonna be pissed," Cleavon said, laughing.

Marshall was nervous. He looked around in both directions, but saw no one coming. "Please hurry," he said. "I really wanna get out of here."

Wilson was examining a huge marble mausoleum with the name THORNTON inscribed over its doorway. Wilson jokingly knocked on the door. "Anybody home?" he asked. He opened the door to the mausoleum and went inside for a more thorough investigation.

Once he was inside, he saw that a tomb drawer on his left was open.

And it was empty.

Where the hell was the body?

Wilson turned back towards the door and came face-to-face with a living corpse, its arms reaching out for him. Its clothing was ripped apart, and it was mostly skeletal by this point. The corpse's eyeballs were long gone and there were gaping holes where they had once been. Pieces of dried, leathery skin hung from the corpse's exposed jowls.

"What the fuck?" said Wilson.

The corpse moved towards him. There was nowhere for Wilson to go.

He screamed, but the scream became a grotesque gurgling sound as the corpse ripped Wilson's head from his neck.

Outside, Marshall and Cleavon were alarmed.

"Wilson?" asked Cleavon.

There was no response.

Marshall said, "Dammit, Wilson, this is no time for jokes. We don't have time for this."

Still no response.

"I'll check on him," said Cleavon, moving towards the open mausoleum. He walked around the thing, entering its doorway, not believing what he was seeing. It was fairly dark in there, so Cleavon couldn't see clearly. There was some sort of grotesquely-disfigured man hunched over Wilson, who was lying on the floor. The man had his head down, obstructing Cleavon's view so he couldn't see what the hell was happening.

"Hey!" Cleavon said. "What the fuck are you doing?"

The man looked up and Cleavon got a clear view of what was happening. When the man raised his face to look at Cleavon, he ripped skin from Wilson's already-torn-apart throat. The bloody meat was dangling from the man's mouth, blood dripping all over Wilson's dead body.

The man faced Cleavon, making a sort of grunting sound as he did.

Cleavon screamed.

He turned to run, took about two steps out of the mausoleum, and was immediately confronted by another of the rotten monstrosities, dressed in a tattered robe that had once been white. Cleavon stared at the thing for a second, realizing it was indeed a rotting corpse. He maneuvered around it.

The thing moved slowly, shambling towards him. Cleavon ran for Marshall, but found that his friend was in trouble, as well. In his peripheral vision, Cleavon could see dozens of figures moving around the cemetery now, but he paid them no mind. His focus was on Marshall, who was lying on the ground, wrestling with another of the dead men.

"Hey, asshole!" Cleavon said, trying to get the dead man's attention. The corpse turned to face him, appearing to look at him even though he had no eyeballs. Marshall, still lying under the thing, reached down to the corpse's side and unsheathed its saber, pushing it up through its crumbling body. The corpse raised up a bit, more frenzied than before, and tried to bite his face.

Cleavon attempted to distract the corpse again. "Hey, asshole!"

The dead man turned towards Cleavon, and Marshall repositioned the saber and brought it up hard through its eye socket. The thing made a dry, growling sound, and fell dead once again. Marshall pushed it off him, and started to get up. Cleavon came forward to assist him, but Marshall saw another dead man behind Cleavon.

"Cleavon!" he screamed. "Behind you!"

Cleavon whirled around and saw the dead man in the white robe. He pulled back his fist out of sheer instinct and punched its chest as hard as he could, his fist going clear through the corpse's body. This had no effect on the creature, and it moved closer towards him. Cleavon pulled his fist out of the dead man's chest, and kicked it hard in the knee. The dead man's leg gave in, crumbling upon contact, and the dead Klansman collapsed. Cleavon moved forward, raised his leg, and stomped hard, crushing the dead man's head. The corpse stopped moving.

Cleavon turned to face Marshall, now standing beside him.

"You believe in walking dead men now?" asked Marshall.

"I know how they kill people," Cleavon said, his voice wavering.

"How?"

"They eat you."

Marshall grimaced, a chill running down his spine.

The two friends suddenly realized they were slowly being surrounded by the slow-moving dead men. There were about ten of them in close proximity, and dozens more behind. It was getting dark now, and they could see the silhouettes of more figures off in the distance, some of them still crawling out of the ground.

"Coming here was a bad idea," said Cleavon.

Marshall looked at him. "I told you, but you don't listen."

Cleavon reached down over the dead man he'd just stopped and unsheathed its saber. The two men turned towards the horde, their backs to one another, sabers of dead Klansmen before them.

"You ready?" asked Cleavon.

"Shit no."

The dead men were closing in.

Cleavon struck first, lopping off the head of a corpse. Within seconds both of them were bobbing and weaving with their sabers, chopping off heads right and left. Both of them were winded with still more surrounding dead men left to battle. Cleavon buried his saber in the cheekbone of a dead man, pushing it through to the hilt. Soon the two men were standing there, back to back, exhausted, with a pile of decapitated Klansmen at their feet.

"Let's get out of here," said Marshall.

"Where do we go?"

"Anywhere but here."

The two of them slowly made their way through the cemetery, fighting off attacking dead men as they walked, chopping off rotten heads and arms at every turn. Finally they made their way back to the gate. They opened it and slipped out, quickly fastening it behind them. A crowd of the dead men was soon assembled there, trying to get out, but unable to comprehend the gate's latch.

"We did it," Marshall said.

Cleavon raised his hand and Marshall slapped him a five.

The two exhausted men then shuffled down the dirt road, looking like dead men themselves.

"The chances of us making it out of this are pretty slim," said Marshall.

Cleavon rolled his eyes. "You always know just what to say to ruin the mood."

"At least we got swords."

Cleavon chuckled. "Two century-old swords against thousands of walking dead men who want to eat us. What could possibly go wrong?"

LOVELY RITA
by Stephen Spignesi

Stephen Spignesi is a New York Times bestselling author who writes about historical biography, popular culture, television, film, American and world history, and contemporary fiction. He is also a university professor, novelist, and musician. Spignesi's more than 60 books have been translated into several languages and he has also written essays, chapters, articles, and introductions to a wide range of books. In addition to writing, Spignesi is a Practitioner in Residence at the University of New Haven where he teaches Composition and Literature. Spignesi was praised for "reinventing the psychological thriller" upon the publication of his acclaimed debut novel, DIALOGUES, and hailed as "the world's leading authority on Stephen King" by Entertainment Weekly magazine. Spignesi lives in New Haven, Connecticut with his grey cat, Chloe. His website is www.stephenspignesi.com.

For Dave and LeeAnn Hinchberger

1
June 8, 1967

One of my biggest regrets in life was throwing away my vinyl edition of the Sgt. Pepper *album. We had cassettes, right? Who needed a record player? It went to the dump with the rest of my albums.*

"Did you buy it yet?"
"Yeah. Yesterday."

"What'd you pay?"

"$2.99. Caldor's had it on sale."

"After only a week? You listened to it yet?"

Peter looked at Jimmy with a smirk that said, *Are you kidding?* "Of course I did."

"And?"

"I can't describe how I feel about it yet."

"Can I borrow it?"

Peter laughed loudly. "Are you kidding?"

"No. I'm serious."

"No way. *Sgt. Pepper* does not leave my domicile."

Jimmy looked down at his bare feet. He was sitting on the edge of Peter's bed and holding a joint in one hand and a bottle of Pepsi in the other. He took a hit of the joint, passed it to Peter and, after exhaling the smoke into the small fan sitting on the bureau, took a swig of the Pepsi.

"I can't afford it."

Peter felt bad. Jimmy could tell. "Can you afford 39 cents?" Peter asked.

Jimmy looked up with a quizzical expression on his face. "Why?"

"Can you?"

"Yeah."

"Okay. Let's take a ride to Radio Shack. 60-minute cassettes are 39 cents. I'll make you a tape."

Jimmy slipped his feet into his lace-less sneakers and stood up. "Right on."

Peter chuckled. "Right on."

2
A Year Later: All Hell

All hell broke loose in the fall of 1968.

What the hell does "hell" mean anyway? People often use that term to describe pretty much any situation where there's confusion, chaos, or violence. Catholics think hell is a pit of fire. Soldiers think hell is war. Students think hell is finals week. Unhappy couples think hell is marriage. The sick and dying think hell is intractable pain. Addicts think hell is being deprived of their drug of choice.

Those of us who lived through 1968 have a completely different definition, one that is so extreme, it sounds like we made it up.

But we didn't.

For Rita, she witnessed hell the moment she walked into her sister Karen's house and saw Karen eating her infant daughter Judy's arm. Thankfully, Karen had suffocated the baby first, and she herself was still cognizant enough to dine quickly before the baby came back.

Karen's mouth was smeared with blood, her eyes were black, and her head lolled from side to side as she chewed, tendrils of infant flesh dangling out of her maw. Rita had her pistol with her (of course), so she walked across the kitchen, placed the muzzle against Karen's head just above her ear and fired. She then noticed that little Judy was making that head-moving motion and guttural moan that signaled a comeback, so she put a bullet in her head as well. Right between her little blue eyes.

Rita walked into the living room and pulled aside the thick curtain on the big picture window. She scanned the street. Two to the left, two to the right, one in the front yard of the house across the street.

Rita checked her gun. Six rounds left. She reached into one of the leg pockets of her cargo pants and confirmed by touch a box of 100 rounds almost completely full.

She looked at her sister and niece, exhaled deeply, and walked out the front door.

She quickly moved to her left and approached the two that were shambling down the street. The moment she was within point blank range, she fired one shot into each of their heads. Down they went. She turned and saw the two in the street and the one in the yard now heading toward her. She walked briskly to each of them and again, one, two, three.

She looked around. Sometimes gunfire attracted them, but the area was all clear. She quickly reloaded.

With a full eight rounds, Rita then pulled a bottle of water out of her left front pocket and took a swig. She screwed the top back on and sighed. "This is fucked up," she said, so softly that to anyone within an arm's length of her, it would have sounded like a whisper.

3

Grocery Shopping

Zombies are stupid. Good thing, too. The very last thing I'd want to see when I got home is an empty cage.

Rita put her water bottle back into her pocket and pulled out of her backpack a rolled-up zippered garment bag. She had discovered that they were quite suitable for transporting a goodly quantity of parts back home to Jimmy. She unrolled the bag and laid it flat on the street. She then removed a portable 10 amp reciprocating power saw from the backpack. She tested it once and was relieved she had remembered to charge it. She glanced around, and then up at the sky. Cloudy. *Hope it doesn't rain before I get home.* Rita took a deep breath and exhaled slowly to a count of four.

Thighs, upper arms, maybe stomach fat slices, she thought. *The stuff with a lot of meat. That should keep him happy for a while.*

Rita had a cassette player in her shirt pocket. She had found a small portable speaker that could plug into the headphones jack. No headphones post-catastrophe. Rita could not block her hearing ever again, under any circumstances. She reached into her pocket and, by touch, pressed play. "Lovely Rita" from *Sgt. Pepper* began playing out of the speaker in her other pocket. She revved the saw again.

Time to get to work.

She approached the closest zombie. It was a thirty-something woman. She was lying on her back. She wore shorts, a t-shirt, and flip-flops.

At least I won't have to undress her.

Rita knelt down on one knee, flipped on the saw, and applied it to the woman's left thigh just below where her shorts ended.

Blood flew as the blade cut through the flesh.

She's still relatively fresh, Rita thought as she squinted her eyes against the flying droplets.

The blade slowed when it hit her femur. She pressed harder and was through it quickly. She then pushed through the remaining flesh and her left leg dropped to the ground. Rather than sever it below the knee in public, Rita simply grabbed the whole thing and slid it into the garment bag.

She repeated the severing on the zombie's right leg, placed it in the garment bag, and then stood and looked down at her.

She's a little overweight, she thought. She used her booted right foot to kick her over so that she was lying on her stomach. Rita reached down and pulled down her shorts and panties. She assessed her buttocks with the eye of a chef.

Meaty.

She revved the saw and, within two minutes, thick slabs of the legless woman's butt flesh were in the garment bag.

4

Day One

Maybe I'm just kidding myself. Survival? How long can I continue to live like this? And if more and more people transform into flesh-eating monsters, what hope does society, our city...hell, the world *have? 'Cause you know this fucking thing will spread everywhere. How can it not?*

Some blamed aliens. Some said it was radiation from a failed satellite that plummeted to earth. Some blamed the Russians. Some said it was fluoride in the water, saccharine in diet soda, marijuana, falling church attendance, or the fact that there were lesbian and gay people. Some blamed the Aurora Borealis. Some blamed Satanists, nudists, atheists, vegetarians, and creationists. Some blamed pro-choice people; some blamed masturbators and fornicators. Some said God was punishing mankind; some said it was the beginning of the Rapture.

And some blamed the Beatles, specifically the year-old *Sgt. Pepper* album. All that "I get high with a little help from my friends," and "I'd love to turn you on" stuff. Heathens.

Regardless of how it happened, though, it happened. Not everywhere, and not all at once, but it happened. The dead began reanimating and resurrecting, and once they were above ground, they were ravenous for human flesh.

The zombies were killable, though. You had to shut off their brain. A bullet in an ear, the temple, the forehead, or between the eyes always did the trick.

There was no denying that after a very short period of time, the term "survival of the fittest" had never been more apt.

Everyone was afraid to leave their home. People stopped going to work, and bands of armed neighbors visited abandoned grocery stories for supplies. For the most part, money became useless, except to buy guns and ammo person-to-person. The pandemic was spreading from city to city, yet the government and the police ceaselessly denied that anything was wrong. (The inside scoop was that they didn't want to panic the public. Most citizens found this hilarious. Seeing an elderly zombie woman dragging herself down the street while chewing on some guy's foot was more than enough to cause a little concern for most people.) The nightly newscasts were ludicrous. The anchors pretended that nothing was going on and flatly reported economic news, foreign news, and, of course, weather and sports.

Everyone knew, though. And after the initial period of rampant rumor, it became clear that the dead were, indeed, rising from their graves and shuffling through cities and towns looking to feed, which ultimately made more zombies.

Rita and Jimmy lived in a small suburb of New Haven, Connecticut called Pomroy. The town had a small cemetery that had emptied out very quickly after the contagion, or the rays, or the toxin, or the curse, or the whatever struck.

Rita loved Jimmy. Enormously. She credited him with saving her fucked-up alcoholic life. She told him – and anyone else who would listen – that she'd have drank herself to death if she had never met him. She adored him. And they were talking about having children.

But Jimmy had been bitten, and he now "lived" in a large, locked, steel dog cage in the living room of their two-story Cape Cod on White Street.

As Rita rearranged the parts in the garment bag, pressed out the air, and zipped it up, she thought back to Day One, the first time she had personally become aware of the calamity.

It had been cold. Low twenties with the wind chill. The sky was dark at noon. As Rita drove home from work around four o'clock, she passed St. Rose Catholic Church and glanced up at the spire. It looked ominous and threatening against the glowering sky. On the corner diagonally across from the church's front steps Rita saw an elderly woman shuffling along the sidewalk, dragging one foot behind her. *No cane?* Rita wondered. *If anyone could use a cane, it was this lady*, she thought. Rita slowed her car and noticed something else about the old woman: no purse. Or shopping bag.

Rita turned onto Saltonstall Avenue, the street where the woman was walking, and pulled into a parking space across the street from her. She watched her walk.

And that was when she noticed the...*fluid.*

As she walked, Rita saw that the woman was leaving behind her on the sidewalk a trail of some type of fluid.

Fuck. This lady is either bleeding or shitting as she walks.

Rita got out of her car and started walking toward the woman.

"Ma'am?" she said as she neared her. "Are you all right?"

Rita looked down the sidewalk and saw the trail the old woman had left behind her. As she got closer, she could see that it was dark red.

It's blood. I'm taking her to the Emergency Room. It's ten minutes up Chapel Street.

Rita reached the woman and extended her arm. She touched her gently on her left shoulder. Rita heard a guttural sound come from the woman and she stopped walking. She turned to face Rita, and that was when Rita met her first zombie.

5

Acts of God

No one put the fire out when St. Rose Church went up in a raging inferno. What was surprising is how well the exterior survived. It was all brick and marble and that does not burn well. Parishioners claimed that the fact that the church itself remained standing was a sign that God had watched out for them. What's a few wooden pews? Those can be replaced. We still have the building itself, they said.

Right after the cataclysm, but before Jimmy was bitten, Jimmy and Rita had a talk about God. Or the lack thereof.

Rita was an atheist; Jimmy believed everything he had been taught in Catholic grammar school. He self-identified as a Christian, and even though he and Rita had agreed never to discuss religion, recent events had resulted in, one, Jimmy questioning God, and, two, Rita questioning Jimmy about how, if there was a God, he could let what had happened, happen.

Rita knew that, for the most part (Jimmy excluded, of course) believers hated atheists. And one day, she concluded that she had figured out why.

"Why should they care?" she asked Jimmy. "Why should the so self-righteously labeled 'people of faith' care about whether or not I, or anyone else, believe in their particular mythological fairy story? Why do they take it so personally?"

Jimmy fidgeted in bed. He had a feeling he knew where this was going.

"I'll tell you why," Rita continued. "Because deep down, in their heart of hearts, behind the doors they never open, they worry that atheists are right. 'What if there is no God and everything I believe is false?' they think. That's the unasked question that goes through their subconscious mind – and probably their conscious mind, if they're halfway honest with themselves – every time they come upon a well-spoken, obviously intelligent atheist shredding their belief system into little pieces."

"Reet…" Jimmy began.

No good. Reet was on a tear.

93

"Show the world what you hate and we'll tell you what you fear. And where you're vulnerable. If the faithful were truly confident in their religious beliefs, they'd laugh off the non-believers and continue believing what they believe. And there are many believers who do just that. But those who are personally offended, and who get rabidly angry every time someone challenges what they believe, even in the generalized, abstract sense of an Op-Ed or Letter to the Editor, those people are the greatest doubters. They'll never admit it, but they are."

Jimmy sighed and turned his head on the pillow. Surrender, Dorothy, was the move for now.

"If I know – or *sincerely believe* – something to be true, nothing you or anyone else can say can sway me. And now that we can look out our window and see…you know what we'll see…I'll ask you this: how can your all-powerful, all-loving, all-knowing, all-merciful 'God' allow something like this to happen?"

Surrender didn't work. Jimmy opened his eyes and sat up in bed.

"God doesn't cause catastrophes, Reet. God doesn't decide to cause a tsunami, or a hurricane, or an earthquake, or a plane crash, or a mass murder, or…whatever *this*…" He gestured toward the window. "…is."

Rita smiled. She loved Jimmy's unquestioning commitment to the myth.

"Really, sweetie? Then why do legal documents and insurance policies define exactly any of the things you just mentioned as an 'Act of God?'"

6
The Stylites

Irish historian William E.H. Lecky on St. Simeon Stylites: For about two centuries, the hideous maceration of the body was regarded as the highest proof of excellence...The cleanliness of the body was regarded as a pollution of the soul, and the saints who were most admired had become one hideous mass of clotted filth...But of all the evidences of the loathsome excesses to which this spirit was carried, the life of St. Simeon Stylites is probably the most remarkable.... He had bound a rope around him so that it became embedded in his flesh, which putrefied around it. A horrible stench, intolerable to the bystanders, exhaled from his body, and worms dropped from him whenever he moved, and they filled his bed.... For a whole year, we are told, St. Simeon stood upon one leg, the other being covered with hideous ulcers, while his biographer (St. Anthony) was commissioned to stand by his side, to pick up the worms that fell from his body, and to replace them in the sores, the saint saying to the worms, "Eat what God has given you."

There were some who considered the zombies to be blessed. They believed the undead were emissaries, or sacred manifestations, or messages from God, and thus, they treated them as divine souls.

Stylites all wore the same thing, and for the same reason: They needed to be able to move around quickly. On the bottom, they wore black shorts, which were either regular shorts looted from stories or homes, or black pants with the legs cut off. On the top, they wore short-sleeved pajama tops. None of them wore underwear.

And in honor of their patron saint, St. Simeon, from whom they took their name and spiritual mission, they never, *ever* bathed. Nor did they clean themselves of any bodily fluids: blood, semen, urine, feces...they believed the mortification of the flesh engendered spiritual growth and fulfillment of the soul. Thus, they reeked to high heavens. And they had lice, and worms, and infections, and boils, and lesions, and all manner of other disgusting physical symptoms.

The Stylite ritual involved dancing around and taunting zombies. They never touched them, but they considered themselves especially blessed if blood, spittle, flesh, or even worms flew off a zombie and landed on them while they were moving about them like whirling dervishes in a bizarre, macabre faux-religious performance.

If one of the Stylites was bitten and transformed, another of them would volunteer to sacrifice him- or herself as food for their former disciple. In a twisted reinterpretation of the Catholic Eucharistic ceremony, the Stylite would walk up to their former devotee and hold his or her arm out for the zombie to bite.

Once they were fully reanimated, the new zombie would become a part of the target group around which the remaining Stylites would dance.

Rita saw Stylites many times during her treks through the neighborhood. She would ignore them unless they approached her, or in any way confronted her verbally. Then she'd shoot them in the head. Living or not, it didn't matter. Rita did not fuck around when it came to zombies or the Stylite lunatics. If they spoke to her, moved a step toward her or, in a few cases, even looked at her, they were quickly dispatched.

On her way home after filling the garment bag, Rita saw a group of Stylites surrounding a male zombie who had probably been in his forties when he reanimated.

The zombie was shuffling along, dragging his left leg. Rita could hear the forlorn, guttural moaning that often issued from the walking dead, and she could also hear the high-pitched keening wail that the Stylites used to elicit a reaction from a zombie. Apparently, the higher range of the squeaky screeching actually got through sometimes, and a few of the Stylites would actually be rewarded by a zombie turning toward them as it reacted to the source of the sound.

Today, Rita was carrying meat. This added an enormous amount of danger to her walk home. Incredibly, physical revenants retained very acute senses of smell. And bloody flesh was their most powerful attractant.

Rita walked slowly, the garment bag slung over her left shoulder, her SIG-P210, her daily carry, in her right hand. Rita had learned that the SIG had the most stopping power for her purposes. It was a single-action pistol that held eight nine millimeter rounds. "Unless you're talking Plus-P-Plus loads, you can forget the thirty-eight," a cop friend of hers named Hank had told her. "Shit, I've seen one of those bounce off a windshield."

That had been enough for Rita. She had wandered through a newly-looted gun store and had been able to find both the handgun she wanted and plenty of ammo. She would have happily paid for everything, but there was no one to take her money, and within 72 hours, the place had been completely emptied out. Rita had made it just in time. She carried 100 rounds with her at all times, and she had another 4,000 rounds hidden in her basement at home. She tried not to think about what she'd do after she had exhausted her ammo stores.

As she walked, her eyes never leaving the group down the street to her right, she saw that the Stylites had noticed her.

She kept walking, and she did not pick up her pace. Some would have been afraid. After what she'd lived through in recent weeks and months, fear was the last thing in her mind and heart. *I'm inoculated*, she'd jokingly think.

One of the Stylites started walking toward her.

It was a young woman with long hair. Her face was filthy, she had lice crawling around on her scalp, and Rita could see shit stains streaking her legs. Her pajama top had been ripped and one large naked breast bounced on her chest as she headed toward Rita.

"The Lord has gifted us with the sacred walkers!" she shouted as she moved closer to Rita.

"Do not come any closer," Rita said in a steady voice and held up her gun.

The woman did not stop walking toward Rita.

"Take another step and I will shoot you," Rita said calmly.

Pajama Girl stopped and held out her arms to Rita. "Won't you please come and join us as St. Simeon would?"

Rita chuckled. *Fucking freaks.*

"The degradation of the body is the only path to salvation," the woman said. "The holy walkers show us the way."

And that's when she started moving toward Rita again.

"One more step and you're dead," Rita said.

The woman extended her arms to the sky, started vocalizing the high-pitched Stylites wailing, and continued to walk toward Rita.

"You were warned," Rita said. She then moved very quickly toward Pajama Girl and, when she was an arms-length away, she placed the muzzle of her pistol against the girl's forehead and pulled the trigger.

The wailing stopped instantly and Pajama Girl fell to the ground. Rita saw that the Stylites and the zombies had noticed what had happened and both groups were now headed toward the fallen zealot.

That's my cue, Rita thought, and began walking quickly down the street away from the scene.

When she was clear, she looked back and saw the zombies feeding on Pajama Girl while the Stylites stood around them in a circle wailing and shrieking.

Headed home, Rita's mind swirled, asking the same question over and over: *How long? How long? How long?*

7
The Holes Were Rather Small

Rita couldn't get one specific joke out of her head: An old woman is very upset at her husband's funeral. "You have him in a brown suit and I wanted him in a blue suit!" she tells the funeral director. "I'm very sorry, ma'am" he replies. "We'll take care of it." He then yells, "Hey Andy! Do me a favor. Switch the heads on one and three!"

Some of Jimmy and Rita's neighbors had gone so far as to install metal, roll-down security gates on all the doors and windows of their homes. They left them down twenty-four hours a day, even when they were home. Rita had visited her neighbor Rachel, and was horrified when Rachel rolled down the front door gate after Rita had entered the house. She felt like she was inside a tomb. Or a missile silo.

Jimmy and Rita had decided on thick, reinforced steel bars on all their windows and doors. They knew that zombies didn't have the strength to break, bend, or in any way get through them, plus the bars came with the added benefit of still being able to look out the window and see what was going on in the neighborhood. Sure, it made looking out said windows akin to peering through prison cell doors, but, overall, it was worth it.

As Rita approached her house, she saw two. One was on her next-door neighbor Stephen's front porch; one was on her own front lawn.

She moved speedily up Stephen's front walk, stopped at the bottom step of the porch, and put a bullet in the zombie's left eye. The old man zombie fell instantly. *He looks like President Taft*, she thought. She then hurried onto her own front lawn and fired one shot into the teenage girl zombie's left ear. Down she went.

Such "clean-up" had become normal for neighborhoods all over. It was just common courtesy, after all.

Before Rita entered the house, she did a tour of their property. She walked into the backyard and moved back far enough to see her roof.

A zombie was hugging the chimney. *He must have smelled Jimmy,* she thought. *This will be a tough one.*

She pointed her SIG at the chimney, lined up the zombie in the gun's sight, exhaled slowly and, at the very end of her breath, squeezed the trigger.

Head shot. Nice.

The flesh-eater's head snapped back, and he then fell backwards, landed on his back, slid down the roof, and fell onto Rita and Jimmy's patio.

Rita pocketed her pistol and walked to the back door. She had to step around the zombie. She kicked it in the ribs just to be sure it was powered off.

It wasn't. Rita suddenly felt a hand grasping her ankle. *Guess I missed the medulla-whatever-blongata*, she thought. She whipped out her SIG and put a bullet in the top of the zombie's head. Its hand instantly fell away from Rita's leg and she kicked the body away from her.

Rita slowed her breathing and reached in her pocket for the keys to the back door. She unlocked the sliding metal bar security gate and was inside in seconds. She had become very good at eliminating any and all vulnerability, and there was nothing that could leave a person more vulnerable than an open door. She triple-locked the door and stepped into the laundry room off the kitchen. She placed the bag 'o body parts in the big slop sink and then removed her jacket and hung it on a hook just inside the door. Her gun stayed with her, as did her cassette player. She pressed Play and headed for the living room. Side 2 of *Sgt. Pepper* picked up where it had left off. In the living room, she could hear Jimmy's guttural moaning. *He's hungry.*

She walked up to the cage and looked down at the man she loved.

This was always hard for her. She could feel that tickly swelling feeling at the back of her throat that always preceded a crying jag.

Not now.

She placed her hand on the top of the cage and Jimmy looked up at her.

And that was when Rita gasped and stepped backward so quickly she almost fell.

Jimmy's eyes were clear.

They weren't black.

He made eye contact with Rita and she could feel her heart skip a beat.

What the…?

Jimmy looked at Rita, and at that moment she would have sworn under oath that he recognized her.

She moved her hand to touch the cage's lock, but quickly pulled her fingers back as though the lock had scalded her.

Am I really considering this? Am I fucking crazy?

But then something shifted inside her consciousness. She was suddenly ultra-calm and at peace. Her anxiety and fear vanished, and she found herself smiling down at Jimmy who, she hoped, was smiling back. It was hard to tell because of the facial degradation and caked blood around his mouth, but deep down she believed he was.

She unlocked the cage and slid open the door. Jimmy breathed softly and in shallow, visceral gasps, and slowly began moving toward the cage door.

Rita stepped back and sat down on the living room floor, her back against the wall. Jimmy crawled out and knelt before her on his haunches. His eyes were locked on Rita but he didn't make a move toward her.

And at that moment, they were together again, and it was as though what had happened had never happened. It was like before.

Before the calamity.

Before the horror.

Before the pain.

Before the fear.

Before the world was brutally torn into vile pieces and all that we knew and loved was trashed like loathsome garbage left to rot in the sun.

Jimmy and Reet were together again. Jimmy the contaminated monster and Rita the vigilante slaughter goddess were a couple again, and both knew, somehow, that their love was still alive.

This was good enough for Rita, and as tears rolled down her dirty cheeks, she extended her arm to Jimmy, looked him in the eye, and nodded.

Rita placed her finger on the trigger of her gun.

Jimmy held her arm gently and bit into the fleshy upper part of her limb.

Rita let him indulge in her flesh and blood a bit before she fired a bullet into his forehead.

Rita sat and cradled Jimmy for a few moments. She knew she didn't have much time.

She looked down at his blood-streaked face and hair, his closed eyes, his stubble-covered cheeks, and saw nothing but her Jimmy.

Inside, she could feel the transformation beginning. It was time.

She placed the black barrel of the SIG in her mouth, squeezed the trigger and—

The echo of Rita's gunshot was long gone when the cassette player automatically shut off at the end of *Sgt. Pepper*.

THE PROTEST
by R.D. Riley

R.D. Riley is a journalist and writer living in Kansas. He co-authored THE STEPHEN KING MOVIE QUIZ BOOK and co-edited TRASH CINEMA: A CELEBRATION OF OVERLOOKED MASTERPIECES.

Bethany Louise Newbold woke up with a brand new name. She would be called "Lily" from now on. She'd decided on the name as she drifted in and out of sleep during the night.

It was dark out when Lily got up. Her head was still a little fuzzy from all the pot they'd smoked as they sat around Mark's shortwave radio, trying to make sense of what they heard. There had been scattered reports of "mass murders" breaking out along the east coast. Just before she'd gone to bed, a Civil Defense bulletin had spoken of shooting people in the head and burning the bodies.

She hadn't gone to bed until sometime after one, and she'd set the alarm for 7 a.m. Their hastily constructed plan called for them all to meet on the quad at nine.

Now that they were finally taking some direct action, Lily felt that a new name was needed to boldly signal her intent to make a clean break with her old life. And whatever kind of weird shit was going down right now, most of the group had decided it demanded action.

Mark, as always, had whined that there was nothing the six of them could do down here in "Bumfuck, Ohio," as he called it, that would make any difference. Mark was forever wanting to cram everyone into his shitty van and drive up to Columbus to join in protest activities there.

"Look, man," Peter had said, "I've told you before. It's just as important that we have a presence here locally at Webberly as what they're doing at Ohio State, or in New York or wherever."

"Come on," Mark had said, "we barely even have a science department at this dump. Columbus is where the action is. You <u>know</u> they're taking DOD money up there, and doing God knows what with it. And whatever the fuck is going on, I'll bet you a million dollars the government is behind it."

"Maybe," Peter had countered, "but if the shit hits the fan, I don't want to be 100 miles from home when it happens. Plus, if this really is some kind of government biological weapon, do you really want to be in a densely populated urban area if it spreads?"

Peter had won the argument, of course. Peter was brilliant and logical always. Mark was a hothead with a lot of big ideas. He did know where to get the best pot, though, so they mostly tolerated him. And he always paid his share of the rent on time, which was more than could be said for the lesbian couple Ursula and Penny, their other housemates and fellow SDS members.

Mark sometimes commented that they must be the smallest, saddest branch of the Students for a Democratic Society anywhere in America. Webberly College was not a hotbed of student activism, by any means. Besides the five of them living in the house, their number included just two others, a black student named Nate, and Carl, a dropout and phone phreaker who generally only bothered to show up when he knew there would be plenty of weed on hand.

Nate had once complained that he felt isolated and alone as part of their "bullshit honky collective," but he'd said it with a smile. Nate was one cool motherfucker, not nearly as angry as some of the other black activists Lily had met, though she figured he had as much right as any of them to be.

As she dressed, Lily's thoughts darkened. She remembered the radio reports from the night before. The world, it seemed, was changing much faster than they had reckoned for.

She went downstairs. Nate was asleep on the couch. He had a dorm room on campus, but often crashed at the house after late night sessions. No one minded. Nate was usually up with the sun and out of the house before anyone else awoke. Today, he'd clearly decided to stay over, which was fine. Today was not like any other day.

In the dining room, she found Mark still hunched over the shortwave radio. He had headphones on. When he noticed Lily, he took them off and gave her a grim nod.

"Anything new?" she asked.

"Nothing but bullshit," Mark said. "All the stations keep saying that the 'incidents' have been 'contained' and everyone should 'remain calm.'"

"That doesn't make any sense," she said. "No one's saying what happened? Or why?"

Mark gave her a smile, one without a trace of humor to it. "It makes perfect sense, Beth," he said. "Mass panic."

"It's Lily now, Mark. I decided last night."

"What?" Mark glared at her for a moment. "Oh, okay. Lily it is."

Lily shook her head. "God, it doesn't even matter right now. What were you saying about panic?"

"Mass panic." Mark leaned back in the chair, and Lily sensed she was in for another one of his lectures. "They want to avoid upsetting the system. It's standard operating procedure. Propaganda 101. Don't tell the sheep anything. Someone was asleep at the switch last night. That's how those reports got out in the first place. But they've cracked down now. Everything is back to normal. Return to your boring lives and continue shopping."

Lily sat at the table across from Mark. "I don't know," she said, a cold fear rippling across her scalp. "If it's really still dangerous out there, maybe we should all just stay here."

"No way," Mark said, raising his voice. "We're never going to get any answers sitting around on our asses waiting for the man to explain it all to us like we're children!"

Lily had argued with Mark before, and she wasn't going to back down now. She opened her mouth to retort, but then Nate came in from the living room, one hand rubbing at his face.

"What's all the fuss?" he asked.

"She's had a sudden change of heart ..."

"Mark is being reckless again ..."

They were talking over one another, voices growing louder. Nate threw his hands up and took a step forward.

"Woah, woah, woah," he said. "Slow down people. Let's be calm here."

"Yes, let's," came a new voice from the living room. Peter entered, still wearing the same pair of worn out jeans from the night before and no shirt. His hair was a mess. And yet he looked perfect to Lily.

Nate moved aside to let Peter take the lead. He generally did, even though the two had founded the Webberly chapter of the SDS together two years ago. Peter was the president of the chapter and had been their delegate to the national convention last year. Nate wasn't even vice-president. That honorific fell to Mark. Unlike those two, Nate didn't seem to need a title to be a leader. He influenced the group in his own quiet, unobtrusive way.

Peter sat with Mark and Lily. "What seems to be the problem? Mark?"

"Beth ... I mean, Lily, wants to cancel the protest."

Lily rolled her eyes. "I do not. I just think we ought to take stock of the situation before we go blindly rushing in. This could be really dangerous."

"Well, it was a little spur of the moment," Peter said. "What's on the radio, Mark?"

Mark repeated what he'd already told Lily, including the bits about mass panic and calming the herd.

"It is a classic disinformation tactic," Peter said when Mark fell silent. "If we don't know <u>what</u> is happening, we won't question <u>why</u> it happened."

"Exactly," Mark said, looking smug.

"Then that's all the more reason for us to be cautious," Lily said. "If they're lying about the worst of it being over, we have no idea what's waiting for us out there."

Nate came forward and took a spot to Peter's left. "That was some pretty scary shit they were talking about last night," he said.

"Look," Mark said, "I've been up this whole time. I haven't heard any gunshots or sounds of mayhem."

Lily raised an eyebrow. "Sounds of mayhem?"

"You know what I mean," Mark said. "No sirens. No cops or ambulances or anything. Besides, we've got strength in numbers. We can get 20 or so people on the quad no problem. More, probably."

"I don't know …"

"Anyway, I've got an insurance policy to make sure we're safe."

"Insurance policy?" Peter looked dubious. "What's that mean?"

"This." Mark reached down by his feet and lifted something from the floor. He set it on the table. A shoebox. He placed a hand on the lid, waited a moment, and then whisked it open theatrically.

Lily gasped and took a step back, even as she realized she'd known what it was as soon as he put the box on the table. A gun. Black and shiny and deadly looking, nestled in the box atop some tissue paper.

"Where the fuck did you get that?" Peter demanded.

"It was my dad's," Mark said, sounding a little defensive. "He took it off a dead German in the war. All the guys did stuff like that."

"Shit," Peter said. "Is it a Luger?" He reached over and pulled the box closer.

"Be careful," Lily said.

"Oh, for fuck's sake, Lily, it's not a bomb," Mark said. "And yes, it is a Luger."

"Don't touch it, Peter," Lily said.

But Peter already had his hand on the gun and was lifting it out of the box.

"Does it still work?" Peter turned the Luger over in his hands.

"Yep. I take it out in the woods every couple of months or so."

Lily's face grew hot. "You've had that thing in our house this whole time?"

"Calm down," Mark said. "I don't keep it loaded. I'm not an idiot."

Lily was seething. The whole point of the student movement was non-violence. She'd known Mark could be a real asshole, but she'd never have thought he was a hypocrite.

"You are not bringing it on campus," she said. "Someone could get hurt."

"You're the one who's all scared about what's out there," Mark said. "I'd think you'd want some extra protection."

Damn it, Lily thought, *he's right. I __am__ scared. But I'm more scared of that damn gun.*

"I have an idea," she said. "Let's call Carl. He lives right on Main Street. He should be able to look out his front window and see if anything seems … weird."

"Good idea," Nate said, rising from the table. "I'll go call him right now."

Mark pulled the headphones out of the jack on the radio. Music burst forth from the speaker, and he reached over to turn the volume down.

"You see?" he said. "They've gone back to regular programming. They want us to forget anything ever really happened. Or is happening."

"Try some other stations," Peter suggested, putting the gun in the box and pushing it back over to Mark. "Surely someone will be reporting on it."

Lily got up and said, "I'm going to go start on breakfast." She gave Peter a quick kiss and went to the kitchen.

As Lily gathered the ingredients she'd need to make pancakes and eggs, she found her hands were shaking. The cold fear she'd felt earlier returned, sweeping now through her whole body. Last night, when they were listening to the terrible events on the radio, she'd been high, and it had all seemed very far away. This morning, stone sober, she sensed that danger was right on their doorstep.

Lily took several deep breaths. She wished she had time for some meditation, but breakfast wasn't going to fix itself. When she felt a little calmer, she went to work. As she did, the rhythm and routine of the work calmed her further.

As Lily was whisking eggs in a big bowl, Nate came into the room. He stood at the counter by her side, and suddenly the big kitchen seemed much cozier.

"What, no bacon?" Nate asked, grinning. Unlike the five of them in the house, he was an unrepentant meat eater.

"Very funny," Lily said. "Did you get hold of Carl?"

"I did. Everything, in his words, 'looks copacetic.' The old folks are gathering at the diner like every morning. The shops are opening up. I think it's going to be okay."

"Hm. Maybe."

"Anyway, Mark found something on the radio. Want to go have a listen?"

"Sure. Breakfast can wait a couple of minutes."

Back in the dining room, Lily saw that Penny and Ursula were up and sitting at the table with Peter and Mark. She exchanged morning pleasantries with them and then turned to the radio.

"So what's up?" she asked Mark.

"Got a news station out of Cleveland," he said. "They're in a commercial break right now."

Mark turned up the volume, and they listened as an ad played. Big Mike's Chevrolet of Cleveland was having a big blowout sale on the latest models. The ad ended, and there was a moment of silence. Then a resonant, authoritative voice came from the speaker.

"Repeating our top story: Officials are reporting to the Associated Press that last night's outbreak of violence along the east coast has been contained. A statement issued by the Federal Bureau of Investigation blames the violence on quote radical elements unquote, and assures the public that there is no further danger at this time."

Mark snapped off the radio and slammed his palm on the table. "Bullshit! 'Radical elements?' Then what was all that talk last night about burning bodies and shooting people in the head?"

Peter looked concerned. Like the rest of them, he knew Mark could be unpredictable when he was angry.

"Look, Mark, you're right. Something's going on that we're not being told. But let's focus on what we can realistically do about it here."

"I'll tell you what we can do," Mark said. "We can shut this school down. We can demand answers. I say we call everyone on the contact list and tell them to be on the quad by nine."

The contact list had been gathered over the past two years. It consisted of anyone who'd ever expressed interest in the SDS and its goals. A few people on the list had shown up to regular meetings of the group, but most had never responded.

"We need to get the media on this if we're going to do it," Penny said. "If we can really get a sit-in organized, it might get some traction at the state level, at least. That might grab someone's attention."

Lily, sensing she had already lost, still fired one last salvo.

"Mark, you are not bringing that goddamned gun. Period. Now, who wants breakfast?"

Mark was angry. Peter was dispirited. Nate seemed a bit bemused.

Lily didn't really know how to feel. Relief mixed with disappointment and a lingering fear that she just couldn't shake.

The Webberly College quad was bathed in bright sunshine. The temperature was in the high 70s. A beautiful day for a protest.

But what a sad protest it had turned out to be. Besides the seven regular members of the SDS, there were six others who'd joined them in front of the library. A small crowd of roughly 10 people had gathered to listen to Peter and Mark (mostly Mark) speak on the evils of the system and the need for answers to the events of the previous night.

Not that the quad was empty. There were plenty of students coming and going. Every so often, one or two would even pause and listen for a few moments before moving on.

"We're being lied to, people," Mark was saying, his voice raised to a shout. "Something terrible happened on U.S. soil, and they're trying to erase it from your minds!"

Lily held a homemade sign over her head. They'd made as many as they could after breakfast that morning. Most of them were laying in a stack behind the protesters. Lily's read "We Want The Truth!" Beside her, Ursula held one reading "Stop The Lies!"

As Mark ranted on, Lily turned to Ursula and murmured, "This is kind of embarrassing."

Ursula smirked and nodded. "I just wish more media had come out," she said.

Penny had called the newspaper, the local radio station and both TV stations before they left the house. The only outlet that had bothered to send a representative was the paper. Said representative looked to be all of 25 years old, probably some junior copy boy, who at least looked happy to be out of the office.

Mark was still yelling. Lily worried he'd blow out his vocal cords if he kept it up. Mark owned a bullhorn (of course), but the battery was dead and there hadn't been time to get over to Billing's Hardware and Supply to buy a new one.

Besides the small group of students, there was one other onlooker—Jerry Benton. Hairy Jerry, as he was called for the thick carpet of hair on his arms and his bushy unibrow, was the head of campus security. He wore his traditional uniform, a crisp white shirt, black tie and black pants, and gazed around the quad, seeming a little bored.

Then Lily saw Hairy Jerry perk up, a small smile crossing his lips. She turned to see what he was looking at. Across the quad, maybe 50 yards away, a trio of uniformed policemen were coming toward them.

"Damn it," Lily said. "Hey, guys, here come the cops."

Mark stopped yelling at the students and turned his attention to the approaching officers.

"This is a peaceful demonstration," he shouted. "We have a right to assemble under the Constitution."

Like that was going to help, Lily thought. But Mark and Peter were already moving, putting their plan into action. While the police were still halfway across the quad, Mark hurried to the front of the library, his big duffel bag in hand. Peter headed around the side, carrying a similar bag.

There were two entrances to the library. Mark got busy chaining himself to the front doors, while Peter was moving to do the same at the side entrance. Meanwhile, the rest of the group formed up and marched toward the police, to give the pair time to get properly hooked up.

"Aw, what the hell," Lily heard Hairy Jerry say. "That's a goddamned fire code violation, son. Don't do that."

"You just had to call the cops again, didn't you Jerry?" Mark asked. "Anyway, there's an emergency exit around back, in the unlikely event a fire breaks out in the library in the next ten minutes."

Lily and the others in the group stopped a few yards from the three officers, blocking their path. Lily glanced back and saw Mark had gotten a long length of chain wound through the handles of the two main library doors. He was wrapping the ends of the chain around his wrists. Then he padlocked them in place. Lily knew Peter would be doing the same, though he only had one door to worry about.

She recognized all three of the cops. They had been the ones who'd successfully broken up last year's war protest. History, it seemed, was repeating itself.

"All right, everybody move along," the policeman in the middle said. Lily remembered his name was Brooks. "This is private property, and you're not allowed to congregate here."

"We're students here," Ursula retorted. "How are we not allowed on school grounds?"

"Come on," Brooks said. He was clearly going to be the official spokesman. "You know the drill. You need a permit from the college. And your security director informs me that you don't have one."

That much was true. They hadn't even bothered trying to get a permit. For one thing, there hadn't been time, and for another, the school had denied them a permit the year before, so there was really no point to it.

Brooks turned to the man on his left. "Phil, go get the bolt cutters so we can separate those idiots from the building."

Phil trotted away without a word. Brooks turned back to the protesters and spread his hands.

"We all know how this is going to go," he said. "You're all going to sit down and link arms, and then me and my buddies are going to go down the line and separate you. Then, you're all going to jail. In cuffs."

The crowd of onlookers had grown now that the police had shown up. A few of them had even crossed over and joined the protesters. Still, Lily knew Brooks was right. That was how non-violent protests worked. The group could almost certainly overpower three cops if they wanted to. But those cops had guns, and there was absolutely no guarantee they wouldn't use them if the crowd became hostile.

So, as if on cue, the protesters did exactly what Brooks said they'd do. They sat down, linked arms, and waited in silence. History repeating itself again.

Then the silence was broken by a scream from somewhere off in the distance. That was new. The scream cut out, and was replaced with an even more ominous sound: gunfire.

"What the hell?" Brooks turned in the direction of the sounds, but Officer Phil was out of sight. Plus, the crowd around them had grown even more, and the two cops were standing like an island between them and the protesters.

"What are you people up to?" Brooks demanded, turning back to Lily's group.

Lily had no idea what was going on, and the sound of gunshots had scared her so deeply she couldn't find words to speak.

"We're not up to anything," Ursula said, unlinking her arm from Lily's and standing up. "Sounds like your man is terrorizing innocent students."

Lily also stood and tried to look over the heads of the crowd behind the police. She could see nothing but several more students on the far side of the quad slowly making their way toward the scene.

"Damn it," Brooks said. He turned to the other remaining officer. "Wilkey, go give Phil some backup."

Wilkey nodded. "I'm on it. You be all right here by yourself?"

"I'll be fine. Hurry up." Brooks returned his attention to the students. "I'm fucking serious. All of you need to disperse immediately."

The protesters stayed right where they were. Some of the other students, obviously uneasy, began to drift away. As they parted, Lily saw something strange. Officer Wilkey had come within a few yards of the approaching group and stopped. He was yelling at them to disperse, but none of them paid any heed. They continued walking right for him.

"Brooks!" Wilkey yelled and took a few steps back. "What the hell? Help …"

Before he could say another word, the group was on him. Lily saw Wilkey reach for his gun, but his arms were grabbed from both sides. Wilkey screamed as he was borne to the ground.

Brooks saw all this and ran to Wilkey's aid. As he moved, he pulled his gun and fired a shot in the air. More screams, this time from the students in the vicinity.

Brooks stopped several yards from the scrum. He pointed his weapon at the group.

"Hands in the air," he shouted. "Goddamnit, get off that man!"

Lily watched in horror. Brooks continued aiming his gun in the direction of the group, but was clearly unwilling to take a shot.

Whether he was concerned about hitting his fellow officer, or just showing remarkable restraint, Lily didn't know.

Finally, Brooks fired once. Unconsciously, Lily took several steps forward to better see what was happening.

Wilkey was on the ground, and several people were clawing at his uniform. Lily gaped in disbelief as one of them bent forward and bit him on the face, tearing a chunk of flesh away. Blood flew from the wound.

When Brooks saw this, he emptied his pistol in rapid fashion. At least two rounds hit home. One caught a strange looking man in a suit in the shoulder. The other blasted a hole in the face of a woman who was bent over Wilkey. The woman fell to the side. No one in the rest of the group as much as flinched.

Around her, there was chaos. Students were fleeing in all directions. Lily felt someone grab her arm. She turned and saw Ursula's terrified face.

"Come on! We have to get out of here!"

Lily gave a nod, but didn't move. There was something wrong with the people in that crowd. Her mind ticked over the scene. The oncoming group seemed larger now, and it split around the site of Wilkey's struggle and pressed forward. Brooks was reloading his weapon. He slammed the cylinder home and quickly fired six more shots into the crowd, to no effect that Lily could see.

Now that they were getting closer, Lily realized that these people almost certainly weren't students. They all seemed to be dressed in formal wear. Lily pulled free of Ursula's grip and went even closer. Something was prickling at the back of her mind, but the horrific spectacle in front of her was overloading her circuits, making it difficult to think clearly.

"Damn it, Beth, come on!" Ursula again, using Lily's old name. The name she had before last night, before …

"Oh, shit." Lily spun around. Ursula, Penny, Nate and Carl were staring at her. "You guys, this is it!"

Lily was strangely excited by the notion that what they'd heard on the radio might actually be happening. On a rational level, she knew that was crazy, that it was just the adrenaline coursing through her system. But it was there nonetheless.

"I don't know what kind of bullshit this is," Nate said, taking her arm, "but we've got to move, now!"

"We've got to get Peter," Lily said. After a second, she added, "And Mark."

Mark, still chained to the library doors, was in no position to see the danger. He was too far away, plus he was sitting down. The damn fool was still shouting slogans.

Lily didn't know what Peter was doing, on the east side of the library. She began to head that way, trusting the others to take care of Mark.

Suddenly, her path was cut off as a horde of people came running from that direction. Lily was pummeled as they raced by her. When they had passed, she saw, behind them, another group.

Like the others, they all wore suits and dresses. But this group was closer, and Lily saw that most of the clothing was filthy and in tatters. She also saw bits of flesh hanging from faces, exposed bone peeking through. Empty sockets where eyes should have been. Skeletal hands, groping forward.

There were more gunshots. Officer Brooks was still standing, apparently. But for how long? And how long could one man hold off a horde like the one that was coming at them now from two sides?

The bright excitement Lily had been feeling drained out of her, replaced with dull, deadly fear. She pushed through the panicked students. She had to get to Peter.

As soon as she was clear of the crowd, Lily began running. She scraped her arm on the brick side of the library as she took the corner too sharply. She spotted Peter standing at the side door.

"Peter!"

She reached him and saw he was still chained to the door.

"What the hell are you doing? We've got to get out of here!"

Peter yanked at the chains padlocked to his wrist. "Um … Mark has the key. What the hell is going on?"

Lily didn't answer. She grabbed Peter's arm and tried to pull the chain free. It was locked tight.

"I already tried that," Peter said. "I didn't want the cops to be able to just take it off, so I cinched it up pretty tight. I need the key."

Lily looked behind her. None of those—things—was moving in this direction. Yet.

"All right," she said. "I'll go get it. Get back in the doorway and keep quiet."

She didn't know why that last part was important, but some instinct told her it was. She reluctantly left Peter and ran as fast as she'd ever run for the front of the library.

The swarm approaching from the east was probably no more than thirty yards away now. The other, larger group coming from the north had apparently overwhelmed Officer Brooks, who was nowhere to be seen. They were even closer.

Mark was just freeing himself from his own chains as Lily pelted up to the front entrance. Nate hauled him to his feet. Carl was there as well, nervously watching the advancing creatures.

"Let's move," Nate said.

"No!" Lily said. "We have to get Peter. Mark, where's the key?"

Mark rubbed his wrists. "In my bag. What the hell is going on?"

Lily ignored the question. She grabbed Mark's bag, and was shocked when he reached out and tore it from her hands.

"I'll get it," he said, unzipping the duffel.

"Hurry it up, man," Nate said. "Bad shit is seriously going down."

"Got it. Let's go." Duffel bag in hand, Mark took off.

"Maybe you guys should just get out of here," Lily said as she went after Mark.

"No way," Nate said, catching up to her. "We should stay together. Besides, Mark's got the gun."

"What? Fuck!" No wonder he'd taken the bag from Lily. "Where are Usula and Penny?"

"We got separated," Nate said. "They got swallowed up in the crowd."

Lily saw that the larger group had swarmed past the other students and was now bearing down on them. The smaller group was less than ten yards away as Lily and Nate led the way around the corner.

But it was even worse than that, Lily saw. Two of the monsters had already reached Peter. He was kicking at them, trying to keep them away, but one of them had hold of his shirt sleeve. Lily tried to run faster. Then the thing took Peter's hand in its mouth and bit down. Peter screamed.

Nate burst forward, plowing into the pair attacking Peter. They flew back and landed on the ground. Mark reached the door and quickly unlocked the chains around Peter's wrist.

Nate had rolled and come up on his feet. He lashed out and kicked one of the things in the head. It fell sideways, but seemed unharmed. The other had already gotten back to a standing position.

Lily made the calculation without even really thinking. "Everyone, get into the library, now!"

Nate didn't hesitate, moving toward the side door. Carl came huffing around the corner … and ran straight into the walking cadavers. They swarmed him, pulling him under before anyone had a chance to react. Lily screamed Carl's name.

Peter had pulled the chains free from the door and pushed it open. He saw Carl go down and yelled, "Oh, fuck!"

Lily stood frozen as the majority of the creatures ignored Carl and pushed on toward her. From somewhere in the crowd, she thought she heard him cry out, and started to move forward, but then she was grabbed from behind and dragged away. She heard Nate's voice in her ear saying, "Come on, Beth. It's too late."

Lily wanted to correct him, but her breath caught in her throat and she could only sob as he pulled her into the library, shutting the door behind them.

They were in the periodicals room. Racks of magazines lined three walls, and various pieces of comfortable furniture were arranged in a circle in the center.

A loud thudding sound came from the door. Lily screamed in shock and they all turned look. The door had a large, single pane of glass in the center, and they could see that the creatures were outside, pounding on it. Grotesque faces were pushed against the glass, rotting faces covered in gore and dirt. And yet the door stayed shut.

"Don't they know how to use a door handle?" Mark asked.

"I don't know and I don't care," Nate said. "We'd better keep moving. Let's check the front doors."

"One second," Mark said. He zipped open his duffel bag. A moment later, he had the evil looking Luger pistol in his hand. Lily glared at him, but said nothing.

As they moved to enter the main library, Lily noticed Peter had his left hand tucked under his right arm. He was grimacing in obvious pain.

"Peter, let me see," she said, moving closer to him.

"I'm fine," he said.

"Don't be an ass. Let me see your hand."

The others all stopped to look as Peter held out his hand. The bite wound was bad. Lily could see that right away. The thing had clamped on to Peter's hand near the pinkie finger, just above the wrist. She could see deep teeth marks through the blood, which was flowing freely.

"We need to wrap that up," Lily said, her voice more calm than she felt. "You're losing a lot of blood."

"Here," Mark said, digging again through his bag. He held out a white t-shirt.

"Damn, man," Nate said. "What else you got in that magic bag?"

Mark shook his head. "I'm all out of tricks, I'm afraid."

Lily took the shirt and wound it around Peter's hand. He sucked in a breath as she cinched it tight and knotted it to keep it in place.

"Okay," she said. "Front doors."

"Wait!" came a voice from behind them.

Mark whirled, raising his pistol as he did. It wound up pointed right at Lily's face.

"Look out," he said.

"Idiot!" Lily stepped aside and turned toward the voice. A young woman was standing behind the periodicals desk, hands in the air.

"Don't shoot," the woman said. "I'm a librarian!"

"Jesus," Mark said, putting the weapon down. "You scared the shit out of us. What are you doing back there?"

"Hiding. When I heard the gunshots outside, I went into the back room there." She pointed at a door behind her. "What's going on?"

The group exchanged glances.

"Don't you listen to the radio?" Mark asked.

"Not really," she said. "It's full of the devil's music."

"Oh, great," Mark said. "A Jesus freak."

The librarian frowned but let it go. "Seriously, what is happening? It sounds like a war zone out there."

"I'm not sure you'd believe us if we told you," Nate said gently. "Bad stuff. Real bad."

Mark was not so gentle. "Dead people are rising from their graves and eating the living," he said. "That's them knocking at the door over there."

Even as he said it, there came the unmistakable sound of glass cracking. A few more thuds, and Lily saw the glass fall away from the top.

"No more time for talk," Peter said. "Let's go."

"I'm coming with you," the librarian said. She came around the desk. "Even rude living people are preferable to … dead ones." She shot a look at Mark.

"Fine," Peter said. "Now move."

"Wait," Lily said as they all crowded through the doorway to the main library. "Does this door have a lock on it?"

"Yes," the librarian said. "I've got the key right here."

Lily nodded. These dead people were relentless and terrifying, but didn't seem to have much in the way of fine motor skills.

"Lock it up," she said. "We might be able to trap them in there."

The librarian closed the door behind them and used her key to lock it.

"Okay," she said. "Now what?"

"We have to check the front doors," Peter said. "Stay close, and keep quiet."

They were at the end of a short hallway. Lily knew that ahead and to their left was the front desk. Mark and Peter moved up and peeked around the corner.

"Looks clear," Peter said. He turned to the librarian. "Hey, what's your name?"

"Patsy."

"Okay, Patsy. Who else is in here with us? I don't want any more surprises."

"There were a few students here when the shooting started. Most of them ran out the emergency exit in back, I think. I had to turn off the alarm. Alice was supposed to come in and run the front desk today, but she never showed. I'm the only staff member here."

"Right," Peter said. "There could still be students in here, though, hiding like you were. So Mark, use your head before you brandish that gun again."

Mark held the gun down at his side and only nodded before disappearing around the corner. Lily and the others followed slowly.

"Everybody keep down," Nate suggested, his voice barely above a whisper. "Let's stay as concealed as possible until we check those doors."

Lily crouched down. Everyone followed suit. Now they were moving even slower.

The front desk was a massive thing, a curving half circle that stretched from the wall on their left around and to the front. They all took cover behind it.

Peter started to crawl forward to take a look, but as soon as he put weight on his injured hand, he yelped in pain and collapsed. Lily scrambled forward and hovered over him. The t-shirt wrapped around his hand was completely soaked with blood.

"Better let me take this one, Mr. President," Nate said. He got down and crept around the curve of the desk. He came scooting back just a second later. "We've got a problem," he said.

"What is it?" Lily asked.

"Better see for yourself. Just be careful."

Lily got as low as she could and crawled. She kept close to the desk, almost hugging it as she went around. The door on her right came into view first. It was closed and looked fine. Then, as she went a little further, she saw the terrible trouble.

Officer Brooks was laying in the left-hand doorway, wedging it open. Three or four of the ghoulish creatures were kneeling over his body, eating at it. They were chewing on the exposed flesh of his arm, ripping away chunks of flesh.

Lily gagged and scrambled backward. She clapped a hand over her mouth, to stop herself screaming or vomiting or both. When she got back to the group, she tried to slow her breathing, but her lungs kept hitching and gasping for air.

"Calm down," Nate said, putting a hand on her shoulder.

"Calm down?" Lily hissed. "You saw the same thing I did, right?"

"I did. But freaking out isn't going to get us anywhere. Just take a deep breath. You can do it."

Just the sound of Nate's voice helped a little. Lily leaned forward and focused all her will on her breathing.

"What the hell is going on?" Mark asked.

Nate explained the situation as Lily got herself under control. Mark groaned. Peter just leaned back against the front desk, his hair lank and face heavy with sweat.

"We've got to help that cop," Lily said. "He may still be alive."

"Why the fuck should we help Officer Asshole?" Mark demanded.

"Because for one thing, he's a human being, jerk. And if you want another reason, we need to get those doors closed."

Mark muttered several curse words under his breath and went to take a look at the front doors. He came back and leaned in close to Lily.

"So how do you propose we go about this?"

Lily hated what she was about to say, but there was no other way.

"You're going to shoot them," she said.

They sent Patsy and Peter to wait by the emergency door, in case they needed to make an exit that way. Peter had trouble standing, let alone walking, but Patsy said she could get him to the back. Lily was really starting to worry about him, but they had more pressing matters at the moment.

Nate had made his way across the library and was crouched behind the new releases rack. The creatures at the door hadn't looked up from their bloody feast as he made his way over.

Lily was next. She moved out slowly, crouched low. As she cleared the cover of the desk, she risked a glance toward the front doors. Brooks was in the same position. The nasty things had finished with his arm, and were now ripping at his pant legs with their claw-like hands.

Lily completed the crossing. Now, it was Mark's turn. He was going to take up a position inside the semi-circle of the main desk. He kept low as well. Lily could just see the top of his head behind the desk as he moved into position. He peeked up over the edge a couple of times, ensuring he had the best angle to shoot from. When he was all set, he raised his hand to show he was ready.

Nate took a deep breath, let it out, and said, "I guess this is it."

He rose from his hiding place and strode out to the middle of the wide aisle between the front desk and the stacks. He raised his hands over his head and gave a sharp whistle.

"Hey, you ugly motherfuckers! Over here! Fresh meat!"

Lily peeked up over the top of the shelf. Her view was partially obscured from this angle, but she saw two of the monsters look up at the sound. The one in front made a gasping, groaning noise and rose, pushing through the door. As it did, two shots rang out, impossibly loud in Lily's ears.

Lily saw both rounds hit home. One took the thing in the side of the throat, blowing a hole there and throwing out a gout of black, nasty looking fluid. The other hit the cheekbone just below its left eye. The creature's head snapped back, and it tottered forward another step before falling over.

Nate whooped and yelled, "Nice!" He looked over at Lily with a giant grin on his face.

"Don't start celebrating yet," Mark called from behind the desk. "Here come the others."

Lily looked back at the door. Mark was right. Three more of the monsters were now crowding at the door, shoving it wide open. They stumbled over the body of Officer Brooks and were inside the library.

Lily was about to shout at Nate to run when she saw they weren't coming toward him. They were going right for Mark's position. He leveled the gun and fired off several more rounds in quick succession.

This time, his aim was off. Lily cursed to herself as several of the shots went wide. The ones that did hit didn't do a thing to slow the things down. They were halfway to the desk, and Mark was reloading.

"Lily!" Nate called. "Come on!"

He ran for the front door. Lily pushed aside thoughts of Mark and the creatures and went after him. She passed within just a few feet of the shambling, groaning things, and caught a whiff of death and the grave as she did.

At the door, Nate was waiting with a grim look on his face. Lily looked down and saw why. Officer Brooks was bathed in blood. His face was red with it. His uniform was soaked. Worst of all, his arm had been chewed to pieces, and was mostly exposed bone with a few bits of flesh hanging on.

"I don't think he's going to make it," Nate said.

"Maybe not, but we still have to get him out of this doorway. I'll pull it open and you move him."

Nate gave a nod, though he was clearly not pleased about having to touch the body. He bent down and grabbed the officer by his uniform's shoulders. Lily opened the door wide enough for Brooks to fit through. Nate quickly dragged him into the library.

Lily let the door go and it began to swing closed. Then a gnarled, twisted hand thrust through the opening. It grasped at the air inches from Lily's face.

"Nate!"

Nate was suddenly there beside her, shoving at the door. Lily looked outside through the door's window and saw several more of the creatures coming toward them. She leaned her back against the door, pressing with her feet as Nate pushed with his hands.

"Push, Lily! We have to break the fucker off!"

Lily tried, pressing with all her might. She turned her head and saw Nate had his shoulder to the door and was hammering with his fist at the hand that stuck through the opening. Lily heard bones breaking. She hoped they weren't Nate's.

The door jerked closed a few inches. Lily took another look and saw that the hand was hanging at an angle now. Nate reared back and threw himself into the door and it slammed closed, snapping the hand off at the wrist. It fell to the floor at Nate's feet and he kicked it away in disgust.

The one-handed dead man immediately began hammering at the glass with his stump. The others surrounded him, pressing against both doors, pounding and slapping at the glass.

"I don't think we're safe in here," Lily said, feeling stupid even as she said it. Of course they weren't safe. Was anywhere safe right now?

"I know," Nate said. "But we've got to figure out some kind of plan. Plus, we've got a severely wounded man over there."

Severely wounded or dead, Lily thought. Anyone who could survive what had happened to Officer Brooks would have to be one tough son of a bitch.

Just as Lily was about to go check on him, more shots rang out from behind her. In the struggle to close the door, she had somehow completely forgotten about Mark. She turned and saw that the three creatures that had entered the library had reached the front desk. Mark had taken several steps back from his original spot and was holding his pistol level in front of him.

Lily realized Mark must have waited for them to get closer to get a better shot. And it had worked. Two of the things were sliding to the floor. Lily saw a black hole dead center in the forehead of one of them.

The last one still standing was pressed up against the front desk, leaning over it with arms outstretched. Mark took careful aim and pulled the trigger.

Click.

Later, Lily would remember that sound and the moment everything went to hell.

At first, it seemed like everything was going to be okay. Mark smoothly ejected the clip from the pistol and pulled a fresh one from his pocket. He slammed it home. He pulled back on the top of the gun, a move Lily had seen in the movies. But instead of shooting the last creature, Mark kept tugging on the gun. That part wasn't in any movie she'd seen.

"Shit!" Mark said. "I think it's jammed."

Not good. Even worse, the remaining walking corpse had stopped trying to go through the desk and apparently realized it could go <u>over</u>. It had hoisted itself up, so its torso was now on the desk. Its feet were kicking at the air as it pulled itself forward with its arms.

Mark was so intent on getting the pistol to work that he didn't see the imminent danger. Even as Lily yelled at him to look out, the creature got itself up on top of the desk and pushed forward, toppling over. It was now behind the desk with Mark.

Lily turned to Nate to see if he was watching this. He wasn't. His back was to her. He was bent over Officer Brooks, doing something to the body. Lily couldn't tell what. Maybe trying to revive him.

"Nate! We've got a problem!"

"I know, I know," Nate said, his voice remarkably calm. "Just one second ..."

"We don't have time for ..."

"Got it!" Nate shouted. He turned away from the body on the floor and held something up. Officer Brooks's gun. "I didn't think I'd ever get it out of his hand." He started to rise from the floor, but before he could do so, Brooks's arm, the one that wasn't all chewed up, flew up and wrapped around Nate's neck.

"Woah!" Nate cried in a choked voice. "Officer, I can explain ..."

Nate's voice was cut off as the arm pulled him down. Lily thought Brooks was reacting to Nate taking his gun. Then she saw his face, pale and dead looking. His eyes were the color of spoiled milk. Nate tried to heave himself away, but the arm held tight. With a look of panic in his eyes, Nate put the gun on the floor and slid it toward Lily.

Without thinking, Lily picked the revolver up. She'd never as much as held a gun before. It was surprisingly heavy. She acted on pure instinct, pointing the pistol at Brooks and pulling the trigger.

Lily's wrist snapped back painfully with the recoil. The bullet zinged off the library floor, closer to Nate's face than to Brooks. Lily tried to take better aim, but now her hand was shaking. The gun wouldn't hold still.

She had an idea that she should get closer. She should run over there and put the gun right against Brooks's forehead before she fired again. But she was too terrified to move. She could only watch in horror as Brooks pulled Nate's head to the side and began biting and chewing at his neck.

Lily screamed and fired the gun again. The bullet whizzed off into some distant part of the library. As Lily fought to control her trembling hands, Brooks opened his mouth wide. Lily could see his teeth, stained with blood. Then he chomped down furiously and shook his head violently, tearing loose a large section of Nate's neck.

Blood fountained from the hideous wound, and Lily realized it must be arterial. She also realized Nate was as good as dead.

Pain and anger ripped through Lily's body, freeing her from her paralysis. She strode forward, holding the gun out in front of her, steady now. The thing that had been Officer Brooks was chewing noisily on its prize, making nasty smacking sounds with its mouth.

Lily leaned forward as she came close. With no time to think, she quickly put the gun to Brooks's temple and fired. She was ready for the recoil this time, though it still hurt. What she wasn't ready for was the gout of blood and brain matter that blew out from the other side of Brooks's head. She nearly vomited, but swallowed it back and went to work.

She pulled Brooks's arm from around Nate's neck and pulled Nate away from the bloody, awful corpse. She steeled herself and took a good look at the bite wound to his throat. It had stopped gushing blood, and was now just dribbling feebly. She knew right away what that meant. Still, she pressed her hand against the hole and applied pressure.

"Nate? Nate? Can you hear me?"

No response. Lily felt tears run down her face, but was too shocked to actually feel the sadness. The only emotion that burned through the numbness she felt was anger.

Lily stood and spun toward the source of her fury. Mark. This was all his fault. If he hadn't pushed and prodded the group, Lily might have been able to talk some sense into them. The stupid son of a bitch …

Was gone. In the sudden silence of the library, Lily heard a small yelp of pain or fear or maybe both. She rushed to the main desk and looked over the top.

Mark was on the floor, his back against the inside of the desk. The creature that had climbed over was clawing and biting at his legs. Mark kicked frantically, trying to keep it at bay. Lily could see he hadn't been completely successful. His left pant leg was shredded and bloody from the thing's attack.

Lily's legs were moving before she could even think about it. She sprinted around the desk to the opening on the far side. She was through and on the scene of the struggle in what seemed like only a second.

Then time stretched like taffy, and she saw the world in slow motion as she kicked the thing attacking Mark in the side as hard as she could. Combined with Mark's own efforts, this had the effect of getting the creature away from Mark so she could take a clear shot. It growled and made a lunge for her, but she was ready. She pulled the trigger and blasted it in the face.

The result was even more horrific than when she'd shot Officer Brooks. The thing's whole head seemed to explode, chunks of bone and flesh flying everywhere. It toppled backward and hit the floor.

"Wow," Mark said. He was breathing hard and his leg was a mess, but he was alive. Unlike Nate. Lily stared at him for a second, then kicked him as hard as she'd kicked the monster. He screeched and tried to scoot away from her.

"What the hell was that for?"

"Nate's dead, you asshole." Lily had to force herself not to kick him again. "I hope you're fucking happy."

"Nate? What?" Mark's face, which had been red from exertion, went pale. "What happened?"

"The cop turned into one of those … things and killed him."

"Jesus. What the fuck is going on?"

"I don't know, you stupid shit! That's the point. That's why I said we should stay home today, because we don't know. But you … and Peter and Nate and …"

Lily trailed off. *Oh, fuck, no*, she thought. She turned slowly away from Mark, who was staring at her with puzzled eyes, to look over the desk at the spot where Nate had died.

He lay there still, unmoving. Lily let out a breath she hadn't even known she was holding. Her vision blurred, tears again welling in her eyes. She wiped them away, blinked, and thought she saw Nate's hand twitch. She pressed her fists into her eyes, told herself it was just blurred vision. She blinked again, and watched as Nate's dead body began to lift itself from the floor.

Lily felt herself go cold and numb. Her mind, her body, were ready to quit, to just give up and let go. She saw Mark come up beside her and couldn't even muster any anger at him.

Then he leaned over to look at Nate. "Hey, Nate's okay," he said.

That was it. That brought the fire back. Lily slapped him hard in the face.

"Goddamn it! Knock it off, Lily!"

"Nate's not 'okay,' you idiot. He's dead, and now he's also one of those things. That's what happens when you die."

By this time, Nate's corpse had gotten to its knees. It turned to look at them, and Lily saw the same dead white eyes as Officer Brooks's. Lily raised the pistol, but her finger would not pull the trigger.

"Um, I think he wants to eat us, Lily," Mark said, his voice trembling. "Maybe you ought to shoot him now."

"I can't." The gun dropped to her side.

"What? Well give me the gun, then."

"No. You're not shooting him, either. We're going to get Peter and the librarian girl and we're getting out of here."

"What if we can't? What if those things are at the back door, too?"

"Then we start shooting."

Mark rolled his eyes. "How many bullets are even left in that gun?"

"We'll worry about that later. We don't have time to argue, Mark. He's coming."

The thing that had been Nate was on its feet, shambling toward the desk. Lily had figured the slow, shuffling nature of the creatures they'd seen was due to decomposition. Apparently, even fresh corpses had difficulty moving. Lucky for them.

Lily grabbed Mark's arm and pulled him through the gap between the desk and the wall near the door to the periodicals room.

"Ouch. Damn, my leg really hurts," Mark said as they made their way toward the back of the library.

"Deal with it," Lily replied through gritted teeth. A part of her was glad he was in pain, glad he was suffering even a little bit.

Lily led the way, slipping between aisles of shelves at random. She moved quickly, and Mark managed to keep up despite his leg wounds. She glanced back and saw no sign of Nate. She did see copious amounts of blood from Mark's leg, and wondered if those things could follow a trail.

The thought spooked her, and she made straight for the back of the library. The faster they could get out, the better. Assuming they could get out. They might be trapped. But Lily didn't want to think about that now.

She and Mark emerged from the stacks into a long corridor at the back of the library. They turned left and Lily broke into a sprint, not caring now whether Mark was with her. All her thoughts now were on freedom. She wanted out of the library, wanted to run as fast and as far as she could from the chaos and pain the place now represented.

Patsy the librarian and Peter were at the end of the corridor, waiting for them by the emergency exit as they'd planned. But instead of being ready to move, they were both on the ground. Peter lay stretched out in front of the door, his head in Patsy's lap. As Lily got close, she saw why.

Patsy held Peter's injured hand between both of hers. There was blood everywhere. It had stained Patsy's hands and dress, and pooled on the floor around the two of them.

Patsy looked up at Lily with wild, tear-filled eyes. "It won't stop bleeding," she said, her voice shaking. "I put pressure on it like you're supposed to but it just won't stop."

Lily knelt down, careful to avoid the puddle of blood. She heard Mark run up behind them. "Oh, shit," he said when he saw Peter.

The blood wasn't the worst of it, though. Peter's face was deathly white, and dripping sweat. Lily turned and handed the gun to Mark, then put a hand gently to Peter's cheek and almost pulled away. He was burning up, seemed to be radiating heat. No fever she'd ever seen had burned that hot. His breath came in tiny, desperate sounding gasps.

"Peter? Can you hear me? We have to go. You have to get up, right now, baby."

There was no response. Lily shook his shoulder, gently at first, then harder. Peter's head rolled to one side, but otherwise he didn't move.

They didn't have much time, Lily knew. Nate—she still thought of the thing coming for them as Nate, despite everything—could be on them at any second.

"All right, you two, help me get him up. We're all getting out of here."

"Um, he doesn't look so good, Lily," Mark said. "I don't think he's going to make it. Maybe we should just go."

"Really, Mark?" Lily spun to face him, fury in her voice. "Is that what you think? I think you're not looking so hot yourself. How's that leg? How many times were you bitten? Because Peter was bitten <u>once</u>, and look how that turned out."

Mark opened his mouth as if to say something, then looked down at Peter. He looked at his leg. He shut his mouth, and Lily saw something in his face change. His eyes narrowed and pressed his lips together hard.

"There's two bullets left in the gun, Lily," he said. "I checked."

"So what, Mark? What are you talking about?" She bent down and grabbed Peter's arm, trying to lift him up. She couldn't budge him. "Come help me, damn it."

"Lily, there's no time for that. Time's up. For Peter and for me. You know that. You know what happens next. So do I, and I don't want to end up like that. Neither would Peter."

"So what are you going to do? Shoot him? Shoot yourself?"

"Lily …"

"If we go now, we can get help. We can save him, Mark!"

Before Mark could answer her, they heard a loud moaning coming from somewhere in the stacks nearby. Everyone froze, and a second later, the sound of shuffling footsteps came to them clearly through the silent air.

"You have to go, Lily," Mark said softly. "Don't make me shoot Peter in front of you. I can't stand the thought of that."

"Fuck you Mark. This is all your fault."

"I know. I'm sorry. But we're up against it here. Peter's not going to make it. And neither am I. But you can. If you leave right now. And be careful."

Lily wanted to lash out at him, to use her words to make him hurt, or maybe just to convince him to help her save Peter. But in the deepest part of herself, she knew he was right. Peter had only a few minutes to live, at best. Because of her cowardice, Nate was a monster now. Whatever else Mark was, Lily knew he wasn't a coward. He wouldn't let the same fate befall Peter.

"Patsy, come on. We're going now. Help me move Peter."

The girl looked at her, eyes red and swollen from crying. Lily wished she could cry right now, wished she had the time to mourn. But she had to be strong and brave, braver than she'd ever been, if she was going to survive.

She started to move Peter from Patsy's lap, but the girl held him tight.

"What's going on?" she asked. "Why are you talking about shooting people?"

Lily realized the poor girl was completely clueless about the situation. She didn't listen to the radio, and she'd come back here with Peter before the things had attacked them up front. Lily didn't know what to say to convince her that they were in great danger.

So she slapped her. "Patsy, I need you to listen to me. The thing that did this to Peter? There's another one in the library. We're going to end up like him if we don't get out of here now."

"I don't understand ..."

"I don't need you to understand," Lily said, sliding Peter gently off of the girl's lap and onto the floor. "I just need you to move."

Lily stood and reached down, pulling Patsy's arm and getting her on her feet. Patsy didn't resist, but neither was she much help. Lily clamped her hand onto Patsy's elbow and guided her to the door.

Lily turned to Mark one last time. A hateful, nasty thought came into her head. She was glad he was going to die. As she saw him standing there, though, looking so sad and fearful, the hate drained out of her. Nate and Peter hadn't been dragged into this hell against their will. And Mark hadn't been alone in not realizing the danger. Lily herself had never imagined anything as awful as this.

She started to say something, to apologize for her behavior, but before she could, Nate shambled out of the stacks behind him.

"Mark! Behind you!"

Nate swung toward the sound of her voice. He was only a few feet away from Mark. Mark glanced around, then hobbled forward as quickly as he could. He moved past Lily and Patsy and shoved the emergency door open. A loud, clanging alarm began to sound. Nate was coming closer, and Lily pulled Patsy forward, but Mark threw his arm out to stop them.

"Let me make sure it's clear first," he admonished. He stuck his head out and looked around. "Okay, go, go!"

Lily and Patsy rushed past Mark and out the door. It clunked shut behind them seconds later, but the alarm kept ringing loudly. It was not loud enough to muffle the sound of a pair of gunshots, however.

Lily choked back a sob and began dragging Patsy forward. They were at the top of a small grassy embankment. At the bottom was the faculty parking lot. It was only about half full of cars. Lily guessed the others had stayed home or fled once the chaos started. But the vehicles still gave her an idea.

"Patsy," she said, "the faster we get out of here the better, and the fastest way out is by car. Can you help me find one with the keys in it?"

The girl, her face ashen except for her eyes, which were red and swollen from crying, managed a short nod. Lily figured that would have to be good enough. She led the way to the parking lot.

"If the keys aren't in the ignition, look under the visor and under the seat," Lily told Patsy. "You take that side." She pointed to the north half of the lot.

Patsy moved to her assigned task, and Lily started down her own row of cars. She went as quickly as possible. Every few seconds, she scanned the area for any creatures that might have been drawn by the sound of the alarm. All was quiet. Peaceful, even. Lily was almost ready to believe that the threat was over, but then she heard a distant chattering sound that could only be machine gun fire.

So, soldiers were on the scene. Lily didn't know if that was better or worse. No time to worry about it, though. They still had to go. She moved on to the next car. It was locked.

"Hey!"

Lily turned and saw Patsy standing next to an old blue Ford pickup with the driver's side door open.

"I found keys," Patsy said, grinning.

Lily jogged across the parking lot. She poked her head into the truck and, indeed, the keys were there, dangling from the ignition.

"Great job," she said. "Hop in."

Patsy didn't even go around to the other side. She just got in and scooted over to make room for Lily, who climbed in right behind her.

Lily had been given a brand new Mustang on her 16th birthday. She had treasured the car at the time. Her father had taught her to drive, strict and stern as always. Lily said a silent thank you to her parents as she turned the key.

As old as the truck was, she expected it to cough and sputter, but it turned over smoothly. The gears were a bit tricky, but she got them out of the parking lot with little trouble.

The question now was where to go. Lily stopped at an intersection and pondered, but in a moment the obvious answer came to her. Home. She had to get home. Her parents lived an hour and a half away, just north of Dayton. Lily turned right and headed for Main Street and the highway.

"Where are we going?" Patsy asked from the seat beside her.

"My parents' place. It will be safe there. My dad ... my dad's a general. In the army."

"Oh. That's good, then."

For the first time in years, Lily agreed with the sentiment.

Watson Avenue, the main street through campus, was devoid of cars. As they passed Webber Hall, Lily saw a group of the creatures shambling down the street a block or so ahead. There were maybe ten of them, and they were going <u>away</u> from the college, toward downtown.

Lily stomped on the accelerator and shifted up to a higher gear. The truck surged forward, and plowed into the group. Two of them bounced off the front bumper and one was slammed by the big mirror mounted to the driver's side door. Another was moving pretty much right down the middle of the road. Lily swerved into it, and felt great satisfaction as the big truck knocked it down and then ran it over with a series of thuds.

The satisfaction curdled into grim foreboding as she drove on. A column of grey-black smoke rose above the trees and houses to her left, and there were more of the creatures milling about in the street. The next block, however, was clear of the things, at least mobile ones. Lily saw bodies piled on the side of the road in three places.

They were two blocks from Main Street when Lily spotted movement again. This time, figures came pouring out from both sides of the intersection ahead of them. She started to press the accelerator again, but pulled back when she saw the figures were all dressed in military fatigues and helmets. And they were all pointing rifles at the truck.

"Soldiers!" Patsy said as Lily brought them to a stop. "We'll be safe now!"

"Maybe," Lily said, watching the gathered troops. They still had their weapons raised.

One of the soldiers stepped forward and pointed his rifle at the truck. "Please get out of the vehicle," he said, his voice raised in command.

"I guess we better do what he says," Lily said.

The two women opened their doors and exited the truck slowly. Lily, on instinct, raised her hands in the air. Patsy just stood by her open door.

"Are either of you injured? Bitten?" the soldier asked.

"No," Lily answered.

"Where'd all the blood come from, then?"

"It's not ours," Lily said. "There were others. We were attacked. They're ... they're gone now."

The soldier lowered his weapon slightly and nodded. "Still gonna have to get you checked out. We've got Main Street cordoned off, serving as a command center. There's a medical tent there."

The man motioned for them to follow him. The crowd of soldiers melted back to the side streets. As they walked by, Lily saw the source of the smoke she'd noticed earlier. They were burning piles of bodies half a block down, right in the middle of Ashland Street.

They kept moving, arriving at a pair of barricades blocking Main Street. The soldier led them through. There were more men in uniforms gathered around a pair of tents. Lily and Patsy were taken to the larger of the two, which was erected in the street right in front of Maeve's Diner.

Inside the tent, they found another soldier and a doctor. The doctor's white smock had a single streak of dried blood across the chest. There were several empty cots as well, and one of them had a large bloodstain on it.

"Did ... did anyone else make it?" Lily asked the soldier who'd brought them here.

"A few," he said. "They've been taken to the fallout shelter in the courthouse. We haven't seen anyone else alive in the last two hours, though. You two were lucky."

She didn't feel lucky. She just felt numb, like her mind was trapped in some kind of dead body. She wondered if that's what those creatures felt. If that's what Nate had felt as he'd come after them.

The doctor approached her with a clipboard in his hand. "First thing," he said, "we need to find out who you are. We're ... keeping a list of survivors. So, what's your name?"

Her name. She could only think of the others, the ones lost to her now. Peter. Nate. Even Mark. Dead. Or worse.

She'd woken up this morning thinking this would be a big day. A special day.

"Miss?" the doctor said. "Your name, please?"

She stared at the blood on his smock, then down at the blood on her hands.

"Bethany," she said at last. "My name is Bethany."

PEACE IN PIECES
by Zakary McGaha

Zakary McGaha is a writer currently residing in East Tennessee. His interests are: Gothic books, horror movies, the month of October, haunted-house attractions, and the supernatural. He believes that good writing, and good storytelling, are the most important things humans can hope to bask in. He wishes to continue writing, as well as living a fun, no-limits life.

His novels SEA OF MEDIUM-TO-HIGH PITCHED NOISES and PARK MASTERS: A COMEDY are published by Burning Bulb Publishing.

Two days was apparently all it took. Forty-eight hours, and everything went down, including morals, safe-feelings, the American dream, and every other Goddamned thing that most people had taken for granted.

But the water was still there. The sand was still there. And the palm trees were still there.

Despite horrifying odds, the thing that Maple loved the most was still there. His home hadn't been totally eradicated. Sure, it sucked more than usual, but it was still a place. Whenever survivors talked about heading to the certain location, they said, "Hey, let's go to Myrtle Beach." And that mattered a lot. At least it did to Maple.

The guitar was cream-colored. Most people would have just called it "white", but Maple didn't believe that kept with the overall tone. Cream was what it was. Cream was a real thing; white wasn't.

About the only thing that wasn't completely covered in blood was the hairbrush. He took it, and combed out his blonde hair, straight down. It was about shoulder length, parted in the middle, and, in his opinion, looked sexy as hell. All of the girls who'd been wanting some experimental *hippie* types had taken a liking to Maple.

That was funny, though; after they'd been termed "sluts," he'd steered clear. No matter what his hormones told him, he wasn't going down the road to Heartbreak City again. No thank you, he was perfectly content in good ole Myrtle Beach, South Carolina.

It was a little known fact that Myrtle Beach was the best damned beach on the Atlantic. The entire state of Florida couldn't even hold a candle to the sheer awesomeness. While all of the other hippies crowded San Francisco, having gay orgies, Maple was basking in the atmosphere of the small, but touristy, town.

Now, dead people were in the streets. Maple had always feared that the year 1968 would bring about something horrible. There was just something about the sound of it. There was a devilish overtone that couldn't be denied.

"Ugh, again, man," he said. He'd combed his hair a little too forcefully, and now his scalp was hurting like a bitch.

The woman on the ground was completely dead. Her face had basically been torn apart, her nose split into two congruent halves. The very tip of her eyeball had also been torn away. Maple had no idea how the zombie had managed to do *that*. Also, he didn't even know why people were even calling them zombies. He'd never even heard that word before. It sounded odd as all hell.

"Damn walkers," he said, mispronouncing the word on purpose. *Why don't people call them walkers? That sounds better. After all, that's what they do: walk and eat. Or waddle and eat. Maybe they should be called waddlers?*

His tie-dye colored t-shirt now had a little more red on it. But he had a hairbrush, so that was the only thing that really mattered.

He meandered about, around the little surf-shop, looking at all of the cool things that were now his for the taking. There were shark tooth necklaces, dried-out sea fish, and tons-upon-tons of knick-knacks. Really, it was overwhelming. Hell, there was even a coffee maker in the back, with a fresh brew. And all of it was all his now.

He poured himself a cup, added cream and sugar, and sat down next to his cream-colored guitar. He sat the java down on the glass counter, which allowed access to different *rare* seashells, and started strumming.

The amp was set up in the back. He played a couple of the Velvet Underground songs he'd learned, and tried his best to sing along. However, this simply couldn't happen. He couldn't break his monotonous *beach bum* accent.

After his fingers started hurting a little, he took his coffee and walked the hell outside. Above the door of the large surf-shop, he saw the shark. Sure, it was fake and navy-blue, but it still freaked him out. Every day before the totally radical dead folk had started rising, he'd been out in the ocean, body-boarding it up. Just the thoughts of fish with big-ass teeth biting him was terrifying.

Now, since the whole dead-people-thing had happened, the ocean was a thing of the past for him. There were way too many things on dry land to be afraid of. It wasn't safe anywhere. At least his odds were increased a little because of the easy movement provided by terra firma. You couldn't travel long periods while swimming. It'd just be too dang exhausting.

But, despite the shock-factor and paranoia of teeth, he loved the shark. Whenever he looked at it, he knew that he was safe. Until he heard the screams, that is.

The screams were coming from down the road.

There was a palm tree riddled motorcycle lot across the street. There were dead bodies slumped over everywhere, tons of walking corpses, and a lot of sound. For some reason, they never left the dealership. Maybe it was because all of the bikers who had inhabited it were all fat boars, so there was plenty of food to last awhile.

Maple took some gigantic beach towels and covered the windows. It was possible that the zombies would see the towels, and decide to go on somewhere else. Maybe the towels would tell them that nobody was home?

"Man, that's a gnarly one," Maple said to no one in particular, holding up a gigantic beach towel with a peace sign embedded in it. "I'd definitely dry my body off with that."

From inside his pocket, he pulled a couple of rings with skulls, all stainless steel. For him, these totally rad skull-rings meant more than just "flashy." They were a staple of a certain time period. And that time period was filled up with disaster.

Back when he'd been dating "THE BITCH WHO SHALL NOT BE NAMED," love had been the symbol he lived for. And not free love, mind you. But real love. Love that was exclusively between one man and one woman. That type of love.

And, damned if it wasn't meant to be. "THE BITCH WHO SHALL NOT BE NAMED" dumped his ass because she wanted to play the field. Experience a life without him. Hell, they'd dated seven months. She was ready for a change by that point.

After the dumping, Maple had decided that life wasn't worth moping about. So, down the hair went. It grew, and grew, and grew some more. A pencil-thin mustache eventually became a scraggly beard, and all else was fucking history. He moved away from his super-Christian town, and wound up in Myrtle Beach. He wasn't a poseur, per say, because he wanted to experience real life. Not fads. Even though he took pride in his fashion, he wasn't a trend-follower. He just happened to have long hair. *His* ideals and *his* philosophies weren't standard hippie code.

Screams arose.

He hated screams. They hurt his head.

He retrieved his cup of coffee, went back inside the surf-shop, and sat down in a decorative beach-chair, complete with an umbrella that's purpose was to provide shade from the harsh, ultra-violet rays of the sun.

Screams kept arising. All around him. Myrtle Beach was going to Hell in hand-basket filled up with power-flowers.

They didn't stop. They wouldn't stop. They were completely consistent, like they were planned out or something.

Eventually, he discerned that the loud screaming was from a single person. And that person was, undoubtedly, a female. A boner appeared, and thoughts of "THE BITCH WHO SHALL NOT BE NAMED" surfaced in his mind. Whenever he'd been with her, she'd never let him touch her. And after she left him, he'd never touched another girl.

Hormones kicked in.

If he was *finally* going to get over "THE BITCH WHO SHALL NOT BE NAMED," he was going to have to replace her with a new bitch, one who could be named. And, if there was a damsel in distress, why not go for her?

Vanessa had been about as sheltered as they come. Nice house in suburbia, church twice every Sunday, and once every Wednesday. But she had urges. She wanted a taste of freedom, wanted a taste of *boys*. She'd dated a little before, but they'd always either been from her honors classes in school, or from church. Needless to say, they were just as scared of her pussy as she was herself.

Now, her family was dead. Dead as dead could be. Well, technically, they were *more* than dead could be, simply because they'd been killed twice. First, they'd been bitten by Mom's sister. Then, Mom had returned, and she bit Dad. Dad returned. After that, Joey, Vanessa's brother, had taken his twelve gauge to them.

The first time, Mom's sister hadn't completely went down. While Mom and Dad had taken bullets to their foreheads, Mom's sister had taken one through her right breast. After Joey had dragged his parents' corpses out back to commence the burying, he'd returned to Mom's sister. And she'd been waiting. She reached up and grabbed his crotch, squeezed as hard as she could, despite the rigor mortis.

With tears running down his face, he'd shoved the gun right under her chin, and blew her top off. After that, he threw up. Then, the pain got worse.

"It hurts, Vanessa," he'd yelled in his country accent, "it hurts!"

Also crying herself, she'd muscled up a stern nub to say, "Go get an ice pack and lie down. I'll take care of it."

With blood and brain-bits covering his face, arms, pants, and hands, he went inside. Clutching himself.

An ice pack wasn't going to do shit. That bitch had grabbed him too good, squeezed too hard. He was busted, and he knew it. He could barely walk. And he certainly couldn't keep from sobbing.

Joey plopped down on the couch, and took one hand away from his ruptured testicles, just so that he could rub the blood out of his eyes.

When Vanessa returned into the house, no blood on her whatsoever, she observed something. Something that made her stop crying. Something that made her want to throw up. It was a high-pitched moaning, more like a squealing, coming from the living room.

"Um, are you okay, Joey," she'd said.

Luckily, she'd picked up the gun. Joey came shambling towards her, not holding his broken balls anymore, and he just kept on coming. A lust in his eyes. Before he could get too close, she pulled the trigger, sending him into oblivion.

One flick of the radio told her all that she needed to know. The emergency broadcast was pretty fucking specific.

She was finally going to be free of her family. Now, she'd be able to meet all the boys she wanted; she just hoped that they weren't dead.

Graveyards were the perfect places for apocalypse shrouding. The young people gathered around the fire in the center of the place, throwing in pieces of the dead to blaze. And burn. And cackle. And snap. And pop.

They all had distinct features: all had slicked-back black manes, and all had black leather jackets, even though they were at the fucking beach. The jackets were more out of style rather than practicality.

"Yeah," one of them said, "show that thing who's boss."

"You're a pussy," another one said, "trying to act all tough-as-shit to a dead body. Fuck you!"

"You saw that fucking thing! It wasn't dead! Thing was chasing after me, tryin' to eat my leg or some shit."

"Fuckin' aye," another one said.

They were all armed with rusty saws. They hacked and pushed and pulled, tearing the limbs from the once-dead-then-rising creatures. Once the limbs were separated, into the fire they went.

"Where do you all think these things came from?" one of them said.

"Who knows," another one said, "they came from the ground, I guess. You can tell because they're all covered in dirt, and they all have suits and shit on. They were buried in these fucking clothes or some shit."

There were a couple palm trees dotting the graveyard. Off in the distance, the Atlantic Ocean could be heard, going on about its normal rhythm, unaffected by the zombie apocalypse. It was the most tranquil thing in the world.

Somehow, there weren't any holes near the tombstones. Apparently, the zombies weren't coming out of their graves. Where in the fuck were they coming from, everyone wondered. But nobody knew.

One of the greasers said, "When you think we'll get a virgin?"

"Well, it might take a while. I'd say, since a lot of them are probably from rich-ass weak families, most of them are done dead."

"No, there's got to be at least *one* virgin out there. At least one."

"Maybe. Maybe not."

"That fucking mausoleum isn't going to clean itself. Anyone here a virgin?"

In total, there were ten greasers huddled around the fire. A few of them were virgins, but none of them raised their hands. Hell, they didn't want to be offered. Being offered would suck ass. They just continued throwing zombie parts into the fire.

The fire was burning in the shape of a pentagram.

Vanessa took the step. It was possibly going to be the longest step of her entire life. Hell, it was the longest one she'd taken so far. And that step was: off the front porch, with her family lying dead on the property behind her. Sadness welled up in her stomach, but she'd long since ceased the crying. She was just too damned excited.

Upon first glance, everything was clear. Everything was fine. There was absolutely no chaos erupting anywhere, no zombies walking about. The coast looked pretty darn clear, and that was her cue to leave, just get the fuck out.

She walked down the road, rubbing her fingers through her brunette hair in an erotic fashion, hoping that she *might* capture the attention of some cute boys. *God, that'd be awesome*, she thought, *boys!*

Vanessa kept right on walking, right on playing with her hair.

The sky was dark now. She hadn't even noticed the night creep up like a bastard.

"Night-time," one of the greasers yelled, "the perfect time for virgin-hunting!"

"Yep. As much as I hate to admit it, you're right. Boys, we need five to stay here and keep the fire going. We need another five to go round up some virgins. Well, technically, we only need four. I count as one of the five who's going, since I have the most *sophisticated* vocabulary of the bunch."

"Hell, I'm goin'," one greaser yelled.

Three more tagged along, and the rest stayed behind, pitching body parts into the blazing pentagram.

Maple walked out of the surf shop, right smack-dab into the *dead* of night.

He didn't like the darkness. Not one bit. In the distance, he could hear moans from the zombified bikers over at the dealership. But they didn't bother him too much. What did bother him was the girl's screaming. It was frantic now, and seemed to be moving. As if she was running away from something.

With one hand, he brushed back his blonde locks from his forehead, and took off on a sprint. Very quickly, he plummeted to the fucking earth. His flip-flop had snapped, causing him to trip. His face planted into the pavement, and blood spurted out of both his lip and nose.

But he was ready to save a damned girl. He wasn't about to let his injured face stop him from reaching his goals. Painfully, he wiped his face off on his tie-dyed shirt, and continued about his journey.

See, Maple was smart. He'd taken off the shirt he'd had on earlier, which had been covered in blood, and replaced it with a fresh one. Apparently, the surf-shop had been run by hippies before the whole dead-people thing, so there were plenty of tie-dyed shirts to go around. And they were all made from good quality cotton, too.

Maple trudged on, just like a soldier. Ready to save the girl from distress. Ready to get over "THE BITCH WHO SHALL NOT BE NAMED." If he could do that, he could live the rest of his life the *right* way. He just knew it. Felt it, too. Deep in his gut. Knew it and felt it. In short, he had to save her. There was no other alternative.

The darkness of the night seemed, oddly, to intensify, as the screams got nearer. Now, he could hear the girl making out statements. "No, leave me alone! Please! NO!"

When it happened, it happened real quick-like. The group of greasers had come upon Vanessa, snorting, making obscene, dirty jokes. For a couple of seconds, she thought about calling out for her parents to come save the day. Then she remembered that they were fucking dead.

"Please, stop," she pleaded. But they kept on. They chased her for a while. Made her scream for a good ten minutes. Got her real sweaty, real fuckable. And she just kept screaming the whole time, as they touched her. Not in a bad way, though. They just poked her with their fingertips, pushed her around, made her scream, made her frightened as fuck.

It went on for a while. Long enough for a couple of people to take notice. However, no one did anything. First of all, they were scared of the gang of thugs. Second of all, they had the freaking zombies to worry about.

Slowly, but steadily, the zombies increased in number. Still, it seemed like there should have been more of them, with the graveyard and everything. Where did the buried ones go? Could they not get out of their caskets or something? They had to be going somewhere. *Had to be. It just didn't make any sense for them to just lie still, while their fellow dead-brethren rose and consumed.*

Maple couldn't believe what he was seeing. Despite the pitch-blackness, he could see the slick, black hair and the deathly leather jackets. They were pushing a poor, small, innocent looking girl around like she was a damned ragdoll or something. Maybe she was to them? Maybe she was.

But what was he going to do about it? He counted five of them altogether, and he wasn't even sure he could take on one of them. Maple definitely wasn't a muscular fellow; that much was for certain.

More pushing. More snorting. And, eventually, they had the girl in their grasp. They started walking in the direction of the old cemetery. The one with the really big mausoleum.

Vanessa was a pretty girl. Brunette. Plump breasts and a little bit of chub, but she didn't flaunt herself around like the other girls at school. She didn't put her hair up, or anything like that. Her parents hadn't raised her that way. And now they were fucking dead.

And now, she was being bossed around by this big group of greasers, getting pushed into a cemetery. If there was one thing that truly terrified her in life, it was cemeteries. Ever since she'd been a little girl, nightmares had haunted her. And they all had one thing in common: tombstones, as far as the eye could see.

Now, her nightmare was becoming a reality.

The cemetery was dark, except for the gigantic fire which illuminated a small area of it. She knew that the tombstones didn't stretch out *that* far, but the fire obscured her field of vision, making them appear to stretch on forever.

For some reason, the greasers were carrying her. They were all far stronger than her, so she had absolutely no chance of escaping. She feared that they might rape her, but none of them were *poking* around at her private parts with their fingers. It was like they had another purpose for her. One that didn't even involve them at all.

In the distance, the mausoleum was silhouetted against the never-ending field of tombstones.

Maple followed them. Better to stick along, he thought. It was far more appealing than going back to the surf-shop. He knew that if he did that, he'd regret his decision until the day he died. And then, after that, he might even come back as a zombie and regret it some more.

No, he thought, *I've got to try to save this girl. Part of it's for me, but the biggest part of it is for her. Totally rad, man. Totally rad.*

Now, the fucking darkness was starting to get on his nerves. He feared that there would be some zombies lurking about, but he saw none. That didn't seem right. Hell, it was a fucking cemetery for Christ's sakes! The place should have been crawling with zombies. But it wasn't. Not at all.

He crouched behind a tombstone, observing silently, like a ninja. From his vantage point, he could make out the fiery pentagram in the distance. *What is going on here?* he thought. *This is just downright bogus! Beyond belief!*

The greasers were just walking around, acting like they were awesome, feeding the pentagram various body parts. There was a large pile of corpses. All of them, at least from what Maple could make out in the dark, were greatly decomposed, like they'd been dead for-fucking-ever.

"Must be coming from the graves," he muttered to himself. Then he took note of the fact *that he was crouching behind a damn tombstone, and there was absolutely no movement under his feet. The ground was still.*

"Where are these gnarly-nibblers coming from?" he muttered to himself.

Then, there was a gunshot.

Jones was walking. Not feeling much, these days. Jones didn't even know that his name *was* Jones. His brain was so *dead* that he didn't know much of anything, other than the fact that he was hungry. Really hungry. Hungry enough to eat a horse, but he preferred humans. From what he'd already tasted, they were similar to beef. He *did*, in fact, remember what beef tasted like. Steaks had always been a normal part of his diet.

His suit was all rumpled, all black and grey and dusty.

He'd been right close to the hole. No, not a vagina, but a grave. He'd been snoozing in his coffin when all hell had started to break loose. One moment, both his brain and body laid dormant, but then, just like the eventual spewing of Mount Fuji, he woke up. And the coffin burst open, he leapt out, and people screamed like dick-sisters. Everyone was scared. Nobody just stood there, saying nothing. Everyone ran.

But running hadn't worked out that well. Zombies were starting to pop up everywhere, not just in graveyards. And not just in Myrtle Beach. The damn things were taking over places pretty far spread out, like New York, New Jersey, Tennessee, *Pennsylvania*. The damn things appeared to be everywhere. And that was definitely frightening to most.

Off in the distance, Jones observed a big light. He didn't know what the fuck it was, just that it was a damn light. Maybe there was food? As he got closer, his question was answered. There was food, but the food wasn't passive. The sound echoed like crazy, and his world turned to black. The first thing that went was the fiery pentagram.

Maple was scared shitless. Now that he knew guns were involved, a fear rose up inside him. And that fear very damn-well near caused him to discontinue his journey, almost made him return to the surf-shop.

But he didn't. There was a damsel in distress, and he wanted to save her possibly-cute little ass. Wanted to save it real good, so that, just maybe, her ass would give him some loving one day. Loving that had basically been vacant from his life for a *long* time.

He walked on, silently. Basically, he had no clue what he was doing. How in the hell was he going to fight off ten tough-as-nails motherfuckers, who also happened to be armed. It was impossible; it really was. But, damned if he didn't want some freaking love.

One tombstone.

Stop… wait.

Another tombstone.

Stop… wait.

Another tombstone. Stop to read the epitaph: *HE WAS A VALINAT SOUL. LOVED OTHERS WELL. WAS LOVED BY OTHERS, AS WELL. GOT KILLED BY A TORNADO.*

Maple thought aloud, "What the hell?"

Then, he moved to the next tombstone, hiding under the cover of darkness, and stopped. Listened. Tried to figure out just what totally-bogus-yet-fully-radical thing was going on. Whatever it was, it was weird. And he couldn't help but notice the mausoleum, lumbering over the miniscule tombstones.

Vanessa had been scared out of her wits. Until they explained that she was going into the mausoleum to meet *boys*. Oh, how she adored that. For the longest time, she'd been super-attracted to a couple. But her parents had kept her on a short leash. But now, they were dead, just like the bodies being thrown into the flaming pentagram.

One of the greasers said, "Be honest, toots. You ever been dorked before?"

"Um… well, to be honest, no. I haven't."

"Would you like to? This isn't a rape. This is something *heavenly*."

She thought about it for a second, then said, "Yes."

That was all it took. "Well, we got her lined up! Men, this is what we've been waiting for!"

Vanessa thought that the comment sounded very strange, but, hell, *boys* were involved. She loved that notion with a passion as bright as the fiery pentagram.

At that moment, the night couldn't have been any darker. The blackness was complete.

Maple crept silently, still using the tombstones to cover his image. There were ten greasers, and they were all walking with the girl, leading her away from the fiery pentagram, right into the gigantic mausoleum structure. *Something completely non-righteous is happening here*, he thought, *and I don't like it at all.*

In less than three seconds, everyone was inside the mausoleum. Except Maple, who stood, silently, on the outside, contemplating his eventual move.

Despite the over-powering tint of the darkness, it grew. And grew. And grew.

Vanessa walked into the mausoleum before anyone. One of the greasers had been kind enough to open the door for her. And when she first set foot inside the creepy, old structure, all traces of light that the pentagram offered were forever extinguished. The beams couldn't butt-fuck their way inside the big ole tomb of death.

The greasers followed behind her. On the walls, little slots lay, containing, presumably, completely dead corpses. But there were sounds. Terrifying sounds. And they were all similar: a deep, guttural moaning.

Right in the center, it sat. A big-ass slate of what looked to be concrete. It was smooth, rectangular, and sat high above ground, about the same height as a bed.

"Lay down," one of the greasers said, as he closed the heavy-as-hell mausoleum door, with the aid of some of his tough buddies.

Now, it was pitch black.

Vanessa sprawled herself on the slab, opened her legs for the first time in her entire life. It felt good, the breeze. She'd never felt such a sensation before. Why had her parents been so intent on keeping her from it?

Then, there was a cold feeling *down there*. It kind of tickled, kind of felt good.

"Mmm," she said, in pure pleasure-mode.

"What's she going on about," one of the greasers said, "we haven't even started yet."

"Huh," Vanessa said, obviously surprised.

One of the greasers had a lighter, mainly used for menthols because he was a pussy. He lit it, and the pretty large portion of the inside of the mausoleum-structure was illuminated, including the pink slit between Vanessa's legs.

And that spot wasn't pink because of her pussy.

It was pink because dozens of night crawlers were wiggling their way into her reproductive system, all while having a jolly-good time. Some of the worms were five inches long, while others were pretty short.

Vanessa screamed, both in pleasure and disgust.

Then she saw the man standing above her; and he wasn't a fucking greaser.

"There he is," one of the tough fuckers yelled, "there's the Devil! We found the tomb of the Devil! Ha! There's the fucking Devil!"

All of the greasers applauded. Vanessa just moaned, with heightened sexual intensity.

There was more than just one Devil. And they were all dripping worms from their decomposing faces, just like the one standing above Vanessa.

Maple couldn't even hear himself think, due to all of the screaming that was coming from inside the mausoleum. Whatever was going on in there, it wasn't good. He listened very closely, but, no matter how hard he tried to make himself, he couldn't hear the girl anymore. Just screaming. And munching. Oh, the munching sounds were horrible.

Soon, there was no more screaming. Just munching.

Well, that sucks, Maple thought, *better luck with the next damsel-in-distress who comes along. Hopefully, her predicament won't be doomed from the get-go.*

Out of sheer boredom, Maple walked over to the massive pile of decomposing zombies. As he got nearer, he observed that they all had bullet-holes in their heads. Apparently, the greasers had went around shooting the hell out of them.

Still, he thought, *why aren't the bodies coming out of the ground?* Then, he thought about the mausoleum screams, and put two-and-two together. All of the tombstones were pretty old. But the mausoleum was a fairly new structure.

Also, there were catacombs in the mausoleum. Perfect nesting ground for *worms*.

He decided that the pile of dead zombies was starting to stink like hell. He walked away, not really knowing where to go.

Then, he noticed the bottles of water lying around. Apparently, the assholes who'd taken the girl into the mausoleum had been somewhat smart. They'd stocked up on water, instead of booze. Still, there was some alcohol.

Maple picked up a couple water bottles, and looked back towards the flaming pentagram.

He'd always been somewhat creative.

Maple walked along the sand, right next to the Atlantic Ocean. Despite his shark phobia, he wanted to go swimming before the apocalypse fucked *everything* up. Now, the sun was starting to rise. Things were getting better.

Back at the graveyard, empty bottles of water lay beside the flaming shape.

It wasn't a pentagram anymore.

The blazing peace sign continued to burn, despite the world going to hell.

THE COMMUNE
by David J. Fairhead

David J. Fairhead was first published in THE BIG BOOK OF BIZARRO with his demonic apocalyptic tale, "The Fall," and his short story "Demoneye" appears in WESTWARD HOES. The latter of which is also being adapted into a comic book with Gary Lee Vincent.

David's current novel THE FALL OF TOMORROW is based on his THE BIG BOOK OF BIZARRO short story and is also published by Burning Bulb Publishing. His website is www.fairlydarkproductions.com.

David has also written a novel titled CHARLIE: A Child's Tale of Terror.

He is also the writer of the comic book series WZWA (World Zombie Wrestling Association) in association with Dr. Jon Towers and Stigmata Studios.

David is currently host of the radio podcast show, KETTLE WHISTLE RADIO, working with co-host Heather Taddy of A&E's Paranormal State fame, where they talk horror, comics, and music.

Devon put the book down on the counter. The rough red cover sickened him, reminding him of the rows of library books back at UCLA that he would never read after dropping out. This one was special. Exhaling, placing the yellow phone handle back in its cradle on the wall, he played with the twine of yellow wires hanging from the phone in Nancy's hallway. He was sure Nancy and her young boy toy were smoking and screwing rather than packing their bags for the trip to Pennsylvania. Back home for him. He wondered when she would tell her young lover that she was pregnant with his child. Keeping high all the time was an easy job, necessary to self-medicate when the world was coming to an end. Equally effortless to avoid talking about serious issues, like marriage, pregnancy, and income. Rebuilding was still in question as the world tried to even out the interrupted equilibrium of rationale.

He scratched at his beard, agitated with the conversation that he had just had with his older brother back in the Pittsburgh area. Never wanting any part of his brother's arcane interactions with authority, he left the commune in Zelienople a year before the "big happening" and all the atrocious shit went down. Long gone were the simple days of selling his brother's popular strain of acid throughout Butler County Pennsylvania. Of course when the unthinkable becomes the new reality, the only positive aspect was that he and his brother had been exonerated of all their charges in Evans City and Zelienople. Devon and his brother Neville had already moved to California to avoid being arrested right away a couple of years before the madness went down. Death, blood, riots all provoked by a supernatural force or disease released by the government. The latter excuse Neville used when he moved back to southern Pennsylvania to start it up again, feeling he could feed off the negativity of a broken kingdom.

"It went down." Chuckling to himself, Devon was still rubbing his unkempt brownish-red beard, now resting his head on the phone box itself that hung on the wall connecting Nancy's parent's kitchen to the hallway. He could hear Nancy and Peter banging the headboard of her mom's bed against the wall. "How in Pete's sake can you two even be in the mood …?" He picked up his knapsack, containing all his belongings, threw it over the shoulder of his army jacket that normally he only wore for protests, but those were dying out now, being that *everything went down.*

"Come on. We have to get going. It's a long walk to Pennsylvania if we miss this last bus out." Not knowing whether he was more perturbed by his numbskull friends' ignorance to what was happening around them or the disturbing conversation he had just had with his older brother Neville. Devon slapped the red hardcover journal on the counter with an open hand. Placing it into the pocket inside his army issued "protest" jacket, as Nancy referred to his favorite coat, he made sure it was secure, tightly close to him. If they were to get robbed, or worse, attacked by the "new forms" he knew that he could give up his knapsack with all his underwear, weed, socks, and his scrap book that he had made on his own with clippings of Porky Chedwick and that crazy radio personality with the great voice, Wolfman Jack. Devon loved music. He wanted to be involved somehow, and now that things "went down" he had to find ways to preserve what he remembered, what everyone forgot, and what he loved. Music.

The Hollies were playing off of his transistor radio in the kitchen, singing about a bus stop during his phone conversation with his brother. Neville was dictating as he normally did during his one sided conversations with his younger brother. This time about finding the book for a second time and buying it back. Devon hated when his brother was right, and this time, book and all, he hit the nail on the head. Neville had tried to start up a following out in California, promising once they became popular at "sit-ins" and concert gatherings that he would buy Devon a guitar and let him begin to perform. Make a name for himself too. As it turned out, Neville did not have what it took to get into the girls pants out east. They were savvier, more progressive, and more prone to follow some of the more practiced madmen, who had better drugs and accommodations. Before the world changed.

As for charismatic fellows with shitty accommodations, Devon found a few. The place that Devon met Nancy—"the future movie star, like Barbara Parkins" as she would say—and the young former mechanic, Peter had just escaped from what had been an acid fueled desert nightmare. They were glad to leave with him.

Come to think about it, she did resemble Barbara Parkins, he thought to himself.

Nancy's parents were gone. She was sure they were dead with the first wave that hit California. With the overgrown influx of population the way it was turning in the east, when it really hit California the wave would be even more deadly than the initial outspurts. The radio warned to evacuate major cities until the National Guard had a grasp of things. So when they had heard about the busses heading to the Midwest, they left the commune out in the desert hills, that nightmare in the making known as Spahn Ranch, in order to go back to her mom's place in Orange County. Things were a bit under control, temporarily, but per Neville and that book of his, the situation was far from over. Most of the activity had happened on the eastern seaboard and if not for folks moving westward, this disease, virus, or whatever in hell it was may never have gotten this far. A ghastly and inconceivable invasion had swooped in but was somewhat under control by local jurisdictions and now his tumultuous brother wanted Devon to head back into the fire.

"Living out in the woods, desert or mountains secured your chances to survive. Less people, more landscape to see the chaps coming," Neville had said on the phone to Devon on the first night when they broke into Nancy's parent's house. He sounded tweaked out on speed.

Devon mulled over his brother's words from that night a couple of days ago, almost as clear as Neville's desperate ramblings rasped in his ear just now. "Did you get the book back? Devon, we need it. You will not believe until you see." Devon could hear the dope crazed voice of his older brother, while some new hippie chick giggled with over-stimulated sensual whispers. Clearly, on the other side of the phone, some girl named Marly was groping him, stroking him or whatever sex fueled frenzy he managed to get his followers into.

"Yes, I went to San Francisco. Found the old shop. I got it. It was dangerous, so many people, so many 'new forms' man, I can't believe you would make your only living relative do that Nev, so uncool man, so fuckin' uncool." He knew Neville only heard the words "*I got it*" referring to the unpublished book with the strange markings inside, no copyright, or discernable date. Neville had sold the journal to a pawn shop on Haight-Ashbury when he was unloading all his belongings to head back east after failing to fit in with the sophisticated western hippies who merely seemed angry at their rich parents and limitless sunshine. He had told Devon, two years back, how he could not handle these condescending pricks pretending to like The Doors because someone said just how "out of sight" the music was. Neville just saw Jim Morrison as another alpha. Competition. Devon started to see a frightening parallel between his brother and others he came across in these unsettling times.

"I'm *out of sight*, bro. I'm leaving. You'd be smart to follow. You ain't getting laid out here, face it. You got looks over me too, but you getting none." Neville had slapped his brother in the face, awakening him from a dope infused stupor and left soon thereafter, leaving their squatter's paradise.

The small red hardcover book that read "People and other Misconceptions" by some unknown pagan preacher that only went by the name Malkyre'. The book made the rounds all about the beatnik scene for a while. Devon could remember going to see Strawberry Alarm Clock at a small club in L.A. with his brother, who broke out the book at the bar deciding to recite some excerpts during intermission between bands. The words got the attention of almost every stinky patron, beatnik, and hippie alike. He had to admit, the words were alluring. More often than not the words form this self-proclaimed "*Seer*" came to fruition. Some predictions had materialized throughout the years that Neville owned the thing during the Beatle invasion when they were kids, consulting it up until that war in 'Nam that they all knew as a waste of human souls. How this book told certain tales ahead of time was something that troubled Devon as much then as it burned now while he was staring at the yellow phone on the wall, waiting for his friends to stop screwing.

"Malkyre'," He said the name aloud. What kind of name is that? He knew somewhere in the book the dude revealed his name, but in his own cloud of pot fueled forgetfulness, he never committed it to memory. No had known who the dude was back then anyway. Probably some fascist hiding behind his own made-up propaganda. Cedric? Nah. He could care less about the made up name, for the words within were the meat on the bone.

They were kids just going through an old book shop on Carson Street in Pittsburgh when Neville fixated on the journal. Obliged, Neville felt he must have this book. Devon looked at it as someone's old family cookbook sold at an estate sale. Yet, the red hard covered curse had made it all the way to California with them.

"Guys, let's get a move on, huh? We do not know how many busses gonna be doin' this trip huh? I don't wanna get crass, you hear?" Devon lit up a cigarette, stepped outside to the front yard of suburbia. Smoke filled the air, cars piled on lawns, bodies …

Devon's stomach fired up with acid at the thought, looking at the bodies torn into contorted shapes with clothes like crumbled paper and entrails staining the grass and streets like red ribbon candy. Fire, Police and EMT personnel scrambled to pick up the pieces left behind by the local posse. He had no fear of lighting up the joint outside the foyer of the ranch. He heard the Dave Clarke Five's "Because" come on from the kitchen, cooling him down some. "Someone was still spinning records, even now." He thought, "Fuckin' California."

Peter must be in the kitchen, he thought, hearing the radio turned up a notch. Tons of pirate stations were popping up in light of the devastation. "Vultures," thought Devon.

Then the younger man stuck his mop of brown hair out the screen door scratching at his pork chop sideburns. He was shirtless and smelled of sex. "Hey, man, we goin? Can I grab a hit off that bro?"

Devon removed his orange tinted sunglasses, rubbing at the rectangular lenses nervously wiping them clean of the steam rising from the burning bodies in the makeshift bonfire in the front yard to the left. Firemen were dumping bodies onto it, careful to be sure none of the victims were still moving. Live or dead.

"Get Nancy. Two of you, clean up. Tell her to change her threads, no more of that brown flower print dress, and you, please, a clean shirt. I'm not traveling for days with you two skuzz buckets in close quarters, and friggin' you two smelling like each other." Devon took a drag, meeting the slight young man's stoned gaze and middle finger. Annoyed, he cynically tapped on the book in his inner jacket pocket. "Fantastic."

"Route 80 had been the best bet for sure," Nancy shouted with a smile, hopping out the side of the blue van. Peter caught her in his bony arms. They shared a smile. Devon waived to the man in the driver's seat, saying thank you for the ride. The man with the paisley collar that hung to his chest, open three buttons down, nodded, after watching Nancy's tight ass in the pastel green slacks when she stepped off.

"Good luck. And stay off of the turnpike. Lots of unfinished business there. There's a gravel road that will take you to a lodge, if that's where you're heading. I'm not prying but there ain't much else out here." The man with the wide rimmed brown sunglasses held out his hand for payment.

Devon did not want to tell the man where they were going, though a road would be nice, he decided it safer to follow his brother's directives, so not to get shot by Neville's own scouts.

"Fifty miles since Ohio. Twenty smackaroos, friend." Louis Armstrong's "What a Wonderful World" hummed from the passenger side window. They had listened to that and the Rolling Stones the entire way. Not many radio stations were playing music again yet and the middle aged gentlemen named "Just Dan," owned only two 8-Track cassettes. He had approached and offered them a ride outside a bar in Elyria, Ohio, where the bus driver claimed he would go no further. Also happened to be a place where Neville informed him there would be many drivers for hire at said bar.

Devon handed him a twenty and the blue van with the bubble windows and grim reaper painted on the side in purple took off in a cloud of exhaust down 40 East. They had come south of Pittsburgh on Route 70 and then by way of 119. The closest "Just Dan" would take them was to the sign that read "Ohiopyle State Park," agreed upon by Devon, as his brother Neville's campground was somewhere outside the park near the Youghiogheny River.

There were few border patrol stops, as most public and government workers alike were busy trying to clear the highways of abandoned vehicles or brush aside some of the "new forms" that still scattered along the roadsides.

"He was a real creep." Nancy twirled her braids that hung down to her chest in tight knots. Big purple bubbly plastic hair ties held them in check at the end.

"Hey Dev, how are we supposed to find your bro from here? It's going to be dark soon. Man, what if he's just as batty as the last buckaroo we stayed with? He's just east coast/mid-west crazy and not California Jive, right?" Peter was tightening his boots under his light blue bell bottom jeans. He wore a matching denim vest that did not cover his skinny waist. "I'm stifled." Taking off his vest, he began to place a red bandana about his head. "Friggin' humid."

"We hike about a mile into the woods, just about where that park sign is. He said we will meet one of his guys there. They are armed, so stay together. This is how he managed to keep his people safe during this mess. Staying out of the major cities, or populated towns, and keeping scouts out around the clock. Some straggling dead may still be wandering the roads so we stick to the woods for now, per him." Devon adjusted a blue bandana around his tight reddish brown wave of hair. Removing his sunglasses, he lit a joint from the top of his army pocket. His thick brown eyebrows were dripping with sweat, irritating him slightly more than the two goddamned love birds he found himself in the company of.

"So, Neville, he's a bit more hip than he was back when you were in the service, Devon? We can trust him … maybe trust his weed a bit more than the skunk we are used to?" Nancy had been nagging him the whole way on the bus to Ohio about the possibility of high quality pot.

"Hey, tweaker queen, keep it cool. He didn't last this long by being stupid. Before it all went down he was selling his shit for a good price. Sold some good trips too." Devon turned on the pretty girl who rarely acted their common age, just pushing thirty. Nancy tended to digress to her younger boyfriend's age bracket.

"Yea, Nance. Don't be a drag. How could it be any worse than staying with that Charlie guy in the desert? Whether he did something really bad, or was about to do something really, really hairy, remains to be seen." Peter, wise for his eighteen years, referred to the commune they had previously holed up in, then promptly left due to the foulness of the company they had found themselves in.

Silence fell between the three travelers, proceeding onto a very narrow trail that broke through the dense forest before them. Night was indeed coming and the trail was only the size of a single bicycle tire.

"Listen you two." Devon turned to look at the young man and the pretty brunette behind them. He liked them better when they were frightened. Seemed to keep them focused. They had all abandoned the last commune together, fearing that something dreadful was coming, even before the "new forms" began walking about. All they had heard, initially, were radio rumors of the horrors out here, before it spread west.

Now they were in the thick of it.

"Walk quiet-like. Listen for crunching brush, listen good. No more talking. We will be found by Neville's guys. If something else finds us first, I want to be ready." He shifted the .45, loosening it from his belt in case of a quick encounter. Each of them had one. Nancy reached for her backpack to get hers out now. Peter had his drawn, almost always, when they traveled on foot. This made Devon nervous. "Neither of them had looked at a gun before this pestilence rocked the scene," he thought to himself.

"Keep the guns pointed down please." Devon whispered.

Taken by surprise several shadows emerged out of the gloom of the forest on either side of them far too quickly for them to respond.

"And so it I tell you, decades under my feet through many guises, I leave these thoughts behind, to not only boast of my many lives and the sizeable tastes of cloaks I wore, but to warn, because it is only fair? Right? Of course. *Natural* occurrences; hurricanes, volcanoes, monsoons and more commonly subduction zones that open a wound in the earth to bleed a malignance on the land are as much to blame as otherworldly projectiles penetrating your skies to fall foul upon your family outing. It happens. (I'm snickering now, for I have seen it).

"I am damned. Therefore I have been given such liberties to see disasters first hand and survive. A purveyor of the dark arts in life, married to a self-proclaimed witch, I was provided more than a glimpse into the netherworld that you fear. I'm a Seer. In life, my name was Cedric Bodnatsen, a long forgotten moniker.

"Of course, I'm not without a sense of humor, tinkering in the dark for the precise genre of art to personify and entertain myself. Yes mostly myself. Watching humans squirm into and out of a situation that was beyond their scope of their very existence also provided decades of loneliness of the type that teaches one how to entertain oneself professionally. Decades of impatience and evil."

–Malkyre'

Neville closed the book, his pointy chin willowed with wisps of a beard he could never quite grow in properly. Dressed in a brown velour leisure suit, he stared at his brother and two loyal friends by his side. "This man was brilliant, and see, he does say his real name Devon, you just never read it all the way through."

"I did. Just didn't care to retain it." Devon sneered.

"I missed this book. Thank you Devon. How much did you have to buy it back for?" Neville paced in front of his new crowd of disciples.

"Thirty bucks. The same turkey you sold it to. Apparently it was a hot item that kept getting sold back to the old San Fran Peddler. Now are you going to read the part. . . "

Ignoring his brother, Neville pranced about the center of the common room in the lodge. His men had ushered his brother and guests into the lodge, offering some Schaeffer's and water bong hits of his weaker blend for guests.

Two men with rifles, long hair under biker hats and open button down paisley shirts stood by the frail white door. Twenty or more folks surrounded the room, like wallpaper, they hung onto Neville's every word. One girl was completely naked in the corner with the exception of a pink scarf on her head holding her red hair back in an unruly bundle. Some giggling blond dude that had to be just out of his teens snapped his fingers like an exclamation after every last word their leader said. Devon and his friends had learned that the young surfer looking dude's name actually was "Snappy" as he dressed in trousers his mom had bought him, cowboy boots and a tight big collared tan sports shirt. Smoke hung down two feet from the low ceiling, concealing the brown wooden paneled walls that encircled them. The nude pink scarfed girl made Nancy nervous, visibly, so Peter held her in his arms tightly, with a fake smile on his own face. To the two of them, this was equally as creepy as the last place they had found residence.

The furniture was a bit better. Couches lined the walls, with big fluffy cushions. Some of these cushions were used on top of the many area rugs for Neville's followers to lay down upon to listen. The sound of a lighter somewhere constantly wisped the air of the room while bongs were lit or joints were passed.

Several of the long haired bearded men sitting around a table drinking beers were eyeing up Nancy's tight pastel pants, noticing the natural beauty, making Peter very uncomfortable. He had reached around her to button up her white blouse. Her cleavage was too welcoming to the creeps from across the room. He knew he was too small to protect her from *that* many grown men.

Neville was as giddy as a kid on Christmas. Devon knew this about his brother, that indeed the end of times as the rest of humanity saw it was Neville's dream come true. He saw himself as more powerful than the average man left standing, for now his foreboding sermons rang as genuine.

"The fascists have lost the god war man. What have I been saying?! Yea, sure, the sheriff and his boys in the 'burgh have things under control, for now …" Silence hung in the air as Neville twirled on his platform shoes, all for show to catch the little surfer boy, Snappy, off guard, mid-snap. They smiled at one another and then laughter filled the lodge common room. Neville of course making it clear that it was fine to laugh at that moment by overcompensating his obnoxious volume.

"*For now*. Yes." The theatrics began anew, tossing the suit jacket onto a couch of onlookers, he raised his white sleeved arms in the air under his tight brown vest. Gold chains, with crosses hung gaudily about his veiny neck when he began to dance about the room, grabbing the attention from all while showing off for his own brother. "... NOW ... local boys in blue and war mongers have control of their own tiny jurisdictions but for how long, really? Cause they're out there! You saw them brother?" He was in Devon's face again. Ripping a joint from a tall handsome man in a green pea coat seated on the arm of an orange couch, Neville took a drag and blew it into his younger brother's face.

"We share here. We have food, running water....the river will continue to provide for us ... Shhh listen ..." Dramatically, Neville put a hand to his ear, some ash from the joint still hanging on his thick moustache. "You can hear the precious flow from here. The river is right down the hill. She will provide." He motioned to the round wood card table in the corner and the tougher looking men, larger, muscled, armed with belts full of visible ammo and rifles on their shoulders. "And they will protect ... As long as Marly keeps them fulfilled." Smiling widely, Neville looked to the nude woman smiling with bright yellow teeth, stone faced in the corner.

Snappy snapped his fingers, grinning through his thick blond locks on his face.

The naked woman stood, her pink scarf falling to her shoulders with her red hair, making her way to the table. In less than seconds, the sound of a zipper "unzipped" while the woman named Marly bowed head deep into the lap of one of the guardsmen.

Devon tried very hard to ignore the moaning in the corner in succession to the slapping of mouth on flesh. Looking to the eyes of every one of his brother's followers, he knew there was not one among them that flew in a straight line to the rational factory.

"Neville, please read *that* section to them. Let our trip here at least make sense please." Devon smacked a joint from Peter's mouth just as the tall dark haired man in the pea coat came over with the dropper to douse the end of the joint.

Peter looked disappointed. Nancy, however, already had a fag from Mr. Pea Coat Man, who was now blotting some of Neville's secret ingredient on the joint. She shared with Peter.

"Are you certain your woods are safe here …? (Cough cough cough …)" Nancy's eyes watered up, feeling the effects.

"No. My pretty Cali lady of the braids. No one can be certain. That is why we take precautions. Scouts out there all the time … well cared for." Neville waived a hand to the round card table with the men and that Marly girl hard at work while new zippers opened. "However, none of my number have perished. The river to one side, mountainous woods of the Laurel Highlands surrounding the other … So my boys, my own posse, can see the *new forms* coming, these, oh what do they call them now on the radio, monster marauders? Ha ha-ha. We are fine as wine here my foxy lady. Even Snappy over here feels safer here than he did in California. Yeah this hodad came from the same place you did!" Neville poked fun at the teen.

"Hey, I surfed, that's not fair …" Snappy laughed back.

"Well not anymore. No one will be surfing for very long if they stay in those overcrowded cities. Here. Well here, brother Devon and friends, bringers of the feast …" He held up the little red hard covered book. "… you will be safe."

Devon prepared himself for the coming reading. They had not been in Neville's commune for longer than three hours and already he could see the brainwashing take hold on his friends. Peter was looking uneasy, taking a beer, sharing a grin with another pretty blond girl in white go-go boots that went to her knees and a purple form fitting mini dress. A purple headband striped across the top of her scalp showing off her impish face and blue eyes.

Devon did not see them leaving here anytime soon. Maybe it *was* safer.

The commune consisted of a cluster of lodges formerly belonging to a Catholic summer camp, (*The Chariot's Comin' Boys Camp*, read the broken sign in the Courtyard by the driveway entrance) just up a steep incline of rocky outcroppings above the Youghiogheny River, deep in the woods.

Vividly it seemed that the guardsmen truly did not mind their work. Like himself, Devon could see that some of the men were ex-military, unless the dog tags around their necks belonged to persons long gone. It worked both ways when he had had attended the Vietnam protests, consisting of both heroes and villains. All of it sickened him.

So did this show that his brother was putting on.

Now tall Mr. Pea Coat dude came by with two gorgeous young ladies, also in go-go gear, hair down to their backs and bedroom eyes. They all had trays of what had to be the window pane formation, crystalized to Neville's standards that he and his brother used to sell up north of Pittsburgh. Soon the tiny crystals were wrapped up, mixed with the buds in a pile on a small TV table near the kitchen unit of the large room. Devon knew what this stuff could do, postulating a euphoria that could put you out for days with its potency.

When it was offered to him by one of the pretty go-go girls, he responded, "No, trying to cut down." The girl tilted her pretty little head like a confused puppy. Someone across the smoky chamber had put a record player on and the tune, "Rain, Park and Other Things" by the Cowsills filled the room with happy pleasant vibes. Some people danced, especially when the music shifted to The Grass Roots, "Let's Live for Today," there was not one person who could not smile. The music deterred Devon's mind briefly.

Peter was beaming now, dancing with both Nancy and the pretty girl in the purple dress and white boots. Devon had not seen the boy honestly happy in months. Maybe his brother had it right? Was he the only "jive bully dulling the buzz in the room?" Nev would say to him.

No. He was not. There was another girl standing by the window, next to the front door. She was wiping her tears on the fringes of the orange, green and white checkered curtains. Was she disturbed by Neville's reading from "Humans and Other Misconceptions?" A book that was more than likely written by some beatnik hipster who sold it for weed money at Golden Gate Park, than the prophet that Neville truly believed him to be.

"Are you ok?" Devon touched the girl on the shoulder.

She flinched. "No." The girl was wrapped up in a wool coat that clearly did not fit her. The mascara ran down her face in rivers. Blue eye shadow caked her eyes too. "Are the contents of that book true? Like, how your brother told us? Was that Cedric guy a prophet, lay it on me… please!?" She looked up. No older than twenty, this girl had genuine fear in her eyes. Maybe she had lost family members to those things? There's no telling what an individual had witnessed.

"Um, I can't deny the truths that I have read. Not now. We had that book for years before this happened, and, well, crazier people than my brother saw it as truth, so I was not prone to believe a lot of the supernatural stuff. I mean who is going to believe some surf Nazi swag dealer claiming to be a warlock from centuries old, preaching about end of the world shit … but then, some of the things happened."

"Who would dare bring a child into this world?" Her tone was threateningly deep. Pushing away from Devon's touch, the girl ran out the door across the lot between the lodges, disappearing into the confines of one of the smaller cabins to the right next to the woods.

"Don't trip on Lara, man, she'll bum you out till the end of time, bro. She was quite the disappointment. Post natal syndrome they call it, this was different though. Born stillborn." Neville had come over, straining an arm around his taller brother, high as all hell.

The brothers watched as her cabin door opened. The curvy woman, healthy by comparison to the thin waif girls surrounding the room they were currently in, threw a white cloche on her head with a big crimson flower on one side then continued to run to the woods on the right side of the campground. Neville seemed suddenly sobered, shouting "WARREN!" to Mr. Pea Coat, the tall handsome man with the greasy dirty dark hair. "It's Lara again. Go get her Warren."

Listening to the conversation, Nancy had come over too, very interested in Mr. Pea Coat Man, now known as Warren. Devon knew that this was just her attention seeking behavior that she performed when her boy Peter was straying with other girls, younger girls. "She's distraught. I'll go to her. Bad trip, right? You say she has a child?" With that, Nancy was running out the door following Warren.

"No, wait… ugh… whatever man." Neville swiped one of his special joints laced with the speckles of window pane. Firing up a match he took a drag. "Dev, take a hit. You'll need it." Neville opened the book again, picking through the pages, "Ah, here we go. This is the ditty that made you come all this way Devon."

Devon reluctantly took the roach clip, sucking in a drag of the sour smoke, staring at his shorter older brother puffing out plumes, fearing that maybe taking their chances out in the wilds or even Pittsburgh, a major city, would have had less risky results than staying with his wild eyed megalomaniacal brother whose delusions outweighed his intelligence.

Peter came over in a sudden frenzy. "Man, she shouldn't go running around like that. Why is Nancy going out in the woods after those cats? What's the deal? She's pregnant you know, two months."

Neville looked at the wild eyed boy, "You're young boy. But yeah, go get your woman. They have a better chance at getting pumped with some iron by one of my boys out there."

"Pregnant. So she told you Peter? You dumb skags." Devon took the roach again, snatching it from his brother's hands and sucked in a much larger drag.

Shaking off the interruption, Neville and Devon watched Peter almost fall across the gravel courtyard, gathering himself in his light blue denim vest, high as a kite, he ran in his heavy boots to the trail where Nancy and Warren had disappeared after the Lara woman.

Gathering around their leader, Devon was uncomfortable with how close the stench of cigarettes, laced weed, beer and body odor had engulfed the air around him. His knees were buckling a bit, nauseated too with the site of his brother in his brown vest and pants (did he think that made him look powerful?) waving around in front of him to get everyone's attention. Devon noticed that some of the armed biker looking types had also gone outside to pursue the distraught Lara chick.

Neville was not one to overtly show concern for another person. No. He was ostentatiously looking out for this Lara's welfare, so something was amiss. Devon stopped caring about it, just trying to get his bearings, shifting in his boots from side to side with the wicked buzz of the window pane strain that had supplied his brother's living expenses up until the dead began to rise from their graves. Yet, he had a fortress of solitude, soldiers that obeyed him and women …

More women removing their clothes. Boots slid off, one piece dresses slid down, giggles with tantalizing teasing echoed around the open common room as bodies fell to the many shag area rugs placed just for such an occasion.

Snappy was rolling around with the cute girl still wearing her purple dress, purple head band falling to her neck so that her golden blond hair fell to her face. Marly, already naked, was snaking her hands up the back of the girl's dress, having her way, while the pretty girl in the white go-go boots continued to ride Snappy the young surfer.

"Jesus, Nev, what is in this stuff ...?" Devon was trying to take in the sights of the orgy beginning around him, striving to keep his own focus on his brother standing in the center with the book before him, open for a reading. Others stood clothed, drinking, smoking, and watching. "Set me free why dontcha babe ..." blared off of the record player.

"Simpler times revered simpler means. Pirates, nautical experts, sailors ... even the best were all misguided when looking to the stars. The blanket of diamonds above their voyages were not telling stories. No. They were all idiots overlooking a mere map for an existential canvas! Fools. My contrition for those before me was in their ignorance. The fear should not come from the stars above themselves weaving tales of honor and brutality. Their true concern should have been what those stars shall bring down upon the Earth!" Neville smiled up at the ceiling to the delight and hollering of his followers. Then he continued to read from the pages.

"A light would explode about the stratosphere, an inconceivable gift radiating from another world will illuminate almost just beyond the naked eyes reach ..." Neville, high on his own window pane laced weed, equally as his love of himself, was feeding off the attention of the women on his legs, groping for him to just look down at them.

Peter wished he had listened to Devon and not taken a hit. Eventually he caught up with Warren the Pea Coat Man and Nancy. They stood in a clearing. He could just barely see the other woman, who had gone running into the woods, yet there she was. Lara was standing in the center of the clearing but the gleam off the river below, a fifty foot ravine, was shimmering bright behind her. He could make out the cloche hat that she was wearing when she had gone running off. Nancy was backing up, getting closer to Peter. Just before them was a makeshift grave, adorned with a wooden cross. Broken pieces of a tiny coffin were strewn about the pine needles next to the hole in the ground appearing to be three feet deep as it was across. A name was carved into the cross. Peter's eyes had not adjusted yet.

Neville was spitting with exhilaration, "The dead shall rise, reminded they are merely a house to those recently released from the lonely dark, tapped on the shoulder by the claws of Hades, AWAKE, dear ones … there is a new shell for you … In the cloak of their coffins a knock came, in the form of radiating heat cast from above and the recently dead …"

"Nancy, what's going on?" Peter asked, the woods lit by the moon illuminating the mist into a frothing blue. A boulder had either fallen on this pine needled splotch of woods, smashing in all directions or a courtyard of rock outcroppings had formed from below as natural run off created the clearing. Objects were shimmering on the ground. Appearing like rocks with the exception that they were moving. Apple sized silver, green, yellow, orange and blue metallic glowing spiders with an odd armor were retreating to holes in the ground by the huge shale stone broken boulders.

"Come here …" Concerned for Nancy, Peter grabbed her hand. Were they all seeing this? He wondered. The trip was intensely bad otherwise.

Eyes adjusting to the dark, Peter looked to where the form of the woman stood. Warren was bent over now, there was a gargling sound in between whimpering. A sound like a lion humming. He could see the name "Cedric" on the wooden cross of what looked like a tiny grave that had been dug crudely.

"Devon...." Neville looked away from the book, to his brother. "We watched the TV... KDKA had everyone's attention, talking about The National Civil Defense headquarters in D.C. Remember? That jive about a satellite that was circling Venus ... The brass claimed they destroyed it! Big Daddy said NASA destroyed the incoming satellite due to high levels of radiation. You all dig?" Now he addressed everyone in the room.

The crowd was shaking their head, whether in the throes of coitus, drink, or like Devon, watching, listening for this to make sense. Most were shaking their head "No" disagreeing with the television reports, and agreeing with this sermon by Neville that they had heard before with prolific certainty.

"The Man Lied." A small chant began in whispers, indicating that what was reported on radio and television had been incorrect. A prophet from long ago had written the words that Neville held dear. The book in his hands was the only proof they required after witnessing the actual Hell on Earth.

"...only the unburied dead were affected, the man on TV said. But oh no ... no. Boys and girls we saw with our own eyes ... before the posse's took some control. We watched loved ones turn after a bite. We saw the dead rise with hunger from graves ... There is more. Our own, *Lara was special*. She came to us with child ... though it was never to be. Her child was born dead to us." Neville looked to the book with voracious eyes behind his thick lenses.

The woman was holding an infant, a newborn to be precise, though the light of the moon shone with inconsistencies. "Stand back, the boy is mine..." Lara looked crazed. Blood was pouring down her neck, her blouse ran with crimson. She was moaning with pain. Warren had fallen to the ground before her, blood gushing from a wound in his neck where something had gnashed at him, soaking the collar of his pea coat.

"No." Nancy understood now.

The *suck, suck, suck* sound coming from the infant in the woman's arms ceased. It turned its gray head, blue veins glowed vibrant in the moonlight now, with eyes blazing yellow at Peter and Nancy.

"That's her child. It was stillborn." Nancy whispered, shocked that the woman stood, dying, watching her own life fluid splash to the pine needles and mud.

"We have to kill it. Her too. She's crossing over." Peter noticed that Warren had ceased moving. It would be minutes before he too would rise. Instinctually, he reached for his belt where his .45 should have been, normally. Where were the other armed men that had followed them down here, he wondered. Both he and Nancy also wished their bags with their guns had not been taken from them when they arrived.

"PETER!!" Nancy shouted.

The woman and child began to approach, her eyes dead blue with moonlight, the baby's eyes yellow. Both mother and child hissed. The baby's arms outstretched toward them.

"Only the watchers, the spiders, would emerge from their lowly depths. These are the scouts who will choose the freshly dead newborn that they would honor with their venomous bites. Messengers of the deep, they are sent to breach the surface to choose a leader, one that would bring wisdom one day in his new legion on Earth as they evolve. Look to cracks in the earth, where ancient outcroppings burst to conjugate with the sky. The watchers show themselves nightly after the comet passes your skies." Neville lost in his own euphoric state broke from the reading.

Something moved out of the corner of his eye, just outside the window. The moon bounced off the river below the campgrounds, hitting the widows of the lodge. "Just the river," he thought to himself.

Devon ran to the sink to splash water on his face, breaking free of the circle of followers committing all manner of debauchery. Neville followed him to the sink. "Do you see? Lara's baby was born dead. We buried it yesterday. It did not rise yet, but I saw the spiders Devon. I saw the watchers coming to deliver their message. They chose Lara's son. Full of wisdom, strength, he will lead them all. I will inherit it all, as his adopted father." Neville's eyes were crazed, glasses hanging off his face.

Devon exhaled, enraged with his brother's insanity. "Read the rest of it. NEVILLE! Finish that paragraph! You say I never finished the book but I did finish that chapter, you fucking fool!" He shouted at him, knowing the words of the last paragraph.

"Awright, man, chill, ok. I got this." He went back to the end of the page he was previously reading. " … And as I am reborn through the human child, *all my legion* shall come to me, beguiled, enthralled by my light …" Neville looked outside, to the river below, just past the cabins. What he earlier perceived as rocks that lit blue with moon glow were actually heads, and now they were rising from the river to join the other living dead emerging from the woods. Shadows moving thicker than the blackness of the trees.

"Oh Shit."

When the horde broke through the windows in the back of the room, knocking down the unbolted side door, very few initially had noticed what was happening around them. Reaching orgasm in the throes of passion, jamming to the music, or under the spell of Neville's new form of window pane, not one of them was prepared as the rushing horde burst into the large common room, able to overpower the naked defenseless cluster of revelers. Wet, dripping bodies, some clothed, some naked as their prey, barged into the common room in such numbers from all angles that there had been no chance to scream. Most of the intoxicated mass did not know they were dying until their own blood was splashing the person under them. Devon saw Marly dragged out the front door by a half dozen creatures wearing business suits. Snappy and Go-Go Girl were smothered, dog piled by gnashing yellow jaws growling for a piece. Then the gargled screams.

Devon and Neville turned to the window above the sink as the horde was concentrating on the mass of people in the center of the room that they had all but torn to screaming shrapnel.

Neville was out the window on his feet when he came face to face with Peter and Nancy in the courtyard. There were living dead feasting on remains of some of the scouts. It was evident to Neville that help was not on the way. Half rotting bodies were tearing people apart in the courtyard, there were some guns among the bodies but too out of reach among the feasting creatures, lumbering from body to body, sometimes consuming all but bone so that the body would never be able to reanimate.

Devon hopped out next, rolled to the ground on top of a man being eaten by three boys dressed in Catholic School uniforms with big patches that read *The Chariots Comin' Boys Camp* embroidered on their shoulders. The undead children were growling like dogs as they pulled at the open abdomen of the dead guard. Their wretched skin was blue and cracking. They dragged the remains of the man away from the rest of the fray to consume on their own, ignoring Devon, briefly. Then their eyes lit up with the moon, acknowledging the man. Devon swiped a rifle from the ground, praying it was loaded.

It was! He pumped out shot after shot. "Go … Run!" Devon pointed to the garage with the flimsy rustic door at the other side of the courtyard.

"What do we do? You have vehicles right?" Peter shouted into the older man's face, holding Nancy's hand.

"Yes, follow Devon to the garage, there's a van." Neville stopped before keeping up with the others. He looked at the broken bodies shambling about, some lumbering in his direction, others still dragging his screaming worshippers out of the lodge.

"Wow. Huge oversight." Neville's mind was broken.

The keys were in the ignition. "Get in Nev! Do it!" Devon revved the engine. Peter closed the side door once Nancy and Neville were inside.

"Recognize this van?" Devon tried to focus on the pedal and steering wheel, his mind still foggy with the window pane speckled smoke.

"Yea, it's *Just Dan's* van." Nancy held her own stomach with one hand, crying, unable to concentrate on their current dilemma.

The van bolted forward, knocking the approaching dead, crunching others feasting upon the shrieking living victims pinned and squirming on the gravel.

"Dan works for me. He was supposed to pick up more the day he got you three. He brought Lara to me. Got a bonus that day." Neville sat in the passenger side, holding his head. "God that stuff is strong. Certainly will make getting through this night easier, haha. Where is Lara? I need to find her."

"There she is ..." Peter's wide eyes peered straight through the windshield. Lara loomed out of the forest to the left of the gravel road. Her white blouse beneath her oversized coat was stained with blood. She turned her head adorned with the cloche now stained a darker hue of crimson than the flower on the hat itself. In her arms, the infant had its mouth of sharp yellow teeth open as wide as its little tiny hands. Unlike its mother, it had yellow eyes so ungodly bright that they cut the distance between it and the approaching van.

"…and there she goes!" Devon plowed into the living dead mother and child reunion, a thump pounded off the grill of the blue van with the purple grim reaper on the side. Under the wheels came a pulpy *crush* compounding a *crunch* from the back end.

There was a shuffle in the back of the van. Peter looked over his shoulder. Under a mess of blankets, ash trays and cans of beer there seemed to be movement.

"Guys…"

"So, you had *Just Dan* … our Dan, meet us to begin with? Was he roving the countryside bringing you people, Nev? I mean really …" Devon was catching on.

"It's over now. Yea, he brought me Lara, and there were a few others, but they either left after a healthy birth … Not too many people getting funky these days." Neville turned to his brother as if he was talking about an old board game or favorite sports team they used to share, "You know, that guy that was interviewed during the early days, on TV, Dr. Grimes, that guy, talkin jive. He had said, and I quote, 'they're just dead flesh,' but they're not, Dev. Ole Malekyre' here, in his book, says it clear as blue cheer man." Neville was rambling while paging through the book. "No more room in Hell."

Devon was disgusted.

Neville was crying, feeling defeated. His head down in his lap peering at the book.

"Guys …" Peter's voice was quivering.

"Peter, *what?*" Nancy turned to touch her boyfriend's shoulder, rubbing his sweaty long hair.

Becoming furious, Devon shouted, "Did you abduct women for this … purpose? If so, people are going to know this van. There's enough people still trying to turn this shit around Nev! What were you …?" Devon's head was clearing from the drugs. Now on PA 43, on the road ahead he could see police cars, men with large hats, red and blue lights flickering. A posse.

"Timing! Looks like they were waiting for *Just Dan* to come back through." Devon could not help but smile at his brother's demise.

Then white hot pain shot from Devon's shoulder to his neck. He looked down to come right eye to left eye with Just Dan, only now his skin was pale going on blue. Dan's eyes blazed with hateful hunger. After the creature that was Dan leapt from the back of the van from under the blankets which he had died, Nancy had pulled Peter aside toward the side door. Just Dan landed on the back of the driver's seat and Devon instead.

Impulsively Devon's foot floored the van causing it to plow ahead. Chunks were being taken from his shoulder and neck while his ear had front row seats for the chewing. Within moments, the posse ahead opened fire on the van, thunderous holes blowing through the shattering windshield. Devon knew pain and then black.

Nancy awoke to the sound of a policeman's megaphone. Moving shadows surrounded her. Men speaking. She felt around, sat up, feeling a body laying to her left. Peter was sprawled out on the road next to her. He had broken her fall from the side door of the van when it swerved off the road. He looked serene, beautiful, laying there with his eyes closed, if not for the fresh gelatinous red bullet hole in his head.

"NO PETER ... NO!" She was screaming. Gasping. "Peter ... Oh no." Two officers picked her off the ground, dragging her away from Peter's body and the van. "I'll name him Peter, I promise, like we said." She wept in an officer's arms, before resuming screaming. "Let me say good bye ... let me ..."

Neville had his hands up in front of a circle of cops, while a man they all referred to as The Sheriff began interrogating him, shouting "Now why don't you listen when you are told to stop? Why the hell you traveling with one of these messed up goons?

HELLO?! I'm talking to you." The Sheriff was in Neville's face. "I didn't like you in the days before the dead, Neville Cordry, mucking up Zelienople with your drugs! Well it is irony that we heard a mass of them were coming this way … and now I get to save your dumb ass this far south! Get him outta my sight." The Sheriff shook his head, taking off his hat, he looked into the van.

"Looks like we got two squirmers in there. Burn it!"

COCAINE CONNIE
by Gary Lee Vincent

Gary Lee Vincent is an accomplished author, musician, and entrepreneur. In 2010, his horror novel DARKENED HILLS was selected as Book of the Year Winner by "ForeWord Reviews Magazine" and became the pilot novel for DARKENED – THE VAMPIRE SERIES, which includes the follow-up books DARKENED HOLLOWS, DARKENED WATERS, DARKENED SOULS and DARKENED MINDS (coming 2015). For series information, visit www.DarkenedHills.com. Gary was a contributing editor on THE BIG BOOK OF BIZARRO and WESTWARD HOES anthologies with fellow horror writer Rich Bottles Jr. He is also the creator of THE TAILSMAN book based on the story of the same name in WESTWARD HOES and is working on a second comic from the anthology titled DEMONEYE, written by David J. Fairhead. Gary is also author of the werewolf/bizarro thriller PASSAGEWAY.

I can't actually say I was pissed off when Connie called, but I must admit any phone calls at 2:30 am on some basic level can be unnerving. I typically don't get to bed until late anyway, but I had drifted off.

The yellowish rotary telephone rang incessantly on the wall and I knew I had to get out of my warm bed and trudge over to answer it because it showed no signs of stopping.

"Yeah, who is this?" I asked, not masking my displeasure, but not being a prick either.

"Uh… it's Connie," came a squeaky-mousey-type of voice on the other end. I knew several Connies, but she didn't need to say anything more for identification, because I knew who this particular Connie was. Never knew her last name, but I always referred to her in my mind as 'Cocaine Connie.' Why? Because she only calls when she needs blow.

"It's a little late to be calling, don't you think?" I asked, not really wanting to make small talk, but just feeling out the waters to have her at least state her business.

There was a deep, nasal draw on the other end. Sounded like she had a cold, but you never knew with her. She always seemed sick and unkempt, even when she was perfectly fine. "Baby, I know it's late, but I'm working a double down at the diner. All of us on the graveyard shift had to work over tonight – a bunch of strange shit going on."

"Really?" I asked skeptically. "If you don't mind, we can chit chat about the news some other time... unless there's *something else* you needed."

"Yea. Uh... I got paid earlier and could sure use a fix."

"You still at the diner?"

"Uh...ha. I'll be on break in thirty minutes. I need a pick-me-up or I won't make it through tonight's shift."

"You know how I feel about meeting at public places—" I had started to say.

"The Evans City Cemetery is just over the hill. It's pretty quiet. Maybe we could do the deal there, like a half hour from now. That's when I go on break. Baby I *need* it!"

"I suppose. Thirty minutes you say? How 'bout I meet you in 45 to give you time to get over there. How much you need?"

"I have $87.00 in my pocket. Whatever that gets me. Baby I'm jonesing right now, *please.*"

I looked at my watch – 2:35 am. "I'll see you in 45 minutes at the entrance to the cemetery. Don't be late."

"Uh... what time will that be?"

Fucking bitch, I thought to myself. *She better not keep me waiting.* "It's 2:35 now, so forty-five minutes from now will be 3:20 am – got that!?"

"Uh… yea… okay. I'll be there. Thanks, babe."

"Sure." *Whatever,* I thought as I hung up the phone.

Although I was upset with the call, business was business. I threw on my cleanest dirty clothes that were piled up in a recent ball in the hamper and headed out into the night with Connie's order.

I arrived at the gates of Evans City Cemetery about ten minutes early. It was dark and desolate, except for one lonely street light, barely putting off enough yellowish lumens with its sodium vapor bulb to see the cemetery's turnoff, which was fine with me. I had just turned off the engine to my 1967 Chevy Nova and cut my headlights when...

BAM! BAM! BAM!

I jumped.

Connie was pounding on my driver's side window, desperation in her eyes.

"Damn, woman! You scared the shit out of me!" I said disgustedly as I opened the door to greet her."

"I got to have it now!" Connie cried. "They think I'm on a bathroom break at the diner and I need to get back right away."

"What in the hell could be going on at that Podunk little diner? You surely can't be *that* busy tonight."

"Uh… ghouls. People are coming in scared. Said they saw ghouls and the radio is telling them to con-ga-gat—"

"You mean *congregate*?"

"Yea, that's what I said… Uh… they want them to congregate in public places."

"Ok," I simply said. It was obvious she must have been on something other than coke from the way she was talking. *Just sell her her fix and get the hell out of here,* my stone-cold sober mind decided. "Your package is in the trunk."

Connie never was a very good looker, but I could see from the dim street light that she looked worse than usual. Her frizzy red hair, oversized hands and feet, and hunchback were only emphasized by the shaky demeanor she was displaying this morning as she impatiently awaited her fix.

I unlatched the trunk and pulled out a small envelope and handed it to Connie. She handed me the cash. I barely got the trunk lid closed when she poured out the powder on the Nova's trunk and started doing lines right there on the spot!

"What the hell, woman?" I asked. "Can't you at least wait until you get back to work? Someone could drive by and catch us!"

"Fuck 'em." she said. "The white crosses are wearing off and I need this shit now!"

I watched in fascinated disdain as she quickly snorted all of the coke right before my eyes. "Connie, you're going to fuck yourself up—" I started to say, but before the words even left my mouth, she stumbled backward and fell into the road.

Shit!

"Connie, you okay?"

She was unconscious. Whatever else she was on… be it cheap trucker's speed or something else … already had her heart overworking and the coke just sent her the rest of the way to cardiac arrest.

"Connie!" I reached down and felt for a pulse. Nothing. *Mother fucker!*

My first reaction was to simply get in my car and drive away. A hundred different things were racing through my mind and no clear-cut solution seemed very good… or at least very humane.

As bad luck would have it, I could hear a vehicle approaching in the distance. *Can't get caught this way!* I thought. How would I explain a girl OD'd far away from her work? They'd put a murder rap on me for sure! I could try to hail down the car and act like I was helping her, but who the fuck would be out at this time of morning running around by the cemetery except a cop or someone *else* up to no good.

There were only a few seconds to react, but I drug Connie's body to the side of the Nova that was not facing the road and hid down, waiting for the vehicle to pass.

A pickup truck sped by, apparently unconcerned with the lonely Nova parked on the side of the road.

After waiting a few precious moments for the truck to return (or someone else to drive by, God forbid), I slid Connie's body over to some weeds. The best thing I could think of was to leave her there and get the hell out of here while the getting was good.

I ran over to the car and got in. I reached for the ignition and… no keys! *I had left them in the trunk lock!*

I got out and went to the back of the car.

Just then my blood ran cold.

Connie was there standing right at the trunk latch.

"Hey, you okay?" I said nervously. "You passed out on me."

Her eyes … something was wrong with her eyes. They had a lifeless look to them and although they were staring *at* me, I could not tell for sure that what she was seeing actually registered any inkling of recognition.

She did not reply with words, only came forward and started attacking me. She clawed and scratched for a few moments; we wrestled there on the trunk of the car. She began trying to bite me viciously, like a rabid dog. I kicked her in the stomach, momentarily knocking her into the tail of the car. She slid down to the ground.

I hadn't planned on fighting this bitch. *Fuck! She was getting back up!*

I quickly reached for the trunk lock to retrieve my keys and realized they were gone! They must have been dislodged from the lock during the struggle.

I am not one to fight a girl, but Connie took one hell of a blow and was shaking it off as if nothing happened.

I looked down, really hoping to see my keys, but it was too dark.

She hissed at me between deep, grunting breaths and came in for another round of attacks.

I punched her in the face and she did not even flinch. She lunged again, trying to bite me, and I kicked her again – this time in the legs, knocking her into the road where she first passed out.

It was here that I realized that I was no longer dealing with a human being but some sort of undead ghoul. Maybe some demon… some *thing* from beyond death. Perhaps this was some kind of judgment from God for dealing drugs.

Ghouls. People are coming in scared. Connie's words from only a couple minutes before sprung to my mind. However, I didn't have much time to dwell on monsters, morals, religion, or philosophical consequences. Connie was back up for round three.

I wasn't sure how fast she could run, but I knew I had to hightail it out of there, perhaps lose her in the cemetery and come back for my keys once she was off my tail.

The cemetery was very dark and I ran for about 200 yards before looking back. I hid behind a large tombstone and simply waited. Within a minute or so, I could hear Connie's weird, raspy breathing noises and realized she was coming right for the spot I was hiding.

I jumped up from behind my refuge and punched at the shadowy *thing* with my entire might. I hit pay dirt and my fist nailed the figure squarely in the throat. However, this was not Connie.

A large man in a tattered suit lay on the ground, quickly getting to his feet. It was very dark, but I could still make out what he was wearing and noticed that he too had that same blank-looking, lifeless eyes that Connie had.

Just as that thought crossed my mind, I felt something grab my shoulder and spun around to see Connie was back, trying to bite me. I blocked her arm and kicked hard at her closest knee, hoping I could impede her strides. I heard a loud 'snap' and was glad to know I must have broken a bone. *Take that you crazy ghoul-bitch!*

The man/ghoul was back with arms outstretched. I took off running again, my mind scrambling as to how in the hell I could get out of this predicament.

The answer came as I noticed a small building... a chapel or mausoleum (couldn't make out what it was exactly in the dark) just up a ways a bit.

I ran for that as hard as I could, thinking that if I could only get away from my pursuers, I could hole up in the building and wait them out. Perhaps they would leave after a while.

When I got to the small building I noticed it had small, wooden arched doors, the kind you would see on any given country church. I yanked at the door and found it was locked. Knowing that my life might very well depend on me getting the door open, I yanked at the door with all of my adrenaline-fueled might and felt it spring loose from the jam.

I swiftly entered the structure, closing the door behind me and hoping with desperation that those *things* had not seen me enter.

I felt for a light switch but could not easily find one. The place was pitch-black and devoid of any windows. Most churches and chapels have some sort of windows, so this building must be a tiny mausoleum. I decided not to try to walk around being that I did not have anything to light my way, but instead simply sat down with my back against the door and waited.

A few minutes passed and my heartbeat began to beat more regularly. I closed my eyes to listen to what might be outside. Perhaps I could hear them approach—

Suddenly, I realized I was not alone. Sniffing and scratching sounds were coming from *inside* the mausoleum. *Holy shit! Holy fucking shit!*

I reopened the door and saw Connie and her "friend" were waiting at the threshold. They were joined by roughly ten or so others huddling outside – staring with the same sightless eyes, mad determination and desperate hunger.

Suddenly, decaying hands grabbed me from behind just as Connie and the ghouls pushed through the door.

I was doomed.

END SCENE
by David C. Hayes

David C. Hayes is an author, performer and filmmaker. His films, like A MAN CALLED NEREUS, DARK PLACES and THE FRANKENSTEIN SYNDROME (and approximately 70 more) can be seen worldwide. He is the author of several novels, collections and graphic novels including CHERUB, CANNIBAL FAT CAMP, KEEPING MOLLY, AMERICAN GUIGNOL, SCORN and MUDDLED MIND: THE COMPLETE WORKS OF ED WOOD, JR. while his short work has graced many anthologies, magazines and journals. David's full-length and one-act plays have been produced from coast to coast with a run Off-Broadway for the comedy SWAMP HO and sell-out performances in Phoenix for DIAL P FOR PEANUTS (winning a 2011 Ethingtony for Best Show). When not creating, David teaches film production, creative writing and communications and speaks frequently at book signings, comic conventions and gatherings of geek-culture.

"Jesus H. Christ, cut!"

The whirring of the Panavision camera slowly tapered off as Robert Crone, hack filmmaker and exploitive genius, stalked from behind the camera and onto the set. The crew shrunk back into the shadows as far as they could to avoid the oncoming tirade. Crone had been in a foul mood for approximately the last forty years, but things had become more and more desperate in the last few. 1968 was proving to be another clunker of a release schedule and there was only so much money the studio could afford to lose and that meant Crone was on the chopping block.

And when Crone was on the chopping block, everyone was on the chopping block. Especially the actors, or as Crone lovingly referred to them, "the talking meat." All of this culminated in the great director's current fury on the set of *Vampire Lust Goddess*, an average Crone film derivative of the genre fare that had made him quite a bit of money in the early 1960s.

He pushed his way through the ring of druidic cult extras and onto the sacrificial altar set (the same one used for *Cannibal Sacrifice*; times were certainly tough) and stood eye to nipple with Faye Worthington, ingénue du jour (real name Penelope Flossom) and current Crone Girl. She was suspended by her arms above the altar and corn syrup blood dripped down her fine, naked body and pooled in her pubic hair. The casting process insured that Crone was quite familiar with that entire region and this was business.

"Awww, c'mon Bobby! What'd I do wrong?" Faye whined, the awkward plastic vampire teeth muffling her a bit.

"Wrong? Nothing, baby. You didn't do anything wrong... you are just horrible!" Crone shot back.

That hung there, thick as fog. The druidic extras shuffled nervously and none of the crew emerged from the relative safety of the darkened studio outside the lit set.

The silence was broken by a single sniffle from Ms. Worthington. This escalated quickly and, in under ten seconds, she was in the middle of a full-blown episode complete with tears, caterwauling and histrionics.

Crone threw up his hands and headed off set toward the office. "Cut her down. Take fifteen. Fuck that, break for lunch."

No one mentioned that it was only nine in the morning as the crew swooped in, lowering Ms. Worthington (soon to go back to Flossom, one would suppose) to the ground, noting that Crone must be getting soft. In the flush years he would have let her swing through lunch.

Crone entered the small office and slammed the door behind him. He was in his seat with a bottle of Old Granddad whiskey to his lips in record time.

"Jesus H. Christ," he said to himself. Not out of any kind of belief, but because it just sounded appropriate.

Crone glanced up at the walls of the office. Lurid exploitation film posters marked the walls. Each of them more successful than the last. *Vampegeddon, Blood Orgy of the Damned, Desert Man-Beast,* and so many more reflected Crone's successes over the previous decade, but things were different now. Just a few years ago, the average mouth-breathing American could turn on the nightly news and see a war. A real, life or death, war playing out on their TV screen and Crone had struggled to keep pace. The kids that went in droves to see *Werewolf Gym Teacher* in droves at the drive-in in 1959 were not the teenagers of today.

Crone knocked back another shot and went immediately to the gallows humor. Most of those kids are dying on that TV screen right now, he thought. How could he compete with that? Naked vampires? Bright red corn syrup and pantyhose filled with cotton? Blood and guts were the new American dinner conversation.

A knock on the door went ignored at first. Another shot. Another knock. Crone sighed.

"Go the fuck away!"

"Sir! This is important."

Muffled by the door, his assistant's voice sounded urgent. Marlene knew not to interrupt him, so what kind of bullshit was this?

Sighing again, Crone stood and opened the door. Standing before him was Marlene. Usually mousy and bright, her big glasses magnifying her eyes to epic proportions, she was no looker (according to Crone). She just stood there, tears streaming down her cheeks. She held a transistor radio up.

"What the hell is this, Marlene…"

"Just listen," she hissed. Crone was taken aback, Marlene was never this direct. When he did take a minute to hear the news broadcast from the radio, the whole world changed for Crone. All at once.

"... again. We must report the unbelievable. It seems, no it is true, it is real, that dead people. People formerly dead have come back to life and are eating the living. This level of mass psychosis or... dear God, I don't know what to call this. The station doesn't want me to tell you this, but... it is the end of times, listeners. The dead walk. The Lord Himself will soon walk the Earth and we..."

Crone slowly wrapped his hand around Marlene's and shut the radio off. Without a word he turned toward the posters and toasted them with the bottle of Old Granddad. Robert Crone didn't really believe he had just listened to the preamble of the End of the World, but he was pretty sure this would be the end of his world. A war was bad enough, how could he compete with living dead cannibals?

Another shot and *Vampire Lust Goddess* stopped production. The world itself went to hell but there was a reason people called Robert Crone the Hollywood Cockroach. He would not go quietly into that night. He would not say die. He was not through exploiting anything he could his hands on.

Six months into the worldwide crisis and Robert Crone finally figured out what he needed to do. He would simply give the people a spectacle. Something they couldn't see out their windows or on their TV screens. He would give them real cinema.

The idea came innocently enough. Los Angeles was a nexus for this zombie, or whatever you called it, outbreak. The concentration of people, filth and an absolute disregard for one another was the perfect formula for the contagion to be very virulent. It wasn't uncommon to see violent clashes between a shambling wreck of a human being and something that used to be dead at any given point in one's day. Sometimes you couldn't tell the combatants apart without a program. Crone was careful, though, and protected himself as he went to and from the studio, trying desperately to get things going again. He noticed that these creatures didn't really feel pain. They were oblivious, like hippies, and only went down with a bit of head trauma. The idea gestated as he tried, in vain, to recoup the losses from shutting down *Vampire Lust Goddess* and then, like a little bit of head trauma of his own, it hit him.

Don't work against the system ... work with it. Crone couldn't believe he had forgotten the golden rule that started him in the business. *Don't swim upstream, you asshole*, he berated himself after coming to THE conclusion.

The film industry was impacted by the global crisis, of course, but you can't kill that beast either. No matter the tragedy and no matter the continent spanning horrors the world faced, everyone still had a couple of bucks to forget about life for a while. The problem, like before, was not being able to trump real life. Crone spent all of his time after the outbreak trying to get to that epiphany that would change his fortunes.

It finally came in the guise of Penelope Flossom, of all people.

Crone pulled into the lot of the small offices he rented after being forced from the studio. He deftly dodged a couple of the dead headers but his mouth dropped as another one of them shambled from the darkness of the alley next to the office building. He knew what he should do. The living all across the country adapted to the presence of the living dead fairly well. It was an odd arrangement but it worked. School curriculums added advanced physiology and outdoor survival classes and each of them stressed using the "head shot" to take out the enemy. The enemy, of, course, were the dead and the good guys were alive. So, men women and children had taken to the streets disposing of as many dead as they could find. This is what Crone was working toward and he trained diligently. He turned the car and pointed the headlight directly at the dead head coming out of the alley.

He stared at the blood-ridden figure and realized it was Penelope Flossom. Fucking Penelope Flossom, Vampire Lust Queen and shitty actress. Crone's foot strayed from the gas to the brake. He stared at the thing that was Penelope. Barely recognizable, the tell-tale sign for Crone were the dead head's tits. Unmarred, even though they were that strange gray color, the dead head still possessed a magnificent rack. The rack that got her the part in *Vampire Lust Queen*... literally. Any number of young, up and coming actresses had straddled Robert Crone to advance their careers, but very few had done so with perfect breasts. He sighed. Even though he didn't give a shit, really, about anyone on the planet, HE still had to live there and another dead head out of the picture just made things safer, perfect tits or not.

He gunned the engine and the big Mercury leapt forward and smack dab into Penelope Flossom. The impact was brutal. Probably due to the decomposition, her body flew apart in an odd manner. Her torso, complete with tits (giving Crone a last look), slid across the windshield as if it were surfing on grape jelly. Arms and legs separated at the shoulders and hips respectively and her head, teeth still gnashing, flew through the air and landed behind the car. Crone heard it crack open like a pumpkin and watched it explode in his rear-view mirror. He smiled, despite the fact it was Penelope, and thought, "Shit. If we could only pull that off on screen. What a freaking picture!"

The epiphany. Right then. Right there. Akin to discovering the power of juxtaposition in the Kuleshov Effect or Edison's brain child and first film studio, The Black Maria, Crone had just changed the film industry for good. It had to be him, though. He needed to keep this a secret and get something shot ... fast.

Crone knew how the infernal business worked. Labor wasn't his issue; there were hundreds of actors waiting for that "big break" where they could get the right exposure and get picked up on a big studio film. Shake a palm tree and they would fall out in droves. So he had his cast. Crone was wise enough to keep the Panavision close at hand and hidden from creditors. Camera, check. Crew? Hell, you couldn't go ten feet in this town without running into competent film professionals, and all he had to do was avoid the union. Check.

The hard part was getting his new stunt team.

Marlene had stuck it out with him through the "plague," the blackballing... all of it. She even stuck it out through that unfortunate paternity case from a few years back concerning the potential Robert Crone, Jr. and the lead actress from his biggest moneymaker, *Blood of the Cannibal God.* There was another pair of tits that could sink ships and Marlene was there through it all.

Crone knew she was in love with him. Or, at least, the idea of him. Film producer. Dream maker. She was a bit mousy and flat for his tastes and there was never a big enough storm for him to sail into that port, but she held that torch high and worked her ass off in the meantime. He knew if he got together with Marlene her work would suffer and he didn't know how to do anything but make movies. She managed everything else.

And she was great bait. It only took Crone a minute or two to convince Marlene that she was the only way his new plan would work, which wasn't a lie, and they found themselves on Sunset. This particular section of the city was a hotbed for dead head activity and Crone knew that putting a perfectly edible, helpless young woman in the middle of the street would attract dead heads like flies.

It was dangerous, yes, but he felt quite comfortable behind the wheel of his Mercury. The headlights played across Marlene's shivering body as she stood in the street, scanning furtively back and forth. The police rarely came this way anymore and the dead heads had really taken root. There wasn't even any power on this side of the city.

It didn't take long for the first of them to peel out from the shadows. Walking on broken legs and stumps and hands and whatever made them mobile, a pack of dead heads slowly approached the girl.

"Mr. Crone!" Marlene screamed out.

Crone flashed the headlights, communicating to Marlene to stay in place and stay with the plan.

The dead heads stepped closer. Robert was nearly close enough to hear the moans and smell the stench of death. Crone wasn't sure how long he could put up with it and mentally made a note to get Marlene some flowers.

Crone waited until the last possible second. Just as the dead heads were ready to bury their faces into Marlene, Crone laid on the horn. Deep and powerful, the blast of sound startled Marlene and, better yet, got the attention of the shambling hoard of the dead.

The herd turned, distracted, and Marlene bolted from them and toward the Mercury. As she slipped into the car breathing heavily, Crone leaned on the horn one more time.

A group of production assistants from Cal Berkley working on degrees in film and in need of screen credit burst out from behind the Mercury. With phone books strapped to their bodies, the howling students moved in unison carrying a wind of chicken wire and flanked the group of dead heads.

Like they had practiced, the students deftly avoided the teeth and nails of the dead (or they deflected off of the phone books). Crone squealed in glee as the production assistants wrapped up five of the dead heads and dragged them back toward the Grand Marquis.

From the safety of the Mercury, Crone popped the trunk and one of the largest American cars ever made was soon filled to the brim with five emaciated, shambling corpses. Once the trunk was closed, the production assistants dispersed back into the shadows, per instructions, to rendezvous at the studio.

Crone sat back in the seat and smiled contentedly. Marlene, still shaking, turned to Crone.

"That was the scariest thing I have ever done!"

Crone nodded. He looked up and smiled, taking Marlene's cheek in his hand. She pushed into his touch, honored.

"And you were great," he said. "Just a few more trips and we'll have the whole cast."

Tears welled in Marlene's eyes. "A few more trips?"

Crone paced back and forth. The lights were set up in the studio. Big, bright HMI's that made the dingy joint look like an All-American living room complete with great big TV and complementing tables for watching and eating dinner at the same time. It reeked of normalcy and Crone managed a smile.

Marlene approached, breathless. She looked up at Crone and nodded.

He took a deep breath and cupped his hands around his mouth.

"OK, people! We are only going to have one take at this! Once we get the cast in place we need to rock and roll, you got me?!"

A chorus of "yesses" and "yups" echoed in the chamber. Crone turned to his cinematographer.

"Roll camera."

"Speed."

Crone turned to the left and barked into the shadows. "Roll sound!"

"Sound speed."

Crone took another deep breath and called out toward the set. "Bring 'em in!"

From the back of the studio three dead heads shambled forward. They were dressed in average American wardrobe:

middle class father, mother and daughter. The make-up crew had done a spectacular job working on the corpses. Relatively fresh, the dead heads looked alive and kicking.

Three grips, each holding a pole with a looped rope end, commonly used for maneuvering dangerous animals, guided the dead heads to the large, paisley couch and sat them down. The dead heads struggled, but the burly film grips, used to a life of hauling cable and lights, managed to get them in place. Mother, Father and Daughter in front of the television set.

The dead heads gnashed their teeth and lurched forward, trying to get to the fresh meat beyond the lights, but the poles held fast.

Tentatively, Marlene stepped in front of them, just out of reach of the grasping arms. She held the clapper, the slate, in front of the camera. It read, "Title - All-American Horror / Director – Robert Crone / Camera – Richard Angst." She shook and jumped every time one of the dead heads swiped at her.

"Hold that steady, Marlene!" Crone called from behind the camera.

Marlene nodded and held it up. She opened the clapper. "*All-American* scene twenty-two, take one." She slapped the slate together with a loud CLACK (so the sound could synch up with the picture) and scooted to relative safety behind the camera.

"All right. Home Invader, take your position!" Crone called out.

The Home Invader, the villain of the masterpiece, took a position next to camera right. Even wearing a ski mask, everyone on set could see just how nervous he was. He danced from foot to foot, eager to get the scene shot and done with. The machete he carried, real metal for this shot, gleamed in the light from the set.

"Let 'em loose and ACTION!" Crone barked.

In a flash the roped poles were loosened from the necks of the dead heads. Being deceased severely affects one's motor skills and the Home Invader leapt into the scene from off camera and brandished the machete before the family could even lurch off the couch.

Like they had rehearsed (with cantaloupe), the Home Invader hacked into the head of each of the family members. Father, then Mother, then Daughter all fell to his blade. He made sure to get each of them right between the uprights first and quell any danger that the dead heads posed to the rest of the cast and crew. After that, every hack, slash and chop was purely an aesthetic choice.

Crone sat behind the camera, mesmerized. Before him one of the vilest and most disgusting scenes in cinema history played out. It was visceral. The Home Invader, character actor and good friend Dick Milligan, swung the blade from side to side, high and low. The Father's jaw separated in a wash of gore and black ichor. The Mother had both arms removed like some decaying Venus. The Daughter caught most of Milligan's attack, being the closest to him, and he nearly cleaved her right in two with the initial strike. This was a cathartic moment for Milligan since he had lost most of his family in the initial wave of dead heads. He had jumped at the role.

Stage blood ran like rivers from the crevices in the family's heads. The make-up department noticed early on that the natural blood had coagulated and, therefore, the things were pretty dry inside. Crone had thought long and hard. He wanted to give the audience reality... the most real reality they had ever seen but if he kept it too real they would think it was some fake-o attempt at horror. He made the command decision to fill the dead heads brain pans up with stage blood, nearly a gallon each, and boy was he happy he did. The set soon looked like some kind of strange modern art done only in reds and blacks.

Milligan was still hacking away and sobbing into the ski mask when Crone ended the scene.

"Cut!" Robert yelled. The whir of the Panavision stopped and the cinematographer sat back in his chair. Nearly everyone stood down, except for Milligan. He continued to hack his way into the dead head family, yelping as he did so and crying out the name of his own daughter who had perished that first day.

Crone considered yelling cut again but didn't. He'd let the crew take fifteen and Don could take out the rest of his anger on the blood-soaked couch and whatever pieces of the dead heads were left.

"Take fifteen!" Crone yelled and gave the thumbs up to Marlene indicating that she could go, too. He sat and watched Don Milligan get himself right. The man chopped and chopped, sobbing and sniffling, the snot running over the knit fabric of the ski mask, until he couldn't move his arms. Milligan dropped to his knees, splashing in the pool of gore he had just created, and dropped the machete. He sobbed, his body heaving with the enormity of it all. Finally, he raised his head toward the burning lights of the studio and wailed … and then collapsed. Every ounce of strength had left his body and he was spent.

Crone stood and walked over to Milligan, helping him up and pulling the ski mask off.

"Robert," Don managed, "they dead yet?"

Crone smiled and nodded. "Yeah, buddy, they're dead. Go have a smoke and we'll do it again in a bit."

Milligan managed a crooked smile. "Thank you, buddy."

Crone slapped his pal on the back and pushed him toward the door. "My pleasure," he answered and smiled. Milligan was so amped up to get some payback he was doing this below scale. Not only was Crone saving money and doing things that had never been legally committed to film before, he didn't have to deal with any unions or prima donnas. And, at the same time, he was helping the community by getting rid of the dead heads. Win fucking win. It took everything Crone had not to cry out in joy. "Keep it cool, cat," he said to himself, "and get everything ready for the next shot."

With a spring in his step for the first time in months, Crone snatched the shooting script off of the floor and paged through. This was going to be a long shoot and he squealed with glee as the maintenance crew swooped onto the set to get the area ready for the next scene.

The next sixteen hours flew by in a blur of gore. Crone took the opportunity to commit to film every atrocious act he could think of and, best of all, it was absolutely budget neutral. Marlene only threw up a few times and the crew seemed to genuinely enjoy themselves. There was, virtually, a never-ending supply of "stunt players" as the living cast and crew had taken to calling the dead heads.

Robert watched in absolute joy as he bashed in heads, sawed off limbs... any manner of debauched death was possible. He actually had a child drawn and quartered. The little boy couldn't have been more than twelve years old when he died the first time. He strapped an old woman to the floor of the studio's garage and ran over her legs, listening to the crunch and crack of brittle bones. The post-production house would insert the screams later but Robert had no problem imagining them.

The story of the film wasn't anything to really write home about. Crone had dusted off an old script, one he had put together years before. Random acts of violence being visited upon ostensibly normal, average Americans would translate to millions at the drive-in. Who wouldn't go and see the awful potential fates that all Americans shared, shivering in their cars and cathartically screaming at the fate of the dead head cast. In all its gory glory, *All-American Horror* would show the world the terror of simply living and Robert Crone would be a millionaire. Even despite the mediocre script.

It was that mediocre script, though, that proved to be Crone's undoing. Written in 1964 in a booze and pot-fueled haze, *All-American Horror* was dutifully scooped up by Marlene after getting Crone into the shower and sent off to the Writer's Guild for registration. The Guild registration automatically renewed each year with a rubber stamp and a check from Marlene. She did this for all Robert's scripts, and that included 1968. So, when the film went into production, Marlene submitted the report to the Guild and corresponding authorities. Marlene was incredibly efficient, after all.

Crone fell asleep in his office, content and happy for the first time in many months. He had released the cast and crew for their eight hour break. They had an eight a.m. call time and he wanted to get back to it fast. As Crone slumbered, though, Hollywood did not.

In a rare move, the International Brotherhood of Electrical Workers Local 45 in a team-up with United Scenic Artists Local 829 sent three members each to visit Crone's studio. In an effort to fly fast and free, Crone didn't utilize any union labor. Not a one. Not the Screen Actors Guild, International Society of Cinematographers... no one. The rough stuff fell to the IBEW and USC. The electricians enjoyed the help from their set design and lighting brethren and after the tip from the Writer's Guild it was a forgone conclusion: *All-American Horror* needed to be shut down.

The big secret about the film was still a little cloudy and the usual crowbar and fire ax entrance method to the rear of the studio resulted in a pretty bad scene. Hell bent on breaking lights and cameras, the union members did not expect to walk, literally, into a pack of 20 dead heads who were not so patiently waiting for their close-up.

The undead tore into the electricians, gaffers, best boys, grips, scene painters, set designers and the rest. Most of them had laughed at one point over a beer or two about how this town would eat you alive if you didn't manage to get into the union. Luckily, the dead couldn't taste the irony and once they chewed their way through the invading force, they stepped out into the night and around sides of the building and headed for the front office.

The screams, shouts and moans rocked Crone awake. He sat straight up and knew, just knew, that some shit had hit the fan. Maybe it was some kind of preternatural sixth sense developed as he swindled and scratched for film budgets, but he knew something was wrong.

Unfortunately for Crone, he figured it out just a minute too late. The door to the front office burst in and standing before him were the stars of *All-American Horror*. Crone swallowed hard and looked around. There was only one way in or out. This was it.

The cast lurched forward and Crone ran to the corner of the office. Every evening they would drag the Panavision into the office for safekeeping instead of keeping it on the set. He pulled it out, got it turned on and made sure there was a full mag loaded.

With a deep breath, Crone stepped forward and in front of the camera. He made sure there was enough light to register an image and he had just enough time to raise his arms as the first of the dead heads dove into him.

"Action…" Crone managed to gasp out as the others joined in. They feasted like Crone was craft service accompanied by the whir of the camera.

Variety reported that *All-American Horror* grossed nearly three million dollars upon its wide release in the United States. Producer Marlene Simmons was quoted praising the film's auteur, Robert Crone, in a press release. She said, "He gave everything to this film and we're just happy we could honor his memory with its release."

Simmons has signed on to produce three sequels and there has been some interest from Charlton Heston to take over the role of Robert Crone.

ELIZABETH'S STORY
by Rachel J. Montgomery

Rachel Montgomery was born in Lansing, and grew up in both the Midwest and the Northeast. She began writing stories in elementary school and signed with her Literary Agent John White when she was 21. Her short stories, poems, and one short memoir appear in the Elm City Review and Trumbull Arts' Commission literary magazine. She completed a Writing Internship with best-selling author Adriana Trigiani and worked as a Research Assistant to Stephen Spignesi for his books, GROVER CLEVELAND'S RUBBER JAW and THE TITANIC FOR DUMMIES. She received a Masters' Degree in English from Oakland University and two Bachelor's Degrees in English and Art from University of New Haven. She currently resides in Michigan with her fiancée and four cats.

I had the list in my hand. Twenty women in my dorm building and ten in my anthropology class signed it. I looked through their names and mailing addresses, written in loopy calligraphy that puts mine to shame. After the break, I'd respond to them in my pointy chicken-scratch, which reminded me of Ms. Bovine in fourth grade, who told me my writing reminded her of a wicked witch.

I planned on sending them information on the first-ever Women's Consciousness Raising Committee on campus- where to go, what time, and most importantly, to remind them of the question we were all there to answer: how, as a woman, do you feel oppressed in your life and how can we as sisters end chauvinism?

I would get the details down after the summer. For now, as I packed my things, I dreamt of another road trip.

"I don't get it," my roommate Jan scoffed as she packed her skirts and dresses to go home for summer break. "How exactly and why exactly, am I supposed to feel oppressed?"

"You're not supposed to, that's the point," I said, sitting in the middle of the box-spring twin mattress and resisting the temptation to sit cross-legged; the hems of my jeans were soaked from the walk back to the dorm through the puddles.

"Then why talk about it?" she retorted, folding some of her socks. She adjusted her headband and looked up at me. "I just don't understand. I'm a woman; I love being a woman. I have loving parents, a loving family and a loving boyfriend who's driving me home in an hour to ask my father if he can marry me! I'm getting a nice home and a nice family just like I always dreamed of! How is that oppression?"

"What about your degree?" I put the list aside, planted my hands on the mattress and raised my legs up and down. When they were up in the air, the puddles that clung on sunk the hemlines well past my ankles. "What about Jan the Oceanographer, or Jan the Actress, or Jan the-"

"There's no law saying I still can't be these things! They just go on hold for a while as I raise a family and tend to the home. Really, I think you're overreacting."

"I don't think I am. What if you wanted to finish your degree before you had kids? What if you wanted to wait to get married before establishing a career for yourself?"

"Maybe I could, but I don't want to?"

"Were you ever encouraged to?"

Jan rolled her eyes and threw the last of her stuff in her bag. "Look, if you feel enslaved as a women or something, OK, but I still don't get it. Maybe once you get back to your family over the summer, you can talk about your grievances with them."

"I'm not going back there for the summer," I exclaimed. "Me and the rest of the SDS gang are going on another trip."

"Whereabouts this time?"

'I dunno. We might go back to California, maybe follow a band around," I cracked a smile. "You should consider going."

"What? And leave Johnny hanging?"

"Well, you can both come!"

Jan rolled her eyes. "It's just... not how things are done. Hey, do you mind helping me bring some stuff downstairs? I'd wait for Johnny, but Old Eagle-Eyes won't let him up."

I grabbed a duffle bag and walked with her downstairs. Old Eagle-Eyes, the dorm matron, made her way down the hall with her clipboard and perpetual scowl under her thick cat-eye glasses and thicker dark eyebrows.

"Did you let her know you weren't leaving until tomorrow?" Jan asked.

"Yeah," I said as I hauled the bag downstairs. "She scowled at me and wrote it on her board."

We reached the bottom of the stairs and opened the door. Johnny's '67 Chevy stood waiting for us in all its red and white glory. He leaned against, it, waiting to greet Jan with a kiss. She offered him a peck on the cheek and a quick hug.

"So get this," he grinned. "Some loons downstate are biting people."

"What?"

"Yeah, a bunch of people are walking around, scaring the living shit out of everyone else."

"What a horrible thing to do!" Jan cried. I raised an eyebrow.

"Don't worry babe," he said to Jan. "Sheriffs will take care of everything. Probably some nutty cult."

"Where did you hear about it?" I asked him.

"All over the radio. Here." He started the car and cranked the stereo. After twizzling the dial past a Patsy Kline and then a Stones song, he got a station with some talking...traffic. He turned the dial again and cranked it:

"... *Just received word that more have been spotted along the interstate near the hospital. Dispatch sent out some state troopers to look into the issue. Authorities remind everyone to remain calm. The situation is being handled and there is nothing to worry about.*"

"Is this a joke?" I asked, amused.

"Shh!" Jan put a finger to her lips.

"*Breaking: authorities are on their way to Memorial Hill Cemetery to respond to a call about a similar disturbance. Apparently, a young couple was attacked on their way to a honeymoon. The wife made her way to a telephone booth down the road and made a distress call...*"

"This has to be a hoax." I rolled my eyes.

"Come on, man, it's the *radio!* They wouldn't lie about this stuff on the radio."

"Maybe it's a serial broadcast?" I shrugged my shoulders.

"SHHHHH!!!!!"

"*Authorities are expected to apprehend all suspects within the hour, as they are slow-moving and easily catchable. Until then, we once again, urge listeners to remain calm and report any suspicious activity...*"

"See?" Johnny said, ruffling Jan's hair. "It'll all be taken care of within the hour. Let's go back inside and..."

Just ahead of the Chevy, a man strolled towards us. He had a funny gait and hunched over so much, that I thought he would topple over.

"Do you think he's injured?" Jan asked with some concern. Johnny shook his head and called out: "Hey! You there. Need some help?"

My breath became more controlled. From far away, I made out the contours of the man's face. His blank expression was uncanny, but intent. He strode closer, passing the birch tree just some yards away from the driveway. He seemed intent on reaching us, but gave no signal back to Johnny that he understood a word he said. *This might still be a joke,* I told myself, *a big, stupid prank. It's most likely the result of some chain letter going around.*

"Maybe he doesn't speak English, or he's deaf," Jan said, waving her arms.

"Stop it!" I snapped.

They turned on me.

"Come on, man! Have a heart," Johnny said. "This poor guy's obviously in some trouble."

"No, I think he's crazy," I said, backing away. *He looks like a patient I saw at Sunnyside,* I thought. As I inhaled, formaldehyde smell shot up my nose, taking me back to dissecting cats in science. "We should get inside, or get in the car and drive."

The man hobbled closer. His skin was pale and waxy and looked as if it were about to melt. Apparently, he was trying to speed up, but couldn't run. Maybe he was just injured...but then...even as Jan and Johnny's hands waved in the air and they cried, "Hey! Hola! Bonjour! Can you hear us?" he never responded.

I grabbed Jan's arm. "Come back in, *please!*" I whimpered.

Johnny smiled. "Oh look, she thinks it's one of those nutty people biting everyone," he laughed. Grinning, he yanked me by the scruff of my neck and pushed me forward. "Hey bite-man!" He called. "Here's a victim for 'ya!"

The man stepped over the driveway and as I stumbled forward, he lunged.

I dove away from the thing in man's clothes. Heart pounding, I raced back to my dorm. Jan screamed in the distance. Too scared to look behind, I threw the door open and closed, pulling my weight against it. I looked through the small window. The zombie was on her, pinning her arms down as she convulsed. Blood poured form under her neck. Johnny opened the trunk and grabbed a crowbar. Roaring for help, he emerged from the car and began beating the strange man, bludgeoning his head as Jan's screams began to die and turn into gasps.

He knocked the man off her. I believed him unconscious. I turned to go to the phone, but I heard Johnny wail: "Jan! Jan! Oh, God, no!"

I looked in fear at Johnny bawling over Jan's limp corpse. The man, the one I thought he beat unconscious, rose to his feet.

"Look out!" I screamed, but it was too late. The man fell on top of Johnny, knocking the crowbar out of his hand.

I took the chair by the door and slammed it against the entrance. Running down the hall, I shouted! "Anyone and everyone! Murder! Murder! Lock your doors! *Murder*!" I raced for the phone and rotary dialed 0. As the circular disc made its way back around, Old Eagle Eyes stormed down the hallway. Her clipboard chopped the air beside her stiff, floral dress and her cat-eye glasses made her look even angrier.

"Operator, how can I help you?"

"Police. Murder. A man jumped on my friend and bit her. He killed her! Get the police, please!"

"Simons," Eagle Eyes barked. "What in the hell is going on?!"

"Jan's dead. Murdered. Man wandered." I tried not to sob as the operator hooked me up to the police. Eagle Eyes snatched the phone away. Down the hall, girls who were still in the dorms emerged. Some looked puzzled. For others, the color was drained from their faces."

"Yes, officer, I am the dorm matron. One of my girls ran down the hallway, white as a sheet, rambling about murder. Apparently, she discovered her dorm mate dead in her room,"

"Not in her room," I gasped. "Outside. On the driveway."

A couple girls on the left side of the dorm went back in their rooms. Their windows had a view of the drive. A girl screamed, then another. Eagle Eyes' thick lips pursed, becoming a tiny hole in her mouth as her eyes under her glasses widened. "Apparently, other girls see the disturbance, too. A girl was murdered on the lawn in front of our building.... Mailer Hall... yes, the university. Please come right away... Her name was Jan Tack.... Five-two, I'd say. Short, brown hair, brown eyes, no glasses... Supposed to be leaving today for home. Her dorm mate found her on the lawn... I do not know, she came in very distressed. Screaming."

"She's getting up!" Someone cried.

Eagle-Eyes' nostrils flared. "Apparently, Ms. Tack has been cured of dying." She glowered at me and pointing a long, withered finger in my face mouthed: *I'll deal with you later.*

"Could someone tell me if Ms. Tack appears hurt."

"She's stumbling to get up," someone called. "There's a lot of red stuff around her neck."

"That's blood, you idiot!" Another girl yelled.

"Ladies!" Eagle-Eyes screamed. "Apparently, some of the girls are saying she is injured... I'm tied to the phone and there are no windows to the scene near me."

"Who are they?" Another girl called.

"There are more people," Eagle-Eyes said into the phone. "I cannot see how many more, I am not near a window! I... I am remaining calm! *Idiots,*" she muttered away from the receiver.

"They're trying to get in, but the door's blocked!" Someone said.

"Don't let them in!" I wailed.

My plea was ignored. One of the girls flounced out of her dorm, glaring at me. She walked to the door and announced, "There's a chair blocking the way! It's stuck! Could someone help me?"

As volunteers rushed to get the door unbarred, I ran out through the fire door back into the open. Alarm bells' tintinnabulation and the faint sound of spraying water hitting the linoleum hallway floor made a chorus, joining the sound of girls' screams. As Eagle Eyes bellowed for order, the fire door slammed.

The day was clear and there was no sign of anyone walking in my view. *At least, there's another way for the girls to get out,* I thought, looking back at the fire entrance.

I reasoned: *I could go back around the building and try to get to Johnny's car. There's bound to be some gas in there to get me the hell out of the area before more of these...what were they? And where would I go?*

I had no family anymore.

I could track down the rest of the SDS, maybe Caroline or Bird. We could get in the van and drive away.

Faint screams kept rising from my dorm building. Girls began to run out the fire exit. I looked back, being far enough away to see the car in the drive...

...And more enemy beings shuffling through the woods to me. It was like being in a war.

This is not war! I reminded myself *This is a bunch of crazy people killing others for fun and getting others in on the action.* But how? Jan couldn't be a part of this; she could hardly keep a straight face when keeping a secret. Maybe Johnny coaxed her into it. After all, he pushed me forward to that creature.

A figure ran towards me. His shaggy hair flew up behind him and he hailed me down. "Liz," he said, grabbing my shoulder. "We gotta run. Med building's been taken over by ghouls."

I followed him. "Jimmy, where are we headed?"

"Bird's dorm. The rest of us are there. We're going to come up with a plan on how to get out of here or how to fight."

I followed him across the lawn. The stampede of women from my dorm scattered in different directions; many headed for the police station, others for another dorm. A few went towards the men's dorms, no doubt where their boyfriends were. I wondered, following Jimmy, if I had a boyfriend, if that's where I'd go?

My interest in men never bloomed. It stopped where it was supposed to start, with my old man. My first memory: him, gun in his hand, stirring me from my white, lacey slumber and telling me to hide under the bed. "They're coming!" He shouted. They were going to kill us all. BANG! BANG! BANG! He fired his gun outside my room. My mother screamed. I crawled under the bed, and cried for mommy, daddy, anyone and everyone, angels, God, Jesus, like they taught me in Sunday School to make it stop!

I learned later from my mother that "they" were the Japanese soldiers my dad fought years before. That was my first lesson in the immorality of war. To keep me safe, my relatives sent him to a ward where they scrambled his brain.

I swore to myself when I was younger that I'd never be scared of anything else in my life. As Jimmy and I slowed to a jog, I thought about dad's operation. As I ran from ghouls, as I thought about hiding under the bed from domestic and foreign enemies, real, but imagined, I thought of the thing that walked towards me, killing Jan and Johnny, as a version of my dad that could walk, but not talk.

I knew it was ridiculous to think what they did to him was contagious, but I just had to think that the catatonia and apathy my dad had, chain smoking in the psych ward every time I came to visiting day, made itself inherent in my surroundings. Jan's indifference to the way things ran for her, coupled with Johnny's assurance that life would go on as normal because the radio said so. Eagle Eyes with her rule of law and order and the girls in the dorm, running to their men for help held back an idea that we could be our saviors. Could I reason this ghoul disease as a contagion, wherein I was one of the pacifist fighters, waging war with my refusal to participate?

Jimmy opened the door to Bruin Hall and I ran in. An RA held up his hand, clipboard in tow. He had horn-rimmed glasses which made him look as much like a bird as Eagle-Eyes.

"No girls in here," he snapped.

"It's an emergency, man!" Jimmy said back. "We're being overrun by crazy people that are biting people and making the dead come back to life."

The RA shook his head and scrawled on his clipboard. "OK. I'm reporting you for apparent drug use as well as the chick..."

SLAM.

Jimmy held the RA up to the wall like he was a shaken rabbit. "Listen, asshole!" he snarled. "There's cadavers walking around by the med building! Don't believe me? I don't give a rat's ass! I've seen them! Now let me through or I'm knocking you into the next century!"

The RA shook and nodded at Jimmy's raised fist. As he crumpled to the floor, adjusting his glasses, Jimmy took my arm and rushed me up the stairs.

"Doesn't anyone have a ground floor dorm?" I asked. "We'll be trapped if we stay upstairs."

"We think the cadavers are making their way towards the other side of campus. They don't move fast, so we have some time to make a game plan and get out of here."

We raced up the next two flights of stairs.

"I don't think they'll be a problem for long," Jimmy explained. "They seem like they're a threat to people they catch unawares, but once someone gets on the move, it's not like they can run after them."

"I don't know," I said. "Once one tried to bite me, he seemed to lunge pretty fast."

"Yeah, but that's the lunge. From what we've seen, they're slow-moving until they get close to someone, then they move in for the kill."

"If they're dead..." I was about to ask, but remembered the ferocity the dead man used to take Johnny down. "They're slow, but they're strong."

"Have to be to catch their prey."

We moved down the hall. The last door on the left was Bird's room, which, when Jimmy opened the door, showed to be packed with the dozen senior members of the club.

"OK," Jimmy exclaimed, "we're all here. Anyone come up with a plan?"

Caroline, the treasurer, raised her hand. "I think we can bunk here until it's settled," she said. "We have enough food to get us through the night, which is when the radio says they'll have this sorted out."

"They said it would be an hour thirty minutes ago!" I cut in. "If they keep increasing the time, we're screwed. Besides, this is a really bad place to hide."

"How so?" Bird interjected. "We have food. We can close the door and lock it if any prowlers come around."

"And how do we know they can climb stairs?" Someone else suggested.

"It seems best to treat this like a sit-in and the creepers outside like a less threatening version of the cops or the administration," Caroline said.

I rolled my eyes. "This is not a protest! The cadavers, ghouls, whatever they're called outside are dangerous and only want to kill us! They will not wait to come up here if they know a big food source is hiding on the fourth floor!"

"Then what should we do?"

"Pile in our cars and get the hell out of here! We can take our rations, some clothes, and pile in the vans and go."

Everyone in the room looked around at each other. Had it really not occurred to them to go while it was safe?

"Our cars are parked in the residents' lot on the other side of the medical building."

I turned to Jimmy.

"You knew this?"

He nodded.

"Then why did you bring me here and not look for another form of transportation?"

"To keep you safe! I thought, we thought, it would be safer if we were together."

"Yes but not here!"

"Looks like there's nowhere else to go." Someone near the window told me.

'What do you mean?"

"Look outside."

I stepped across folded legs and feet to get a look outside. Out the window, girls in various states of dress and undress stepped forward...forward...forward toward Bruin Hall. I recognized some of them from Mailer. Jan and Johnny went up the stairs and got everyone. I wanted to lean out and see if more came from the medical building, or elsewhere. But that would tip the dead ones in front of our room where we were.

"Can we get access to a room across the hall, so we can see if we're flanked on the other side?" I asked.

"I'll see," Bird said, getting up and brushing his thick, black hair out of his eyes.

"Meanwhile," Jimmy declared. "We should put everyone in the hall on high alert. Perhaps everyone in the building as well. Maybe we'll get to the ground floor."

"No!" Caroline shouted. "That's where they'll hit first."

"But we may have a better chance of escape down there than up here."

"Hey, I have an idea," Bird said. "How about we seal off the entrances on the lower level, alert the building and we can hide out wherever we want here?"

"Good idea," Jimmy conferred. "But once you're in, you're in. No going out. No letting anyone in from out there. Everyone got it?"

The room nodded. I looked out the window again at the lawn full of ghouls. I turned away and knocked on the door behind me. No one answered. I pushed down on the door and it opened. The room looked lived in, but like someone had flown out of there. From the window, I gazed at young men running down the stairs. I peered out the window. To the left, I saw cadavers from the medical building on the horizon with an army of newly dead corpses walking towards us. I saw nothing to the right, but did I want to take that chance?

A scuffle could be heard downstairs. "Bar this hallway," Jimmy said. Yells and bangs and clashes echoed up the stairs to where we were.

Jimmy came in and grabbed the bed sheet. "We're tying the doors shut and getting the rest of the fellows up here to help us patrol the halls," he said to the rest of the group. "Food will be distributed every four hours to people who are still awake."

"Will it be enough?" I asked. "If they're coming up the stairs, it's already too late."

"Shut up!" He told me. "Everyone needs to stay calm!" Caroline began to cry. He yanked the sheets around the door and tied it closed. "Can someone help me pile these beds?"

Bird and another young man came in the room where I was and maneuvered the bed to the door. They propped it on its legs and piled some other furniture on top.

Scuffling and murmured voices carried across the hall. Barricades were made at the stairs on the other end. Men asked whether or not anyone had baseball bats, hockey sticks, or even kitchen knives and utensils that could be used as weapons.

"We need all food in Room 45 for rationing! Unless you want to starve while we're up here, get everything: candy boxes, soup cans, out here and into this room!"

"Anyone got matches or lighters?" Someone else called.

Some people talked about cigarette rations. Someone else asked if anyone had alcohol, Mary Jane or stuff for a trip. Before anyone could answer, Caroline came in the bedroom and shut the door. She had a bag of food, a baseball bat and a knife.

She moved the desk and slammed it against the door. She tied her scarf to the doorknob and wrapped it to the front of the desk and tied it to a leg of the chair.

My face blanched. "Caroline," I said, in the calmest voice I could muster. "How are we going to get out if they come?"

"Jump out the window for all I care. Besides, it's not the ghouls I'm worried about."

Chills went up my torso. I saw the night go on and the result of drunk college men getting bored and looking for something, or in our case, someone, to do.

"Jesus I hear them outside!" Someone yelped from the other side of the hall.

The men outside shuffled to the barricade. I heard someone climb on top and whisper, "Shit. A bunch of the ghouls are on the stairwell."

Someone else climbed up. "Is that Patty? God, it looks like they turned half the girls' dorm."

"If they're girls, we can take them," someone else exclaimed.

Patty Beauregard, or Patty Perry, I wondered. Both were in my building and one of them was on my list for raising consciousness. I think Beauregard signed up; Perry was a freshman who wanted to pledge into a sorority. She told me she wouldn't have time, in a silky voice girls use when they don't want to condescend too much.

The idea that this was the last room I may ever enter crept through my brain. I looked outside again. A handful of ghouls stood around the entrance. Some hung around the windows. I recognized my history professor from freshman year, the one who spoke about evolving from cave men who yanked women by their

224

hair and dragged them into their caves for rape. He used it as a springboard for how advanced the human race became. "We treat women better and better every year," he droned on. "In our progressive society, women can have everything they want and more..."

His testament spoke for me, but not about me, I remembered writing in the margins of my history notes.

I spied a notebook on a shelf and grabbed it. Full of graph paper and equations, the writing on the first page told me it belonged to a Peter Shrub who had slanted, messy print and was in Calculus 1. I flipped through the page to the next blank one.

"Have you seen a pen?" I asked Caroline.

She shook her head. "Why do you need one at a time like this?"

"I need to write something. It's important."

I opened a drawer in the desk not obstructed by the pink, paisley scarf. A ballpoint pen and several pencils hugged the side of the drawer in a crevice between the metal side and untouched stationary.

I grabbed the pen and began to write: *My name is Liz, Elizabeth Simons. I was twenty years old, Vice President of Students for a Democratic Society and Founding Member of the Women's Consciousness-Raising Committee. I have no family. I have no boyfriend. I had some, but nothing serious.* I crossed the last sentence out. It should be of no importance if I had a boyfriend. *I didn't know what I wanted to major in, but I was going to convince the dean to let me in the pre-med program. I wanted to go into pediatrics.*

I scribbled everything else. I wrote about my father and mother and where I went to school. The rock n' roll bands I listened to, my first bike, my first car... How the ghouls killed Jan, what we were doing when they came, and how I got this far.

"What exactly are you writing?" Caroline asked me, after an hour. Her arms wrapped around her knees. A trigonometry textbook was open in front of her, which she apparently threw down.

"My life," I said. "If they find my body, moving or not, I want people to know who I was and what I did with myself before all this mess."

Caroline nodded and began to poke around the shelves. She found a novel, from the looks of it, then another and another and put it down next to her, but kept searching.

'What are you looking for?" I asked.

"A radio. Maybe there's a transistor somewhere in here that we can listen to, to let us know what's going on."

"Do you think the boys know we're in here?"

She looked at the door and furrowed her brow. "No idea, but the silence is killing me."

"Hey," I said. "There's a stereo over there. We could put on some records."

She looked through them and nodded. "Decent selection. Motown. A couple Beatles albums. No Doors, though. Shame. I think Jim Morrison's dreamy."

"Me too. I like John Lennon too, though. He's very deep. Morrison seems fun, but someone you'd go on a trip with rather than have good conversations about life and stuff."

"You like Dylan?"

I channeled my voice through my nostrils and started singing "How Does it Feel" like I had a cold. She laughed.

"I dig the lyrics," I laughed, too. "And the guitar, but really, he needs a tissue."

"Blue Cheer?" she asked, puzzled, holding a navy-colored album up.

"They're pretty good."

She shrugged and threw it on. I got up and made sure the dial was turned down low and sat back down to write.

I jotted down the basics of my life: what high school I went to, who my friends were, maybe major life events, but I didn't get too much into detail. I'd add stuff as time went on, but I wanted my story told in its entirety before the ghouls broke in. I decided to add in when I read Betty Friedan and how she led me to make up my mind that I was going to college. I named the newspaper I started, wondering if any copies were left in the world. If the ghouls wiped us out and aliens landed on earth a thousand years from now, would there still be a copy of my press? I continued writing about college. Some words about Old Eagle Eyes and rooming with Jan graced my page. I mentioned taking a road trip to California last summer and the friends I met in Ashbury, which brings me to the ghouls...

"I might go into journalism if we live," I said aloud.

"I was going into accounting. At first, it was to meet a banker guy, but why? Why can't I be the banker?"

"Exactly." I felt my list in my pocket. I pulled it out and extended my hand to hand it to her.

CRASH!

Something banged on the door. There was a period of silence between us only pierced by a fast drum beat picking up after Dick Peterson declared over the stereo: "There ain't no cure for the summertime blues."

CRASH!

Our door shook. The wave came from the barricade, rattling the hinges.

CRASH!

Someone had a stereo going outside. The Doors' synthesizer began playing up, and I heard the first riffs of "Light my Fire." For a few seconds, the melody danced with the rapid drums of

"Summertime Blues" coming from out stereo. Caroline got up and turned it off. She grabbed her baseball bat and stood at the door.

Someone knocked.

"Girls! We know you're in there! We need all hands on deck! They're breaking through!"

I jotted down some last words: *The pounding continues on the other side of the door. I hear glass shatter on a window downstairs and wood splinter from the bloody fist of persistent monsters outside. Bird turned up "Light my Fire." As the synthesizer instrumental whirred its way in the room on vinyl, the ghouls shattered the glass and began reaching their hands in, grabbing at us live ones. Bird and Caroline and Jimmy stabbed them with pokers, sticks, broken curtain rods and glass, getting them through their eyes to their brains. They fell back. Some we got good enough where they stayed dead, others...*

The note trailed off there. Officer Dwight Beulah pocketed the blood-stained note and looked at the young body piled on top. Mrs. Peters strode over to him, her floral dress covered in blood and dirt. A face mask covered her beaky nose and mouth.

She straightened her cat-eye glasses and nodded: "she was one of my charges."

"If you could fill out an ID form so we can tell her family..."

"She had no family, as far as I understood. She was at the university on scholarship, active on campus, too. She was a rabble rouser, though, seemed to be mad about something all the time." She tutted.

"Still, we need an ID."

"Of course, Officer."

As Helen Peters filled out the form, Beulah read through the note one more time. No trust for the man, and what the hell was consciousness-raising? Sounded like some drug scam to him.

He turned to give the note to evidence, but decided against it. His superior told him to burn everything found on the bodies, and

Beulah figured that included testimonies, lest they be covered in ghoul-making germs. It was nothing anyway, the writings of a nobody he was about to douse in gasoline and immolate for the community good. He surveyed the round, red dot in the middle of her forehead and the halo of blood and brains in her long, hippy hair.

That was his doing. They cleared the building of ghouls early in the morning and last, went upstairs. They opened fire on a mass of ghouls around a broken-down barricade. As each one swooned down, a bullet in his head, Beulah wondered if this really came from the dead rising, or if it was some bad drug the kids were taking.

They went farther down the hall. They moved slowly, except to kick down the doors and shoot ghouls inside. CRASH! CRASH! BANG! As Beaulah's heart began to race, screaming in his chest, he took deep breaths and told himself: *they don't move fast. We got guns, they don't.*

She emerged from the end of the hall, looking dazed. She stumbled over some debris with a blood-stained bat in one hand. Her long hair was caked in ceiling dust; the front of her was splattered with black human fluid that Beulah, with his years of investigations, associated with John Does they found half-rotted in the woods.

He had his gun on her and before his forefinger squeezed, he thought he heard her speak: "Don..." BANG!

"It was the wind," he muttered to himself. "You're hearing things."

He told himself again that ghouls couldn't speak, not even the pretty ones. When he went down, gun back on her head to make sure she stayed dead, he noticed she wasn't like the others. Her skin still had some warmth to it. *Recently turned,* he shrugged, and began his police report.

He shook his head again. "You were no one," he told the corpse, pouring gasoline over her face and on her clothes. He lit a match, and instead of flicking it on the bodies, he lit a corner of the girl's note...and threw it on the pile.

DEADHEADS
by Paul Victor Wargelin

Paul Victor Wargelin is a mild-mannered copywriter for a major metropolitan publishing house, and the author of more than a dozen short stories, two of which garnered honorable mentions in The Year's Best Fantasy & Horror. He has also reviewed over a dozen films, books, and comic books for Feo Amante's Horror Home Page (feoamante.com).

TWISTED TUMBLEWEED TALES is his first short story collection. Visit Strangecoach, Paul's weird western blog at strangecoach.blogspot.com.

Axe to Grind led the charge, striking up a militant rendition of "Sgt. Pepper's Lonely Hearts Club Band" as a call to arms against the politicians and the parents and their stupid war. Alex sang the Lennon/McCartney composition with an edge even Hendrix's Monterey Pop performance a year ago couldn't match. In her voice, the words of The Beatles' invitation to tea for a civilized brass and string concert became an accusation against the American war machine. Twenty years ago, the band wasn't taught to play, it was taught to kill.

But it never learned how to die.

"How do you teach people to die?" Alex screamed into the mic, startling Chris in the midst of his solo, spraying feedback onto the unsuspecting crowd. He recovered with furious rhythmic slashes, pretending the noise was intentional, throwing a rabid dog-eyed glare at Alex as he fought to get the song back on track.

Peering back at him through strands of sweat-soaked bangs drooping down her face, she mouthed "fuck off" before snarling the final verse and letting the mic slip through her clammy hands. It landed on the wooden stage with a thud that echoed in a monotonous drone as she whirled off through the wings. She could hear Kyle's bass match the tone, twirling root notes around it, while Davis beat out a funeral march on his drums. Chris dropped to the low end, getting them all in sync before ending the song on a sinister final endless note, reminiscent of the Sgt. Pepper album's last track, "A Day in the Life."

The crowd roared at the conclusion, a wave of sound that invited Alex back onstage to take a bow, but those tripping and drunken worshippers meant nothing to her. College students in registration name only to continue avoiding the draft while turning on, tuning in, and dropping out. Now, without the pressure of obtaining barely passing grades for three months, these children are celebrating a second Summer of Love at the Smith Point Park Pop Festival.

But 1968 has no Summer of Love, just an endless winter of discontent that's numbed the nation's very heart and soul. Smith Point Park is not Monterey. The local bar bands performing here have no hit records, no television appearances, no fame or notoriety to attract a large audience willing to travel east of New York City. The ethos of 1967's Flower Power movement that fueled California's three days of peace and love and inspired this Long Island gathering wilted under the relentless reality of Vietnam's victims.

In 1967, Randy was still alive. In 1968, what was left of Randy after stepping on a mine was buried in the national cemetery at Pinelawn. Alex attended her brother's funeral less than a week ago, and changed Axe to Grind's entire set list without consulting the rest of the band. She would not sing the blues covers they performed throughout Suffolk County, as if white middle class college kids really believed that their complaints about life entitled them to share the music composed from the hardship of an oppressed minority. If the band wanted her to sing, it would be the pop songs that made everyone smile, twisted and delivered in anger.

She was trembling when Connie appeared beside her, pulling her into an awkward embrace, hindered by the acoustic guitar slung over her back. "Hey, it's okay."

"What the hell Alex?" Chris's voice pounded her ear drums, bringing the first pulse of a headache. "We've got six more songs on *your* set..."

Alex pulled away from Connie and punched Chris, knocking him back against Davis and Kyle. Before she could swing again, Connie pinned her arms against her sides, and the band's rhythm section stopped their lead guitarist from retaliating.

"You *bitch*."

"Fuck you Chris."

"What's going on?" Frank Wilton, owner of the pub unimaginatively named Frank's Place, Axe to Grind's usual performing venue, and the money man behind the festival, stormed over. Unlike most World War II veteran business owners, he didn't view politically-savvy college kids as the enemy, and actually enjoyed their music, which benefitted Frank's Place with packed patrons every weekend. "Your set isn't over."

"Mine is," Alex said. "We're done."

"Oh for Christ's..." He took a deep breath, pulled a joint out from behind his ear, lit it and took a hit. "Connie, get out there before the natives get any more restless."

Connie looked at Alex, who nodded. Swinging her guitar around, she sashayed her way on stage, hugged by a mini-dress that drew welcoming cheers and catcalls.

"Bert," Frank said to a technician with a transistor radio glued to his ear. "Get out there and set up her mic."

"Huh?" With an annoyed wave of his hand he said, "Just a minute. I wanna hear this..."

Frank yanked the radio from Bert's hand and everyone heard the stoic voice of a newscaster intone "...scientist believes the phenomenon may be related to space probe radiation..." before he shut it off.

"Get out there. Now."

Bert scowled, but went onstage. Two minutes later, Connie was singing "Mrs. Robinson."

Looking at Axe to Grind, Frank said. "Get it together. Now."

"Frank..." Alex started.

"I don't care what your problems are. People paid money to see and hear you, and you're gonna play. You've got thirty minutes." He dropped the last of his joint and consulted his clipboard, heading for the trailers where the talent were housed. "Where are the Rough Diamonds? They're up after Connie."

Davis and Kyle were relieved when Chris asked them to give him and Alex a moment.

"I know you're hurting..." Chris said.

"You don't know a damn thing."

"...but you don't take it out on us. On *me*."

Alex massaged her bruised knuckles. "I never took you for having a glass jaw."

Anger flushed across Chris's face, but laughter bubbled up out of him before it could take hold. "You've got a mean right hook."

"Taught by the best," Alex choked on the last word, squeezed her eyes shut to keep her tears from falling.

Chris hugged her before she could protest. Connie's cover of "The Sound of Silence" flowed around them.

"He never should have gone," said Alex.

"It was his choice. College wasn't his scene."

"He could have tried harder."

Chris kept quiet. Alex was grateful.

"Dad was so proud of him."

"Your Dad's an asshole."

"He could've run to Canada."

"Randy? Never."

Alex sighed, pulled away.

"What do you want to do?"

"Finish our set."

"You sure? Frank's not our…"

"If I'm going to be angry, I'd rather sing it than break my hand against your face."

Chris rubbed his chin. "Agreed."

"We're still doing <u>my</u> set."

"You're the boss."

Connie joined them. They hadn't heard her finish. "The crowd's getting bigger." She didn't sound happy.

"Really?" Alex peered around the curtain from the side of the stage. The sun was setting, but she could see the audience had indeed grown. Their shadows undulated like waves crashing together on the beach. The drunken newcomers in the back reeled against their neighbors and scuffles broke out between the revelers. Alex felt Connie shiver beside her.

"What is it?"

"There's gotta be a couple thousand people out there. It's getting out of control."

Alex looked again. The crowd was surging closer to the stage.

"Axe to Grind," Frank called out. "On stage. Now."

"What about the Rough Diamonds?" said Chris.

"Their drummer's sick. I think the punk's on heroin."

"Jesus…"

"Get out there. They're getting agitated."

"I'll get Kyle and Davis," Chris said.

Alex headed for the stage, but Connie grabbed her arm. "Don't go out there."

"You're being silly. I've faced rougher crowds in bars."

"Something's *wrong*."

The audience screamed louder.

"That's my cue," Alex joined the rest of Axe to Grind. With three strikes of drumstick against drumstick, the band erupted into "Last Train to Clarksville." Her rage fueled the lyrics beyond the song's metaphor to represent the true anguish of young American soldiers, singing an altered refrain of "and I *know* that I'm *never* coming home."

Lost in the music, she didn't notice the blood covered girl until she was already on the stage, sobbing. Her sudden appearance brought a round of applause from those who thought she was part of the act. Alex tore her blouse off, bringing yet another appreciative roar from the audience, and tried to staunch the girl's wounds.

"Help me," she said, quieter than a whisper. Her body wasn't just cut, it was torn. Parts of her flesh had been ripped away.

Alex looked up. A warring mob clashed at her feet. Stoned kids fell beneath swarms of bloodied, ashen-complexioned people who clawed and bit them like starving animals. Many were trampled as others stampeded to escape.

Chris swung his guitar at a slack-faced ghoul crawling onstage, snapping its neck upon impact. The lolling head swung with a pendulum's rhythm, its red-foamed mouth opening and closing as if it were a fish out of water. It turned its black rimmed eyes to Alex and licked its lips.

How is it still alive?

The injured girl sighed her last breath. Alex shuddered, then flinched as Chris pounded the broken-necked creature until its head caved in, splintering his guitar. He raised the instrument again, but Alex stopped him.

"That's enough."

"What about them?" said Davis, clutching his drumsticks like knives in white-knuckled fists.

The ghouls that weren't feasting on their fallen prey continued their shuffling advance.

Alex shrieked when the dead girl grabbed her arm, gnashing teeth lunging at her face. Kyle's bass guitar crashed into the girl's mouth. Alex pulled free and Kyle shoved the girl into the oncoming horde.

"Go, go…" Chris pushed Alex and Kyle ahead of him backstage and towards the trailers. Davis held back, slapping and stabbing his drumsticks against the attacking mob. Alex cried out for him to follow but Davis was surrounded and lost from sight.

Behind the stage, the park was chaos. People ran everywhere, directionless. Some fought the ghouls, most fought each other, and others were too wasted to realize the danger around them. Cars screeched away in frenzied panic, colliding with one another like a demolition derby.

The surviving members of Axe to Grind were speared in the headlights of a Volkswagen bus. "Get in," Connie ushered them into the open door, and then they were racing out of the park and onto William Floyd Parkway. Alex didn't even note who was driving until she recognized Rick, the Rough Diamonds' bassist, behind the wheel.

"Pull over," Alex said. "Kill the lights and let the rest of these lunatics go."

Rick obeyed and parked on a grassy patch under a canopy of trees, while the traffic sailed past them at reckless speed. Alex relaxed long enough to take inventory of the bus's occupants beyond Connie and Rick. Frank was in the passenger seat, a roach clutched between his lips. The other two Rough Diamonds, guitarist/lead singer Adam and drummer Danny were behind her, the latter lying across the back seat, alone and unmoving.

"Turn on the radio," Alex said.

Frank giggled. "You kids got yourselves a gen-u-ine apocalypse. Isn't that what you wanted? Viva la Revolution."

Alex ignored him. "Rick, please."

Several channels of static assaulted their ears before Rick found an emergency broadcasting announcement. A voice with the concise diction of a Kellogg's commercial pitchman delivered a grim report.

"...continue to come in from Pittsburgh, Atlanta, Los Angeles, Chicago, New York, and other US cities. As unbelievable and...ridiculous as it sounds, citizens of the United States are being attacked by the reanimated corpses of the recently deceased. These...things are consuming the flesh of the living. The President has declared a state of martial law, urging all citizens to return to their homes and remain indoors until order can be restored..."

"Did the Zombies ever cover 'Turn, Turn, Turn'?" said Frank, before taking a long toke. "Why the hell are the Byrds singing 'a time to die' instead of the Zombies?"

"Shut up Frank," Alex said. Cars continued to fly out of the park onto the highway and she could see teetering undead following in their wake, oblivious to the sudden violence of vehicles crushing them beneath their wheels. She exchanged looks with Chris and Kyle, then turned to Adam. "How long's Danny been dead?"

Adam's eyes widened. "He's not..."

"Yes, he is. And he could get up any second and try to kill us."

Without warning, Adam vomited. Frank broke out in hysterical laughter as the rest of them left the bus. The last outside, crawling on all fours, Adam emptied his stomach until all he could do was dry-heave.

"Help me," Alex told Chris. They removed Danny's body from the bus. "We have to destroy it."

"Oh my God," Connie said.

"Can't we just leave him here?" said Rick.

"So he can eat someone?" said Alex.

"That's enough Alex," said Chris.

238

"You saw that girl come back. You saw how *quickly* she came back."

"So why hasn't *he* come back?"

Alex looked at the body.

"That girl was bitten," said Chris. "Danny overdosed."

Rick knelt beside Danny. "So he shouldn't come back?"

"I don't know," said Chris. "But I don't think we should risk it."

Adam stopped dry-heaving long enough to ask, "So who's going to do it?"

Rick got to his feet. "Fuck this. I'm outta here."

"Rick..." Alex started.

"No. This is bullshit. Crazy fucking bullshit. You wanna destroy *it*, be my guest."

"He was your friend."

Rick open the passenger door and dragged Frank out.

"Hey, what the fuck..?"

"Hitch a ride to Hell. I'm outta here."

"Oh for Christ's sake," Frank reached into his coat, pulled out a .45 caliber pistol Alex recognized from her own father's military cache, and shot Rick in the chest. Connie screamed as Rick collapsed. Keeping the gun pointed towards them, Frank searched Rick's body for the car keys.

"Jesus Frank..." said Chris.

"Shut your trap. I just saved our lives. This piece of shit was going to abandon us...Goddamn it." Frank stood up. "Connie, find the keys."

She was crying, shaking her head.

Frank stepped towards her before his attention was torn away by a high-pitched scream. Danny's face was buried in Kyle's thigh, chewing through the denim of his jeans and into his flesh. Pounding his fists against Danny's head proved useless, and Kyle lost his footing as the ghoul brought him to the ground.

Pulling the trigger again and again, Frank emptied the clip into Danny and Kyle, but they still thrashed in a violent embrace.

Chris pulled the tire iron from the bus. "You have to hit it in the head," he snarled as Frank struggled to reload his gun with a second clip. Alex winced as Chris swung the iron to finish off the thing that used to be Danny, and fell beside Kyle, sobbing.

"Thanks for the advice kid," said Frank. He put a bullet in both Chris and Kyle's heads.

Alex ran and buckled beside Chris's body, cradling him. "You fucking bastard. Why?"

"We've attracted company," Frank went back to Rick's body. "Fresh meat should keep them occupied."

They appeared in the dim illumination cast by the highway lamps, lumbering at a geriatric pace, unconcerned with how long it would take them to catch their prey. Watching them approach, Alex knew they would never tire, driven by their insatiable hunger. Even if their legs rotted out from under them, they would drag themselves by their hands to find sustenance for their decaying bodies.

"C'mon," Frank muttered, keeping an eye on the approaching dead, patting the ground.

"Looking for these?" Connie jangled Rick's key ring, standing in front of the bus.

"Clever bitch," Frank swung the gun towards her, just as Rick sat up and bit his arm. Howling, he tried to pull free but Rick held fast and in their struggle he dropped the gun.

The dead were just about upon them.

Alex dragged herself from her friends' bodies, scooped up the pistol and dove inside the bus. Connie was already behind the wheel, putting all her weight atop the gas pedal. It leapt onto the road, slamming walking corpses from its path. Alex turned in her seat and watched Frank vanish beneath the dead. His screams seemed to follow them for miles.

Then the women heard a moan from behind them. Alex whirled around, finger on the trigger and stopped herself from pulling it when she saw it was only Adam, curled up on the back floor in his own vomit. He must have crawled back inside during the melee.

"Where to?" said Connie.

Alex closed her eyes. "Pinelawn Cemetery."

"Are you crazy?"

"You don't have to go, but I do. I can drop you off somewhere first, but I'm going."

Black letters on white marble spelled out Pvt. Randall Close, April 1, 1946—June 17, 1968. Alex knelt on the still fresh soil covering the coffin that housed what remained of her brother. The mine had taken most of his body, but his head was intact.

She knew he was awake, could hear his mewling cry, and feel him pounding the inside of the lid, even though there was six feet of dirt between them.

Randy gave his life for his country in an unjust war.

It was Alex's responsibility to give him a just peace.

After leaving Connie and Adam at a hospital, she crashed Pinelawn's locked gates, damaging the bus. It limped along as she ignored the concrete paths, driving across the graves until she reached her brother's. From behind the windshield, she stared at his tombstone until the sun rose.

She didn't know how long she waited before the ground shifted. A broken hand pushed through, followed by another. Randy's head emerged, sunken eyes blinking in the harsh sunlight before focusing on Alex and snapping his teeth together.

"Welcome home Randy."

Alex raised the gun to his forehead and pulled the trigger.

PHILBEAR

by David F. Walker

David F. Walker is an award-winning journalist, filmmaker, and author of the YA series THE ADVENTURES OF DARIUS LOGAN. His publication BADAZZ MOFO became internationally known as the indispensable resource guide to black films of the 70s, and he is co-author of the book REFLECTIONS ON BLAXPLOITATION: ACTORS AND DIRECTORS SPEAK. His work in comics includes the series SHAFT (Dynamite Entertainment), NUMBER 13 (Dark Horse Comics), DOC SAVAGE (Dynamite Entertainment), THE ARMY OF DR. MOREAU (IDW/Monkeybrain Comics), and THE SUPERNALS EXPERIMENT (Canon Comics). Walker's work in film includes directing the award-winning shorts THE DAY THEY RAN OUT OF BULLETS and BLACK SANTA'S REVENGE, which he also wrote and produced.

☠

The phone wouldn't stop ringing. At least five people had called him, and he didn't pick up for any of them, because he hated talking on the phone. Fewer than a dozen people had his phone number, which meant that Barry knew whoever it was that was calling. And he knew that they knew not to call him at this hour—if at all—because he hated talking on the phone.

It wasn't that the ringing phone had woken him, because it hadn't. Barry barely slept since his return home from Vietnam in the spring of '67. He'd learned a lot during the war, and picked up a ton of new habits—so many in fact, that he often thought of himself as someone else. He'd become the other Barry. In Vietnam, he became Philbear. That's what the other soldiers called him—Philbear. It was a combination of his name, Barry, and the city he'd come from—and returned to—Philadelphia.

The other guys in his platoon had taken to calling him Philly Barry, which was quickly condensed to Philbear. Fewer syllables. Easier to call out in a crisis. Unless, of course, it was someone who didn't know him that well, or had forgotten his name in the middle of a crisis—like a piece of shrapnel tearing their guts open. During those times, they'd just scream out, "Medic!"

The phone started ringing again. He knew it had to be important. Someone needed help at the clinic. Mom was worried about Dad. Dad was worried about Mom. His older brother, Joe, was worried about Mom and Dad. Barry went down the list of the handful of people with his phone number, wondering who the hell it was that kept calling.

"They should've gotten the hint by now," he said to himself. Or maybe he simply thought it. There was a time when Barry could differentiate the things he thought to himself and the things he said out loud, but it wasn't that easy for Philbear. And on some days, he wasn't sure who he was.

Philbear was the one who hated answering the phone and talking, while Barry wondered—with genuine concern—who it was that kept calling. After more than a dozen calls, in which the phone rang at least ten times before the caller hung up, Barry decided to answer the phone.

"What?"

"You okay?" asked the voice on the other end. A ton of noise in the background made it difficult to hear, but Barry recognized the voice as his older brother, Joe.

"You the one been calling all this time?" asked Barry. He hadn't talked to Joe in at least two months.

"What? No. Listen," said Joe. "Something's wrong. Something's going on."

Barry strained to hear his brother over the noise in the background. He couldn't be sure, but Philbear was fairly certain he'd heard the sound of gunfire. Not automatic weapons, but maybe shotguns, or hunting rifles. He also thought he heard screaming. "What's going on? Where are you?"

"Not sure. Somewhere north of Pittsburgh. Close to Evans City. My car got run off the road…"

"Your car got what?" Barry demanded.

"No time to explain. I can see a saloon down the road—I'm gonna go there, see if anyone can help."

"I'll come get you."

"No. Go check on Mom and Dad. Been calling, but their line is dead. Something's going on."

"Something?" asked Barry.

"I don't know, baby brother. People are going crazy. Heard some crazy bullshit on the radio about mass hysteria, or maybe some outbreak of rabies. I just need you to …"

The phone went dead.

Barry immediately dialed his parents' phone number—one of only three numbers he had committed to memory. The other two numbers were his own, and the number of the health clinic, where he pulled long hours, pretending to be a doctor, when all he really knew how to do was stuff a person's guts back into them, and patch them up enough to keep them from dying immediately.

The phone at his parents' house didn't ring. No busy signal either. Just a weird static. He hung up, made sure there was a dial tone, and then tried calling again. Nothing.

Barry placed the phone back on the cradle. That's when he noticed the sound. Sirens. Police. Ambulance. Fire department. All of them. He'd never heard that many sirens all at once. Every siren on every cop car, ambulance and fire truck in Philadelphia was blaring all at once, like the opening overture of a coming apocalypse. He couldn't believe that he hadn't heard them all before.

Then he heard the voice of his brother, as clear as if Joe was in the room, "Something is going on."

Joe had called him to get him to check on Mom and Dad. But he also called to warn him—something is going on.

Without thinking, Barry reached under the pillow and grabbed the .45 automatic. He didn't bother to check the weapon—it was always loaded. He made a quick sweep of his tiny apartment, gathering up all the loaded magazines he had strategically hidden, and stuffed them into the small duffle bag. Real doctors carried black leather satchels filled with whatever it was they carried around with them. His bag was filled with a first-aid kit, a canteen full of water, a few MREs, and now ten fully loaded clips of ammunition for the sidearm that had returned home with him from Vietnam like a best friend.

Philbear opened the door to his studio apartment. The screaming sirens were louder in the hall. He could hear radios and televisions blaring from the other apartments. News reports of mass hysteria and civil unrest flitted through the air like bugs as he rushed past the doors of neighbors he didn't know by name, down two flights of stairs, and out on to the street, where something was clearly going on. Something bad.

The health clinic he worked at was located in North Philly, near the headquarters of the local chapter of the Black Panther Party for Self Defense. After he came back from Vietnam, Philbear met some other brothers who had joined up with the Panthers. That wasn't his thing—at least not completely. Philbear was done fighting, but Barry still wanted to help people, especially his people, and he respected that part of the Panther's Ten-Point Plan.

Joe had warned him about getting involved with the Black Panthers, saying they were too militant. Like Joe was one to talk. Barry's older brother had a reputation for being one of the most outspoken black men in all of Michigan. He spent most of his time out near Detroit, where his job kept him traveling, but his reputation in Philly still lingered. As a kid, he'd grown up in the shadow of Joe.

Joe had always been a man of action. "Get the job done," was his motto. He'd picked it up from his parents, who passed it on to him and Barry. The brothers shared their parents' tenacity, but not much else. Joe had objected to Barry's joining the Army, and Barry ... well ... he seemed to disagree with Joe simply on the principles derived from sibling rivalry.

Barry thought about his brother and his parents as he stepped out on to the chaotic streets. He and Joe disagreed on just about everything, except for one thing—they both loved their parents unconditionally. And as he looked around at what could only be described as madness, Barry—or more specially, Philbear—prepared himself to go to war for his parents.

The sun hung low in the sky, retreating for the day, and making way for the night. It would be dark soon, though not that dark. The light from several fires burning throughout the city had already started a weird glow that would illuminate the city once the sun had completely set.

Philbear's first thought was that there must be rioting going on. Riots had become regular occurrences throughout a nation struggling with Civil Rights, and many cities had gone up in flames. Parts of Philly had taken a beating back in 1964. Only those fires had always been confined to certain parts of whatever city had been set ablaze—the parts of the city where black folks lived. As he looked in all directions, Philbear could see that there was no rhyme or reason to these fires. Knowing the city like he did, and knowing how to measure distances like any decent soldier, Philbear constructed a mental map of all the neighborhoods where he could see fires. None of them was contained to any specific racial or ethnic enclave, nor was economic status a factor. There were fires burning everywhere—from the richest parts of Philly, to the poorest slums, where his parents still lived, because they refused to move somewhere better.

He took off on foot, moving with a quick pace and sense of purpose, knowing that if he walked at a regular pace, it would take him only twenty or thirty minutes to get to his parents' apartment in the Raymond Rosen Homes Housing Projects. Barry wanted to run, but Philbear reminded him to take it easy. Between the insomnia, the ringing phone, the pre-med classes at Temple University, and a double shift at the clinic, he had only slept about four hours in the last three days. Not that lack of sleep was unusual for him—he'd gone days without sleeping back in 'Nam. But this was America—North Philly, and even though it looked like home, it also looked like a battlefield.

Philbear had to leap out of the way of an ambulance that either didn't see him crossing the street, or didn't care. He dove between two parked cars, landing on the hard concrete sidewalk at the mouth of an alley. Picking himself up, he swore at the ambulance driver, when he heard a scream from the alley.

At first he thought it was a mugging—some punk not much younger than him attacking an old woman. Then he realized it was the punk who had screamed for help, and that it was the old woman doing the attacking. Philbear started to laugh, thinking about how what was clearly a mugging had gone wrong. This little thug had messed with the wrong grandmother.

He moved in closer to break up the scuffle, and that's when he saw it. Something was wrong with the old woman. Her face was a sickly color—a color Philbear had never seen on anyone that was actually alive. Her left arm was still attached, but much of the skin and muscle was missing. It was a grisly mess that looked like she had been attacked by some kind of wild animal. But that wasn't the most disturbing part. The most disturbing part was that she was still able to use the arm, and that the undamaged hand attached to the mangled arm was reaching and grabbing for the punk kid.

Philbear stared for a moment, unsure of what was going on. The punk kid called out for help, and Barry realized he wasn't the juvenile delinquent he'd mistaken him for. In an instant, he recognized the kid as Leroy, who worked three blocks down the street at Caruso's Market. Leroy stocked shelves and bagged groceries, which he often carried home for some of the older residents of the neighborhood.

Two bags of groceries lay on the pavement of the alley, their contents spilled out and mixed in with the garbage that littered the alley—garbage that was splattered with blood. Lots of blood—the massive amount of blood that only comes when a major artery is torn open.

A few feet from the bags of groceries lay an old man. Philbear didn't know his name—because he didn't know the names of most people who lived in his building—but he recognized him. The old man lay motionless, most of the blood having left his body through the gaping wound in his throat.

Only a few seconds had passed since Philbear entered the alley, though it seemed like minutes, and he wasn't even sure if he was really there. Maybe he had finally fallen asleep, and this was just another nightmare, like all the others that made sleep so difficult.

No, this wasn't a nightmare. He could smell the garbage and the piss in the alley, which were mixed with the scent of fresh spilled blood. He knew that smell all too well. It was the smell that told him he wasn't asleep—that this wasn't a nightmare.

Philbear moved into action. He grabbed the old lady from behind, trying to pull her off of Leroy, and surprised at how strong she was—especially since she was missing most of an arm. Philbear managed to pull the woman off Leroy, but then she was on him, clutching and clawing, and trying to bite him.

The old woman's mouth was smeared with blood, her breath stank of it, and what looked like raw meat hung from her gnashing maw. Philbear cast a quick glance at the old man, laying dead amidst the garbage, spilled groceries, and his own blood, his throat torn out by what looked like an animal attack.

With all of his strength, Philbear pushed the old woman off him. She stumbled back a few steps, and then began moving back towards him. He swung his duffle bag at her, smashing her in the face and knocking her to the ground.

His adrenaline pumped, and Barry realized that he hadn't felt like this since the war—hadn't felt this much like Philbear in a very long time. There was a part of Philbear that was with Barry every moment of every day, but it had been a while since that side of him had come out with so much force.

Philbear rushed to Leroy. The young man was covered in blood, but Philbear couldn't tell where the blood had come from. His training as a medic kicked into overdrive as he checked Leroy for injuries. "Where are you hurt?" Philbear asked.

"She…she just attacked us," said Leroy. His voice had the sound of someone struggling to keep it together—trying not to go insane.

"It's okay. I've taken care of her."

The words had barely left his mouth, when Barry felt the hands grab him from behind—surprisingly cold hands. The look of shock and fear on Leroy's face told him all he needed to know. Philbear had made the mistake of thinking he'd knocked the old woman out, when in fact he'd just knocked her down.

None of it made sense. His mind raced, trying to assess everything he knew. Then he remembered what Ben said on the phone. "Something is going on."

Philbear struggled to break free of the old woman's grasp, but she was relentless. Like a … rabid dog. Hadn't Joe said something about a possible rabies outbreak?

She pulled him back toward her, and they both fell to the ground of the alley. In the fall, their positions had shifted, and the old woman was no longer behind him, but on top of him. Philbear had fought hand-to-hand before. He knew what it felt like to struggle with another human being, when either your life or theirs was at stake. This wasn't like that. This was something else.

The old woman made a growling sound as she tried to bite Philbear. In his mind, he swore at her. Or maybe he swore out loud. He couldn't be sure of anything, other than the fact that he wasn't having a nightmare, rather, he was living in one.

Leroy smashed the old woman in the back of the head with an object clutched in his hand. The can of soup he'd picked up from the spilled groceries did little to deter the crazed creature disguised as an old woman.

"Hit it again," said Philbear.

Leroy brought the can of soup down on the old woman's head a second time, and there was a disgusting crack. The third blow to her head made an even more disgusting squishing sound, as the woman's skull cracked open at the same instant that the can of soup exploded.

She shuddered for a moment, then collapsed on Philbear, who pushed her off, and rolled away from her. He gasped for breath, lying on his back in the alley.

Leroy stared down at him for a moment, and then hurried away to vomit.

Philbear turned his head to see the old woman laying just a few feet away from him. Her skull was split open, her brains seeping out; mixing in with what Barry assumed was cream of potato soup, and whatever else was splattered on the ground in the alley.

Leroy stumbled back over to him, his legs unsteady, his steps uncertain, like the first steps of someone who has just become a killer. Philbear knew the steps well. He'd walked them himself, seen countless other guys make that journey as well, and he knew that young Leroy, who bagged groceries at Caruso's Market, would never be the same.

"You okay, mister?" asked Leroy.

"Thanks. You saved my life," said Philbear. He sat up, immediately feeling the exhaustion from the struggle with the old woman whose brains continued to trickle out of her ruptured skull.

A faint groan filled the alley. Both Philbear and Leroy looked at the motionless corpse of the dead woman. They'd both heard her moan like that as she attacked them. With the second moan it became clear that it wasn't the old woman making the noise.

They both turned to look at the old man. The old man whose throat had been torn out. The old man who had been dead, because there was no way anyone with any injury like that could be anything but dead. But there he was, slowly starting to sit up, his skin a similar sickly shade to that of the old woman—to that of the lifeless bodies Philbear had helped bag back in 'Nam.

Leroy took a few steps back. Philbear scurried away from the old man, while scanning the alley, looking for something. He spotted his duffle bag on the ground, next to Leroy.

"My bag! Toss me my bag!"

It took Leroy a moment to figure out what Philbear meant. By now, the old man had gotten on his hands and knees, as he tried to pick himself up off the ground. His moves were stiff and slow, marked by a clumsy uncertainty. And yet, he had a sense of purpose, made clear by the way his milky eyes darted back and forth from Leroy to Philbear. The old man was a predator, determining which prey to attack.

Leroy reached down and tossed the duffle bag to Philbear, just as the old man got to his feet. Philbear fumbled with the bag for a moment, pulled out his Colt .45 automatic, and flipped off the safety as he pointed it at the old man.

"Stop," said Philbear. His voice was stern and absolute in its resolve. He could've said more, but anything more would've been wasted breath.

The old man took a clumsy step toward Philbear, who on the ground, and within closer reach, must have seemed like the easier target. Philbear fired a single round, hitting the man in the leg. The old man took a second step.

Leroy let off a string of profanity that echoed those uttered by Philbear.

Philbear shot the old man a second time, in the left shoulder, just above the heart. The bullet tore a decent sized hole in the man's body, though there was almost no blood from the wound. All of the old man's blood had spilled out on to the grimy ground of the alley.

The old man paused after the second shot tore into him, though Philbear could tell that the momentary hesitation hadn't been caused by pain or fear, or anything like that. The old man had merely reacted like an animal that had been momentarily distracted. The bullet from the gun may as well have been a fly buzzing around.

The old man took another shambling step toward Philbear. Two, maybe three more steps at most, and he'd be close enough to grab him with hands that Barry knew were ice cold.

Philbear fired a third shot, hitting the old man right between the eyes. The body fell so fast that it hit the ground with the same speed as the brains that erupted from the back of his head and splattered on the wall behind him.

Philbear started to pick himself up. Leroy reached down, offering a helping hand. They looked each other in the eye, without saying a word. There were no words—at least not any that were appropriate for the moment. They had both just killed people in an alley in Philadelphia—two people that were not ... well ... like other people. They had been more like animals.

It should not have taken them as long as it did to travel the relatively short distance they traveled. Philbear and Leroy were just about to leave the alley, when Barry stopped and looked back—not at the corpses that they were leaving behind, but the spilled groceries. A voice in his head told him to gather up the food, that they might need it for later.

"We don't have time for this," said Leroy. He was a kid and terrified and had no clue what it meant to survive in a truly hostile environment.

Leroy pointed out that paper bags that had carried the groceries were drenched in blood, and some of the food was covered in blood and bits of brain.

"You do what you think is best," said Philbear, removing the coat of the old man, and fashioning it into a makeshift gunnysack. "Can't tell you what's going on, but this food might prove to be valuable."

Leroy thought about it for a moment before helping Philbear gather up the groceries. The two of them then decided they should check both bodies for some sort of identification. And then they took the money they found, because as Barry explained it, "We may need this, and they sure as hell don't have any use for it."

They said a quick prayer over the corpses, not so much because either of them really wanted to, but because Barry felt it was something that his parents would do. And then they took off, having spent more than five minutes longer in the alley than either of them had intended, before heading north and west.

By the time they left the alley, the sun had gone down. More of the city glowed from new fires that had sprung up. Sirens screamed from every direction. More people had taken to the streets. Across the street and at the end of the block, a family of three defended itself from a group of five shambling attackers that looked like those that Philbear and Leroy had just killed. The father swung a baseball bat, trying to keep himself between the vicious assailants reaching for his wife and crying baby.

Barry stopped to consider the family for a moment. Philbear urged him to move on—to get to his parents' place as quickly as possible. He wasn't sure which part of him ran across the street and down the block toward the family, as he argued with himself, but it was definitely Philbear who carefully placed a single round through the heads of four of the attackers. The fifth went down when the father caved its skull in with the bat.

"Gracias," said the father. He introduced himself as Max, his wife as Juliana, and their infant daughter as Rosa.

"Hey, man, we need to get moving," said Leroy. He pointed to the other end of the block, where three more people, with grey, lifeless skin began shambling towards them.

No one spoke a word, but they moved together as a group. Philbear led the way, not because he wanted to, or even because he cared about the others—he just headed where he headed, and the others seemed to follow. Every few seconds another vehicle with flashing lights and a blaring siren sped past. Screams came more frequently, as did gunfire.

They moved methodically, Philbear leading the way with the cautious steps of a man who understood the dangers of combat. He didn't know what was going on, what they were up against, or what might be facing them as they moved steadily toward a destination that seemed miles away instead of blocks.

By the time they reached Caruso's Market, Leroy understood why Barry had taken time to gather up the food that had been dropped in the alley. Looters poured out of the tiny market, carrying whatever they could get their hands on. From their corner across the street, where they stopped for a moment to watch the looters, it seemed like the world was coming to an end.

"This is bad," said Max.

As if to drive home the point, Thomas Caruso, the son of the original owner of Caruso's Market, stumbled out of the store. Blood flowed from a wound across his forehead, his skin had the same sickly, grayish tone as the people from the alley and those that had been attacking Max and his family.

Old man Caruso didn't say a word, but he made an animalistic growling sound as he lunged at one of the looters. The old grocer grabbed on to a young man, pulled him close, and bit down on his arm. The young man screamed as Caruso's teeth ripped through the fabric of his coat and tore into his flesh. The young man pushed the shopkeeper away, though a huge chunk of his arm remained in the grocer's mouth.

The screams of the young man caught the attention of some of the other looters. They turned to see what had happened, and then Caruso lunged at another one. This one he caught and pulled close, biting into their throat. Arterial blood spray erupted from the torn jugular, as Caruso and his victim fell to the ground—the old man continuing to bite into the looter as they hit the sidewalk.

Juliana gasped in terror. Leroy gagged, and had he not thrown up earlier, he felt like he would throw up again.

Two more grey-skinned figures lumbered out of the market. One was Caruso's son, Tommy Jr., and the other was Gladys, a cashier. They lunged at the group of looters, who were trying to save their friend from the clutches of the elder Caruso. Within moments, more blood sprayed onto the streets.

"We need to keep moving," said Philbear.

By the time they reached the Church of the Advocate on the corner of Diamond Street and 18th, they'd picked up four others. Two had been on the run, just like Philbear and his group, and the other two had to be rescued from crazed attackers. Nine strong, they arrived at the Advocate to find it overrun with people. More than a dozen Black Panthers, armed and ready for action, formed a perimeter around the church.

Philbear led his group toward the church. They stopped dead in their tracks when a young black man leveled a shotgun at them.

"Ain't room for nobody else," growled the young Panther.

Philbear didn't recognize the young brother, and wondered if he was part of the chapter from over near Germantown. He knew pretty much every Panther than hung out at the headquarters on Columbia, and they knew him. That wasn't the case with the cats from the other side of town. Philbear looked into the eyes of the young man whom he figured was somewhere between his age and the age of Leroy, thinking how easy it would be to get the gun away from him. He considered it for a moment, then let his better half take charge.

"Don't want no trouble," Barry said. "Just looking for some place safe."

"Then get to steppin', 'cause this ain't the place for you," said the Panther.

"Let them through," commanded a voice.

Father Paul Washington was the leader of the Church of Advocate, and one of the most respected men in North Philly. He'd become a close ally to the Panthers, and to the people on the hard-knock streets of Philadelphia. There was a saying in the neighborhood that if there was a fight of some sort, you'd find Father Paul with his sleeves rolled up. His sleeves were rolled up, and his black shirt glistened, soaked with either sweat or blood, or both.

Father Paul pushed past the Panther pointing his shotgun at Philbear, gently placing his hand on the weapon and lowering it so that it no longer pointed at anyone. Tall and lanky, with a dark complexion offset by grey hair, Father Paul had a serious look on his face, but an inviting gaze in his eyes.

It had been years since Barry had set foot in the Advocate, though it was clear that Father Paul recognized him. The man of God opened his arms, embracing Barry.

"Brother Barry," he said, "we've missed you around here."

Philbear offered a grim smile. "Wish it was under better circumstances," said Barry.

"God welcomes all children into his house, no matter what the circumstances," Father Paul said, leading Philbear and his group past the Panthers standing guard, and towards the church.

Tables and chairs had been set up outside on the sidewalk. "As you can see, we don't have much room, but as long as I draw breath, no one gets turned away," said Father Paul.

Barry handed the makeshift gunnysack full of groceries to the priest. "Here's some food," said Barry. "Have you seen my parents?"

"No, son, I haven't."

Father Paul had a sad look on his face. Like everyone else, he had no idea what was happening, but he knew that it was bad. His church was overflowing with proof of how bad things were getting. People sought refuge from a wave of violence that tore through the streets. Nearly everyone seeking the safety of the Advocate had a horrific story to tell of being attacked by another person—sometimes a friend or family member, and sometimes a complete stranger. Over the course of half a day, Father Paul had now heard similar versions of same story at least one hundred times. He had even heard—as outlandish as it sounded—some people claiming the dead were coming back to life.

He explained all of this to Barry, who thought of the old man in the alley. The old man's throat had been ripped out. There's no way he could've survived that wound, and yet he'd gotten up and attacked Philbear.

"I'm going to find my parents," said Philbear.

Before the priest could say anything, Philbear had taken off, heading west on Diamond Street towards the Raymond Rosen Homes Housing Projects. He didn't bother to say goodbye to Leroy, or Max, or any of the others that he'd accompanied thus far.

Saying goodbye meant too much of an emotional investment in folks he doubted he'd ever see again.

Barry and his older brother Joe had grown up in a small house in the Strawberry Mansion neighborhood of North Philly, near Fairmont Park, within spitting distance of James W. Johnson Homes public housing projects. Shortly after Joe went to college, their father lost his job, and the family moved to the Rosen Projects. Barry had hoped they'd get to move in to Johnson Projects, as he knew more people there, and Rosen, which was in another neighborhood, was technically enemy territory.

Without his older brother around to protect him, Barry had to either learn how to hit harder, or run faster, if he was going to get by. He chose the former over the latter, and earned quite a reputation around the block. He hated everything about the Rosen projects, though he'd be the first to admit that whatever it was that kept him alive in Vietnam had been forged in the hellish world of public subsidized housing.

The four blocks separating the Church of the Advocate and Raymond Rosen Homes never seemed longer than at that moment, with the moon high in the night sky, and fires burning throughout the city. People rushed past Philbear, and some stopped to ask if he knew anything about anything. He told them that the Advocate was near to bursting. He asked a few people if they knew what was going down inside Rosen. All he heard was the same thing, over and over again. Stories of people attacking and being attacked. One person claimed he'd heard something on the radio—the dead were coming back to life—but that was impossible to believe.

Philbear scanned the faces of the people who rushed past him on the streets, looking for his mother and father. Rosen Projects consisted of nine buildings, all crammed with poor people who couldn't afford a better place to live. Joe sent his parents money every week, and Barry begged them to leave at least as frequently, but Dad and Mom remained steadfast in their conviction.

A half block away, the Rosen Projects in sight, a wave of people came rushing from the various buildings. Some were carrying their belongings; others were just looking to beat a hasty retreat. They looked like the villagers who would try to flee whenever American soldiers showed up in some tiny collections of shacks in Vietnam.

Something caught Philbear's attention—something out of place. A white police officer, carrying two small black children was part of the crowd. Police were a rare, and definitely unwelcome sight in Rosen, as well as a good many other parts of North Philly, and this one looked especially out of place amidst a sea of black faces.

Philbear rushed toward the cop, grabbing his arm before he could get away. The two black children were crying.

"What's going on in there?" Philbear asked.

"All hell's breaking loose," said the cop. "Me and my partner went in on a call—dispatch has got the entire force running all over the city. Outbreaks of violence everywhere. Never seen anything like this."

"What happened to you?" asked Philbear, noticing that the cop's hand was covered in blood.

"Someone bit me. Can you believe that?"

"I was a medic in the Army. Let me take a look."

"I'm good. I'll get it taken care of later," said the cop. "Right now, I just need to get these kids some place safe, and then come back to look for my partner—lost track of him in all this madness."

Before Philbear could ask any more questions, the police officer took off, blending in with the rest of crowd looking to put as much distance between themselves and the Rosen Projects as possible. Barry couldn't blame any of them. Even under the best of circumstances, Rosen wasn't the sort place most people wanted to be.

As he entered the courtyard that sat in the center of the towering buildings, Philbear saw the first of them. He knew they were there, because he could hear screams coming from all nine of the buildings. Some of them shambled about in the courtyard, seemingly going nowhere in particular. They all had discolored skin. Some were covered in blood, or had obvious wounds, and all seemed to stir whenever someone ran past.

Philbear checked his gun. He'd already used an entire magazine, and wanted to make sure that in all the confusion, he had remembered to reload his weapon. He worried that the remaining magazines would not be enough for whatever he had to face. He wondered where his brother Joe was at that moment, and hoped that it was some place much safer than Rosen Projects. Hopefully Ben would find a nice, safe place to hunker down until everything blew over.

Crouching low, and moving fast, Philbear made his way to the third building in the southwest corner of the projects. There was movement in and around some of the buildings, but not the one where his parents lived. The lights in the lobby flickered, and as he moved closer, he could see two, maybe three of them just inside the entrance of the building.

Philbear stood inside the lobby, not twenty feet from them— three of them—and he couldn't believe his eyes. They were crouched around the dead body of a white police officer, and they were eating him. He knew the cop was dead. No one could survive the sort of damage his body had sustained. One of them was gnawing on the officer's arm, while the other two clawed at his guts. One had a handful of intestines, and the other reached in and pulled out … something.

Philbear gagged. It was all he could do to keep from throwing up. The people—the cannibals—didn't seem to notice him. As he moved closer, one of them looked at him, and stopped tearing into the flesh of the cop's arm just long enough to consider Philbear, and then moved back on to its meal.

His parents lived on the fifth floor, and whether he took the stairs or the elevator, he had to get past the cannibals. He thought about the brief conversation he'd had with Joe. "Something is going on."

The violence seemed to be everywhere. He'd seen some horrific things in the war, but nothing like the horrific, cannibalistic gorging going on in front of him. He realized that this is what the old woman in the alley was trying to do to Leroy—she wanted to eat him. Same with the old man. And the group that had been attacking Max and his family.

The world had lapsed into some sort of insanity, and there were those that had emerged from this madness in a dazed stupor and a hunger for human flesh. It seemed like something out of one of those terrible monster movies his brother took him to see on Saturday afternoons, where he would cover his eyes, but still peak through the cracks between his fingers.

Philbear leveled his gun and aimed at the head of one of the cannibals. He remembered that he'd shot the old man in the alley twice, and that neither shot did any good. It wasn't until he shot the man through the head that something happened. Philbear didn't know if that was the only way to stop the killers, but he didn't have enough bullets to risk finding out otherwise. He picked his target, and with three shots, he took out the three cannibals.

He slowly moved past them making sure that they were in fact dead. He was a few feet away, when he turned to look at the cop. The cop's body was torn to shreds. His torso looked like it had been hollowed out. Bits of his flesh and muscle and organs were splattered on the floor around him. And in the holster of his belt was a gun.

The thought of it disgusted him to no end, but he had dealt with blood and guts before, and he needed the extra gun and ammunition. Philbear fumbled with the corpse and nearly slipped and fell from stepping on what he thought was the cop's spleen, and after a few minutes, managed to work the entire belt free. He had the gun, the bullets, and the nightstick.

Philbear turned to walk away, and that's when he heard the groan. It was similar to the sound made by both the old woman and the old man in the alley. It came from the dead cop.

He closed his eyes for a brief moment. He wanted to think he was having a nightmare, but again, there was the smell—and not just the smell of blood. Philbear opened his eyes, and turned to see what he hoped he wouldn't see.

The cop's corpse struggled to sit up. So much of his guts and eternal organs had been eaten or spilled out on to the floor that he essentially had no middle. The cop rolled over, and his exposed, bloody ribcage made a terrible scraping sound against the floor. He reached his one good arm out toward Philbear, groaning a low, mournful wail—the sound of the living dead.

It wasn't possible, and yet there it was, right in front of him, reaching out for him. Back at the church, Father Paul had mentioned that some people claimed the dead were coming back to life. It sounded ridiculous then, and it still sounded ridiculous. But as unbelievable as that statement sounded—the dead were coming back to life—it was drowned out by the sound of a deafening roar of reality.

Philbear looked down at the dead police officer pulling itself toward him, its bloody ribcage making a wet, scraping sound as it moved across the floor. He pointed the gun at its head, took careful aim, and then stopped himself from squeezing the trigger. He only had so many bullets, and there was no telling what he might run across on his way to find his parents.

Philbear lowered the gun. Or maybe it was Barry who lowered the gun. He couldn't tell which part of his persona was in charge at the moment. He was becoming someone new, just as he'd done when his family moved from Strawberry Mansion to Rosen Projects, and as he'd done when he went to Vietnam. His very survival had necessitated transformation. Deep down in the core of his being, he knew that this is what needed to happen. If he was going to survive this night of the living dead, Barry and Philbear were going to have to reconcile their differences and become one.

He thought of his brother Joe. The smart one. The calm, cool, and collected one. Someday, hopefully, soon they'd be together again, and they could swap stories about how they survived this night. The thought of that made him smile—not Philbear or Barry, but both, at the same time.

He turned and headed toward the staircase that would lead to his parents' apartment on the fifth floor.

The reanimated corpse of the police officer dragged itself after him, and for now he was totally aware of the awful thing that was coming closer and might catch him.

WRONG PLACE, WRONG TIME
by William Vitka

William Vitka is a journalist and writer and native New Yorker/Pennsylvanian. He's written for The New York Post, CBS News, Stuff Magazine, GameSpy, On Spec Magazine and The Red Penny Papers. He is currently a writer for Permuted Press, Post Hill Press and Curiosity Quills. Facebook: facebook.com/VitkaWrites Twitter: @Vitka.

Clay Jones holds his Colt M1911 pistol against the back of the bank teller's head. "Way this works is: You give us the money, you don't die. Dig?" Clay's eyes flit over to his partner, Howie Matheson—who's got one foot planted in the small of the Doylestown Trust Co. guard's back and a Remington 1100 shotgun trained on the poor sucker.

The teller, a balding man in his late fifties, nods with nervous agitation. "Y-yes. But, please, don't hurt any of us."

Clay feigns a soothing voice. "Hey, bud, we don't wanna kill you. We just want the money, then we're gone." Clay sniffs. He adjusts the M14 rifle slung over his shoulder. "Frankly, I find excessive violence rather distasteful."

Howie smiles. "Yeah, man. Gets messy." He prods the bank guard's spine with the shotgun barrel.

The guard's just a kid. Maybe twenty-five. Way over his head. His .38 revolver is tucked into the waistband of Howie's jeans.

There are four other people inside the bank, all on the ground. None of 'em have made a peep so far. Which's good.

Clay and Howie slipped in a moment before the bank's 5 p.m. close to minimize the number of potential civilians. They drew guns and had the placed shuttered. Locked. Curtains drawn.

Wasn't too hard. Surprise was on their side.

Plus, Howie's shotgun up against a pregnant woman's stomach convinced the bank teller to stop in his tracks and not hit the panic button until Clay could disable it.

Now the sun's starting to set. Yellow rays turn orange against the two-story brick bank on Court Street.

Clay returns his attention to the teller. "Truth is, none of this shit'd be happening if you pigfuckers had given me that loan." He taps the back of the teller's head with the Colt. "I coulda saved my house. My wife and kids wouldn't have high-tailed it to her family in Chicago. This is really just ... y'know ... restitution. That's a nicer word than robbery."

The teller stammers. He turns around to face Clay. "B-b-but we, I mean, I—the people here had nothing to do with that. We had nothing to do with any of that." He loosens the blue tie he's wearing over his white shirt.

Doylestown is a sleepy place in southeastern Pennsylvania. It's surrounded by farms. It's known for being quiet—if a little quirky.

People don't even remember bank heists *happening* here.

Clay meets the teller's eyes. Squints. "Well, bud, I guess it's just a wrong place-wrong time kinda thing." He puts the Colt up against the teller's forehead. "Now, the money."

Clay thinks: *Two goddamn tours in the jungle. I come home and get spit on. I lose my house. I lose my family. I ain't gonna get wishy-washy about taking what I'm owed.*

He watches Howie's face. Watches the creepy bit of glee on his Army pal's face as he totes the shotgun amid their prone captives.

Clay arches his eyebrows. Thinks, *Still ... Any dead bodies would be bad.* He looks to the aging bank teller. "Hey, bud, I'm gonna have a brief chat with my friend over there—" he nods his head toward Howie "—you get any sudden urges to be the hero, just remember that my bullets might disagree. And .45 slugs can make real big holes in people."

The bank teller grumbles. "My name is Ed. Not 'bud.'" He stuffs stacks of money into a burlap sack for Clay.

"Well then, Ed." Clay smiles. "Better 'Ed' than 'dead,' right?" The smile vanishes. "Don't do a *fuckin' thing* other than stuff cash in that sack."

He walks out from behind the teller windows. Tucks the Colt into its holster on his waist. Pops an unfiltered Lucky Strike cigarette between his lips. "Hey, Howie."

Howie's got his Remington laid against his shoulder like some prison pit boss. "Yeah."

Clay jerks his head. "C'mere." He walks off to the side, where they can't be heard. Lights his Lucky with a Zippo. He offers one to Howie, and his comrade snatches it up.

"Thanks." Howie takes a drag.

So does Clay. "You all right?"

Howie nods. Blows out a plume of smoke. "Yeah, man." He wrinkles his nose. "Wait, why?" His eyes bounce away from the civilians for a moment to meet Clay's.

"This's gotta stay peaceful. No shooting. We'll be outta here in a minute. Soon as the bag's full." Clay sucks another lungful of smoke. "We ain't even hitting the vault. Just the registers. Should be a good, easy haul for both of us. We hop in your Olds 442 and blow town. Quiet."

"Jesus fucking Christ." Howie's eyes get suspicious. "After everything we went through against the gooks in that jungle, you think I'm gonna shoot some unarmed Americans on the *ground*? I'm not even doing this for the fucking money. I'm doing this for *you*." Howie's nostrils flare. "Even if that bank pig stood up right now, I wouldn't shoot him. You think I want cops on my ass? Or the Feds? For a murder rap?"

"I'm just—" Clay flicks the ash from his cigarette "—I'm just saying. Sorry, man. No offense." He looks to the pregnant woman on the ground. She's on her side. Eyes glistening with tears. Staring at him. Hands over her belly in a protective way. Clay sighs. "I think this is getting to me. I wanna get gone."

Howie nods. "Yeah. Agreed." He storms behind the teller windows. Brings the Remington to bear on old Ed. "Finish up pops."

An air-raid siren screams across Doylestown. It howls.

Howie shouts: "The fuck did you do, old man?"

Ed drops the stack of twenties he's holding. "I didn't do anything!"

"Bullshit!"

"You disabled the panic button! I couldn't do anything if I tried!"

Clay stamps his cigarette out. "Christ." He unslings the M14 from his shoulder and readies it. "Okay, folks." If the cops are gonna come, they're gonna come. But he wants the hostages away from the doors and the windows. He wants 'em inside the vault. "Everybody up." No quick escapes. No random people caught in the crossfire.

Clay and Howie never planned on a siege. They've got bullets and magazines in the pockets of their cargo pants and plaid shirts, but not enough for a *fuckin'* siege if it all goes sideways. Maybe thirty or forty rounds apiece.

Clay's worried about snipers, too. There are too many goddamn windows in the bank. The whole front hall is a prism of glass.

He can imagine the negotiator or whoever it is that might end up on a bullhorn outside: *What is it that you want?* He chuckles to himself. "My house and my family, you pigs." He shouts to the hostages and the guard who pick themselves up from the floor. "Let's get a move on." He leads 'em at rifle-point, their hands up.

The air-raid siren continues its haunting, steady whine.

Police sirens join the cacophony.

Clay snaps his finger at Ed. "Lock the hostages in the vault."

Ed shakes his head. "I am not going to help you turn these people into prisoners."

Howie greets Ed's refusal by ramming the butt of his shotgun into the old teller's stomach.

Air explodes out of Ed's lungs. He drops to his knees.

The civvies gasp.

The young bank guard takes a step forward. Looks down at Clay's M14. Then seems to change his mind about further action.

"That's smart, man." Clay nods his head. "A wise decision." Clay offers a hand to Ed. "Lemme help you up."

Ed glares up at him. He reaches for a desk. Steadies himself with that instead. Stands. He holds his gut. Walks slowly over to the vault door. Ed closes it while muttering, "I'm sorry. I'm very sorry." When there's just a sliver of opening left: "It will be all right."

Then it's just the three men outside the vault.

Clay checks his M14 to make sure there's a bullet chambered. "Howie, watch the old man. I'm gonna have a look outside."

"Sure."

Police sirens wail.

Clay leans his face against the glass of one of the front windows.

A cop cruiser barrels down West Court Street toward the bank. It passes Doylestown's Colonial homes and stores that've stood for a hundred years. Some longer. Flashing red lights turn the street into a dance hall.

Clay's grip on his rifle tightens until his knuckles go white.

The cruiser gets closer and closer and—

Blows right passed the bank and makes a right onto North Clinton Street.

Clay cocks an eyebrow. "What the hell?"

Howie shouts from the back: "What's goin on out there?"

"Dunno yet. Hang on."

Another cop car screeches through the intersection of Court, Clinton and State streets. This one heads east, full tilt, the opposite way of the other cruiser.

Across the street, there's a family loading suitcases into a nice new powder blue Cadillac De Ville. The father tosses luggage into the trunk. The mother escorts two little boys into the back seat. They're talking to each other, but Clay can't hear the words. All he sees is the father shouting and rushing the rest of the family. A second later, he's in the driver's seat. He guns the big V8 under the hood, and the whole group shoots away.

Clay turns away from the window. He yells to Ed. "You guys got a radio in here?"

"I think there's one in the manager's office."

"Well, get it. Something's goin on."

"Mr. Bailey—the manager—he left early today. His office is locked."

"So unlock it."

"I don't have the keys to his office."

Clay rubs his face. Mutters to himself. "Wrong place, wrong time didn't seem to hit that fuckin manager." He storms back to the teller windows. "Ed, show us where the damn manager's office is."

"But it's locked."

"*Jesus Christ*, Ed, did I stutter?"

"Fine, fine." The old man walks out from behind the bullet-proof glass. Howie follows.

Ed leads the way down the back hallway. The last door reads MR. BAILEY – MANAGER. Ed gestures toward it. "Here you go. But it's solid oak. You'll prolly just hurt yourselves if you try to kick it down."

Clay sticks another cigarette between his lips. "Why in living shit would we break it down like that?" He nods to Howie. Flicks his Zippo.

Howie grins. He shoulders his Remington and sends a load of 12-gauge buckshot through the heavy door's lock. Splinters fly. "That's what we like to call a 'masterkey.'"

Clay pokes the door open with the barrel of his M14. He tilts his head from side to side. Just checking it out before walking in.

He sees the radio there on the manager's desk. A gorgeous Grundig 1968 portable Concert-Boy transistor with the fake wood and fake leather on top that surround the chrome buttons.

Howie spits. "Fucking Germans."

Clay doesn't disagree. "But they make good shit." He hits the FM button atop the Grundig and scans for frequencies.

He catches one.

WMMR in Philadelphia.

Bill something—Clay doesn't catch the whole name amid the static—announces on the radio: "We've got reports as far as Pittsburg and as near as Warrington ... Ah—" The sound of papers shuffling "—there seems to be an epidemic of wide-spread violence, according to authorities. One engulfing the entire eastern seaboard. Police and civil authorities are urging people to stay in their homes."

Howie shoots Clay a look. "We should go, man. Hop in my car and get on. Warrington *ain't* that far from here. We can boogie up 611. Head north."

Clay holds up a hand. "Hang on, man."

Radio Bill keeps going. "The most disturbing report ... that we've received so far comes from Sheriff's deputies in New Britain who are saying ... I can't believe I'm about to announce this on air, but, deputies in New Britain are saying that victims of this outbreak appear to have been ... partially devoured ..."

Howie grabs Clay's shoulder. "He just said people are fuckin' eating people?"

Ed scoffs. "Americans don't eat one another."

Clay rolls his eyes. "You're a *banker*, asshole." He looks to Howie. "We're leaving." Gets up and walks away.

Howie follows with a "Fuckin' A."

Ed yells at the two former soldiers. "You're leaving?!"

Halfway down the hall to the front of the bank, Clay stops. "That's what I said."

"B-b-but the radio says there are crazy people out there."

"Howie and me killed ourselves a lot of Viet Cong overseas. Crazy doesn't scare us much." Clay stomps behind the teller windows. Grabs the sack filled with cash. Looks like two-hundred thousand. Weighs a ton. "So *we* are leaving. You take your time. Let the civilians outta the vault when you want. I don't care. You are all officially not our problem."

Howie puts the Remington on his shoulder. He looks old man Ed over. "It's something else, ain't it." He laughs. Digs a Lucky from the front chest pocket of Clay's Wrangler button-up. "Old Ed here's afraid." He sparks the cigarette with a match. "Ed wants our *guns* here. In case of those crazies outside."

Clay rolls his eyes. "If there even are crazies outside."

Ed adjusts the collar of his shirt. "Well I just think it might be prudent to—"

Clay licks his lips. "You realize we're robbing you, right?"

"Given the possible conditions outside, that are on the news—"

"What? Better the devil you know? Motherfucker, you don't know us."

"I think you're ... d-desperate, but you haven't harmed any of us."

Howie puffs his Lucky. "I hit you in the gut with a scattergun."

Ed inhales slowly. "All the same, it—"

Clay adjusts the weight of the money on his shoulders. "You can suck my dick. We're leaving." He struts across the lobby. Walks through the open antechamber doors. Rests his hand on the lock to the two front doors.

Ed grabs his wrist. "Please—"

A blonde woman slams her face against the front doors of the bank. Her nose crunches up against her skull. The cartilage goes to mush. Blood spurts in rivulets along the wired glass. It gets in her hair and makes it sag. The woman's eyes ...

Howie dips his head like a bird. "What's wrong with her eyes, man?"

The bloody woman is less than an inch away from Clay's face through the glass. She chews the air at him. Teeth clicking clicking clicking. Like she really wants to gnaw on his cheeks. His lips.

Clay eyeballs her. Lights another cigarette.

Ed points. "Oh, my God. Do you see? The radio said they were all crazy out there. You have to stay. You have to ... You have to defend us."

Howie uses the barrel of the shotgun to push the old teller away from the front doors. A guy leading a cow away from slaughter with a cattle prod. "We gotta do what now?"

Ed shakes his head. "That's Annie. She works the register at Herb's Hobbies on Main."

"She don't no more."

Clay breathes smoke through his nose. "Why is this dame a reason for us to stay? She's 'crazy' now, right?" Clay grabs the old teller's keys from his belt. Opens the door to the bank. Lets the leggy blonde into the antechamber then locks it again. She seems disoriented. Confused. Clay puts the M14 up against her forehead. She pushes against it. She swipes at Clay.

He bites his lip. "Lady, this is a military weapon. A keepsake from Vietnam. It will run a seven-point-six-two bullet through your forehead. That's a skullfuck. The back of your head is gonna look like red coleslaw. I need you to retreat, or I will fire."

The blonde pushes harder and harder against Clay's gun. Blood appears as she splits her forehead against the barrel.

Clay pulls smoke into his lungs. Lets it out through his nose. "Annie? Annie you gotta quit that. You gotta walk away. Radio says you've all gone nuts, so give me a reason to believe you ain't."

Her pupil-less eyes go wide. Clay sees nothing but milky white insanity there. She swipes at him again. Drool drips from her chin and splats against the ground.

"Damn it, woman, talk to me!" Clay spits his cigarette out. "Say something." He shakes.

This can't be real.

The blonde woman moans. Wheezes. Then she growls.

Clay pulls the trigger.

The M14 cracks.

Annie's brains fly in ropey sprays of blood and bone and tissue.

The spent bullet casing *clinks* against the tiled bank floor.

The young woman's body drops in a heap. Red oozes from her head.

Clay thinks: *Fuck. I shouldn't have done that. But she was going to bite me. Or someone else. Radio says they're all nuts.*

Clay's brain is an engine that can't quite turn over. It just clicks and chugs. His heart jumps around in his chest. "She was a crazy."

Howie pushes Ed aside. "Man, no argument here. Let's *go*."

Ed shakes where he stands. His hands tremble. "You killed ..." His lips quiver. He looks like he's in the middle of a panic attack— but who wouldn't be? "I've known Annie since she was ten. She used to come here when I was getting off my shift and we'd go to Ed's Diner—no relation—for food. Her family lives outside of town, on East Butler Avenue." He kneels next to her shattered face. Tries to pull strands of yellow hair from the pool of blood. "But this ... *husk*. It wasn't Annie. She was so sweet. My God. What is happening here?"

The old bank teller weeps.

Then, in a finger snap, instead of one crazy person at the front doors, there are five. Each moans and chews on the air. Each one drags their dirty face across the glass. Each has the same dead stare that Annie did.

Clay looks to Howie. Howie matches his gaze. Unspoken words pass between 'em. Words effectively summed up by: *This shit is fucked.*

Ed snaps out of his emotional coma. "T-the doors and windows here were all designed to withstand a r-riot." He sniffs "They should hold un-t-til the police can handle the situation."

Police sirens still shriek through Doylestown, but they're distant. If there are cops still doing their jobs, they're nowhere near the bank.

Clay approaches the doors. The crazies follow his movement like cats after a toy. Their moaning gets louder and louder. Clay flips his hand at 'em. "Doesn't take much to get 'em agitated. The hell do they want?"

Howie pulls Clay back. "Man, what are you doing?" He taps the glass with the barrel of his shotgun. "Okay, forget fuckin Ed and all his bullshit. Okay? There's just five of these cocksuckers out there, smearing the glass like a bunch of mongoloids. We put rounds in their heads, and we *go*." Howie huffs. "Man, we went from one crazy to five. *Five.* You can see these cocksuckers drooling right now. We need to *leave.* You want a town of crazies all over these doors?"

Clay backs away from those doors. "Where the fuck're we supposed to go?" He twitches his head. Rubs his neck. Tries to calm down a little. He puts a hand on Howie's shoulder. "I ain't leaving till I know where I'm going. You're talking about five crazies here on the doors? There could be a couple thousand outside waiting for us around the corner. We ain't packing that kinda ammo."

"Clay?" Howie grips Clay's neck. "Clay, we don't gotta do shit except grab this money and get to the Olds—that 442 will take us right outta here. It'll make it to Chicago. Hell, it'll blow through a goddamn roadblock." Howie smiles. "You know that. Nothin' can stop that big V8. We can go right to your family. Your wife and kids."

Clay hangs his head. "Thanks, bud. Thanks." He inhales slowly. "We still gotta make sure the way is clear. And it's getting full dark, which ain't no good." Clay snaps his fingers at Ed. "I wanna get to the roof and have a look around. Bring the radio."

Night settles over Doylestown. Blackness spreads across the steeples of the old churches and the roofs of the aging homes.

The streets are anything but quiet.

Screams. Howls. Pleas for help. Moans. Gunshots. Store alarms. Car horns. Crashes.

This is the soundtrack that greets Clay, Howie and Ed on the white-tiled roof of the two-story brick building.

They can see fires and broken windows. Chaos. Vehicles driven through homes and storefronts. People run in every direction. The crazies chase them on stilted legs—they lumber, arms outstretched.

There's a pile of crazies at Court and Hamilton on top of a woman. Nobody wants to acknowledge what's going on, but there it fuckin' is: the freaks are chewing on her. They dig into her abdomen and stumble away with handfuls of guts.

In the streetlights, it's hard to tell if it's blood or chocolate syrup all over.

Old Ed makes a gagging noise. He vomits over the side of the building. Wipes his mouth with the back of his hand. He starts:

"Do you think the Russians, maybe ..." But doesn't finish the sentence, because it would sound goddamn stupid.

Clay and Howie run to the rear of the roof. On Wood Street, behind the bank, there's a German Shepherd defending two young kids—a boy and a girl around ten—from their moaning, crazed father. They cry at him: "Daddy? Daddy, stop. Stop! Why did you do that to Mommy?" Both children back away.

The dog lunges at the former father. It sinks its teeth into his hand and tears a few fingers off. The dad doesn't shout in pain or even shriek. He just acts annoyed and continues to stagger toward the kids.

Clay shoulders his M14. The wood stock smooth against his cheek as he lines up a shot on the crazed father. Clay pulls the trigger. The bolt snaps back. The bullet flies. The man's back explodes in a waterfall of gore.

But the crazy sonuvabitch doesn't stop. He grunts. Acts like his spine isn't exposed and his lungs ain't Swiss cheese. Reaches for the boy and girl.

Clay furrows his brow. "No way. No fuckin' way." He readjusts his aim.

The German Shepherd returns. It clamps its jaw down on the father's outstretched arm and pulls the crazy to the ground. Which is goddamn great—except the commotion brings three more staggering, moaning lunatics to bear on the kids.

Clay sends a bullet through the psycho dad's skull. Bone and brains splatter against the sidewalk. The dog yips in surprise then scuttles to the children.

Howie grunts then yells, "Hey! Hansel and Gretel." He points. "Get to the front of the fuckin' bank. We'll meet you down there, all right?"

Both children nod through tears. They duck reflexively as rounds from Clay's rifle ring out and burst through the heads of the three loons nearest to 'em. The German Shepherd follows at their heels as they duck between buildings.

Clay slings his M14. Snaps his fingers at Ed. "Grab the radio. Follow us down." He nods to Howie. "You ready?"

Howie's already ahead on the stairs. He shouts over his shoulder, "For what? This hero shit? You're such an asshole. We shoulda left."

They jump the last few steps to the tiled lobby floor. The magazines and loose ammunition in their cargo pockets *clack* and jingle as they jog to the front doors.

There's nine psychos outside now. One's missing his lower jaw. He drags a bloody tongue across the reinforced glass and leaves great dark streaks. The others gawk and gape. Their moaning reaches a fever pitch once Clay and Howie get close enough.

Howie grimaces. "Not too smart, are they? They can see us, but they don't get that there's a damn door in the way. They ain't even figured out the handles."

Clay shrugs. "Not sure they need to be smart, y'know? A lizard's prolly smarter than an ant. But get enough ants together and—"

"Yeah, only thing left'll be bones."

Clay pulls his Colt. "Headshots put 'em down for good. Dunno what's making 'em crazy, but you saw that sonuvabitch I blew the back off of. Shouldn'a been walking, but he was."

Howie checks the Remington. Makes sure there's a shell chambered. "Yep."

Clay unlocks the doors. Both men raise their feet. They kick the doors open. The crazies stumble away. Stagger. A few fall.

Howie moves right. His shotgun barks. Twelve-gauge buckshot sheers off the face and top half of a psycho's head. Howie pumps the Remington and obliterates a second skull.

Clay moves left. He executes two lunatics struggling to pick themselves off the ground. "Where are the kids?" There are a lot of dark shapes and shadows on the street. Clay's tempted to pop a few rounds their way, but it's hard to tell who's nuts and who's just fleeing. He whistles. Hopes that'll call the dog over. And maybe the kids will follow the German Shepherd.

Howie takes down another shambling shithead. "It's getting hairy out here, man."

Clay turns to look.

The gunfire's attracted more of an audience. Twenty or thirty lumbering figures appear down the street. Black silhouettes against the fires and stuttering store lights behind 'em.

Clay turns back to his side. Yells, "Come on kids, get over here." Then puts ragged .45-caliber holes in the heads of the three remaining psychos on his side. "All clear."

Howie loads fresh shells into the shotgun. "Clear on my side too. Not counting the brand-new assholes heading this way."

The young boy and girl peek their heads around the corner of the bank. They stare at Clay with watery eyes. The German Shepherd licks its bloody chops next to 'em and shoots Clay a look like, *Well, we're here. What now?*

Clay motions to 'em. "Come on, come on. Get inside. It's safe there." A bullet *pings* off the sidewalk next to him once the kids are in the antechamber. "What the *fuck?*" If the psychos are using guns now, they're screwed.

But it ain't the lunatics.

Howie levels his Remington at a cop halfway down the street. The cop made it through the crazies. He's marching right for the bank. Howie shouts, "Jesus Christ, *now* you show up. What're you doing? We're trying to get these kids where it's safe."

The cop keeps his revolver pointed at the two robbers—a Smith & Wesson .38 Special. "Looters. You're *looting*, like parasites."

Clay points his Colt at the cop. "Goddamn, you are some kinda stupid." He lies. "We ain't doing shit. You see this mess around us? We're trying to help."

The cop laughs. "I don't believe you thugs for a second. You're using rifles and shotguns at a *bank* to keep people safe, huh? It looks like armed robbery to me." He opens fire.

A bullet barrels through Howie's thigh. Another round skims Clay's side. It tears out a canal of flesh. It keeps going—and hammers into the young boy's chest.

The boy tumbles to the floor with a sickening thud. His head hits hard. The German Shepherd whines and paces. The girl screams, "Davey!"

Ed rushes from behind the teller windows. He grabs the bleeding boy and pulls him farther into the bank lobby. He checks the kid's pulse. Rips off his blue tie and tries to halt the flow of blood pouring from the boy's breast.

Clay and Howie shout in pain and rage. Buckshot from Howie's Remington rips up the cop's leg. Clay pops off the last two bullets in the 1911's magazine, but they go wide. The Colt's slide locks back. Clay drops the mag and slams another home.

By the time Clay's ready to open up again, the cop's stumbling away. Bumbling down the block. The cop shouts, "You won't get away with this. You won't—"

A shape lunges from the shadows. It grapples with the wounded cop. They both go sprawling. The cop groans. Cries out. "Help me! Help me!" More shapes converge. The cop's pleas become wet gurgles as the crazies reach for him and tear him apart and chew on him.

Howie leans on Clay for support. "Fuck that pig. Get me inside."

The men stagger through the antechamber. They leave trails of red with each step. Clay makes sure to lock the front doors and the second set.

Howie collapses into one of the crummy, cushioned chairs that line the waiting area of the lobby. Clay offers him a Lucky Strike. Howie grabs it. Lights it. Considers it for a moment. "'Lucky' my ass." He sticks the cigarette in his mouth and yanks a red bandana from one of his pockets. He wraps the cloth around his thigh and tightens it.

Clay holds his side. He raises his eyebrows.

Howie exhales a cloud of smoke. "Bullet went through. Didn't hit an artery. I'll be fine. Just don't ask about any marathons for a while. You?"

Clay grimaces. "Ain't as bad as it looks." He shouts to Ed. "How's the kid?"

The young girl's sobs are a tragic hint.

Ed looks up from the body. His hands are smeared red. His blue tie is crimson. He looks to Clay, then Howie, then shakes his head.

Clay hobbles over to the girl. He kneels. Grips his shoulder. Turns her away from her brother's lifeless stare. "I'm sorry."

She talks through tears. "Daddy hurt mommy and then you killed Daddy." She wails. "Now Davey is dead." She glares at Clay. "You did this! This is your fault! You said it was safe." She throws weak punches at Clay's shoulder before falling into him with shudders and sniffling heaves.

The German Shepherd whines. It sits next to Davey's corpse.

Clay pats the girl's back. He doesn't bother trying to reassure her or apologize any more. He diverts her attention. "What's your name, honey?"

Ed stands. "There's a table cloth in the b-break room." He walks away without another word.

The girl mumbles into Clay's chest. "My name is Rebecca. Rebecca Connolly."

Clay holds Rebecca. "How old are you, Rebecca?"

"I'm eight."

Clay smiles for a brief second. "My little girl is eight."

"Where is she?" Rebecca's heaves die down.

Ed returns. He drapes a large, floral pattern table cloth over Davey. Then he cradles the boy in his arms and puts him in one of the side offices, behind a closed door.

Clay nods to Ed—*Thanks*—then tries to soothe Rebecca. "Clare ... Clare is in Chicago with her mom and her sister."

Ed disappears again. Down the hallway toward the manager's office. He comes back with a big bottle of Evan Williams and hands it to Howie—who chugs a mouthful then splashes the whiskey on his ruptured flesh.

Rebecca sniffs. "Do you think this is happening in Chicago?"

Clay inhales and exhales. Very slow. "I hope not. I really hope not." He looks at the German Shepherd. "What's your dog's name?"

"Brando."

"He's a very good dog."

"I know he"—her throat catches and she weeps again—"he fought Daddy to keep us safe." She bawls. "I don't understand. I don't understand what's going on. Why would Daddy hurt Mommy? Why would Daddy try to hurt us?"

"I don't know, Rebecca. I think something"—Clay scratches his chin—"I think there's something making people awful sick. It's making 'em ... not be who they really are." He brushes Rebecca's hair back from her face. "It wasn't your daddy anymore, honey. Whatever this sickness is, it made him not be your daddy."

Rebecca lets out a long sigh. "Sick. Everybody's sick." She leans hard against Clay. And in that moment, she is very much like his daughter Clare. She sighs again. "I wonder if Mister Giles made daddy sick."

Clay rubs Rebecca's back. "Why do you say that?"

"Mommy said our neighbor Mister Giles had a problem with his heart and was real sick. Daddy went to check on him before

281

dinner and bring him mommy's chicken noodle soup. When daddy came back he said Mister Giles bit him."

Clay raises his eyebrows at Howie.

Howie shrugs. "Biting is on the crazies' resume." He gets up. "Maybe this shit's like rabies—don't get goddamn bit." Walks stiff-legged to the radio where Ed left it at the teller windows. Turns it on and cranks the volume so everyone can hear.

Radio Bill is still broadcasting from WMMR. "—And the facts, as unbelievable as they seem, are still the facts. Civil authorities are repeating their urgent request that people who can get to one of the shelters that we will be naming every ten minutes. Those shelters are under the protection of the National Guard and Army units. If you *can't* make it to one of the announced shelters, then *please* remain in your homes. What's worse ..."

Clay picks Rebecca up with a grunt. He holds her with a strong arm.

She glances down at his damaged side. "You're bleeding."

"I know, sweetheart."

Brando circles around the two. He pants. Watches this robber hoist up his ward. But doesn't bark or protest.

Clay offers the German Shepherd a good scratch behind the ears.

And the dog seems content.

Radio Bill keeps at it. "The ... infected are carrying some kind of highly-communicable disease. One that drives them to murder and consume their victims. Those victims of the infected then get up and seek new victims ... You are hearing me correctly. The dead and recently deceased appear to be *returning* in some capacity. We still don't know the source of this epidemic. Some are speculating that a satellite carrying high levels of radiation that was exploded by NASA over—"

Howie laughs. "This is some Saturday morning cartoon shit."

Ed unbuttons his shirt a little. The white Hanes underneath is stained with sweat. "I hope that f-fella gets a Peabody. Can you imagine s-staying on the air at a time like t-this?"

Howie mouths the bottle of Evan Williams. "Can you imagine hanging out in the bank you were robbing at a time like this?" He chugs a little more Kentucky whiskey.

Rebecca pulls away from Clay. "What does that—"

Clay shushes her. "It's nothing, sweetheart. Just a bad joke." He clears his throat. "Howie, can you turn that down in case it attracts more attention than we want?"

One of the infected slams its face against the front door. Then another. Ten more join in. There are others at the windows. Ghastly faces with pale eyes and hungry mouths. The sounds. The moaning.

It's maddening.

Clay hefts Rebecca. "Don't look, honey, okay?" He pulls her head down against his chest. "Don't look at 'em. We're gonna put you somewhere safe until we figure a way out of this mess. Okay?"

The young girl nods. "Missus Wilmarth is at one of the windows."

Ed frowns at the infected outside. "You wanna put her in the vault?"

Clay pats Rebecca's head. "Remember, it's not Missus Wilmarth anymore." He glares at old Ed. "You got some *other* place that's actually secure and she don't need to look at people she knows trying to eat her?"

Ed holds his hands up. "I was o-only asking." He walks toward the vault behind the teller windows. Clay follows a few feet behind. Brando stays at his heels.

The old teller enters the combination and spins the big handle. The vault door begins to open.

Brando barks wildly.

Clay's gut screams at him. *Close it back up. Close it back up!* But the instinct doesn't make it to his mouth in time.

The sloppy sounds of wet chewing flows into the lobby. Then the stench of guts and animals turned inside out. The floor is red. Slick with blood. Viscera.

Through the widening crack, Clay can see the young security guard struggling with one of the four civilians they'd shoved inside to keep them protected. Dumb fuckin' luck.

Clay yanks Ed away from the opening. He shoves Rebecca into the old man's arms and hisses: "Get to the manager's office. Close the door. Keep the lights off. Stay away from the windows."

Ed doesn't argue.

Clay pats Rebecca's cheek. "Be brave. I'll come get you in a couple minutes."

She nods. The two bound around the corner.

Clay snaps his finger at Brando. "Stay."

The dog obeys, even though it obviously wants to run in and tear the crazies apart.

Howie clasps the heavy vault door with a free hand. He keeps the shotgun low. Waits for Clay to pull his Colt. The two give each other a wordless *Let's go* with their eyes.

The door swings wide. They're greeted by a slaughterhouse nightmare.

There are pieces of people all over. Fingers torn loose. Slabs of skin. Streaks where the fights happened when ... whatever it is finally broke out here.

Clay and Howie rush in. Howie kicks the infected bastard off the bank guard. Almost slipping in the slick layer of bodily fluids on his way.

The bank guard kid starts to say, "Thank you so—"

Howie shakes his head. "Shut the fuck up and get outside." He raises the butt of the shotgun and slams it into the face of the infected over and over until its skull cracks. Until its brains are scrambled.

The bank guard hauls ass to the lobby.

The pregnant woman sits in the far corner. She's slack-jawed. Her eyes roll. Her arms end in horrid little nubs where the hands have been chewed away. The belly below her swollen breasts has been carved open. Hollowed out. There's nothing there anymore. She's a shell. A husk. Clay can see straight through to the woman's spine.

But she ain't dead. Not the same kinda dead that's normal.

There's a fleshy thread leading away from what's left of her womb. Clay follows it with the iron sights of the Colt. Slow. It trails away. Just under two feet. The two other ghouls are there. Hunched over.

His mind mumbles: *They're sharing a meal.*

He wants to vomit.

Clay steps quietly behind the damned things. They don't seem to give a shit about him, long as they're eating. He puts the barrel against the back of the nearest one's head. Pulls the trigger. The infected slumps forward with a spray of brains that blows through its face and falls to the side.

The final crazy turns a little to Clay. It opens its mouth.

What remains of a tiny arm falls free.

The infected moans.

It holds the half-devoured body of a baby in its bloody hands.

Clay's nostrils flare. His lips form a thin, bloodless line. He pistol-whips the lunatic. Plants his foot on the fucker's neck as he falls. Grinds the heel of his Corcoran boot against this rotten sucker's throat until he hears the windpipe squish.

Then he stomps.

And stomps. And stomps.

Until the ghoul's head is paste and those dead, white eyes don't stare.

Clay breathes heavily through his nose. He offers the infected mother who had her child ripped from her body a pitying look. Then sends a .45 slug through her brain.

Howie steps in front of Clay. Puts a hand on his buddy's chest. "You all right?"

Clay digs a Lucky Strike from his pocket. "Yeah." He flicks his Zippo. Breathes smoke.

They step out of the vault together. Howie slams the vault shut. Spins the wheel so, unless you're Ed or you've got some special skills, it's never gonna open again.

Clay grabs the bottle of Evan Williams and chugs it. He lifts his shirt. Douses the bloody caterpillar-looking shape on his side where the bullet burned through. Then he chugs the whiskey again. Puts the Lucky Strike in its rightful place between his lips.

He squints. Points the Colt at the young bank guard. "What's your name?"

It takes the bank guard a second to tear his eyes away from windows, where there are countless faces of people he probably knows. "I, uh ... Kyle."

"Okay, Kyle. Can you tell me what the *fuck* happened in there, Kyle?"

"One of the"—he glances back to the dead stares from the windows—"one the guys you shoved us all in there with. He fuckin ... He kept saying he was claustrophobic. He kept pacing. Back and forth just—pacing pacing pacing. And uh, Jesus Christ. You had that door closed for hours. He went nuts. Real *crazy,* you know? He had like, uh"—Kyle taps his head—"like a Swiss Army knife on him or something. He pulled out the fuckin' ... the fuckin' blade and he slit his wrists, man. Then when he was bleeding out and one of the other guys tried to help, he stabbed 'em, man."

Kyle starts to cry.

Brando whines in the lobby.

Clay takes another drink. His aim with the Colt never shakes.

286

Kyle wipes sweat from his forehead. "Me and the pregnant lady and the other guy, man, we thought they were dead. But then ... but then ..." Kyle gets a weird look in his eyes. "They came *back*. They started ... eating her. It sounded like ... They pulled that woman's baby out."

Clay nods. Blinks. "Did they bite you?"

Kyle hesitates. "Yeah, I mean, they were all nuts."

Clay rolls his head back. "Sorry, Kyle. Wrong place, wrong time." He pulls the trigger on the Colt and blows Kyle's teeth through the back of his head. The bank guard's body drops.

Howie grabs the bank guard's gun belt and all the .39 ammo on it.

Clay stamps out his cigarette. He looks to Howie. "You do the same for me, if it comes to that. And quick. No fuckin' dramatic bullshit. I don't wanna spend my life like a psycho."

Howie plucks a cigarette from Clay's shirt pocket. "Comes to that? I'll do us both. Ain't no pride in living like some mindless cannibal."

Clay screws the top on the big bottle of Evan Williams. He walks over to the sack of cash and stuffs the booze inside. "Time for us to leave, brother."

Howie grins. "How's it gonna work?"

"I drive. You sit shotgun. Old man and girl in the back. Dog laid up behind the seats on the floor."

Howie puffs his Lucky Strike. "Gonna need smokes. Booze. Food."

Clay adjusts the weight of the money on his shoulders. "I think we'll manage."

Brando growls in front of the door they hid Davey's body behind. The little office with the dead boy.

Clay tilts his head to Howie. "Do it before we get the girl and the old man."

Howie holds his shotgun at the ready. "Jesus, really? Can't we just leave it alone?"

Clay shakes his head. "The girl. Rebecca's gonna have to walk by that door. She don't need to hear her dead brother on the other side." He grabs the collar around Brando's neck and holds the good dog in place.

Howie opens the door. Slow.

Davey stumbles out. Arms raised. The child-thing moans.

Howie pulls the trigger.

What used to be Davey disappears from the neck up.

Howie drags the boy's body back into the office and closes the door.

Clay releases Brando's collar. "Ed. Rebecca. Come back to the lobby."

The old man and the little girl make their way forward. Ed carries something that looks like a big lunchbox or a tin briefcase. "This was in the lunchroom." He hands it to Clay. "I f-figured"— he looks to Clay's side and Howie's leg—"some medical stuff might be useful."

Howie trades the first-aid kit for the dead guard's .38 Special he had stuck in his waistband. Plus the belt with the ammo. Howie buckles it around the old man's hips. He cocks an eyebrow at Ed. "You know how to shoot?"

Ed frowns. "Not even a little."

"Jesus." Howie scratches his cheek. "Point the gun at the thing you want dead. Pull the trigger. Make the thing dead." He claps Ed's shoulder. "There, that's how you shoot."

Clay puts his palm around Rebecca's cheek. "We're gonna leave now. All of us." He squints. "All you need to do is be brave, okay? Can you be brave, Rebecca?"

Rebecca nods. "Yeah."

"Good. You're a brave girl, Rebecca. But don't look at anything either, okay? Just keep your eyes closed. Me and Howie are gonna keep the crazies away and Ed ... Ed's gonna get in the back seat of the car with you and Brando, and we're gonna just get the hell out of here. Okay?"

Rebecca closes her eyes. She nods against Ed's throat.

Clay eyes Howie.

They kick the front doors open one last time. Their guns cry out with noise and light in the darkness. Ed ducks with Rebecca while the robbers mutilate and disintegrate the crazies around them.

They fight their way to the Olds 442. Through bullets and blood and bones and shattered faces.

Clay unlocks the car. He pushes the front seat forward. Brando jumps in. Then he runs to the trunk, where he tosses that heavy sack of cash. One of the crazies gets too close, so Clay lights the fucker's face up.

Howie pushes his seat ahead and fires over the top of the car, breaking faces with buckshot.

Ed and Rebecca slide into the backseat.

Clay turns the big 442 engine over. Finally.

Howie slams the passenger door but keeps the shotgun up. "Let's move."

Rebecca opens her eyes. She leans forward. Grabs Clay's ear. "Where are we going?"

Clay hits the headlights. The devastation of Doylestown flares into view. All the bodies in the streets. All the broken glass. All the ruined homes and stores. All the lumbering, shuffling shapes of the crazies that are attracted by the rumble of the 442's big engine.

Clay shakes his head. Looks down at the fuel gauge. There's only a quarter of a tank left. Clay keeps that information to himself.

He meets Rebecca's eyes. "I have no idea."

FELICITY MARMADUKE REDUX

by Rich Bottles Jr.

After an unillustrious print journalism career in southwestern Pennsylvania, Rich Bottles Jr. moved to West Virginia at the age of 32 to pursue a career in technical writing. He spends his free time visiting and hiking at the many state parks in the Mountain State, which is also where he develops the concepts for his novels. He has produced a trilogy of WV-themed "humorrorotica" books, the most recent of which is THE MANACLED, set in vicinity of the West Virginia Penitentiary. Other books in the series include LUMBERJACKED and HELLHOLE WEST VIRGINIA.

Rich was a contributing editor on THE BIG BOOK OF BIZARRO and WESTWARD HOES anthologies with fellow horror writer Gary Lee Vincent. He also helped create THE TAILSMAN comic book by adapting Gary Lee Vincent's story into comic book form.

He has also written stories for the StrangeHouse Books anthologies STRANGE SEX, ZOMBIE! ZOMBIE! BRAIN BANG!, STRANGE VERSUS LOVECRAFT, A VERY STRANGEHOUSE CHRISTMAS and many others.

Felicity Marmaduke often found solace in her powder room, as she called it.

The bathroom was her own private retreat, which she always visited when she was troubled or anxious. She found the sounds of water, splashing above her in the shower or swirling beneath her on the toilet, to be comforting and rejuvenating.

But one morning, the serenity she had become accustomed to experiencing in her sanctuary was shattered when she dashed to the toilet, clutching her stomach, and projectile vomited into the bowl, much of which splashed back up into her face.

"Oh my god, this can't be happening," she said to herself, her naked, kneeling body shaking on the cold linoleum floor.

"Oh my god, oh my god, oh my god," she stuttered as another rush of vomit traveled up her esophagus and was directed toward the toilet bowl, the acidic puke burning her eyes as her arms embraced the porcelain base. "Oh my god, oh my god, oh my god."

After her stomach was emptied of its volatile contents, she fell backward onto the floor, leaning her back against the cabinetry. Cold sweat covered her body and her throat felt scorched from the wretched regurgitation.

"Dammit, dammit, dammit," she cursed, trying to revisit the last time she had had her period, but knowing full well she was long past due.

She jumped up from the floor, flushed the toilet and walked to the mirror, instantly regretting her decision to inspect her condition in the looking glass. She immediately turned on the faucet of the sink full blast and began splashing the water onto her face. As she cupped her hands under the fast-flowing faucet, the water cascaded across the countertop, over her naked body and spilled onto the floor.

Ignoring the flood she was causing in the bathroom, she scooped palmful after palmful after palmful of water toward her gaping mouth, gulping it down like a parched Parkinson's Disease sufferer trying to take his meds with only one small Dixie cup of water in his shaky hand.

Felicity felt her belly filling up with water, but continued guzzling the lukewarm liquid to sooth her throat, until she started feeling dizzy and passed out on the damp floor. Water flowing over the sink counter and splashing onto her pale face eventually brought her back to consciousness.

She realized that she needed to throw up again. She used her hands to climb up the side of the wet sink basin and reach across to shut off the water. She then crawled on her hands and knees back to the toilet.

A panicked miscalculation caused her to throw up all over her hands as she tried to lift the seat. This time her violent and vocal heaves were mixed with the moans and cries of a morose mother.

Soon the foreign residents below her apartment were banging on their ceiling with some foreign object, complaining about her leaking bathroom in some kind of angry foreign gibberish.

"Hundir Palos! Hundir Palos!" they screamed from below.

"I am fucked," she admitted, before she vomited yet again.

Four Hours Later

Felicity was able to make an emergency appointment with an obstetrician and arrived at his office about an hour before it closed. Once she was in an examination room, she sat on the paper-covered table and nervously awaited the doctor.

"Miss Marmaduke, what brings you to the office on such short notice?" greeted the doctor as he entered the room.

"I think I'm pregnant."

"Well congratulations, we can get you onto our regular pregnancy program and we'll help you through the entire process."

"No, no, no, I need you to hook me up with one of them abortion doctors in New York, where it's legal and all if it's done in a hospital."

"Let's not jump to conclusions even before we know the results of the Wampole test," he laughed. "Besides, New York is pretty far away."

"We're in Pennsylvania, doc, New York is a border state if you didn't already know."

"All right, all right, how late is your period?" asked Dr. Kirkwood.

"Over three weeks."

"Well then, it's still rather early to be contemplating an abortion, so I'd like to counsel you on other alternatives," he added, taking a moment to study his freshly manicured fingernails.

"I don't need no family counseling, doc, I need an abortion. I'm almost forty years old, I'm single, I work at a damned mortuary, and I can barely afford my one-room apartment. So, please get out your little rolodex and find me an abortionist."

"Tell me this, Miss Marmaduke, is the baby's father aware of your pregnancy?"

"Hell no, he's dead and buried."

"I see… was he in an accident or did he die of natural causes?"

"How should I know? They just brought him into the mortuary one day."

Two Hours Later

"So, Miss Marmaduke, explain to me how you met the deceased father of your baby at the mortuary where you work," asked the detective once Felicity had been escorted to the interrogation room of the local police station.

"Hey, wait a second, isn't there some rule about doctor and patient constitutionality?" she asked the man before turning in her chair and looking at a large mirror where she assumed other law enforcement officials were observing her.

"If you're talking about doctor-patient *confidentiality*, the answer is 'no' if the physician believes a serious crime may have been committed."

"Serious crime? Are you shittin' me? Maybe I need a lawyer before I say anything else."

"Okay," he agreed. "I'll get you the obit section from today's paper. Maybe you'll find a good deceased lawyer who can relate to your case."

Eight Months Later

"So, Miss Marmaduke, explain to the jury how you met the deceased father of your baby at the mortuary where you worked," asked the male prosecutor on the day of Felicity's speedy trial.

From the witness stand, Felicity looked over to her public defender for guidance, but the man was just sitting behind the defendant's table and staring off into space like he wasn't paying attention. *Maybe the motherfucker is dead*, she thought.

"Like I've said before to my doctor and the police, I used to work down at the Mourning Glory Mortuary just outside Evans City. My job was to prepare the Dearly Departed for their funerals by washing their bodies, fixing their hair, applying makeup, etcetera. Well, one day I arrived at work and there was this old guy on a gurney, covered with a sheet, in the prep room. Just like any other day, I gathered what I needed to give the D.D. a sponge bath, and then I removed the sheet. As I'm washing him down in the privacy of the prep room, I eventually moved the sponge down to his crotch area. Well, as I was scrubbing on his privates, I noticed his you-know-what starts to…"

"Miss Marmaduke, we're all adults here," interrupted the prosecutor, "you don't have to be shy about describing body parts, especially since sexual organs are an integral part of this trial."

From the witness stand, Felicity once again looked over to her public defender for guidance, but the man was still just staring off in the distance. *I'm going to kill that motherfucker if he ain't already dead*, she thought.

"You mean, I shouldn't say stuff like 'his you-know-what' or 'his privates'?"

"Precisely," answered the prosecutor, nodding to the judge to indicate that an understanding had been reached on the testimony. The public defender also nodded, but was actually nodding off.

"Okay then," Felicity continued. "Like I was sayin', I was scrubbing down his ball sack when I noticed his cock starting to twitch. So I began sponging his shaft and pretty soon this dead guy has the biggest frickin' boner I've ever seen in my thirty-eight years! I mean this thing was monstrous, like a frickin' work of art!

"Well, I'm the type of woman who is not into, like, heavy commitments or serious relationships, but I'm also the type who won't pass up an opportunity for casual sex, if you know what I mean. Anyway, I made sure the prep room door was locked and then I stripped off my clothes. Unfortunately, because the guy was dead, he couldn't check out my rockin' hard bod, which is pretty damn hot for my age, if I do say so myself, so he started experiencing a little shrinkage. But I quickly remedied that with my hands and my mouth, and before you know it, he was back to his former glory – I mean I could literally wrap both of my hands around his shaft, one on top of the other, and there was still so much cock meat above my hands that I could barely fit it into my mouth. [Makes motion of thumb entering her mouth].

"My tongue was lapping furiously at his big knob, like a dog with its first ice cream cone, but I found that I kind of missed the excited vocal responses that men usually provide during my awesome blow jobs. I mean it really wasn't his fault, bein' dead and all, but I figured why waste my time trying to please him if he can't appreciate it. That's when I decided to satisfy myself by climbing up on the gurney with him, 'cause I was curious whether my little pussy could take the whole length of his big dick.

"The only problem was I couldn't stand to look at the old guy's sullen, blank expression. It kind of freaked me out, you know? Then I thought to myself, it's time for a little reverse hippy chick. If any of you folks in the jury don't know what a reverse hippy chick is, it's when the girl sits on the guy's cock, but doesn't face him, which was a perfect position in this situation. Hell, it's not like he'd be able to grab onto my titties anyway. So I slowly start squatting over his crotch, using my hand underneath to direct his dick to my slit. My cunt was just dripping wet, so I didn't expect any problems, even though the head of his cock felt like a fist bangin' at my front door. [Taps knuckles on wooden frame of witness stand for effect].

"Well, it took me a couple tries to answer nature's call, but I finally managed let him into my humble abode. It hurt like hell at first, but I kept workin' my hips up and down on his cock until the shaft started to make its long journey into my narrow love canal. Eventually, when I thought I had it most of the way in, I tried to sit straight up on his dead stick and I immediately felt the last couple inches bury themselves into my crypt. My eyes immediately crossed and my vision became blurry as my pussy was skewered deeper than it had ever been before and I let out a loud moan that could've woke the dead (well, not really).

"Although I felt light-headed and my face and chest were burning, I still found the fortitude to continue on and to make my throbbing pussy ride his slick pole. My hips slammed onto his crotch effortlessly, over and over again, like a perpetual motion machine that I had no control over.

"I thought I was just dizzy with desire, but then I realized that my frenzied efforts were causing the gurney to move across the floor of the prep room. I saw that the gurney was headed straight toward the open cremation oven, but I didn't care since I was on the verge of coming. I also figured his cock must be turning into ashes inside my own little oven. I came hard just as the gurney crashed into the wall, and then I felt something warm and thick shoot into my slit as I tumbled onto the floor. I panicked, realizing that this dead dude just shot his load into my snatch, and I considered tossing the evidence into the crematorium, but then I thought, like, dead men tell no tales, so I just douched out real good with formaldehyde and tried to forget the whole thing."

Felicity looked down at the female court reporter typing away and asked, "Did you get all that?"

"I-I-I think so," sputtered the embarrassed woman, looking up to the judge for support.

"I object," announced the prosecutor.

"To what?" asked the judge. "She's your witness for crying out loud!"

"Your Honor, I believe anyone would find her testimony objectionable."

"Be that as it may, I am going to allow the testimony and I'm going to request a short recess. I would like the court reporter to follow me to my chambers, so that she can read back some of the testimony."

After the recess, the prosecution rested its case and the defense rested his head on the table. The jury met briefly for deliberation, announcing shortly thereafter that they had unanimously found Felicity Marmaduke guilty of Desecration of the Dead and Necrophilia.

The judge reiterated the jury's verdict and asked the defendant to stand, which prompted Felicity to elbow the public defender so that he would wake up and stand with her.

Once both the public defender and the public offender managed to stand, one leaning on the table for support, the judge proclaimed, "Upon reviewing the facts of this case and the proven charges, Miss Marmaduke, you also got pregnant and your immoral perversities were revealed. Do you have anything to say for yourself before I proceed with sentencing?"

The public defender belched and said, "Allow me to speak for my client, Your Honor. This trial has firmly established that a sexual relationship did occur between Miss Marmaduke and the deceased, and that relationship resulted in an unwanted pregnancy.

Throughout her pregnancy, my client has attempted to receive a legal abortion, but has been stonewalled and denied her rights every step of the way.

"First off, her doctor is widely known for his almost fanatical anti-abortion views. She discreetly went to him for an abortion referral, but his referral could only be filled down at the police station, where she was ultimately placed under arrest. Unable to make bail, my client has remained in custody since her arrest and her pregnancy is now too advanced for a safe abortion procedure. Consequently, since Miss Marmaduke has been forced to carry her unwanted pregnancy to term, we are requesting that the court mandate the family of the deceased to pay her monthly child support payments. The state, which also prohibited her from obtaining an abortion during her incarceration, should also be responsible for child support."

The judge rolled his eyes and answered, "Go back to sleep, counselor."

"I would like to say something, Your Honor," Felicity spoke up. "Is it too late to ask for a different lawyer?"

"You get what you pay for, Miss Marmaduke," the judge responded. "I hereby sentence you to time served. I do not see any point in keeping you in custody once the baby is born. Perhaps the responsibility of caring for a child will keep you from making careless and selfish decisions in the future. I understand that Dr. Kirkwood has graciously offered to deliver your baby *pro bono*, so that you will not incur any additional expenses. I highly recommend you take him up on his offer."

"It's an offer I can't refuse, Your Honor," she admitted, "especially since my water just broke."

Two Hours Later

Within hours, Felicity Marmaduke was admitted to the Butler County Memorial Hospital, under the supervision of Dr. Kirkwood.

"Let's get this over with as quickly as possible," greeted Kirkwood as he walked into the delivery room while a nurse was placing Felicity's legs in the stirrups atop the padded table. "I'm working off the clock, you know."

The doctor took his time washing his silky-smooth pampered hands at the sink inside the delivery room, ignoring the screams and groans which were already emanating from the center of the room. After patiently drying his hands on some unfortunately rough and unlotioned paper towels, he snapped on a pair of plastic surgical gloves.

As he rolled a stool up between Felicity's spread legs and looked toward her contracting cunt, all he could think about was the woman climbing up on top of some poor dead guy who was not allowed to rest in peace. He thought about pushing himself away from the table – and he vocalized his intention.

"Push!" he finally commanded, deciding not to abandon his patient. "Push, you whore!"

"Hey!" squalled Felicity between screams. "Watch your mouth! Ahhh! I'm in a lot of pain here! Owww! Isn't there some kind of shot you're supposed to give me!"

"Sorry, epidurals are not in the budget. Now push!"

Felicity became delirious with pain, hallucinating that she was onboard a boat in a rowing competition with the coxswain yelling "row, row, row," or on a dogsled with the driver yelling "mush, mush, mush," or at a Reggae concert with Max Romeo yelling "Lie down girl, let me push it up, push it up; lie down girl, let me push it up, push it up; lie down girl, let me …"

"Push, push, push!" yelled the doctor, making his voice heard over Felicity's caterwauling, while twisting his wrist to look at the time. "It's starting to crown!"

As the baby's head appeared, Kirkwood cradled the child's skull and tried maneuvering the newborn so that the shoulders would slide out. But now it was the doctor's turn to shriek.

"Ow! Dammit!" he hollered, jumping up from the stool and shaking his hand. "The little bastard bit me!"

"Bit you?" questioned the nurse, running from the side of the table to see what the commotion was about. "Don't be ridiculous, doctor, how could the baby bite you?"

The nurse circled around just in time to see the baby reach his small arms out of the womb, grab onto the labia with his tiny hands and push himself completely back into Felicity's vagina.

"Oh my god!" exclaimed the nurse. "Did you just see that?"

"We need to get the hell out of here, nurse," responded Kirkwood. "Just leave this bitch here to deal with her evil spawn. She made her bed, let her sleep in it!"

"Wait, wait!" bawled Felicity. "Please don't leave me, something doesn't feel right! It hurts like hell, please help me!"

As the doctor and nurse ran from the delivery room, Felicity began to experience extreme abdominal pain, like something was tearing her open from the inside. Little did she realize that her spawn was making a meal of the freshest placenta that had ever been consumed.

Felicity began pounding on her belly with her fists, trying to alleviate the torment, but the gnawing sensation inside her stomach continued like she had just finished a large meal at an authentic Mexican Restaurant.

At one point, her arm bounced off her body and her hand brushed an instrument stand beside the table. Desperate to find respite, she grabbed a shiny scalpel from the tray and brutally began a self Caesarean, slashing her stomach open. But when the tool became slimy, it slipped from her fingers and fell to the floor. Felicity fainted at the sight of her sprout bursting through the open wound, with organs and flesh still hanging from the moppet's mouth.

Crawling up its unconscious mother's torso, the nipper began nursing at her breast, tearing a nipple off with one bite. Felicity had intended to bottle feed.

Ten Minutes Later

Dr. Kirkwood and his nurse were waiting to get through the cashier line in the cafeteria when they saw one of the hospital security guards paying for a cup of coffee. The doctor had ordered the special, which was a steak salad.

"Excuse me, officer," Kirkwood spoke up before the guard walked off. "Are you on break right now?"

"No, why?" the uniformed man responded.

"There's a disturbance on the fifth floor. You may want to check it out."

"I'll get there when I get there," the middle-age man enthusiastically agreed.

When the guard eventually reached the fifth floor, he didn't hear or see any type of disturbance, stopping every few steps to sip his hot coffee. He almost slipped on the linoleum floor when he walked past the delivery room.

The guard looked down and saw a gory trail of entrails leading from the delivery room to the adjacent nursery. "What the fuck? Can't somebody clean this shit up? That's just nasty," he mumbled to himself as he carefully walked toward the nursery.

He tried glancing into the room via the large window in the wall, but all he could see under the flickering fluorescents were a few fidgeting babies waiting for their moms to recover from their med-induced slumber. Still curious about the gore trail, he decided to enter the room and assess the situation.

As soon as the door closed behind him, he felt a sharp pain just above his ankle, which caused him to toss his coffee cup to the side and attempt to grab his stinging leg. When he reached down, he saw Felicity's bloody ankle biter clinging to his pant leg and chomping down on the soft hairy flesh beneath the polyester blend.

The guard's knees weakened and gave out, sending his big body plummeting to the floor. He tried desperately to shake the child from his leg, but he felt like a wild animal helplessly caught in the type of cruel leg hold trap that is banned in many states.

He saw other babies crawling toward him, displaying gray unhealthy skin and licking their blue lips like they'd already been approved to eat solid foods. They climbed onto the officer and began their feast of flesh.

Between screams, the officer managed to grab his two-way radio from his belt and broadcast a warning: "Attention, attention, this is officer Reciffo, we've got sick babies in the nursery! They're dangerous. Something's wrong with them. We've got an emergency up here! Evacuate the fifth floor immediately and close off the nursery! Repeat ... Evacuate the whole fifth floor and close off the nursery! Oh my god, somebody, please help me ..."

When a tyke began munching on his neck, the guard gave up his struggle and submitted to the babies' collective will. He tried pressing the transmit button on his radio one last time and whispered the obligatory: "Over and out."

The panicked guard's incredulous colleagues heard his emergency call and rushed to his assistance as quickly as their minimum wage salaries could justify. Peering into the window of the nursery, they saw ravenous and rambunctious bambinos dining on raw Reciffo and lapping up creamy, coffee-diluted blood from the floor.

The other guards immediately barricaded the nursery door and ordered everyone removed from the fifth floor. According to their standard operating procedures, their next course of action in such an emergency would be to call their Point of Contact at the U.S. Department of Health, Education and Welfare.

Four Hours Later

In the bleak and dreadful Fairmount section of Philadelphia lays the ancient crumbling ruins of the massive Eastern State Penitentiary. The facility was slated to be closed in 1971, at least that's what the public was told. Six of the seven stone-encapsulated cell block wings had long been considered uninhabitable, but the barest of maintenance expenditures still allowed the seventh to remain viable.

Actually, the Federal Bureau of Prisons managed the seventh wing and used it to incarcerate a handful of the nation's most criminally insane inmates – the ones who no mental health facility wanted or could handle and the ones who were awaiting trials which would never come.

U.S. Department of Health, Education and Welfare Special Agent Clarice Cherish was sent to the Seventh Wing when her agency was notified about the disturbance in Butler County. The H.E.W. had already taken over the investigation at the hospital and had placed Dr. Kirkwood under protective custody.

Agent Cherish, who was dressed in sharp business attire, was led down the dark corridor of empty cells, cracked cement floors and leaking ceilings by a hefty sloppily-uniformed B.O.P. officer. The iron bars of the cell doors were rusting in the damp and dreary atmosphere, while a distinct scent of backed up sewage emanated from every vacant cell. Clarice listened for miserable moans and lunatic laughter, but could only hear the echo of the couple's footsteps and the sound of endlessly dripping water.

The B.O.P. officer suddenly stopped, almost causing Clarice to walk into him from behind. He turned around and told her, "Kermit is past the others in the last cell. I'll be watching. You'll do fine."

Clarice continued on the rest of the journey alone, passing numerous cells with huddled men in corners hiding from the fleeting ray of dusk shining down through the skylight of each cell. The men appeared to be barely alive and caused her no problems as she hesitantly approached the final cell, which contained the infamous abortion doctor known as Kermit "Late Term" Lector.

"Good evening, Clarice," softly greeted a small elderly man in gray prison garb as he stood behind the bars of his small gray cell. "Welcome to Cherry Hill."

"You know my name? They told you I was coming?" asked Clarice with some concern. She stood back away from the cell door and had trouble focusing on the features of the old man's shadowy face.

"Please Agent Cherish, come closer, closer," the seventy-year-old encouraged before breaking off to breathe in the presence of his visitor. "You use Stayfree scented sanitary napkins, and sometimes you use Summers Evening Irish Splash Douche... but not today."

"You perceive a lot," thirty-year-old Clarice responded, taking a slight whiff of air near her underarm, making sure she remembered to apply her deodorant that morning. "But if you know my name, you must also know why I'm here. Will you consider helping us?"

"Terms?" he asked. "If I help you Clarice, there must be terms. Late terms or early terms, but there must be terms – terms between myself and the government and terms between us too. Quid pro quo. I do things for you and you do things for me. I've been in this cell for two years now. What I want is a view that doesn't remind me of Philadelphia. I want a window that's not cracked. I want to see a tree that's not dying. I want to drink water that's not polluted. I want to be in a legitimate mental institution, far away from Philadelphia."

"The Department of Health, Education and Welfare is prepared to move you to such an institution in New York if you help us. I've even got them to agree that you would be in charge of any abortions needed at the institution which result from patients' conjugal visits. But to be frank with you, doctor, I am not comfortable entering into any personal terms between just you and I."

"You're not very ambitious, are you?" growled Kermit. "You know what you look like to me, Clarice, with your faux-leather bag and bargain-bin shoes? You look like a jigsaw puzzle. A unfinished jigsaw puzzle with just a center piece and a couple side pieces missing. You're not more than one generation from steel town Hunky trash, are you Agent Cherish? And that accent you try so desperately to hide – pure south-western Pennsylvania. Who is your father, dear? Is he a steel worker? Does he smell of the Iron City? And, oh, how quickly the jag-offs found you in high school… All those toothy blowjobs underneath the bleachers, while you could only dream of getting out and finding some real men to satisfy your desires – some real men, like they have working in the Federal government."

"Dammit, doctor, what is it you want from me?"

"That you come to me with your first unwanted pregnancy."

Six Hours Later

It was in the middle of the night when Clarice and Kermit arrived at the Butler County Memorial Hospital. Awaiting their arrival was a large plastic bag labeled with the name of a local hardware store.

As soon as Clarice removed the handcuffs from Kermit, the man snatched the heavy bag from the Visitor's Desk and pulled out two new manual hedge-trimming snips.

"Ah ha!" he exclaimed. "These are exactly what I ordered! These will make our job much easier, Clarice!"

He handed one pair of the giant scissor-like trimmers to Clarice, and then began waving the other pair in the air, snapping the blades open and shut, like a kid getting a toy snap gun for Christmas.

"I used to have a specially-made pair of surgical scissors at my office, which I used to snip the spinal cords of unwanted babies," he excitedly explained. "But even those would be too small for what we need tonight. The short length and lightweight design of these hand-sharpened, high-quality, American-made blades are ideal!"

"If you say so," Clarice answered.

Feeling the length of the handles, from the smooth surface of the aluminum bars near the blades down to the cushioned hand grips, he continued, "But don't you love the oval tubular handles and comfortable soft grips?"

"Yeah, they are… they're really awesome. So what's next?"

"Now it's on to the fifth floor!" he announced.

Taking the service elevator to the maternity ward, Kermit whistled along with the soothing instrumental folk music while Clarice fidgeted with her white smock. Both had borrowed lab coats for their mission.

When the car stopped at the fifth floor and the door opened, Kermit and Clarice stepped out into an eerie silence. Scattered emergency lighting illuminated the vacant halls, bathing the scene in a dreadful artificial hue.

The duo stood still, trying to acclimate themselves to their unfamiliar surroundings – neither of them ever had the desire to visit a maternity ward. Soon they heard some light crying, almost like a howling, coming from somewhere down the hallway.

"Lambs," whispered Clarice. "They are screaming."

"Let us follow their call."

The belabored bawling continued as Kermit and Clarice carefully walked down the abandoned hallway, but the wailing ceased when the pair approached the nursery. Both crusaders immediately noticed that the window of the nursery had been smashed.

They looked through the hole in the wall where the window pane had been and were shocked to see a bloody mass in the middle of the floor, which represented the fallen security guard. A two-way radio, which may have been used to break the window, was suddenly heard beside their feet, and it screeched out a staticky warning which indicated all was not well.

"My god, how much can their tiny tummies hold?" Clarice commented, still staring at the partially consumed body.

"We don't know how many babies were infected in the nursery," Kermit observed. "We may have a larger problem than we thought. But I wonder where they all went."

"According to Dr. Kirkwood, there may be another dead body inside the delivery room. Maybe they crawled there."

The swinging doors of the delivery room swung open to darkness as Kermit burst into the room like a thirsty cowboy hurrying into the only saloon in town. Clarice followed him inside and fumbled for the light switch. There was a rank stench in the room which made Clarice hesitant to locate the switch.

"Anytime now, Clarice," Kermit whispered while taking a few practice snaps with his trimmers.

Finally, light shocked the room; the room of blood, gore and mayhem. The body of Felicity Marmaduke was still splayed across the padded delivery table. Her midsection looked as though she had been a suicide bomber armed with an incendiary suppository.

"If this was an abortion, then it's very sloppy work," Kermit commented.

"My god, doctor, how can you even stand to look at it?" Clarice asked, lifting the top of her smock to cover her nostrils.

Once light from the delivery room could be seen seeping under the doors and into the hallway, the door to the room across the hall creaked open and a small army of infected infants silently marched in lock-crawl toward the light.

Kermit and Clarice did not hear the delivery room doors swing open, but Clarice did sense the unmistakable feeling of tiny hands pulling down on the back of her smock and climbing up her legs. It sounded like the mounting ragamuffins were moaning "ma ma, ma ma."

She twisted around and saw two gray-fleshed babies ascending her back. "Eww, get them off, doctor. Get them off me!"

"Ma ma, ma ma."

Kermit turned around with his trimmer blades open and reached over for the highest climber, which was already halfway up Clarice's back and was reaching for her hair. It took a bit of strength on his part, but once the blades were around the tyke's neck, Kermit was able to snip the head off like a stubborn oak branch.

Blood splashed down on the climbing child below, but it didn't lose its grip on Clarice until the headless kid fell onto it. The active baby tried another ascent but was met with Kermit's persistent pruning. Now there were two small skulls rolling across the delivery room floor, eventually spinning to a stop on their soft spots.

As Clarice turned around to face the doors, she saw another four gray grunters approaching on hands and knees. "Ma ma, ma ma."

"You get the two on the left and I'll get the two on the right," Kermit commanded.

Clarice dropped to her knees to be on the same level as her attackers. She placed her pair of hedge trimmers in front of her on the floor and stretched out her arms toward the oncoming brood. They crawled toward her like a mechanical insane posse to a magnet.

"Ma ma, ma ma," they chanted, one spying Clarice's left breast and the other focused on the smock area containing the right breast. "Ma ma, ma ma."

As soon as one urchin was close enough to match the length of the trimmers, Clarice snatched up the tool, spread open the blades and pushed them under the child's chin bone. Squeezing hard on the handles, the offspring's top sprung off.

But now the other enfant terrible was getting terribly close to Clarice, so she had to whip the snapper around to catch its head in the snips and snap off the whippersnapper's skullcap. A chip off the old block, thought Clarice as she excitedly watched the cranial cap pop off.

The release of enraged energy and the rush of omnipotent power over her enemy caused Clarice to become flushed with desire. She desperately looked for more kiddies to kill.

Meanwhile, Kermit kicked one of his kids across the room and into the wall. He knew the impact would not stop the scamp, but the maneuver gave him time to pick up the other cub by the scruff of the neck and carry it over to the wall of the fallen one. Being careful to avoid the gnashing mouths of the pair, he meticulously placed one on top of the other, and then held them in place with his foot. He jammed the open blades down onto their stacked necks and cut through both cervical vertebrae at once.

"I've always wanted to do twins!" he ecstatically yelled, looking over to Clarice for some type of acknowledgment of his feat.

What he saw was Clarice pulling off her smock and tearing open her blouse. She was looking directly at his crotch and its telltale bulge, which usually accompanied his specialized family-planning operations.

"Drop those damn snips, doctor; I am burning up over here!"

"I see you've experienced the euphoria associated with snuffing out a newborn," smiled Kermit as Clarice continued to strip off her clothing. "Now that you've tasted true blood lust, maybe you and your kind won't be so judgmental of my chosen profession!"

Clarice violently stuck both of her hands simultaneously into the open cavity which once represented Felicity's belly, coming back up a few seconds later with hands full of clotting blood, ripped organs and decaying flesh. She fervently rubbed the macabre mixture across her chest, around her stomach, between her thighs and down her legs.

"Ah, yes," muttered Kermit, approaching the agent. "She rubs the lotion on her skin."

Seeing his steady approach, Clarice wasted no time shoving Felicity's body off the slippery table and inserting her own legs in the stirrups. Although forty years separated their respective ages, all she could think about was connecting with the older man who had just slaughtered a slew of sickening swine.

Kermit unzipped his pants as he strutted up to the side of the table where Clarice's chalice was on full display, wet and ready to quench the desire of any man. "Tell me, Clarice, have the lambs stopped screaming?"

Clarice didn't answer, but soon she was the one screaming as Kermit's engorged cock filled her gorge. Kermit hadn't had a young piece of ass like this since he raped his last patient years ago. He had trouble keeping his footing as his shoes began slipping on the slime-covered linoleum, but he was determined to show Clarice that he could still fuck as good as any of the hometown studs she schtupped in western Pennsylvania.

But endurance was an issue that all older men face and Kermit was no exception. He suddenly clenched Clarice's waist and screamed an obscenity which isn't even appropriate for a tale such as this.

Clarice raised her head up and snarled, "Don't tell me you already came, old man!"

"I-I-I am sorry, Miss Cherish, but it has just been so long, I mean I've been locked up so long that..."

"No excuses, you old fool," she yelled. "You need to get your head between my thighs and finish me off!"

Soon Kermit tasted his own cum, mixed with the carnal carnage of Felicity's sanguineous viscera, and vice versa. Now it was Agent Cherish who was in control – and Kermit had to endure what any too mature premature ejaculator must endure.

As soon as Kermit rose back up once Clarice reached orgasm, the woman removed one leg from its stirrup and kicked the old man firmly in the chest. His slippery shoes skidded out from under him and he crumpled to the gory floor. Before he knew it, Clarice was putting pressure on his back and pulling his wrists together. He then felt the handcuffs snap on from behind.

A Half Hour Later

Besmocked Special Agent Cherish led the Besmirched Dr. Lector to a small conference room on the first floor of the hospital, which was being guarded from the hall by a local deputy. They walked into the room and Clarice helped Kermit get seated in one of the chairs. Kermit immediately noticed another man seated in the conference room, wearing the same kind of smock that he wore, but this man was not handcuffed. The man's hands were crossed on the table and displayed a small bandage on one finger.

"Dr. Lector, this is Dr. Kirkwood," Clarice introduced. "Both of you are considered material witnesses to the events of the day.

311

You'll both have to be interviewed and debriefed before you can leave. I must go now to find a shower and file my preliminary report."

After the agent left, Kermit glared at the doctor on the opposite end of the conference table. "I've heard about you," he spat. "You're that anti-abortion obstetrician who refuses to refer for abortions. It's the archaic beliefs of people like you that cause doctors like me to be incarcerated."

Kirkwood stared silently at his hands.

"So you believe unwanted pregnancies should evolve into unwanted persons, is that it? Have you ever felt unwanted Dr. Kirkwood? I doubt that you have, being born with the proverbial silver teat in your greedy little mouth. Mommy never left you home alone while she went out whoring, did she? Step-daddy never snuck into your bedroom in the middle of the night, did he? Have you ever been shuffled from one abusive adoptive family to the next, realizing that no one will ever let you fit in anywhere? And I bet you never had to put your trust in some slave wage social worker who doesn't really give a shit about you. No, no, Dr. Kirkwood, when you rest comfortably in your ivory-towered gated community with your ebony-toned trophy wife, you never think of the multitudes of unwanted children suffering downtown in putrid public housing and shitty city shelters. But I want you to know that I was one of those abandoned children, Kirkwood."

Kirkwood still refused to acknowledge the abortionist.

"Just can't bring yourself to support pregnancy termination, can you Dr. Kirkwood?" Kermit continued. "It's not so hard, once you get used to it. The key is to never think of the fetus as a person, but as an infection, like gonorrhea. You have to think of the fetus as subhuman – a zombie, if you will...a zombie that you just have to *immobilize*."

As Kermit was waiting for a bible-inspired response, he studied Kirkwood's face. The man's complexion was dull and listless, and when the man looked in Kermit's direction, his lips were blue and his eyes were milky white with no irises. The man slowly rose.

"What's wrong with you, man? Sit the fuck back down."

But the man didn't sit the fuck down. The man limped toward Kermit and stretched out his arms, eventually falling on top of Kermit and causing them both to tumble off the chair.

"Guard! Guard, help!" shouted Kermit toward the closed door of the conference room, but soon his vocal chords were sliced by the sharp incisors of Dr. Kirkwood. And Kirkwood didn't stop there…

One Month Later

Clarice Cherish often found solace in her powder room.

THE MORNING AFTER
by Douglas Brode

Douglas Brode is a novelist, graphic novelist, screenwriter, playwright, film historian, and multi-award winning journalist. His work in the science-fiction vein includes ROD SERLING AND THE TWILIGHT ZONE, co-written with Carol Serling. Brode's fantastical short-story "The Ides of Texas" appeared in the anthology MORE STORIES FROM THE TWILIGHT ZONE, edited by Carol Serling. Brode co-edited a two-volume anthology of essays on STAR WARS for Scarecrow Press. His forthcoming books include a similar two-volume set on STAR TREK for that same publisher, as well as FANTASTIC PLANETS/FORBIDDEN ZONES/LOST CONTINENTS: THE 100 GREATEST SCIENCE FICTION FILMS for University of Texas Press. Author Douglas Brode and illustrator Joe Orsak co-created the popular graphic novel VIRGIN VAMPIRES, OR ONCE UPON A TIME IN TRANSYLVANIA (McFarland).

The darkest hour, Steve repeated over and over again in what little remained of his once fertile mind, arrives just before dawn. A cliché, to be sure. Then again, as life had taught him, clichés serve their purpose, have their reasons for existence. Oft-repeated phrases reassure us as nothing else can that there are patterns, discernible patterns, to life. If only we can link our individual experiences to greater, wider paradigms that have defined the human condition since its onset, we may survive, even in times of trauma too terrible to be believed. Like, for Steve, right now. Of course, clichés, in one's own personal drama, may or may not prove true. Still, if a physically lame man needs a crutch to navigate his way down some winding road, an emotionally, intellectually drained person must likewise depend on an idea he can believe in – hoping that in his case it will prove an altruism, not some false myth. Though time had long since lost meaning, become a blur rather than a scientific formulation, Steve knew that even if the dimension we refer to by that term appears to have stood still, that is only an illusion. So the seemingly endless night of horror must be almost over now. If so, then the morning would arrive up there, in the world, shortly. The only remaining question had to be: how long should Steve remain here, crouching in this dark cave? If time can be calculated, yet another cliché might determine whether Steve lived or died: Timing is everything.

Call me Steve. That is not my name. Where I come from, we humans, or more correctly distant descendants of humans, no longer go by names. Nor numbers either, if that were your next question. We have arrived at a system of cognition that stretches beyond the limits that were thought to exist eons ago. Mentally we are advanced, if physically diminished, from earlier incarnations of homo-sapiens. We would, if only we could, conquer the universe, travel wide and broad in deep space, a dimension even you denizens of the 20th century's second-half had come precariously close to conquering. We would stretch further still, come to know all there is to know about fantastic planets, forbidden zones, and lost continents beyond the stars. We would add, multiply, divide ... yet instead we huddle together deep in the bowels of the earth, our torches burning just beyond a perimeter to keep the Ghouls away. Those Ghouls, characterized by their glassy eyes and uneven gait which, in the year you calculated as 1968, began their conquest of the earth's surface, forcing us underground. Into the caves, humans returning to what were the species' initial homes at the beginning of history. We scaled back the great projects we might have embarked on, our scientists concentrating their immense energies not on travel to the stars but through time. Our sole purpose: try and undo what had been done. If, we must inject, such a thing is possible. For even in our distant future, we daily struggle with that issue which has haunted mankind from his humble origins: Is history set in place, planned out long before mankind had been conceived? Or is it not such an inviolable narrative-paradigm, only one version of what might have been ... and, as such, replaceable by another – an alternative line of events, leading to an entirely other conclusion?

For Steve, or more correctly the living breathing creature who would allow himself to be called by that name while visiting earth in the year 1968, the scenario he had barely survived and which he knew to be all at once coming to a close, for better or worse, had begun with an open road. A wide-open country road of the sort that might have existed pretty much anywhere in the U.S. of that time and that place – before super-highways all but eliminated the winding back ways in rural stretches of the nation. Thanks to the Elders and their genius for calculation, Steve had arrived precisely when those in charge of this, the third and likely final experiment in time travel, agreed that he ought to. Though in fact Steve had, in other guises, been sent flying backward via an invisible apparatus several times before ... on that first journey, a full three years previous to the moment that he ... *it* ... 'Steve' to us ... now inhabited.

Here is how we see it, the Elders had explained to the volunteer shortly before his first attempt. The Ghouls were inadvertently created by a NASA space launch. When the satellite veered too close to Saturn's rings, it picked up an extraordinarily intense form of radiation that would prove destructive should it return to earth. With our time-travel apparatus workable if not yet tested or by any means perfected, we will launch you back in time to the days when that project was initiated. We dare not wait; if we do, the Ghouls will likely break through the ring of torches (they have been experimenting, in their crude but cunning way, to find a means to extinguish the flames) and devour us before we try to eliminate the initiation of their existence in 1968. You will take the guise of a bright young scientist who, owing to knowledge and acumen, is accepted onto NASA's team. Gradually, all others committed to the Saturn Probe will turn to you as their natural leader. Democratically, they will promote you to chief. They will feel particularly good about this, as you will appear to them in the guise of what they politely referred to as a Negro, in those days before all races merged into a single race, our own modern humankind. In the late-1960s, Civil Rights dominated; this adds to the pleasure and pride they will take in acknowledging you as the best of the best. They will not, of course, realize that, step by step, you are sabotaging the very project you appear to shepherd.

If only enough energy sources remained so that, after he was drawn back to the future later this morning, he could set out again, all would turn out right. And if time remained, in that threatened future, for the Elders to propel him once more, before the Ghouls finally invaded their last outpost. Still, he was and would be a fallible if advanced form of the human species. Subject to emotions, whims, distractions. Steve's mind drifted back to his first attempt to enter the past in 1965 and create an alternative history, and how those elements, as essential to the human as they were impossible for Ghouls, caused him to fail ...

Small details in blueprints and drawing-boards will purposefully be set wrong; progress will cease to move forward on the Saturn probe. All the great minds involved, even as everything crumbles, will shortly be blaming one another. Everyone but you, their great hope. So the launch will not take place. The probe will never near Saturn, and as a result it will never be infected. That at least is our plan...

In 1968, on the initiation of the third attempt, Steve had observed as the car glided by. This reoccurred in each version of the never-ending story. At that precise moment, even as he had been instructed to, he made his way three miles southeast to the roadhouse. As the Elders had explained, he would there find a car in the nearly-deserted parking lot. He was to slip inside, attempt to start it up by setting and resetting wires in the absence of any key. Then he would drive on in the direction that the other car had gone. Even as he set about doing that, everything exploded around him. A truck, with a pair of terrified drivers at its helm, spun around a bend in the road with at least a dozen Ghouls, identified at once by their glazed-over eyes and awkward movements, chasing after. Losing control of the lumbering vehicle, the driver threw his hands across his face as the eight-wheeler slammed into the roadhouse. At once an explosion, not unlike some miniature nuclear bomb, was unleashed. Both men in the truck died instantaneously. Steve feared something far worse for anyone inside because they were burning to death. Before he could rush to try and help, there were more Ghouls. Here, there, everywhere. They had spotted him, sensed his presence, lumbered toward him in that off-balance way of theirs. Steve had to run. Not so much as he feared for his life, though of course he did. More though as he was there on a mission more important than himself, his own personage. This, he had agreed to risk.

During that first journey back, everything that could possibly go wrong did. Steve, in his mid-1960s guise, had made the mistake of falling in love with a young female scientist. Inspired by the man she believed him to be, the lady had worked diligently alongside him, convinced that here was a mission for the greater good of

318

mankind. He had allowed her to grow too close, their relationship ever more intimate. Steve, filled with hubris and self-delusion, had believed he could control everything while venting his passions, newly awakened in the strange and wonderful Ghoul-less earth of 1965, while diligently completing his mission to sabotage the technology. But she was no fool, noticing his purposeful inversions of necessary formulations almost at once. Enraptured as he had never been in his own far-removed era, in which descendants of mankind's struggle to survive left little room for such luxuries as romance, Steve allowed his sense of narrow purpose to dissipate, leaving himself open to detection. No one had any idea that he had arrived to save them, and their progeny, from a dark future. She believed him to be a Soviet agent who had used her sexually to gain her trust. She reported him. He had been arrested though, before any official trial process could begin, The Elders had drawn him up and away, off to their own time. You failed miserably, they said. I know, he wept. But allow me one more chance. I have another idea that might yet accomplish what we all so sorely want.

He must find a child after she had been bitten by a Ghoul but before the infection took her over entirely. The time-travel apparatus was sophisticated enough to bring these two, owing to Steve's slightness of frame and the child's small stature, forward-—though no one else could be transported, as additional weight would cause complications. If as the Elders believed, there may indeed be alternative versions of the past, then history may yet be changed, with an outcome that bodes well for mankind's survival and, conversely, the destruction of the Ghouls.

Why should we trust you a second time? The Elders wanted to know as Steve approached, begging for another chance. Because I have learned from my previous mistake, he insisted. Because I am the youngest that you have available, therefore will more likely succeed than an older man. And most importantly because I have an idea that may allow me to redeem myself in your eyes. Tell us, the Elders said. Another entry point, Steve explained. Allow me to arrive one month before the probe comes too close to Saturn and is infected. This time, I will win myself a place in the military, even as I previously did with NASA. After the probe comes in contact with Saturn, they will initiate a debate as to how to handle the situation. I will have won their respect, admiration, trust. And I will convince them to destroy rather than salvage the returning probe. The sophisticated piece of metal and technology will be eliminated by super-sonic weapons somewhere in deep space. Any potential infection will drift off into unknown regions, dissipating as it goes long before the sickly forces can reach and endanger any other sphere. Then, this future will never occur. Of course, that means none of us will be here as we are now, at some distant point, which we perceive as the present, the Elders mused, Yes, Steve quickly replied. But that does not mean we will never be born, only that the Ghouls will never come into being. As to ourselves, we will instead enter into not this dark world we inhabit but a better place, in which all of us will live ordinary lives – unawares of the alternative reality of a post-Ghoul existence leading directly to man's end-game.

During Steve's second journey backward in time, as he and the Elders had swiftly planned it (the Ghouls could be heard outside, stomping out the torches, their minds having gradually learned to function over the many years since their inception, Ghouls like the humans that preceded them on earth subject to evolution), Ben had arrived precisely as they planned. Yet while everything had seemed so simple, so clear, so easy to pull off during his discussion with the Elders, again nothing turned out as they had planned. Thanks to his abrupt, unsentimental education during the first time-travel trek, Steve had learned the hard way not to become involved with any of the attractive young women who had recently been allowed to assume their rightful places alongside men in the military. He remained focused. Then, the moment of truth had come. NASA launched the Saturn probe for what they believed to be the first and only time, though for Steve there existed a sense of déjà vu, that feeling he had been here before. If not in this precise place, a secret room in the Pentagon, then not too far removed as what had, for him, become a ritualized experience occurred once more.

The aim of the Elders was to create a serum, thanks to their advanced capabilities, far beyond those of scientists in 1968, that could be distributed in the areas into which infected materials would descend. The plague would be defeated by science before it could come into being. Mankind would live happily ever after, the Ghouls never coming into existence ...

That second time around, the probe had brushed too close against Saturn's rings and was infected, as all could see on the immense tele-screen. Even as others in this room within a room scurried to make phone contact with NASA and the White House, Steve had shifted positions, nearing the button that would set off a rocket and obliterate the Probe, along with any heinous viruses that it carried. But as he moved to situate himself for that early rocket launch, he heard a voice call out: "You!" Stunned, Steve turned. The young woman from NASA, the one who had become his lover and had turned him in, stood before him, as shocked to see Steve as he was to encounter her. He mumbled something incomprehensible while she, in a garbled way, replied; somehow, through their mutual surprise, Steve grasped that she had been sent here from NASA as a liaison only to now encounter the 'traitor' who, after her declamation nearly three years earlier, had somehow managed to disappear without a trace.

Yet here he was now, a miracle of ... bad timing. That concept once again ...

The moment had arrived; Steve readied himself to step into the lift-off spot with a ghoul-bitten comatose girl. He knew what would happen next; a split-second later, they would be home – his home, however horrible that potential future-earth might be – where the scientists, with their genius and technology, would rapidly create the serum, working diligently even as the sound of the Ghouls at their gateway grew ever louder, closer. Then, and for the fourth time, he would return to earth, circa 1968, with the serum. He would use his skills of persuasion to convince the authorities that they must distribute this to the populace. The infected materials would again fall from the sky, though this time there would be no fear of infection.

During that second 'go,' Steve – desperate at the unexpected sight of the one person who could devastate his plan – awkwardly turned to launch the rocket. Noticing what he was about to do, and certain that this was the Soviet spy she had loved and then exposed three years earlier, she leaped forward, seizing Steve in her arms. Others, also in a state of shock, rushed over, unsure which of the two struggling people they ought to help. Who was the 'good-guy,' who 'the bad one?' As always, that had less to do with the struggling people who scratched, bit, wrestled on the floor than any onlooker's perception of the event. Finally, Steve fought his way free, leaped toward the control panel, slammed his fist down on the button. The rocket launched, but those precious seconds had altered everything. On the vast screen, he hopelessly watched as the rocket grazed the probe, sending debris falling downward. At that moment, he understood a terrible truth: In trying to keep remnants of the probe from re-entering earth's orbit and infecting people, turning them into Ghouls, he was in fact the one who had caused this to happen. He, Steve, brought about the eventual end to mankind even as he tried to stop such a thing from occurring. In this one of an infinite number of potential scenarios for the past, present, and future of human life on earth, he had been the agent that destroyed humankind.

Could this have been his fate? Was it written in the stars long before time, as humans calculated it, had even begun? Or was it simply a terrible irony, a cruel joke played on him and the world of man by the exigencies of time and the paradox of timing? As such, a joke that could yet be reversed. If only he were given a third chance.

Please, let me go back one more time, he had begged the Elders. They appeared strained, frightened, knowing that the Ghouls could not be held off much longer by fast-fading torches. We must find another who will journey back, as you are clearly not capable of completing this task. But I can, Steve insisted. I will. You have revealed to me that a child will be infected. I'll go back and bring an infected child here. You can then swiftly prepare a serum or antidote and I'll take it back ...

The Ghouls, the Elders sensed, were ready to end what little was left of humankind. Still, people, or descendants of people, anxiously awaited Steve's presence in the invisible bubble, with the infected child alongside him. Every second became an eternity, for if Steve did not appear soon, very soon, then even if he did break through the time barrier, it would be too late for them to have the hour or two they required to create a serum by analyzing the blood of the child ...

The Ghouls were at the final barrier, where human troops did what they could with fire-throwing weapons to keep them at a distance from the cave's deep, dark recesses. But the fuel had run precariously low. The Elders gasped, then turned back to their controls. Steve? Where are you? Why haven't you returned? This is it!

Hurry, Steve. Hurry. Come back to us with or without the infected child. Even if you cannot bring her, a fourth return may yet—

I'll travel back once more, Steve thought. I'll arrive two days earlier this time, contact the lawman out there, with his rifle, so that we can begin the hunt for Ghouls earlier, hours earlier, meaning there will be less of them to destroy, thus less chance that one might survive and breed...

Too late, The Elders sensed, as the Ghouls broke into and over-ran their hidden laboratory. Nor could these last humans run, for the Ghouls had mastered at last an ability to walk more like 'normal' people, even if their horrible eyes still gave them away. Yes, the Ghouls screamed as they cannibalized the helpless scientists, we have evolved. And if we lacked the emotions of you human beings, then we always possessed your intellects. Our brains evolved, even as did yours, at precisely the same rate. Naturally, we created a time travel device even as you did ... and we have countered your plan.

The lawman's eyes, Steve noticed even as the shot rang out that would claim his life instantaneously, are not the eyes of a human. He is one of them, a Ghoul, this supposed lawman. The shot just now fired will end any hope of a fourth return; Steve could not know that the simultaneous (if in different but parallel and intersecting eons) destruction of the Elders would render that impossible anyway. No, that policeman, attempting keep the human deputies around him from noticing, did not have human eyes. He is a Ghoul. But how? Of course! Sent back in time, even as I was, to ensure that history turned out the way they want it to.

324

If there were even a shard of a second in which an idea might pass through Steve's mind before he fell down dead, it was that his lifelong question had at last been answered.

Yes, time can be altered. Things can be changed, even as they have clearly been owing to my visitations. Some things. Minor things. Yet history is indeed a force, with a way of asserting itself, with time as its accomplice. Changing the little details does not alter the big picture. Perhaps once the meek were likely to inherit the earth. Now, something else has come into being, been born by accident or plan, that will spread far and wide. It may not long succeed, for it may well have set into place its own doom by eliminating the humans that it needed to cannibalize to remain alive ... or, more correctly, some form of the undead. Even as ours did, its time will come. Then, something else will take its place. The cannibalizer of the cannibals, whatever that might be. That is not my concern, the dying Steve considered. I tried and failed. Whether a more capable person could have accomplished this task, or if the future, the larger and all-encompassing future, cannot be altered, that I can never know for certain. I do know now, though, that mankind's time, like those of previous species, has reached its conclusion. And, that for a time at least, we will be replaced by these creatures.

The lawman, or at least the time-traveling Ghoul who has assumed the guise of a lawman even as Steve had assumed the shape of a NASA scientist and a Pentagon official, lowered his gun. Momentarily, he would convincingly lie to his human deputies, insisting that he never would have fired if he had known this was a human staring out at him, not another Ghoul to be destroyed. They would accept that. Everyone makes mistakes. As they would do when they accepted his lie. The job, so far as everyone was concerned, had been done, the task accomplished.

325

THE MORNING AFTER

Even as they burned the bodies of that first wave of Ghouls, they could not know that their leader, with that badge of honor proudly pinned on his shirt, would as soon as the group had broken up begin cannibalizing unwary inhabitants of the area who had heard, on radio and TV, that the threat was all over. No one grasped that he had arrived from the future to insure that the past remained if not inviolable then at least fundamentally unchanged. Not even the young woman who, just then, arrived from NASA to aid in any way that she could. When she inspected the body of Steve, the young woman returned to assure the sheriff that he ought not to be overly saddened at killing another person, for this was some agent – perhaps from the Soviet Union, maybe from something more sinister still – and that, as she could verify from her two previous meetings with him, had come here to end mankind. The lawman thanked her for relieving what he pretended to be his human element, even as this Ghoul wearing a star marveled at the timing that had brought them all together at this moment in time.